Above Suspicion

Frank Lean

Above Suspicion

William Heinemann: London

First published in the United Kingdom in 2001 by William Heinemann

1 3 5 7 9 8 6 4 2

William Heinemann
The Random House Group Limited
20 Vauxhall Bridge Road, London SW1V 2SA

Random House Australia (Pty) Limited
20 Alfred Street, Milsons Point, Sydney
New South Wales 2061, Australia

Random House New Zealand Limited
18 Poland Road, Glenfield
Auckland 10, New Zealand

Random House (Pty) Limited
Endulini, 5a Jubilee Road
Parktown 2193, South Africa

The Random House Group Limited Reg. No. 954009

www.randomhouse.co.uk

A CIP catalogue record for this book is available
from the British Library

Papers used by Random House are natural, recyclable products made from
wood grown in sustainable forests. The manufacturing processes conform to
the environmental regulations of the county of origin

Typeset by Palimpsest Book Production Limited,
Polmont, Stirlingshire
Printed and bound in Great Britain by
Creative Print and Design (Wales), Ebbw Vale

ISBN 0 434 00745 5

To Darley Anderson, Kerith Biggs and Lynne Drew
With grateful thanks

1

'Get out of here, you maggot!' I shouted when Clyde Harrow poked his nose round my office door, but a glance at what he was wearing should have told me that the man was well armoured against any insult. The old coat draped over his shoulders did little to filter the glare from garments as bright as the flag of any newly emerging nation. Royal blue suit, red shirt with a livid white collar and a dazzling silver tie all said, '*Hey, I may be old, fat and bald but I'm still a famous TV presenter.*'

'Is that any way to speak to one of your oldest friends?' he asked, his chubby features creasing into a grin. 'I come bearing gifts, Dave. Spare me a moment of your precious time.'

As he spoke he withdrew a bottle of Lagavulin sixteen-year-old single malt from the poacher pocket of his Barbour. He pushed aside some of the files that I'd been half-heartedly studying and placed it on the desk in front of me.

'Is this the Argus-eyed sleuth who tramped his size tens through a thousand cases that I see before me?' he said, gesturing to the piled-up papers everywhere in the room. 'Or do these rheumy old eyes of mine alight on a man transformed? *Cunanus Bureaucraticus*, a prime specimen of the desk-bound, big-bottomed species that passes for male humanity in these parts?'

'What you see, Clyde, is an angry man whose size tens are capable of coming into rapid contact with your own big bottom if you don't remove it from my office, along with the rest of your putrid flesh, *tout de suite*.'

'There! I knew you were a changed man, you pin-striped pen-pusher! That proves it . . . "Putrid flesh" and French, indeed. Whatever next! I came here seeking a man of action, not a tuppenny ha'penny intellectual.'

Clyde waved his arm in a dramatic flourish. Frustrated Shakespearean actor, television personality and sports reporter though he is, the old ham is nevertheless extremely astute at gauging the mood of his interlocutor. That's his trade, after all. The truth is that I was bored to the point of distraction but I had no intention of allowing Clyde to see that he'd hit the nail on the head.

Running a failing detective agency, Pimpernel Investigations, something I'd done for many years before success came my way, had kept me alive and alert. Well, more or less alive. The knowledge that the next callers through your office door might be the bailiff's men sharpens up your instincts. My life in those none too distant days had a raw, on the edge quality that I miss now. I never knew then if the story that was being spilled over my desk might lead to a worthwhile fee and an interesting case. I followed clues where they led me – frequently into the casualty wards . . . as an emergency patient.

My eyes focused on the extremely costly bottle Clyde had deposited in front of me. Clyde Harrow is not one to pay in advance for information. Blackmailing his mark with the threat of slanted television revelations is more his scene. I smelled something interesting.

I nodded to the expensive stainless steel and leather chair next to my desk. Clyde allowed an expression of triumph to flicker across his face. I knew that look only too well. I'd risen to the bait and he intended to reel me in. Before seating himself he discarded his Barbour and flicked the rain off it in my direction.

'Thanks a bunch!' I grumbled as water landed on my desk.

'Fussy, aren't you?' Clyde remarked conversationally. 'Do you want to check that I wiped my boots before daring to tread on your luxury shag pile?'

'A moment is all you asked for and a moment is all you'll get,' I muttered grimly.

'Dear, oh, dear, Dave! Must you take being a chief executive quite so seriously? Can't you tear yourself away from your account books and your computer screens even for a second?'

'I have to check these files.'

'Surely one of your many minions . . .'

Here again Clyde was striking near the knuckle. There were indeed minions only too keen to relieve me of executive responsibility. I tried not to let my irritation show but Clyde Harrow is almost telepathic at times.

'Ah,' he observed, glancing at his fingernails. 'Do I detect the symptoms of executive stress?'

'Can it, Clyde!' I growled. 'And get to the point.'

'I'll do that all the quicker if you share the lovely gift I've brought and oblige me with a wee dram.'

'I'll oblige you with a wee kick up the arse in another second,' I offered but it amused me to remove the expensive malt from my desk and replace it with a bottle of the blended Scotch I keep for my police visitors. I fished out a couple of glasses from a drawer.

'A low blow,' he muttered, watching as I poured him a very small dram.

'So what's all this in aid of?' I asked.

'Aren't you going to join me in a drink? For old time's sake, at least.'

'Clyde, I'm running a business here.'

'Are you sure the business isn't running you?'

I shook my head at that one, poured myself a small whisky, added water from the fountain and settled down to listen to his spiel.

'As you know, Dave, I maintain an interest in the

sporting activities which contribute so much to the fame and fortune of our fair city.'

'You mean you get your fat snout into the trough at the Alhambra TV suite down at the Theatre of Dreams as often as you can.'

'No, no, Dave, that's unfair. I won't have my reputation besmirched. I do match commentary on TV. My opinions on the Beautiful Game are still much respected.'

I shrugged and for once Clyde looked slightly crest-fallen.

'Sneer if you will, young Dave, but that's not bull-shit.'

'No, it's horse manure. Can we come to the object of this exercise?'

'The proof of what I say is that a certain famous footballer . . . one whom we may even call with *King Lear*, Act One, Scene Four, "a base footballer" . . . has sought my assistance.'

'Clyde, if I have to listen to any more Shakespearean allusions from you I swear I'm going to hit you in the mouth.'

'Dave, like the late Dr Goebbels, you reach for your gun when anyone tries to raise the abysmal level of your intellect.'

'You're confusing Goebbels with Hermann Goering . . . I should think Goebbels is one of *your* role models.'

'A mere quibble. Anyway this footballer, Jamie Piercy . . .'

'Hold on! Did you say Jamie Piercy?'

I was startled. Unless he was merely name-dropping, something at which he was adept, Clyde was claiming intimacy with one of the most famous footballers in the country, a man for whom the Reds had reputedly turned down a transfer fee of thirty million.

'The very same,' Clyde boasted. 'I thought that would get your attention. Nowadays you're only interested in helping rich people, aren't you, Dave?'

4

'Not at all,' I snapped, peeved because there was a tiny element of truth in what he said. Most of the current clients of Pimpernel Investigations are big insurance companies.

'Getting to you, am I? This young man with the world at his feet has sought my help . . . our help, I should say . . . in a matter of some delicacy.'

'What? His girlfriend's pregnant and he wants someone to head her off before she goes to the *News of the World*?'

'Nothing like that. This young man has the quality to deliver us the World Cup if he isn't blown off course by the scandal that's threatening him.'

'Which is?'

'I don't know, except that it's nothing sexual or vulgar in the way you imply. He's asked me to find him the best private investigator in Manchester to pursue in the utmost secrecy a matter that could affect the whole future of football in this country – so naturally I thought of you.'

'Do I detect a slight whiff of exaggeration there, Clyde?'

'It *could* affect the whole game. Jamie is that big.'

'I didn't mean that.'

'You may be the best private investigator in Manchester, but then I don't know many others.'

'Thanks.'

'He's waiting to meet you now. All I ask in return for this introduction is that you allow me to be the first to hear of it if you find that young Jamie is in no real danger. If he's in a genuine pickle of his own devising, then naturally I wouldn't wish to be the conduit through which his predicament became public knowledge.'

'Oh, naturally not, Clyde!' I echoed. 'Heaven forbid you should scent a story and reveal it to the media. I'm surprised at you. Normally you'd have come along with some copper-bottomed method of blackmailing me into helping you. Today all you can manage is a bottle of Lagavulin and an appeal to my finer feelings. Here, take your bottle back and get out.'

I retrieved the whisky from the drawer I'd stowed it in and pushed it across the desk towards him.

'No, Dave, Jamie Piercy really is in trouble. No b.s. this time, honest.'

I smiled cynically.

'Dave, I'm appealing to you,' Clyde said, gathering himself up and putting on his coat with what dignity he could muster. 'I sense that this boy's career is going down the tubes if he doesn't get some help.'

I said nothing. Clyde looked at the bottle on my desk as if uncertain whether picking it up would spoil his exit. He turned to go without a word, leaving the bottle where it stood.

I let him reach the door.

'Hold it, Clyde. Where is this meet, then?'

'I knew you'd see reason,' he said, turning, his fat face wreathed in a smile. 'Jamie Piercy is a once in a lifetime, heaven-sent talent. We've got to do what we can for him. He's waiting for us at Loony Leary's.'

This is one of the swanky new theme bars on John Dalton Street, situated in a former methodist chapel.

I turned to pick up my own coat from a cupboard behind my desk and when I turned round again just caught sight of the Lagavulin disappearing into Clyde's poacher pocket.

'Oh no, you don't,' I said. 'Put it back.'

'I just thought . . . if you didn't want it. Jamie gave it to me actually.'

Loony Leary's attracts crowds on Friday and Saturday nights. Some inspired PR man dreamed up the story that the ghost of a former minister now haunts this shrine to the demon drink. It gives the boozing den just that extra little frisson of naughtiness that draws in the punters.

Clyde and I got some odd glances when we entered. It wasn't his age or his clothes but the fact that they thought I was a copper! It's something I'm used to, the curse of

6

heredity that's landed me with the physique and bearing of the long line of law-enforcers from which I spring. I saw a barman scuttle round a corner when he eyeballed me. Doubtless spliffs were already being extinguished in secluded nooks, but Loony's isn't really that sort of place. It's too upmarket. Any illegal substances are down to the customers not management. I suppose they were making enough on the bar not to bother selling the other stuff. Even on a Tuesday afternoon the place was heaving with young people. I imagined the teetotal preachers who'd performed in this roomy hall spinning in their graves like steam turbines. Darkness, throbbing music, weird décor now made a hellish scene where earnest 'Methodies' once imbibed nothing stronger than blackcurrant cordial.

We quickly found Jamie Piercy.

Not that he was easy to recognise.

He was in the upstairs room, nervously evading the adulation of the multitudes by hiding behind a pillar. The face that earned millions when tagged on to an advert for crisps or caramels was now hidden behind reflective shades and the hood of a sweatshirt. We spotted him through the fashionable gloom when he pulled back the hood and removed the shades for a peek at the new arrivals. The trademark dark locks, startling blue eyes and sallow complexion were like a neon sign saying 'Jamie Piercy, football idol'.

Clyde introduced me.

'Hello, Mr Cunane,' Jamie said.

It was hard to see him clearly but his face was so familiar from television that I had the illusion of seeing more than I actually did. The voice didn't match the figure at all. In person Jamie Piercy had that pared-down, taut look you associate with professional athletes, like a greyhound straining at the leash. But when he spoke the effect was completely spoiled. This perfect physical specimen could only speak in the thin, high-pitched London accent that a long line of comedians has told us is funny.

7

It is.

The mismatch between man and mouth was so pronounced that I had to suppress an involuntary laugh. Clyde caught me at it and glowered darkly.

'Look, I can't stay here,' Jamie Piercy explained urgently. 'I think someone's seen me and they'll be after me.'

'Who?' I demanded, as he slipped on the shades again and pulled up the hood of his sweatshirt. I felt a tingle of excitement, something that hadn't happened for months. Who was after him? Hitmen, paparazzi, outraged fathers? The possibilities were interesting.

'Yeah, like fans, teenage girls, older women,' he whined. 'I don't go out much in town,' he added, making a sort of hopeless flapping gesture with his hands.

'Is that all?' I asked disappointedly. If he only needed a minder then he'd come to the wrong shop, or rather I had. The pretentious boozer chosen for our meeting was beginning to irritate me already.

'It's worse than you think . . . dangerous, like. Something horrible's happened.'

Piercy showed no sign of the aggressiveness that had cost his team two penalties yesterday. Was he an athlete who needed turf under his studs before he felt self-confident? I mentally calculated how much he'd earned while we'd been talking to him.

'Well, if you're worried we can go somewhere else,' I suggested.

'Yeah, good idea, but I don't want it to look as if you two have come to arrest me. Mr Cunane, you look more like a copper than a private eye. It'll be all over the tabloids tomorrow if I go out with you.'

'Feel these threads,' I joked, offering him my sleeve. 'Too smooth for a copper, believe me.'

Piercy lowered his shades to check if I was taking the piss.

'Yeah,' he agreed, 'but it's too dark in here for anyone

to check out who your tailor is. Tell you what – I'll meet you on the street. You duck out and I'll join you in a minute.'

'Listen, Mr Piercy,' I said, 'if you don't like my looks and you want me to butt out that's fine by me. I'm only here because good old Clyde here said you needed my help.'

'No, it's not that I don't need you . . . Christ! I need somebody.' His voice sank to a level that was almost bearable. 'This is so difficult . . . the papers . . . publicity. I do have a problem, a stinking awful one.'

He took the shades off again and looked at me searchingly, then seemed to make his mind up. I got the impression of a drowning man clutching at a straw.

'Yeah, it might be better if you left us now, Clyde, before I say too much.'

'What?' exclaimed Clyde, bristling. 'But . . .'

'You've been very good, like, a real mate helping me, and I won't forget it.'

'Yes, Clyde, I won't forget it either,' I added.

He looked first at Jamie and then at me, as if unable to comprehend, all injured innocence. I was reminded of a professional footballer being shown the red card and I gave him an ironic smile to speed him on his way.

Neither of us spoke until Clyde had disappeared from view down the stairs.

'This isn't about me, it's my brother,' Jamie began.

I'm afraid I cracked a smile at this. If I'd invested ten pounds for every time I'd heard a client begin an interview with those words I'd be well wadded by now. 'What's so funny?' he demanded, temper flaring at last.

'Look, you can tell me what it is. Believe me, I don't shock easily.'

'It really is my brother who has the problem.'

'All right,' I said equably. 'Suppose we start at the beginning?'

'No, I can see you don't believe me and I don't suppose

9

I can blame you. What we'll do is to go and see my brother. He can tell you what the trouble is. And what he wants doing about it.'

At that moment someone nudged my arm. A youth of about nineteen in a red shirt was pushing a drinks menu towards Jamie. 'Will you do me an autograph on this, Jamie?' he asked. As I looked on stupidly, thinking this was a new way of paying for drinks, the youth said, 'Pity about yesterday's game. Do you think the Boss will drop you for the Chelsea match?' Jamie, disguise penetrated, sighed heavily and removed the shades and hood.

I tensed, ready to send the aggressive youth on his way. Jamie laid a hand on my arm. 'No, I've got to do it. It's bad luck if you don't.'

He signed the menu, pushed it back into the punter's grasp and stood up.

'We're not going to get anything done in here, mate, let's go.'

The intrusive youth seemed poised to block his exit but Jamie swerved round him with the inborn talent that has made him a fabulous footballer. One minute he was there, the next he was at the top of the stairs beckoning me to follow.

'Here, are you the police? Is he in trouble?' the youth demanded as I passed. He grabbed my arm. 'Are you from the FA?'

I gave him a sharp rap on the ankle to discourage pursuit and headed for the stairs.

Looking out at Manchester through the tinted windows of Jamie's Italian Red Ferrari 550 Maranello gave me a new perspective on his earning power. He confided that it was the third Ferrari he'd owned.

'I had a 360 Spider until January, and then I got myself the 550 as a late Christmas present. This does two hundred m.p.h.'

'Really, where?' I enquired sceptically.

'Yeah, there is that,' he conceded regretfully.

We turned out of the town centre on to the Princess Parkway heading south. Traffic was heavy and as we passed slower vehicles their occupants craned round to see who was in the Ferrari.

'Listen, Mr Piercy . . .'

'Jamie.'

'Jamie, if you don't want to be spotted, this is hardly the vehicle . . .'

I barely had the words out of my mouth before he slowed down and swerved into the inside lane. 'Jesus, you know that never crossed my mind,' he said, as if I'd made a blinding revelation. For a second I thought he was being sarcastic but he was perfectly serious and seemed to be thrown into a panic by the observation. The shades were off and he was peering round anxiously in all directions.

'Don't worry, we only need some wheels that are a bit less conspicuous,' I said soothingly.

'Right,' he agreed, and made that same flapping gesture with his hands that I'd noted at Loony Leary's. I guessed it was the signal for someone to rush in and solve his problems. So I did.

'Take the next right for Chorlton. I've got a Mondeo in a garage behind my flat. We can switch cars and no one will be any the wiser.'

'Yeah,' he agreed. His face cleared and we set off again at a fair speed. I now realised how soccer managers earn their money.

There was no one about at Thornleigh Court, the block where my girlfriend Janine White and I inhabit adjacent flats. The presence of the brand new Ferrari in the car park made everything else look slightly shabby so I was happy when Jamie made no fuss about locking it in my garage. It was on the tip of my tongue to ask him upstairs for a fuller explanation before proceeding any further. I still wasn't convinced that the 'brother' was anything but a convenient way of distancing himself from whatever trouble he was in.

A glance at his earnest expression made me think again. Jamie may have been one of the greatest dribblers in the history of soccer but his powers of verbal deception were strictly limited. There really was a brother, there really was a problem and I was going to find out what it was.

2

The journey to meet the mysterious brother at Wilmslow was not incident free. An employee phoned me twice on my mobile. It all sounds fairly innocuous when you put it like that. An employee phoned . . . nothing to it.

Nothing to it except if the employee in question is Celeste Williams, my PA. A bold, beautiful black girl from Old Trafford, Celeste doesn't easily take no for an answer, even from her boss. She has a lot to do with the day-to-day running of Pimpernel Investigations. And then you've also got to consider that I don't just employ Celeste . . . I employ several of her relatives, not least Marvin Desailles, her cousin. Marvin is gay, intensely focused and since working for me he's gained all kinds of qualifications. He's a terrific man to have on your side, particularly if the Old Bill start taking an interest in your affairs. He has a way of looking at police officers that seems to shrivel them up. On the other hand he knows so much about employment law that I have a secret fear about what might happen if I ever did something to upset him. Not that I would deliberately do anything to upset him or Celeste.

Still, it's there, the friction, that tiny piece of grit in the works that you get when you employ human beings and not robots. When I was a one-man business I only had to worry about pleasing myself and keeping a smile on my bank manager's face. Now . . .

'Mr Cunane, where are you?' Celeste demanded. 'You've got an appointment with your accountant at four . . .'

13

I grimly noted the use of the formal term of address instead of the usual 'Dave'. My absence was resented.

'Listen, Celeste, something's come up. Can you get Peter Snyder to go over the last quarter's figures with him? I should have mentioned it before I went out. They're on my desk. There shouldn't be any problem.'

Peter is the office manager and senior investigator after myself.

'Hmmph!' she grumbled. 'But where are you?'

'I'm with a potential client,' I said, glancing across at Jamie. He frowned at the word 'potential' so I gave him a reassuring nod. 'It's a very important piece of business, Celeste. I'm not bunking off, honest. Anyway, I'll call you later. I'm in traffic now,' I said, ringing off.

'You will take the case?' my passenger asked anxiously. 'It's a risk for me and me brother even to tell you what's happened unless we know you're going to help us.'

'I've never been known to let down a client,' I said coldly. 'On the other hand, I've no intention of getting into anything illegal.'

'Oh, yeah,' Jamie said.

At that point I was manoeuvring the Mondeo across three crowded lanes to join the M60 at the Princess Parkway interchange, a tricky task at best. We were silent as I followed the M60 along the Mersey Valley and then turned off for the A34 taking us on to Wilmslow.

No sooner was I on the A34 than Celeste rang again.

'Shall I start the clock going on your client?' she enquired in a deceptively calm voice. 'If it's an out of office meeting the client ought to start paying the moment you set foot in the street. After all, it's not as if there isn't enough work for you to do here.'

'That's very true,' I agreed, waiting for the punch-line.

'So what name shall I put on the file, then?'

'Oh, leave it blank for now. No, call it Red . . .'

14

My passenger glanced at me then, showing there was nothing wrong with his hearing.

'Red what?' Celeste demanded.

'Just leave it at that,' I snapped.

'A file called "Red" and a mystery customer . . . that's great! Listen Mr C, you know how awkward the Inland Revenue were last time you did *pro bono* work on the firm's time.'

'It's my firm,' I said pettishly.

'I know that, but if you swan off in the middle of the afternoon with that Clyde Harrow it makes it hard for me to stop other people skiving off.'

'I'm sorry, Celeste, but I've no intention of becoming desk-bound to suit you or the Inland Revenue. I'll sort things out tomorrow.'

Celeste broke off the call before I did. She's hot-blooded but she had a point. The boss is supposed to set an example. My 'employees' are worse than a bunch of frogs round a pond. Clearly some sharp pair of eyes had observed my visit to the 'pub' on John Dalton Street. Not for the first time it crossed my mind to get myself premises separate from the Pimpernel office. I switched the mobile off.

I must have looked grim because Jamie said, 'Bad news, Mr Cunane?'

'Not really,' I said with a sigh. 'It's just that I seem to have problems with being spotted in the streets and I'm not even a famous footballer.'

'Yeah, it's a bugger, in't it?' he murmured without a trace of irony.

At his instruction I headed off the A34 when we reached Wilmslow. Jamie supplied directions and as we turned into the road leading to the private Wilmslow Green estate I noticed a Rolls-Royce showroom on the corner. This clearly wasn't the sort of neighbourhood where they sell used cars on their forecourts. Jamie's brother lived in an elegant turn-of-the-century house in its own grounds. He was waiting on the doorstep when we pulled up on the gravelled drive.

I could tell they were brothers so that part of the story seemed to be true. I wasn't sure of Jamie's age, well under twenty-five I guessed, and this guy looked perhaps four years older than him, say twenty-seven or twenty-eight. The family resemblance was strong but strictly surface level. They were tall and athletic with the same long bony face, dark hair, sallow complexion and very blue eyes, but the brother had a dark flame of anger in his which I hadn't detected in Jamie. Three days growth of dark stubble awaited the razor. By contrast his head was closely shaven.

Jamie's expression was open and guileless, whereas his brother's darting eyes were restless . . . shifty even. It wasn't hard to believe that he had a problem. There was a menacing quality about him. His hunched posture radiated impatience and tension. I try to avoid taking an instant dislike to anyone but I was on my guard.

'This is my brother, Lee Parkes,' Jamie began.

I looked from one brother to the other. Why the different names?

'For Christ's sake, don't start the poor bastard on the family history, Jamie! He'll have enough unravelling to do before he's finished,' snapped Lee, picking up on my unspoken question. 'And what are you gawping at?' he snapped at me. 'Come in the bloody house and we'll get down to business.'

My jaw didn't drop by more than a millimetre but Lee's words were like a slap in the face after Jamie's comically unassuming way of speaking. The client seemed to think he was hiring a flunky. Too bad! If Lee Parkes expected me to show 'respect' he'd be waiting a long while. Looking from Lee to Jamie I realised what it was I'd been missing about Jamie's character . . . he was shy. Lee was the exact opposite.

16

As for me, I know what I am . . . bloody-minded.

'No,' I said, 'I'm going nowhere until I get an explanation.'

'Cheeky bastard! We're paying your wages, aren't we?' Lee snarled. 'Who the fuck do you think you are? Are you trying to prove you're hard or something?'

'Listen, Mr Parkes, I didn't come here to join the Kray Gang. I came because I was told Jamie needed help. And no one's paid me a penny yet.'

'The bloody Kray Gang?' Lee chortled. 'Well, you're good for a laugh if nothing else. You're forty years too late to join them but then you probably think anyone from "dahn Sarth" who talks a bit rough has to be a major league criminal.'

'Are you?'

'I'm a legitimate businessman.'

'He is,' Jamie corroborated.

Lee continued to laugh. 'Come in, you daft bugger. I'm not trying to recruit you to knock off the Crown jewels or something.'

I followed him into the house.

'Drink?' Lee offered when we entered the big, comfortably furnished lounge. There was a little stage in one corner complete with a set of drums and amps. Perhaps they wanted me to join their combo?

'Drink?' he repeated, flicking his hand towards the long bar counter which was supplied with more kinds of liquor than Loony Leary's. 'Name your poison. Whisky, brandy, anything you like, but I'm not making any fancy cocktails today.'

'Any kind of whisky'll be fine.'

He poured me a hefty shot of Bell's, gave himself an even more impressive brandy and passed a can of Diet Coke to Jamie.

'He's in training,' Lee commented as we all sat down. The sofa he steered me to was more like a bed than a seat.

17

Lowering myself, I sank well below his eye level. I struggled back to my feet and took a chair from behind a table and sat on that instead.

'Like to be in charge, do you?' Lee quipped.

'Best to be comfortable, isn't it?'

'I suppose so,' he muttered. His mood seemed to have darkened. 'Right, well, I got you here because I want you to root out the scum who kidnapped my daughter.'

'Kidnapped?' I repeated stupidly.

'Yeah, that's right, Mr Cunane,' put in Jamie. 'What sort of a person would kidnap a baby?'

Lee gestured impatiently at him to shut up.

'We need you as an investigator not some kind of psychic,' he continued. 'I can do a lot of things but investigation's not one of them. No patience. But I want them bastards punished.'

'Whoah!' I said. Like a rock climber taking a downward glance I had a sudden rush of vertigo. This was clearly no footballer's prank.

'No, I've got to say this now or I never will. Here, look.' Lee snatched up a silver-framed photo from a coffee table and thrust it into my hands.

'That's my wife and child. The wife killed herself in a car accident and now some bloody freak's nearly let my little girl die this weekend. What do you think of that?'

His eyes were glittering with rage. I cleared my throat to speak but no reply was required.

'Coldest weekend for months,' he continued, 'and they leave her in the boot of an abandoned car. Poor little thing's had leukaemia from birth. She's had transfusions and everything. We were building her up for a bone marrow transplant but now she's in hospital again because of what's been done to her.'

He clenched his hands into fists at the thought.

'Those filthy nonces! What am I supposed to do? Fold my arms and sit quietly like a plaster saint? No way! They

18

kidnapped my baby, took two hundred thousand off me and didn't give a shit whether she lived or died. Tell me, Mr Manchester Private Eye, do you think I'm a criminal for wanting payback for that?'

There was silence for some time after this outburst. I looked at the photo. The child resembled its mother, a natural redhead with a vacant expression. The baby looked sickly. Various thoughts went through my head. Did Lee want them caught because they'd cheated him out of two hundred thousand or because the child had been brought close to death?

'Tell us,' Jamie insisted, voice high-pitched with emotion, 'what sort of a person would kidnap a baby and leave her like that?'

'Was there any, er, interference?' I asked diffidently.

'No!' Lee barked 'None of that! But in my book anyone who neglects a sick baby is asking for the chop.'

'It's usually disturbed women who kidnap babies and neglect is the last thing on their minds, but this is different. It was a man, you say?'

'Two of them,' Jamie muttered.

'What happened exactly?'

Lee turned away and banged his fist on the bar before slugging another measure of brandy into his glass.

Jamie was left to answer my question.

'They told us she was being looked after but when we finally got to her at midnight . . .'

'Midnight, mind you,' Lee interjected. 'Those dirty bastards!' He underscored his grief by kicking the base of the bar savagely.

Jamie fluttered his hands in a pacifying gesture before continuing.

'Now she's on the critical list at the Alexandra Hospital. They had her all day and didn't feed her, change her or even keep her warm. Who could do that? It was so cruel.'

This time there was no way I could evade offering an

opinion. 'There are some people who don't play by the rules,' I murmured. 'How did you find her?'

'They ran us ragged all day and all night and then finally sent us to an abandoned car in a back street of Wilmslow. And there she was, barely alive.' Jamie struggled to maintain his composure but couldn't suppress the tears as he spoke.

The room felt cold.

'What about the police?' I asked eventually.

'Out of the fucking question!' yelled Lee. He shot out of his chair and went over to the bar to pour himself yet another shot of brandy. His hands were shaking. 'I can't have them involved, do you understand? There's to be no police.'

'This business you're in – it wouldn't be drugs, would it?' I said.

'Suspicious bastard, aren't you? No, it isn't drugs, as it happens, but that doesn't mean I can afford to have a bunch of Plods sniffing round.'

I must have looked doubtful because he turned to Jamie who was clutching his can of Coke as if his life depended on it.

'Tell him, bro. Fill him in on what I do for a living.'

'Yeah,' mumbled the soccer star. 'Yeah,' he repeated. 'Lee's like, well . . .'

'Spit it out,' he commanded.

'Lee's a professional gambler. He makes money on the results of soccer matches, among other things.'

'So?' I said.

'So, all right,' Lee continued. 'Nothing illegal about gambling, is there? Except you make more money if you know the results in advance. Isn't that right, bro?'

'I've done nothing wrong,' Jamie protested feebly.

'Try telling that to the gutter press when they find out I've taken money from Malaysian Chinese bookies to fix matches,' Lee shot back. He seemed to be taunting Jamie.

'I've never fixed anything,' Jamie insisted. At that moment he looked more like a teenager wrongly accused of something than a famous professional footballer. I felt sorry for him.

'I know that,' Lee said, 'but will the police when they find out that we're blood brothers?'

'I've done nothing wrong! It's not my fault you've always wanted more than you're entitled to.'

'You told me who was susceptible to a little offer. Very thick with some of your England team-mates, aren't you?'

I cleared my throat.

'Yes, well, that's not what we're here for, is it?' Lee conceded. 'There's no need for anyone to know that I'm a professional gambler, Jamie. We were adopted, Mr Cunane,' he explained, turning his attention to me. 'Our parents died in a car crash when I was seven and Jamie was three. He took the name of the couple who adopted him while I kept the name of our natural parents. Funny you should say that about the Krays . . . I did live in Bethnal Green for a while when I was little, just round the corner from Vallance Road where the twins lived, but they were before my time and my adoptive father was perfectly respectable. Poor sod died of cancer six months ago, as it happens.'

'Sorry,' I muttered.

'Yes, cancer at the age of sixty-three. That's what an honest life gets you. He drove a bread van. Imagine it, stuck behind the wheel of a bloody van for forty years to provide for your family and then you get cancer as your reward. Well, not for me.'

He took a long swallow of his drink before turning back to Jamie. It was hard to read his expression as he looked at his brother.

'Jamie and I used to see each other every weekend. It's just the luck of the draw that he turned out to be a fantastic footballer. I played for Millwall myself, mainly

21

in the reserves . . . first team, once or twice, but they let me go. They said I was too slow on the turn — not that I was sorry to leave. Right bunch of bananas some of those old professional footballers. They treated me like shit. What a bollocking I got if I didn't give them easy passes! The youngsters were expected to do the running for them while they took the glory, and then the snide bastards said I was slow.'

He paused and looked reflectively at Jamie.

'Well, I soon showed I wasn't too slow in other ways, didn't I?'

'Yeah,' his brother agreed. 'You wouldn't believe it, Mr Cunane, but he started gambling when he was still at school. He made money at it, loads of the stuff. He's clever. He went all over the country gambling at racetracks. Lee's one of those punters who has the lucky touch . . .'

'Luck!' he interjected. 'Inside knowledge is the only way to get ahead in gambling! You get that by knowing the right people.'

'Yeah, like the Malaysian Chinese,' Jamie agreed gloom-ily.

'I still don't know how they found out that Jamie and I are brothers,' Lee continued. 'It wasn't common knowledge when we were kids. Jamie's new family thought they were a cut above mine. Jack Piercy had his own contracting business — still does. They discouraged us from meeting, and my people took the hump at them being snobs. Naturally, the more they were against us seeing each other, the more that encouraged us. We kept in touch in secret and never missed seeing each other at least once a week. That's right, innit, bro?'

'Yeah,' Jamie agreed. I looked at him. His expression was as unfathomable as his brother's had been a moment earlier.

'OK,' I said. 'You're both publicity shy but now I need to know exactly what happened to the little girl.'

22

'Cheyenne,' said Jamie. 'She's called Cheyenne.'

'And nothing goes to the pigs, you clear on that?' Lee growled.

'Crystal!' I muttered. While Jamie's face remained inscrutable, big brother Lee was coming over all menacing again. I smiled at him. *That's ten per cent on your bill*, I thought, trying to keep my expression bland.

'Leave it out, Lee!' Jamie said sharply. 'Mr Cunane doesn't need to be told.'

'Just as long as he knows.'

'I know,' I said quietly, while thinking that Lee had just bumped his bill up another ten per cent. 'Suppose we get on with you telling me what happened to Cheyenne?'

'It's all that bloody girl's fault . . .'

'What bloody girl?'

'Her nanny, Naomi Carter.'

'Lee, you know it wasn't her fault,' Jamie interrupted.

'She was in charge of Cheyenne, wasn't she?'

'Only because you'd made her take the baby out for a walk on the coldest morning of the year.'

'She'd been crying all night. I needed a break.'

'This was last Saturday?' I asked.

Lee nodded.

'What time?'

'Time? What does that matter?'

'Just tell him, Lee!' Jamie ordered.

'It was nine o'clock. I told her to bring the papers back with her. I only sent them out to give the kid some air.'

'You sent her out while you packed off that stupid bimbo Keeley!'

'She's not a bimbo. She's the wife of one of my oldest friends and I can spend the night with whoever I please. I don't ask you who you sleep with.'

Bemusement must have clouded my open features.

'My wife . . .' Lee began.

'Cheyenne's mother?' I interjected.

23

'Who else, you cheeky bastard?'

'You never know these days,' I said unapologetically.

Lee seethed for a moment and glared at his brother. Then he took a deep breath and went on with the story.

'My deceased wife, Mel,' he said between clenched teeth, 'who was Cheyenne's mother, got herself killed about ten weeks ago. Wrapped her Porsche round a tree at a roundabout on the A34, the silly bitch.'

'I'm sorry,' I said, making a mental note of the choice of words.

'Gee, thanks! I lose my wife and you're sorry.'

'Lee, just concentrate on what happened,' Jamie advised.

'Mel's gone and Keeley rallied round to help. Only it turned out she had something else in mind other than just helping . . . What if she did share my bed? It was only the once and I had to tell her that afterwards. Her husband, Kimball, is one of my oldest mates. She got a bit emotional.'

'So naturally you wanted your daughter out of the house for a short time?'

He studied my face to see if I was winding him up.

'In view of what happened I have to know if the kidnappers were expecting Cheyenne to be out in her pram at that time,' I explained.

'Yeah,' Lee agreed. 'She often went out in the mornings, but that didn't stop Carter from complaining every time she had to go out. Idle cow! If I'd let her have her way she'd have had Cheyenne propped up in front of the telly while she had her head stuck in some daft magazine. The doctors told me fresh air was good for Cheyenne. I mean, what do you think I am, some sort of monster?'

'I told you, I don't think anything.'

'Cheyenne's been delicate from birth, but a walk lasting an hour or so would have done her no harm. She had the best clothing and pushchair money could buy.'

'I saw to that,' Jamie confirmed.

24

'*I saw to that*,' mimicked Lee. 'Do you think I'm incapable of looking after my own kid?'

'I just meant that I love her too,' Jamie muttered.

'Right, OK,' Lee agreed. 'All Carter had to do was to walk Cheyenne round a few streets and bring her back safe and sound. She didn't.'

'That's not fair, Lee,' Jamie said, 'and you know it. She's just a teenager.'

'She could have done something – fought them, got help – but she did nothing.'

There were a hundred things I needed to ask but for the present they boiled down to one.

'Where's the nanny now?'

'She's upstairs, in a right state,' Lee said gloomily.

'How have you explained what happened to Cheyenne? The doctors must have asked.'

'I told them the nanny kept her out in the cold too long.'

'That was a bit rough. No wonder she's in a state,' I commented.

'Do you think I don't know that?'

'I don't want to be morbid but is there any chance Cheyenne would have fallen ill whatever happened to her that day? I mean . . .'

'I know what you mean and the answer is no. Either Carter or me would have seen there was something wrong if we'd had her here with us. Those animals left her in the boot of an abandoned car and I want them.'

'They shouldn't be impossible to find,' I said after an awkward pause.

'I know that but I can't do it. That's where you come in.'

'The question is, though, what are you going to do if I do find them?'

'No one's asking you to get your hands dirty.'

'You must know the law better than that. If I find the

25

names of these people for you and they end up with their heads bashed in, it won't be long before the police come knocking on my door.'

'Find them and I'll deal with them well away from you. I've got contacts. You don't grow up in the East End of London without knowing where to find certain people.'

'I don't seem to be getting through to you, Lee.'

'According to Clyde Harrow you aren't always so finicky,' Jamie put in.

I looked at him, unable to make up my mind. Though capable of petulance on the football pitch Jamie had seemed mild enough in private but now he was openly baying for blood.

'Don't believe everything Clyde Harrow tells you,' I growled.

'Well, he spoke very highly of you,' Jamie replied.

'I just want to know who they are,' Lee said wearily. 'Mr Cunane, I'm appealing to you. You seem like a normal sort of bloke and not some arty-farty social worker. These people deserve seeing to. It's not as if they're even going before a judge for a tap on the wrist.'

'It isn't fair, but me going to prison for conspiracy to murder or commit GBH isn't fair either,' I said quietly.

'But don't you see? Unless you do something they'll have won. They must have known I couldn't bring in the police. How will Cheyenne or me ever be free from them now? I've got to find them or they'll bleed me dry. I don't want to kill them, I'm not crazy. I don't want to spend Cheyenne's childhood in jail. Getting my money back would be nice but I must know who they are. Next time Cheyenne might not be so lucky.'

'As a point of interest, how much money did they originally ask for?'

'They wanted half a million at first but I managed to persuade them that I don't keep that kind of money lying around the house.'

26

'You beat them down to two hundred thousand?'

'Are you trying to make me look cheap?' he snarled.

'No, I'm just trying to get my head round your Oliver Twist theory.'

'What are you on about?'

'You said they'd come back for more. In most cases I'd say they wouldn't. It's not blackmail these folk are interested in but a quick score and no trouble from the law.'

'And in this case?' Jamie asked.

'It's just possible they might come back as they asked for half a mill and they know you're a famous footballer. *They* might feel that you two got the better of them.'

'So you'll take the job?' Jamie asked eagerly. 'For Cheyenne's sake, not Lee's or mine?'

'I haven't said that,' I replied quickly. 'I need to know a lot more first.'

Experience has made me very distrustful. This could be some kind of complicated scam.

'I'm interested in the case . . .'

'Hark at you!' Lee said scornfully. 'Interested!'

'. . . I'm interested, but I'm not going to take it until I've listened to what Naomi Carter has to say.'

'Get Carter!' Lee ordered Jamie.

'I want to see her on her own.'

'Take him up, then.'

Jamie stood and nodded towards the door. I followed him out and up the stairs.

'Lee's not as bad as you think,' he said. 'He likes to give that impression of himself.'

'I don't think anything,' I told him.

'You see why it's all got to be kept secret, don't you?'

I nodded.

'But I can't quite make you two out,' I said. 'One minute, Lee seems to be at your throat, the next you're calming him down, looking out for him. A bit one-sided, isn't it?'

He shrugged.

'We're brothers.'

'So were Cain and Abel.'

He looked at me blankly.

'Cain killed his brother Abel,' I explained.

Light dawned. 'Oh, it's in the Bible, innit? I don't know much about that stuff. Religion's a load of bollocks. No, looking after each other is what I believe in. Lee and I were stuck in a children's home. He looked after me there. Then the Piercys took me in but not him. Lee once walked fifteen miles to see me, wouldn't let us be separated. I've always respected him for that no matter what else he's done. I mean, you have to, don't you?'

There didn't seem to be any short answer to that so I kept my mouth shut.

We reached the upstairs landing and Jamie knocked on a bedroom door. I could hear the sound of sobbing from within.

'Don't tell her my name,' I cautioned. I still felt that I might pull out.

'This is someone who's come to talk to you about Cheyenne,' Jamie said when Naomi Carter opened the door. She was in a 'state' all right. One hand clutched a sodden handkerchief while the other was holding the front of her dressing gown tightly shut. Hair all over the place, tears streaking her chubby face, and she'd dribbled on to her nightdress. Seeing my ugly mug brought her no relief. She started another bout of wailing. When she raised her hands to shield her face she looked like a frightened child. I noticed that the fingernails on both hands were bitten down to the quick.

'Now, miss, this won't do,' I said. 'I need to talk to you. You can leave us now, Jamie.'

Naomi Carter waited until he'd gone downstairs.

'Are you the police?' she managed to gasp between heartrending sobs, the hands partly lowered so she could look at me. She was a solidly built lass with strong arms and shoulders. Her mousy brown hair, which was plastered to her face by the constant crying, made it difficult to see her expression.

'I'm not the police,' I said as gently as I could, 'but Mr Parkes wants me to catch the men who took Cheyenne away from you. I need to talk to you.'

'Why won't he get the police? Is it because they'll blame me? I want to tell them what happened . . .'

'Miss Carter, may I call you Naomi?'

There was a lull in the gulping and gasping which I took for consent.

'Can we sit down and talk, Naomi?'

She nodded.

'Mr Parkes wants me to find the men who did this. Wouldn't you like to help me do that?'

She nodded her head vigorously and I noticed that her nose had run. I took out a handkerchief and offered it to her. She blew her nose with a sound like Gabriel's horn and handed the handkerchief back. I folded it carefully and put it away. There were chairs in the wide upstairs hallway, fancy Sheraton replicas, and rather than go into her bedroom I led her towards these. She sat down with her head hanging.

'I'm a detective but not a policeman, and I'm going to catch the men who took you and Cheyenne. Nobody's going to blame you for what happened.'

'Mr Parkes does, I know he does.'

'No, he doesn't. He's got problems of his own. All he wants now is to catch these men.'

'Will I get into trouble? I mean, is this a criminal thing?'

I studied her for a moment. She wasn't as stupid as that hysterical weeping made her look. I took out the card identifying me as a member of Pimpernel Investigations and passed it to her. I was being drawn into this case whether I liked it or not.

'I'm a private detective, Naomi. I don't do anything illegal because I'd be the first person the police would come down on if I did. You want these men caught, don't you?'

She nodded her head vigorously.

'They should be strung up by their balls until they scream for mercy,' she said viciously, 'then cut down and shot.'

'Good, Naomi,' I said. 'We're not going to do that, but if you help me there may be ways to catch them and stopping them hurting anyone else. I'm not asking you to do anything against the law. Do you understand that?'

She nodded her head so strenuously that the chair she was sitting on creaked. Her story came rattling out, so packed with detail that I could scarcely take it in.

'I was wheeling Cheyenne on the main street in Wilmslow – Alderley Road. We had to wait ages at the pedestrian crossing to get to the other side, it's such a busy road. She has a lovely pushchair, by the way. The most expensive they had in Daisy and Tom's – that's the posh children's shop on Deansgate. It's a German make and very easy to push. Mel got all Cheyenne's clothes there as well, Baby Dior and such, all designer stuff.'

She looked at me to see if I was suitably impressed. I struggled to show no sign of impatience but smiled as if to say that the ways of the rich were a mystery to me too.

'It can get boring, wheeling a baby round the streets, but the shops in Wilmslow are totally upmarket. It's not like wheeling a kid round the back streets of Nottingham, like I used to do before. Anyway, I knew I had to stay out for at least ninety minutes . . .'

'Mr Parkes said he only told you to go out for an hour.'

'No, it was always more like two. He never likes me coming back too early.'

'Go on, then.'

'Well, I was taking my time. There was a freezing wind

and Cheyenne was better wrapped up than I was. I went in the Grove Arcade. At least you're sheltered there. It's covered, you know.'

'I see.'

'Then I thought I'd grab a cup of coffee to warm myself up. My nose had turned blue but I can't go inside a coffee shop.'

'Why not?'

'It's one of high and mighty Mr Parkes's rules. I'm not to go inside anywhere and leave Cheyenne outside or take her in with me. He's frightened of germs. I don't know what he thinks I'm going to do with her. Anyway, there's this little café on Grove Street, that's just round the corner from the Arcade, called the Gusto. They let you drink outside there.'

'So you had a cup of coffee?'

'Yes, and a packet of crisps – cheese and onion.'

'All right. Did you notice anyone watching you?'

'No, it's a busy street. Why should I think anyone would be watching me? Was I supposed to be on the lookout?'

'Don't worry, I was only asking. What happened next?'

'I thought I'd go down Hawthorn Lane. That runs along the back of all the shops and you come out on the main road at another pedestrian crossing. It's like a circuit of the town, I do it most days that I take Cheyenne out. There's this nice baby shop on Hawthorn Lane called Bambino. I like looking in the window there and sometimes I pick up something for Cheyenne but not on Saturday. It was freezing. I just looked in the window and checked that she was OK, which she was. She was fast asleep, the little pet, and completely shielded from the wind.

'I walked on a little way and that's when it happened.'

Naomi buried her face in her hands and gave herself the comfort of another little weep.

'I see.'

'You don't!' she wailed. Indignation roused her from

31

self-pity. 'You don't know what it was like. It was horrible!'

'Tell me everything you can,' I soothed.

'I saw this ambulance facing me. At least, I thought it was an ambulance. There was a flashing light. A man got out, the driver. He had a peaked cap and he stood right in front of me, blocking the pavement, but I didn't stop. I only slowed down, like. He asked me for directions. I thought it was funny. I mean, an ambulance man, he should know where everywhere is. So I was going past him when he rapped on the side of the ambulance and the back door opened and this other horrible thug got out. He had a clown's mask on and he was huge. He sprayed something in my face and then he grabbed me and put me in the van. It all happened so fast, it was unbelievable. I had no time to open my mouth before they were driving away.'

At this point Naomi halted her breathless narrative and began trembling with fear. She shut her eyes tightly. I thought she was going to pass out. I touched her arm and after a long pause she started talking again.

'I think I must have become unconscious, like, then,' she said timidly, 'because the next thing I remember is coming round on a bench in the car park outside Willows Lane Baptist Church in Cheadle Hulme. It was terrible. I was so cold I could hardly move and my face was all stuck up with some sort of chemical.'

'Was it Mace or ammonia? Did it sting or burn your eyes?'

'I don't know.'

She put her head in her hands and sobbed bitterly.

'Can you remember what happened next?' I probed.

'It was the most horrible moment in my life, even worse than being snatched up off the street. I looked round and I saw the pushchair. Its back was towards me. I went over. The blanket I'd wrapped Cheyenne in was there but she wasn't. You must think I'm stupid but I howled. I screamed my head off but nobody came. The car park's behind a thick hedge and there was no one in the church. Then I remembered I had the mobile. I thought I'd dial the police but I wasn't sure about the number . . .'

'Nine-nine-nine,' I said gently.

'But I wasn't sure if it was the same on a mobile so I pressed the button to speak to Mr Parkes instead and he said not to tell the police, that it might be some friends playing a trick, and he came for me.'

Naomi started wailing again. She buried her head in her hands. I guessed this was the state she'd been in since Saturday. Lee Parkes had done nothing to comfort her. I patted her arm as gently as I could but this time she didn't come out of her crying fit.

I knew I was taking the case. It was stupid and dangerous and might wreck the business but I didn't care. The truth is that I'm an adrenalin junkie. I can do a boring desk job but I can't hack it for long.

'Listen, Naomi,' I said gently. 'Go and get a shower now. Then get dressed in your outside clothes and we'll go over the route you took with Cheyenne. Is that all right? I mean, face it, lovey, you're doing yourself no good sitting up here sobbing your heart out. You might as well pack up.'

'I'm already packed up. There's no baby here for me now, is there? Cheyenne'll need a nurse not a nanny. I wanted to go yesterday but Mr Parkes said to stay.'

'Have you any relatives you can go to?'

'I've got my mum, but she won't have me back. She split up with me dad and she's got a new partner who doesn't like me.'

'What about your dad?'

'He's in Strangeways for armed robbery. That's why I took a job here, so I could visit him.'

'Naomi, if I find you somewhere to stay, somewhere that doesn't remind you of poor Cheyenne all the time, will you come with me?'

33

Mention of Cheyenne set off a new round of bawling but she looked me in the face this time and nodded her agreement. Then she got up and strode purposefully to her room.

I went down to the brothers.

'I'll take the job,' I said, 'but there are some more questions and then we need to sort out one or two little problems.'

'Fire away,' Lee said. 'The sooner we get started, the sooner we catch these scum.'

'I need to know everything that happened after Naomi phoned you to tell you that Cheyenne had been kidnapped.'

3

'I knew you'd take the job,' Lee smirked. 'Not many people could resist prying into the affairs of Jamie Piercy . . .'

'That's not it!' I said harshly, wanting to wipe that knowing grin off his face.

'All right,' Lee said, holding his hands palm up towards me. 'I surrender, Cunane. You're a noble knight on a white charger righting wrongs and rescuing ladies in distress. How much do you want for the job?'

'Lee, will you leave it alone?' Jamie pleaded. 'He's said he'll do the job.'

'But on his own terms,' snarled Lee.

'What does that mean?' I asked. 'I've already promised to keep your dirty little business secret. You must trust me to that extent. Now if you don't mind telling me everything that happened after Naomi . . .'

'Oh, it's *Naomi* now, is it?' he interjected peevishly.

'. . . after Naomi took Cheyenne out on Saturday, I'll get down to business.'

It felt as if I was speaking lines in a play. I wasn't comfortable in my skin with this man. I took out a notebook and the feel of the pages under my fingers restored me a little.

Lee glowered, but like a thunderstorm disappearing on an April day, his dark mood vanished. Perhaps he was right, I couldn't resist prying into the affairs of Jamie Piercy. But then his affairs were also Lee's. I made a mental note to read the reports of every match Jamie had played for the Reds over the last three years.

'*Naomi* left the house just after nine,' Lee said. 'You'd think I'd asked her to go on a Polar expedition, the fuss she made.'

I made a note to check Saturday's weather.

Lee watched me write and it seemed to please him. He swallowed a mouthful of brandy.

'Then Keeley came down and left. That didn't take long. We hadn't much to say to each other.'

'OK,' I said, making a further note. 'What then?'

'I got a call about ten, or not much later. It was that sad cow upstairs. I couldn't make out what she saying except that she wanted me to call the police. I told her to can that, sharpish.'

'Naturally,' I commented.

'Yeah, well, I went there to pick her up. She was sat on a bench with the pushchair and no Cheyenne. I felt somebody was pulling my strings and it was all I could do not to hit her but she gabbled out this tale about being picked up off the street so I figured maybe somebody who thought I owed him money was trying to collect some security.'

'And is that possible?'

'No way! I don't owe anybody anything, but in my game there's a lot of sharks and it was possible one of them might have thought it was worth his while to try and put the bite on me. Anyway, I know now it wasn't one of them. Can we get on?'

'I have to ask,' I muttered.

'Hmmm, well . . . I got the silly bitch into the back of the Volvo and got her home and as soon as I pulled into the drive I could hear the phone ringing in the hall.'

'Interesting timing,' I commented.

'Right, so I dived in and grabbed the bloody phone and there's this heavy calling me a Cockney arsehole and demanding five hundred thousand for Cheyenne.'

'Hold on! How did you know he was a heavy?'

'I could tell . . . deep voice, choice of language. I know the type.'

'Really?'

'Don't try to be sarcastic.'

'No,' I agreed. 'Did you recognise the accent?'

'Local, or somebody doing a good imitation of it. I thought it was Bernard Manning for a minute.'

I wrote 'Local heavy??' in my notebook.

'So you started bargaining?' I asked.

'No, Mr Smart-arse, I didn't. He put the phone down before I could say anything and then a few minutes later there was another call. This time I knew the guy wasn't phoning to sell me double glazing or to threaten me. He was smooth as silk but more frightening than the other bugger. He said that if I didn't play ball they'd abandon Cheyenne in some woodland. He wanted the five hundred thousand but I managed to persuade him that I didn't have that sort of money. I offered him two hundred thousand in readies, and as cool as the proverbial salad ingredient he said he'd put the offer to his associate. Then I phoned Jamie.'

'Yeah, that's right,' he agreed. 'The match was on Monday not Saturday that week, thanks to Sky Television. I got round here quick.'

'And not long after the first guy phoned again, the one with the Bernard Manning accent,' Lee continued. 'He was checking that I hadn't got the five hundred thou. I was sure they were going to kill her.'

'I wanted him to phone the police,' Jamie told me.

'But I told him then what I'll tell you now,' Lee said. 'We both have too much to lose. We wouldn't have needed you if they'd stuck to the bargain and handed Cheyenne over safe and sound. What they did was completely out of order and now they've got to pay for that.'

Jamie hung his head and remained silent.

'Tell him the rest,' Lee ordered.

Jamie looked at me. He seemed to be on the verge of

tears. 'I'd have done anything to get Cheyenne back safe and sound. You've got to believe that, Mr Cunane.'

'I do believe it,' I soothed him.

'He phoned again, the smooth one. Lee said he had his brother with him – and he knew who I was! It was afternoon by this time, two o'clock. We were both going frantic. He said he wanted to speak to Jamie. Told me they'd settle for the two hundred thousand but the handover had to be after dark so we couldn't see who they were. He said Cheyenne was being well looked after. He gave me the instructions about what to do . . .'

'Go on.'

'It was incredible. The money had to be divided into two parcels wrapped up really well.'

'We did that,' Lee said impatiently.

'They kept us waiting. I couldn't stand it but eventually they rang again, hours later. We had to make the drop at Alderley Edge.'

'You mean the town?' I asked.

'No, he means the flipping beauty spot. They had us trailing about round the woods and cliffs in the pitch dark,' Lee said angrily.

'Yeah, first they had us waiting in a lay-by on the Macclesfield Road just where a white sign pointed to a footpath over the Edge. He said we'd be under observation. So we waited.'

'We waited a full hour,' Lee added.

'Then they phoned again. We had to take the money across the Edge to the Devil's Grave.'

'I beg your pardon?'

'You heard!' Lee snapped. 'The Devil's Grave! I ask you. They were playing games with us.'

'It's this, like, cave on top of the Edge,' Jamie explained.

'I know, it's a well-known beauty spot.'

'Anyway, when we got there, there were these two luminous sacks like post bags under a stone and we had to put money in each of them and then the bags just disappeared like a conjuring trick.'

'It wasn't a conjuring trick,' Lee said. 'There were cords fastened to the bags and they jerked them down this sheer drop so we couldn't follow without parachutes. Not that we would have tried. They'd told us we'd be under view with powerful night glasses.'

'When we got back to the car they phoned and told us to go home to wait for the instructions about where to pick up Cheyenne. They kept us waiting until nearly midnight. We found her in an abandoned Skoda car on Cleetor Lane in Wilmslow. I thought she was dead when I saw her. It was the worst moment of my life.'

'It was the same guy who gave you instructions throughout, the smoothie?'

'Yeah, and I'd love to meet him again,' Jamie said softly.

'And he knew who you were?'

'He knew everything about me. Taunted me, the sad bastard!'

'Careful, bro!' Lee said sarcastically. 'You'll alarm Mr Cunane if he thinks you want vengeance.'

'I've said I'll take the job, and I will, but there are just one or two things we have to get straight first.'

'I thought there might be,' Lee snapped, nursing another large brandy. 'What is it? Do you want a split of the money when you recover it? Fifty-fifty, is that it? A hundred grand for you and a hundred for me – or do you want the lot?'

'Why don't you shut up, and listen to what the man's got to say?' Jamie muttered. 'It's your big mouth that got us into this mess in the first place. If you'd paid what they asked, Cheyenne might have been returned safe and sound.'

'We don't know that,' I interjected. Fraternal strife was the last thing I needed. Judging by the venomous expression on Lee's face, blows were only a short distance away.

'I'm sorry,' Jamie said. 'I didn't mean that. It's just that this is all too heavy, know what I mean?'

'Are you going to say you can't do it?' Lee put in.

'No, I've already told you that it's possible. Just because the police would put fifty officers on this case doesn't mean they're fifty times more likely to succeed than one man. Those fifty spend a lot of their time coordinating things, telling each other what they've had for breakfast, jockeying for promotion, going to the boozer, etcetera, etcetera. Believe me, in a lot of police investigations it's really one man driving things along and sometimes the mass of information the others turn up just gets in his way.'

'Right, I get the message,' Lee said impatiently. 'What's your first move?'

'If the kidnappers are from round here, as the Manchester accent suggests, then we're looking for local villains with two hundred thousand to spend. Criminals who get caught do so because they spend too much or talk too much. They always have plenty of mates ready to grass them up, especially when there's a reward involved.'

Lee smirked. 'So you'll want money then.'

'Yes, I'll need some money on account – but, I'm sorry, I'm not free to start work straight away. I'm supposed to be going to Holland with a friend called Bob Lane to visit his brother. I could cry off that but it's difficult.'

'Bob Lane?' Lee repeated. 'Not the one they call "Popeye"?'

'Yes.'

'Then you're a hypocrite, Cunane. Talk about two-faced! You ask me if my money comes from drugs and then casually mention you're friendly with the biggest importer of marijuana in the north-west of England.'

'He's never been arrested for it.'

'His name's well known in certain circles.'

'So you are familiar with the local crime faces?'

40

'With some of them,' Lee confirmed.

'When I first knew Bob he was just a club bouncer. What he's done since is his own affair and I've told him what I think about it. When he gets caught I'll not lift a finger to help him, but he is my friend. He keeps saying he's going to get out of the weed business and swears he's never brought in any hard drugs. We were going to see his brother. Clint's handicapped and really looking forward to seeing us . . . but I suppose I might be prepared to put the trip off.'

I was waiting for Lee to be magnanimous.

'Oh pass the sick bag, Cunane,' he muttered disgustedly. 'Next thing you'll be asking for a subscription to Oxfam.'

'All I'm trying to explain is that I have other commitments. I can give you the name of another investigator, if you like?'

'And we'll have to go through all this rigmarole with him? No, thanks. I'd rather try on my own. I *can* drop everything. What have I got now? No wife, sick kid, no fucking life at all until these fucking bastards are found.'

Lee whirled round and grabbed the brandy. He started to pour himself another healthy belt but Jamie snatched the bottle off him.

'That's no solution.' He pulled his brother by the wrist and tugged him over to the conservatory that opened off the lounge. They held a whispered and urgent conversation with Jamie taking the lead and making his points by poking Lee in the chest with two fingers. First impressions can be deceptive. The Premier League player was forceful enough when he wanted to be.

It was Jamie who took the lead when they came back.

'We want you to do the job, Mr Cunane . . . Dave. And it's to be kept strictly confidential. We'll hold you responsible if anything gets out to the press.'

'What do you mean, responsible?' I asked.

'Just that,' barked Lee. 'If the boys in blue find out

anything about what we told you then you'd better start watching your back.'

'Take no notice of Lee,' Jamie said smoothly. 'He doesn't know how to deal with people. This is how we'll play it. We'll give you ten thousand pounds now to start this investigation, pay for information like you said and your expenses, and we'll pay whatever your firm bills us at normal rates. Then there'll be a personal bonus of twenty thousand pounds in cash for you if our anonymity remains intact plus ten thousand pounds in cash for the name and current location of each of the sickos who kidnapped Cheyenne.'

'You believe in cash incentives, then?' I asked with a smile.

'I'm a professional footballer.'

'And the downside of this munificent offer is?'

'I'll take you to court if you reveal our identities to the press in the course of the investigation. We'll sue you for every penny you have.'

'Confidentiality is part of our standard contract but you introduced yourself to me through Clyde Harrow, one of the biggest newshounds in the country. I can't guarantee he'll keep his mouth shut.'

'I know Clyde,' Jamie said awkwardly.

'Fair enough. But what do you intend to do with these bozos if we catch them?'

'When we catch them,' Lee interjected.

'All right, when we catch them.'

'We thought we'd discuss that with you now.'

'You mean, you thought,' Lee said bitterly.

'Yeah, well, we can hardly turn them over to the police,' Jamie said, fluttering his hands in that now familiar helpless gesture. 'Listen, Dave, if you're prepared to turn a blind eye to what happens to the scumbags, I'll let you have my Ferrari.'

I'm afraid I laughed at this. It was the wrong thing to

do. Both brothers scowled fiercely and I took a quick glance over my shoulder to see how far I was from the door.

'Sorry,' I said, holding my hands up. 'It wasn't you I was laughing at. It was the thought of me driving round Manchester in a Ferrari Maranello. Anyway there may be a way round the crime and punishment issue without Jamie having to give up his wheels. These punks are hardly likely to be beginners . . . sit down for a minute and I'll explain.'

The brothers scowled at me again. Lee was all for clocking me one but Jamie led him back to his chair and seated him *sans* brandy.

'Go on,' Jamie said, very tight-lipped now.

'As I say, this was a professional job. They knew what they were about. It can't be the first time they've done something like this. Think about it – they're a class act. They extort money from people who can't go to the police . . . in fact, the last people in the world to go to the police.'

'The criminal fraternity, you mean,' Lee muttered, 'like your underworld friend, Bob Lane.'

'So illegal gambling and match-fixing are OK then?' I stared at him.

He looked away.

'Go on,' he muttered.

'All I'm saying is there must be other people they've done this to, perhaps even some fatalities. They threatened poor Cheyenne with death right from the word go, didn't they? If we can track down some of the other victims you might find yourself at the end of a long queue waiting to do the business on these creatures.'

'Sly bugger, aren't you?' Lee said.

'No, just experienced.' I was beginning to enjoy baiting him. 'There's something concrete you can do, Lee. You must have some idea who the other people in your line of business are. Put the word out discreetly. Find out if

43

anyone's had a sudden unexplained cash loss. Think of some way to warn others that there's a gang of extortionists on the prowl. Don't tell them what happened to you, just say that you've heard a whisper. It could surprise you what that turns up.'

'Don't want much, do you?' he snarled. 'I've no fucking idea if I can do that.'

'Oh, and I shall want both your signatures on my standard contract. Just to say that I'm acting for you both and to cover me if I need it.'

4

I never got to hear if Lee and Jamie agreed to my plans for retribution at second hand because Naomi Carter arrived downstairs just after they'd signed the contract. She knocked on the lounge door but remained standing outside in the entrance hall. Her appearance was transformed. She was in denim jeans and a pale green sweater with her hair combed back and gathered in a ponytail. Her face was still red and blotchy from all the crying she'd done but otherwise she looked like a normal, if rather stoutly built, teenager. Putting down a Reebok sports bag, she announced, 'I'm ready.'

'What's this?' Lee demanded aggressively, starting up from his chair.

'Naomi's going to stay somewhere else. I thought it would be good for her to get away for a while,' I put in.

'Who the hell asked you to start disposing of my staff? And incidentally you must have done it before you even agreed to take the case.'

While he spoke, Naomi seemed to shrink into herself. She licked her lips nervously. I realised she was scared of her employer. It was possible she had good reason but I hadn't seen any signs of actual physical brutality.

'Listen, Mr Parkes,' I said in my most officious tones, 'it's obvious even to a person of my limited mental capacity that Naomi needs a change of scene if she's going to be able to help us to catch the men we're looking for.'

'So your concern is only for the job?'

'No, just have a bit of sense. She's been through an awful experience.'

'Proper Sir Galahad, aren't you?' he sneered, close enough to give me a whiff of his breath. He must have been on the brandy for several days.

'If you say so,' I retorted.

'Leave it, Lee,' Jamie warned.

'I can catch the bus to my auntie's in Scunthorpe if this is going to cause so much trouble,' Naomi ventured. She sounded much more normal than earlier. The prospect of an escape from Wilmslow and its troubles had galvanised her.

'Forget it,' I said.

'Where are you taking her then?' Lee asked.

'I thought she could stay at my girlfriend's until we find somewhere more permanent for her,' I improvised. I realised as I spoke that I had no idea if Janine would be agreeable. Oh, well, I thought, there's always my parents.

'You have a lot of bright ideas, don't you?'

'Yes, another is that Naomi can show me the streets she walked Cheyenne along, and that Jamie can take us to where you went to pick her up.'

Lee pursed his lips and considered this for a minute. Then he nodded his head.

'Wait here a minute,' he ordered. 'I've got to get you that stuff we talked about. The folding stuff.' He turned and walked off to what I presumed was the kitchen.

I gave Jamie my car keys and asked him to let Naomi into the Mondeo then turned to follow Lee into the kitchen, but when I reached the door he was holding it shut.

'Stop right there,' he growled. 'You know enough about me already without discovering where I keep my money.'

'Why, do you keep it in the freezer like me?' I asked. This lucky shot produced a reaction. He ground his teeth audibly.

'Mind your own damn business.'

46

'I only wanted to remind you that this might be a good time to pay Naomi what you owe her. I shouldn't think this house holds many happy memories for her. I doubt if she'll be coming back.'

'You should have been a social worker, Cunane, not a detective. I was going to give her what I owe her but you just keep your nose out of this room.'

Well put in my place, I retreated to the outside entrance.

Jamie passed me with a smile on his face. 'I'm going up for the rest of her luggage,' he said. I didn't volunteer to assist him.

Sounds of pulling and pushing and grunting began emanating from the kitchen. Lee obviously had his stash behind some bulky piece of equipment. There was a limited range of those in any kitchen. While I speculated, the man himself suddenly came out of the door, his face puce with effort.

He looked at his brother who was tottering down the stairs with a massive stereo system in his hands.

'Hell!' he muttered. Then, 'Come here, Cunane, you big sod! I need you to help me, I'm too pissed to move the bloody fridge-freezer.'

'I thought you wanted secrecy?'

'Don't get too smart. You already know enough about me to really fuck me up if you want to. Now get your arse in here and pull this damned thing out.'

Such is trust among the gambling classes, I thought as I followed him into the expensive fumed-oak kitchen. Always a kitchen fancier, my eyes roved over the cluttered surfaces and worktops. It was obvious there hadn't been much cleaning done recently. The double sink was crammed with pots and there was a mild stink of decay emanating from an overflowing rubbish bin.

'Don't rub it in,' Lee said, following my gaze. 'My cleaner's due back tomorrow. Just get that big shoulder of yours behind this bugger. It's supposed to be on tracks but it seems to have slipped.'

I did as I was told and then stood and watched while he opened the safe. He made no effort to shield the contents from my view. There was easily enough in there for him to have paid the ransom in full, which implied that the person who'd demanded it had a fair idea just how much dosh Lee kept about the pad.

'For ten K I want results,' Lee said as he handed it over. 'I want you to report on progress as often and as soon as you make any. Do you understand?'

I nodded.

He split a bundle and counted out several hundred pounds for Naomi then pushed past me to go out to the car. His brother was in the front passenger seat and Naomi in the back. She wound her window down.

'Here,' he said brusquely, giving her the cash, 'take what you've earned and thanks for keeping your mouth shut.'

Naomi folded the money up but didn't make any fond farewells. I got in and we drove away.

Following Naomi's directions we followed the same route she'd taken with Cheyenne from Lee's house and drove slowly down Station Road and on to Hawthorn Lane. Grove Street, where the coffee bar was, is a pedestrian precinct but we parked at the end and looked along it. I made a note of every place where people were likely to have congregated. We moved along Hawthorn Lane, past Bambino's and parked near where Naomi and Cheyenne had been lifted. I only stopped for a moment because I could hear her snuffling into her handkerchief and didn't care to risk another outbreak of hysterics. It was almost pitch dark but I made a note of the businesses on the narrow street. There were some private flats as well. They'd all have to be covered.

The thought struck me that even now, late in the evening, it wasn't the ideal spot for a kidnapping. There were too many people about. Too many doors which might suddenly bring witnesses on to the street. This gang must have relied on split-second timing and they must be well practised.

We went to Cleetor Lane where Cheyenne had been dumped. The Skoda was still there only it was red and scorched as a result of the intense heat it had been subjected to. It had been burned out and the plates removed.

'Interesting coincidence,' I said to Jamie.

He nodded; the sight appeared to have rendered him speechless. I thought about it for a few minutes. Even if I'd had the car intact, or if the police had had it, it was unlikely that there would have been much forensic evidence from it. This gang was far too careful.

We finished off with a trip to the church car park in Cheadle Hulme. Deserted when Naomi was dumped, it was now jammed with cars. We only discovered that when we drove in. The high perimeter hedge screened it completely from the road. There was some sort of production going on in the church hall. The fact that it was full of cars now and empty when the villains had wanted to drop off Naomi implied once again that they had local knowledge and were careful planners. There aren't all that many places where you can dump someone out of a van on a busy Saturday without being observed.

'I'd like to drive up to Alderley Edge now,' I suggested tentatively.

'I've got training tomorrow morning,' Jamie said, 'won't it do another time?'

'All right,' I agreed. I drove back to the A34 and then on to the M60, taking the turnoff for Chorlton.

Naomi had been very quiet throughout the checking of her route. She hadn't volunteered any information apart from the bare essentials.

'Where are you taking me?' she asked anxiously. 'I'm not going into Moss Side or anywhere down there. I'll catch the bus to Scunthorpe.'

I suppressed a smile. God only knows what stories she'd

been told about the alleged evil dealings going on in inner city Manchester. In my experience most of the really nasty stuff that goes down in this town is dreamed up in the leafy outer suburbs from which I'd just delivered her.

'Don't worry, I'm going to ask my girlfriend if she can put you up for tonight. She's a nice lady with two children. She'll make you feel at home and then we'll think about finding you somewhere more permanent tomorrow.'

This seemed to go down well. She relaxed back into her seat.

Before I let Jamie out of the car I took his mobile number. I bustled Naomi into the entrance of the flats without much ceremony while Jamie made his own way to the garage where his sports car was parked.

'Who is he?' Naomi asked to my surprise as we watched Jamie's back disappear round the corner. 'He's much nicer than Mr Parkes.'

'Oh, don't you know him?'

'This is the first time I've seen him.'

'Really? Well, he's an old friend of Mr Parkes's,' I said wonderingly. I couldn't quite take in what she'd said for a minute. It was hard to grasp that there was a single person the length and breadth of this country who wouldn't recognise Jamie Piercy. It was vaguely possible, I supposed. Maybe she'd only seen the back of his head in the car, and it was dark. I didn't enlighten her.

'Mr Parkes was out most of the time. It was just me and Mel at home until . . . she had the accident.' Naomi gave a sort of whimper at this recollection. 'Then he had that Keeley round a lot but I didn't see many of his men friends.'

We reached the door of Janine's flat. I felt a faint stirring of butterflies in my stomach. Maybe that's why I'd rung the bell as I opened the door. Like rabbits popping out of a hole the faces of Janine and Jenny and Lloyd, her children, appeared at the end of the

50

passage as I swung the door open. Janine came forward.

'Dave! Where have you been till now?' she asked. 'It's after nine.' The expression on her face was what I call transitional. It hovered between affection and irritation. 'Celeste has phoned about four times asking if you've got back.'

'Never mind that. This is Naomi Carter. She's been having a bit of bad luck and I wondered if . . .'

'If I can put her up for the night?' Janine stood with her hands on her hips looking at Naomi who was peering out nervously from behind me. Janine is a determined-looking woman by anyone's reckoning. Then her expression softened. 'It's Liberty Hall here, Dave, you know that,' she said mildly, beckoning Naomi to come forward

'Liberty Hall at the weekends only,' I commented ruefully.

'None of your moaning!' she said, giving me a friendly thump on the arm.

Janine and I have adjoining flats but I spend most weekends in her flat. Alas, efforts to extend the arrangement to the rest of the week have failed so far. Janine is fiercely independent. She's wedded to her career not to me, as she's pointed out many times.

I kissed her and when we uncoupled she led Naomi into the living room of the flat. It was cluttered with children's games and videos. Lloyd and Jenny sank shyly back on to the sofa.

'Where's this man had you? You look as if you're half starved,' Janine said to Naomi.

'We had to check one or two things out,' I explained.

'I know you, Dave Cunane,' she replied. 'I bet you've dragged the poor girl over half of Manchester.'

'No, it's all right, Mrs Cunane,' Naomi said apologetically.

I smiled at Janine, daring her to correct the girl.

51

'It's just Janine White,' she said firmly, 'and this is Jenny White and Lloyd White.'

Since her spot of bother with their father she's had the children's names legally altered from Talbot to White.

'Yeah, we're all Whites here,' I muttered, 'except me.'

Naomi's brow furrowed as she took in this information.

'Are you ready for something to eat?' Janine continued. 'Bacon and eggs all right? Then you look as if you need a good night's sleep.'

Naomi looked flustered. I wasn't surprised. An extended stay in the Parkes household wasn't likely to have accustomed her to civility.

'My things . . . they're in the car.'

'Dave will bring them up, won't you?' Janine said in a tone that didn't invite argument. 'You settle yourself down, Naomi.'

I found myself back at the car. It had started raining again. I opened the boot. It was jammed to the top with Naomi's gear. There was the stereo and a large suitcase, a pile of CDs, a television, a computer system and loose coats on hangers.

I made a start with the stereo system and when I reached the door of her flat Janine was waiting at the door, arms folded.

'Your place with that, I think,' she ordered. 'Naomi told me she has a lot of goods and chattels.'

I pulled a face. My back was aching.

'You'll never guess who loaded these into the car for her.'

'Let me think,' she said. 'Was it a famous footballer?'

'How did you know?' I demanded angrily. 'It was Celeste wasn't it?'

'Oh, come on, Dave. You're not the only one in the investigating business. Don't forget I have the key to your garage. There aren't many people who own monogrammed

Ferraris or many footballers with the initials JP. Could you ask him to give me an exclusive interview . . . "Manchester's Most Eligible Bachelor" . . . I can just see the headlines.'

Janine is a journalist on the local paper. I could tell by her expression that the suggestion wasn't lightly made. Lately she's been finding it hard to juggle her career and the care of children. Her profession's crammed with younger, unattached women who can spend any amount of time hunting down a story.

She opened the door of my flat for me and I staggered in towards the spare bedroom.

'I'm under a heavy penalty clause to maintain Jamie's anonymity,' I said, which wasn't strictly accurate but close enough to the truth. It provoked one of those hundred-and-eighty-degree changes of tack which make reading the tabloid papers interesting.

'Is she his girlfriend?' Janine asked, wagging her head in the direction of her own flat. 'What's the muscular brute done? Raped her or something? You can tell she's been crying a lot.'

Janine doesn't have a high opinion of sportsmen.

'No!' I said, dumping the stereo on to the bed and turning on my partner. 'She doesn't even know who he is, or so she claims, and I'd like it to stay that way. If you must know, she was the nanny to Jamie's baby niece who was kidnapped and left half dead on Saturday.'

'There was nothing in the media about that.'

'That's the way it's going to stay,' I said firmly. 'I'll fill you in later.'

Janine was looking very serious now.

'It's always wheels within wheels with you, Dave,' she commented wonderingly. 'What are we doing about the sleeping arrangements? I don't want to turn one of the children out of their room.'

53

Our flats each have three bedrooms. I use one of my spare bedrooms as a home office.

'She can't come in here with me,' I snapped. 'She's nervous enough already and distrustful of men. She wanted to run off to her auntie in Scunthorpe when she thought I was taking her to Moss Side. Someone's been filling her head with daft tales.'

'Then she can stay in here on her own and bolt the door behind her and you can come in with me. I know it isn't the weekend but I'm prepared to waive the rules for once.'

'Well, wham, bam, thank you, Ma'am!' I said, reaching out for her.

'Stop it!' she commanded. 'Put those hands down. This is an exception because of the emergency and because I want to hear every tiny detail about what's gone on between you and this soccer player.'

I returned to my activities as a Sherpa. Although there are many more stairs up to my flat than in Lee Parkes's house I had to marvel at Jamie's fitness. He'd loaded the car in minutes. Now, as I struggled with burden after burden, I could only regret my foolishness in not moving to somewhere with a lift. It took me a full half-hour by which time Janine had managed to feed Naomi, set her at her ease and also put the children to bed and tidy up.

There was no trace of food for me when I made my final delivery. I must have looked pathetic.

'Dave's a wonderful cook,' Janine said to Naomi in that mocking tone the female sex reserve for discussing men in their presence. 'He'll whip himself up a meal in no time.'

5

Breakfast with Janine made a pleasant change to my mid-week habits. She was very affectionate when we woke up.

'We must do this more often,' she commented.

'What, sex?' I asked.

'No, break out of our routine.'

'Your routine, Janine.'

'Mmm, maybe,' she muttered languorously.

'I want us . . .'

'I know what you want, a little wifey at your beck and call, but that's not going to happen, mate.'

'You'd rather be bullied by some spiteful editor and exhaust yourself trying to hold down a job and look after your children . . . all in the name of greater female freedom.'

'God, Dave! Have you been reading some anti-feminist tract?' she said, grabbing my shoulder and giving me a painful nip. 'Or has your old man given you one of his pep talks?'

'Neither,' I muttered, rubbing my shoulder. 'I can occasionally think for myself, you know.'

'Sorry, mustn't damage the fragile male ego. You might go out and start rioting at football matches if I say the wrong thing.'

'Janine!'

'It's just that you seemed a lot more pleased with yourself last night than you've been for some time. I like you better when there's this hint of danger in the air. Can't you see that we'd get horribly bored with each other if we settled down to married life?'

'No!'

'Race you to the bathroom,' she challenged. Then she was up and heading for the door. I leaped after her and we reached the bathroom at the same time.

'Don't wake the children up,' she giggled as I squeezed in with her. Cold showers were not on her mind. It was some time before we disentangled ourselves. Ablutions completed, Janine woke up the kids and started getting them ready for breakfast while I went next door to get my razor.

It was then that I hit a snag.

Naomi wouldn't open the door, which following Janine's suggestion was bolted on the inside. My front door is a work of art. Following a break-in some years ago I'd had a special security door fitted. The door looks normal from the outside but it incorporates a plate of case-hardened steel five-eighths of an inch thick. Moreover, it's anchored to the specially reinforced wall and floor at top, bottom and both sides. It would be easier to knock a hole in the wall than to force that door open.

I kept my finger on the buzzer for three minutes.

There was no response.

I started imagining things. Had Naomi done away with herself in my guest bedroom?

I went back to Janine's.

'She's asleep!' Janine exclaimed. 'Have you never come across a teenager before? When I was a student I slept through a fire alarm in my hall of residence. It took two firemen to wake me up.'

'Fire-fighters, you mean, Mummy,' Jenny said.

'No, these were firemen,' her mother said sharply. 'I remember one had nice fair hair.'

Jenny grimaced as only an intelligent eight-year-old can.

We tried phoning, with no response. There was no phone extension in the bedroom. Eventually I went downstairs and stood in my dressing gown with my finger pressed on my own outside bell. That has a noticeably louder ring than the front doorbell. I got some funny looks from the neighbours but after pressing for five minutes I got a response.

Upstairs again, I thought it was better if Janine coaxed the slumbering nanny into opening the door, which she did willingly enough. The girl was befuddled with sleep. Her eyes seemed to have shrunk into her face. There were deep crease marks in the flesh around her shoulders.

'I feel as if I haven't slept for three days,' Naomi said by way of unapologetic explanation. 'Do you mind if I go back to bed?'

'Hold on!' I said anxiously. 'I can't have you barricading yourself in again.'

'Oh, I wouldn't need to do that against you, Mr Cunane,' she said dreamily. 'Janine told me all about you last night.'

'And?'

'I think you're safe.'

'So why did you put all the bolts on?'

'Janine thought it would help me sleep better. Now can I go back to bed?'

'No! I need a recent photo of you.'

'Why?'

'Because I'm hitting the mean streets of Wilmslow, Cheshire, today and trying to discover if anyone saw what happened on Saturday. I need to be able to show your photo.'

'Oh, I see,' she said. 'But there are no mean streets in Wilmslow. It's a very rich place.'

'There are,' I said.

Naomi's brow began to furrow and I thought I'd been stupid enough to set the waterworks off again. Her round, open face and wide-set, very blue eyes gave her a look of childlike innocence. Naomi's face was puppyish. Blurred by sleep, it was hard to read. I caught a momentary flicker of something in her eyes, though. Was it anger or was it calculation?

There was definitely more to Naomi Carter than appearances might suggest.

'Dave's only joking,' Janine reassured her.

Solemn-faced and awake now, Naomi began rummaging through the large suitcase which I'd nearly given myself a hernia with last night. The mystery of its incredible weight was solved. She hadn't filled it with bricks as I'd guessed. The small dressing table was already groaning with female beauty aids and bottled concoctions of every sort and colour. The suitcase contained more. She'd also set the stereo up in one corner. I suppose music is as essential as sleep and make-up.

Eventually, Naomi came up with a couple of photos. There was one of herself on her own and one with her pushing Cheyenne in the pram. I eagerly snatched both of them out of her pudgy fingers.

'Satisfied?'

'Not quite,' I said. 'I want you to spend some hours with an artist doing a reconstruction of the phoney ambulance man who spoke to you on Hawthorn Lane. Janine's going to ask a mate of hers called Granville Courteney to come round and make a sketch of him which we can show people.'

Janine raised her eyebrows at me to say it was the first she'd heard of it then nodded to say she'd do it anyway.

Naomi looked at me, at Janine, and then at her bed with a curious expression on her face. For a second I had to wonder how seriously she took Saturday's events now that she'd left the Parkes home behind her. You never know with teenagers. Their minds are not as our minds. It was possible that if she spent a lot of time watching the soaps she thought a street kidnapping was a fairly run-of-the-mill experience.

'Can I go back to bed first?' she asked with a weary shake of her head. 'I'll be able to remember things better with a bit more sleep.'

I must have looked impatient at this response but fortunately Janine stepped in again.

'Yes, you sleep, dear. Mr Courteney isn't an early riser either. It'll be an hour or two before I can rouse him into activity and then I'll come round with him and pick you up for lunch, but don't bar the door. I'll let myself in and wake you up gently.'

This diplomatic intervention was rewarded with a warm smile. I obviously have a lot to learn about sleep deprivation among the under-nineteens.

'Oh, and I'd like to talk to you about your experience as a children's nanny,' Janine concluded with the ghost of a smile on her face.

I was instantly alert at this.

'You're not thinking what I think you're thinking?' I said as we left Naomi to her interrupted rest.

'She seems a nice girl,' Janine said noncommittally, 'and as you're going to need to have her around for some time I thought I might give her a trial. It would kill two birds with one stone. It'll give me a chance to see how I get on with a live-in nanny and it'll help you if I keep her busy.'

'Hmmmph! She looks like a girl who needs a lot of sleep.'

'Leave her to me, I'll soon put her through her paces.'

A few minutes later I headed off to work to meet the other impossible female in my life, Celeste. As usual recently the skies were dark and threatening. There was rain in the air but I had a mac with me, an authentic detective-style Burberry. I intended to spend the entire day out of the office. If necessary the entire week, even month.

When I reached my workplace the cleaning staff were about to leave. Celeste swept in before the last of them had departed. She was wearing pink lipstick and flashed me a bright smile as she went to her desk in the open-plan front office and peeled off her long black raincoat. I waved a reply. A faint aroma of expensive perfume wafted through the connecting doors as she hung her coat up. When seated she started listening to overnight messages on the answermachine.

I'll say this for her: apprentice dominatrix though she may be, every morning is different with Celeste. She must spend a large amount of her not inconsiderable salary on clothes. Today she was wearing a long slate blue jacket reaching to her knees over a delicately shaded lilac sweater with slim-legged trousers to match the jacket. She was the very model of a rising young executive. Just looking at her made me feel jaded, thinking of the endless meetings with accountants, graphs to study, reports to write, business seminars to attend, that she had in mind for me. She belongs to a world of order and planning and decisions made and conclusions underlined.

It's not her fault.

It's not my fault that however hard I try, that world will never be my world.

I smiled when she came to the door of my room and she reciprocated warmly. Yesterday's harsh words were forgotten and forgiven.

'There's a message for you, Boss,' she said cheerfully. 'Ring this number.'

'Thank you, Miss Moneypenny,' I muttered in my best Connery accent.

'Oh, James! I don't think it's M,' she said, quick as a flash.

She handed me a Post-it note with an Irish Republic number on it. I moved towards my office. I knew that our usual conference when she reminds me of all the things I

60

don't want to do, but which must be done, was scheduled to start with the morning coffee.

I picked up the phone and dialled the number.

'Is that you, Dave?' a familiar flat north Manchester accent enquired. 'Thank Christ you caught me. I'm having to move about fairly swiftly.'

'What's the prob, Bob?'

'This is no joking matter,' Bob Lane replied. 'I'm having to keep on my toes here, moving swiftly. Listen, Dave, we're going to have to keep this chat short.'

'Why?'

'Because you never know who's listening on an open line. Sorry, mate, but they know I'm a friend of yours. They might be getting an earful of this to try to trace me.'

'And who are they? Police?'

'No, Customs and Excise.'

'Oh, no, how many times have I told you to get out of that business?'

'Don't jump to any conclusions, Dave. It's not the weed they're after me for but the ciggies.'

'Ciggies?'

'Ordinary cancer sticks, duty free, not the wacky baccy. There's nearly as much money in it and far less risk.'

'I see.'

'Yes, Customs found a container load that was on its way to me from Hull Docks. Hah! It was supposed to be a load of engine parts. Luckily, the driver was clued up enough to tip me off before they worked out where he was delivering the stuff but I think I got out just a few minutes ahead of them.'

'So you're on the run?'

'You could say that but it's not as bad as it sounds. They only want me for evading the excise duty, not drug smuggling, and my brief thinks we may be able to get them off my back by paying the duty on the fags.'

'On a container load?'

'It's better than doing time. Of course they confiscate the load and the lorry.'

'You know your own business best, Bob.'

'Yes, but there's a little problem and I need your help. We won't be able to go to Holland to see Clint.'

'I understand that . . .'

'Wait, there's more. The people he's staying with on the farm are associates of mine . . .'

'Oh, yes?'

'Don't jump to conclusions, Dave. They're straight.'

'I see.'

'The trouble is they were expecting us to come and look after Clint. They're taking their holiday now and have people coming in to look after the farm animals. It's not something I can just ask them to drop.'

'Right.'

'And they won't be able to look after Clint any more. I'd arranged to bring him home for good anyway. As we're not going for him, they're putting him on the shuttle to Manchester. He'll be arriving at the airport at four. Terminal Three.'

'And you want me to meet him?' There was obviously more that Bob could have said about Clint's need to leave Holland but now didn't seem like the best moment to quiz him about it.

'Would you?' He sounded desperate. Bob may not be a model law-abiding citizen but the shining page in his life story is his treatment of his educationally challenged brother.

'There's something else, Dave. I don't have anyone to look after him in Manchester. Could you keep an eye on him for a few days until I get something fixed up here? He's done well at the farm work. It suits him, being with animals and everything. I've noticed he's improved in a lot of ways. He's never going to be what you'd call bright but

62

his understanding seems to have got better and you know he likes you, Dave. He always asks about you when I phone.'

I sighed.

'Terminal Three?'

'Thanks, Dave, I knew you wouldn't let me down.'

'How long for, though?'

'Just a few days. Got to go, I'll be in touch. I owe you one, mate.'

He hung up, leaving me with dozens of questions I wanted to ask. Looking after Clint is not exactly a stress-free activity though it does have its compensations. If you know the expression 'built like the proverbial brick outhouse' then to describe Clint you have to think in terms of a concrete bunker. He is quite simply a giant with the mind of child. If he sees a friend, such as Bob or myself, being attacked he springs to their defence. A fight is just a casual romp to him but unfortunately he has the strength to detach heads from bodies. Not that he's ever done anything like that. Yet. But I could hardly ignore Bob's request in his hour of need.

Celeste came in a moment later with a pleasant smile on her face. She sat at the desk in front of me with her notebook open and pen poised.

'So how did you get on with your private client?' she asked coyly.

I took the ten thousand out and laid it on the desk. I wanted to impress her. I pushed nine thousand in her direction and left a thousand in front of myself.

'I'd like you to bank this in a special account . . . call it "File Red". It's the retainer from the private client. Not a pro bono job, far from it.'

The sight of ten thousand casually stacked on the desk looked notable enough to me. There'd been many years when my net earnings had been nothing like that but Celeste's face remained totally impassive.

'About the client,' she began. 'Is he a footballer?' She

63

has a deep, rather husky voice, which is very easy on the ear, but this morning I didn't want to listen to it. I shook my head and she trailed off into silence.

I could see she was bursting for more information so I decided to tantalise her.

'Even if you guess it, his name must never be mentioned in this office. I'm under all kinds of threatened penalties if his business goes public . . .'

'But Clyde Harrow . . .'

'Yes, I know. It's going to be difficult to keep anything involving Clyde Harrow out of the news.'

'No, I was going to say, after I phoned you yesterday he came in here with a camera crew. Said he was testing the feasibility of a fly-on-the-wall documentary about the agency. That you'd given him the go-ahead.'

I swallowed. I could taste copper in my throat. I felt the veins on my neck and forehead pumping up to the size of tractor tyres.

Celeste watched this process with fascination.

'You didn't give the go-ahead?'

I shook my head and struggled for breath.

'I tried to reach you.'

I nodded.

Eventually rational thought returned as my heart gradually stopped trying to propel a jet of blood through the top of my skull. That's what it felt like anyway.

'How many of the staff did he get sight of?' I asked.

'There was just me, the secretaries, Peter Snyder and the accountant. He wasn't best pleased . . . the accountant, I mean. Most of the investigators were out.'

Many of my employees seem to find outside jobs to attend to late in the afternoon. I don't mind, as I'm always telling them this isn't a nine-to-five job.

'Were there any references to our latest subject?'

'File Red?'

I nodded.

'He didn't say anything but as he was going I'm sure he was humming the music from *Match of the Day*.'

'Right, as soon as you've banked this,' I said, pushing the unimpressive mound of cash at her, 'you must do a circular to all employees. They are not to speak to Clyde Harrow under any circumstances. They are to read it and sign it. I want you and the secretarial staff to do the same. Place the replies in File Red.'

'Like the Official Secrets Act?' she said sarcastically.

'Exactly.'

'I can get our Leon to punch his lights out, if you like.'

'An attractive idea, Celeste, but I don't think so.'

Leon is her brother. He works as a minder for an agency that supplies protection for various local celebs.

'Just warn everyone to stay out of Clyde's way. I'll be out all day on File Red business.'

'But . . .' she began.

'Listen, Celeste, if it's admin that you're worried about you can give yourself as much overtime as you like to do what I usually do. Signing expenses slips and sending out invoices isn't what I'm best at.'

'Surely somebody else . . .'

'There is nobody else to do this job. All investigators including Peter Snyder have ongoing enquiries. It's time I got out from behind this desk.'

'But . . .'

'I'll be on the mobile. Don't call unless it's really urgent, and by that I mean life-threatening. If any of the staff do get curious . . . I'm on urgent enquiries.'

'Right, Boss! I'll run that up the flag pole and salute it!'

6

I was in a fever to begin. I started in Wilmslow. I always find going over the ground is the best way to start an investigation. I need to be able to see things through the eyes of perpetrator and victim.

I parked in sight of Lee Parkes's house.

It was one of those typical English days when the weather can't make up its mind. Dark and stormy skies one minute, rapidly clearing the next. Shafts of sunlight, sudden squalls of rain. I pitied detectives who had to work in the monotonous sunshine of places like southern California.

Lee's house is on a private road which runs parallel to the River Bollin which itself crosses through Wilmslow at right angles to the main Manchester Road/Alderley Road. The public road on which I was parked borders the western edge of the exclusive neighbourhood but there's now a bypass between this area and the town. Until recently long-distance traffic used to crawl through Wilmslow, but not any more. The new road, the A34, is ancient as well as modern. It's really the old route from the north-west of England down to the Southampton area. Henry V's Cheshire archers marched down it to Agincourt, but now it sidesteps to the edge of town and slashes its way through a newly engineered cutting. To reach the shops from Lee's house you cross a bridge over the bypass that takes you into town around the back of the railway station.

I took my time studying this terrain.

When I set out to follow Naomi's footsteps I was looking for mums or nannies out taking the air. I may not be a practising parent but I do know that the people most likely to notice a woman struggling along the cluttered footpaths with a pushchair were others doing the same. As Naomi had said Wilmslow is a rich town and the walls of the shops along the main street were festooned with security cameras. I walked the complete route and then back again.

There were no blinding flashes of inspiration except that I reasoned that the kidnappers must have had a spotter keeping tabs on Naomi from the minute she left the house. There were many different routes she could have taken but not many places where it wasn't too risky to bundle a nanny and child into the back of an ambulance. Also, if I were the criminal mastermind I wouldn't leave an ambulance parked on a side street for too long. Ambulances are too conspicuous. People get nervous when they see one parked near a neighbour's door. You'd need someone to tell you in what direction your victim was heading. Then you'd position yourself in a suitable spot for the snatch just a minute or so ahead of her.

From the spot where the car was parked I could see the house but someone from the house would be equally able to see me. I walked down the road until I came to the last possible spot from which you could observe the house. Bushes screened it but from a car or van you'd be able to see the house well enough.

I examined the area.

I didn't do a fingertip search but then I wasn't the Cheshire Constabulary. There were oil stains on the road at that particular spot. They were dark stains that you get when an old banger's been leaking for some time . . . days possibly? Then in the same place there were three cigarette butts. I wouldn't have thought they were significant except for their being three clustered together. I picked them up.

There was an inch to an inch and a half of tobacco on each, which argued for a nervous smoker . . . someone who was aware of the risks of smoking a cigarette right down to the filter. There was no trace of lipstick, so I was probably dealing with a man old enough to be aware of the dangers of smoking . . . over thirty? It could be.

Mastermind that I was, I followed the gutter as far as the grid. There was a sodden Silk Cut box wedged in a corner. I fished it out. 'Silk Cut, the low tar cigarette' it said on the box. I threw the cardboard and the butts away. I wasn't collecting evidence, just looking for clues.

Satisfied that I'd gleaned all I could for now, I set off towards town again. This time I had the photos of Naomi and baby Cheyenne in her pushchair fixed to a piece of board under a plastic sheet. I find that it helps to have a clipboard in your hand as you approach the public. They think you're doing market research and that you might be handing out free goodies. I had a cover story ready. If questioned I would say that I was an insurance investigator checking up on an accident. That was close enough to the truth to be convincing.

I soon found witnesses. At the Gusto coffee shop and restaurant on Grove Street a waitress remembered Naomi. She came to the shop about once a week and always drank her coffee outside, clinging on to the pushchair as if she was terrified someone was going to run off with it.

'I told her she could bring her baby inside but she seemed happier sitting out in the cold. There's no pleasing some people. She always had a large mug of coffee with a chocolate biscuit or sometimes a blueberry muffin. What's she done? Shoplifting?'

'Nothing like that,' I said. 'I noticed you have a VCR trained on the front of the shop.'

'Oh, you have to. They've had ram-raiding and all sorts round here.'

I showed her my investigator's card and photo. She

68

looked suitable impressed. I smiled. Charm has always got me results. I noticed that she had a Mills & Boon romance open behind the counter and decided to appeal to her sentimental feelings rather than spin the yarn about an accident.

'The girl's run off,' I said in a low voice. 'Her parents are frantic. I'm trying to establish which of several young men she may have gone with. If I could have a look at the VCR I might be able to see if she met anyone.'

'I don't know. Rafiq sees to that.'

'Who's he?'

'Rafiq Shah, he owns the place. I only work here.'

I opened my wallet and put a ten-pound note on the counter. She looked at me stupidly. I smiled again but she started getting nervous. There were only a couple of old ladies in the place and she might have thought I was propositioning her.

'Give me one of those biscuits,' I suggested.

With a sigh of relief she gave me a biscuit, tilled the note and rang up my change.

'Keep the change,' I said.

'Oh!' she said, light dawning.

'Would it be possible to see the video?'

'I can let you in the room but you'll have to go through the tape yourself. I don't really know how to work it. I do know Rafiq changes the tapes every so often.'

'Since Saturday?'

'I don't think so.'

It took me thirty minutes to spool back to the right place but there was Naomi sitting on the cold bench outside, right in the frame. She kept looking up and down the street nervously. Then with jerky, rapid movements she put the cup down and left. There was no sign of anyone following, but the spotter might have been on the other side of the street.

I considered taking the video, but there was no point. A

freeze-frame view of one of the gang on my first try was a bit too much to hope for.

I left the shop and went on to Hawthorn Lane. Unfortunately there were no conveniently located cameras. It was one of those streets you find on the edges of town centres with low-cost business premises: a property rental agency, minicab offices, a Chinese takeaway, a charity shop or two. The houses proper began lower down the street, well beyond the spot where Naomi and Cheyenne had been lifted.

They knew Naomi at Bambino, but had seen nothing of her on Saturday. There were part-timers working then. To question them I'd have to come in next Saturday.

However, fortune favours the bold or at least the persistent. As I went from door to door flashing my clipboard and my investigator's badge I got mixed results. In an insurance salesroom a jolly salesman hailed me from behind his counter. I was in conversation with his young blonde assistant and getting nowhere fast.

'You ought to ask old Mrs Latham,' he said. 'She sits up in her window all day long watching the street. She's certain to have spotted any ambulances – the old dear's expecting one to come and cart her off at any time.'

'Where does she live?'

'That's for me to tell and you to know,' he said with a grin. 'Meanwhile, can I interest you in changing your car insurance?'

'No.'

'Buildings, house and contents?'

'Listen, mate, this is serious. I need to know if there was a witness to this woman being taken into the ambulance.'

'Yes, but you're only private, aren't you?'

He smiled at me infuriatingly. I knew that I was providing his day's distraction from a totally boring job so I decided to give him a treat. He obviously needed a spot of intrigue in his life.

70

'It isn't just an accident I'm looking into. Those men weren't helping her into an ambulance, they were kidnapping her. This girl is married to a wealthy Arab from the Gulf. If I told you his name and you were a racing man you'd probably have heard of the family . . .'

'Sheikh M—'

I put a finger to my lips and shook my head wisely. He shut up.

'He's a connection but it's not him personally. Anyway, this girl, my client's daughter, has split up with him and she was in hiding near Wilmslow. Somehow he's found out where she was living and had her kidnapped. The baby is his only child and he wants her but probably not the mother. She's likely to end up in some jail in the Gulf if we don't find her before he gets her out of the country. My only lead is the ambulance.'

'But how do you know it was an ambulance?'

'I've checked the videos in the shops on Alderley Road. An ambulance was following her. If I can identify it, or find out who the men were, then there's a chance.'

The grin had faded from his face. 'Mrs Latham's next door above the furniture restorer's shop.'

'Thanks,' I muttered.

'Stop a minute! I can speak to her on the intercom. She knows me. I meet her every morning when she gets her milk in. She has cats.'

'OK.'

He folded back the flap on his counter and came out. We went out of the shop and he spoke to the old lady from the street on the intercom.

'Is there any chance of a reward?' he asked when she buzzed the door open for me. 'George Merrilees, Top Line Insurance.' He passed me a business card. I carefully opened my wallet and tucked it away.

'There could be if the girl and the baby are found.'

'Sound!' he said, retreating to the doorway of his office.

71

When I knocked on Mrs Latham's door it swung open. A gush of stiflingly hot air blew out to meet me. She was sitting on a rancid worn sofa with not one but three cats to keep her company. Her face and the white lace-trimmed blouse that she was wearing were clean enough but the long fingernails of the hand that beckoned me into the room were black. She fixed me with a piercing stare. Her very pale blue eyes focusing intently out of an ancient face reminded me of a Van Gogh portrait.

'Are you from the Sanitary?' she asked.

'No, I'm an investigator,' I said, proffering my ID.

She didn't look at it.

'It's not fair, you coming like this. Who's going to look after my cats?'

'I don't want to take them away from you.'

'I know them buggers underneath keep complaining about me but I've got a lease on this place and they can't shift me unless they can prove that I'm endangering their health. It's not as if they're selling food or anything. I ask you, all they have down there is a few rotten old chairs. How can my cats endanger them?'

'I'm sure they can't. Do you want me to speak to them?'

'Them? Waste of time speaking to them. All they understand is solicitor's letters.' She fingered a pile of grease-stained envelopes.

'May I?' I asked.

She nodded wearily.

I opened the first envelope. It was a threatening letter from a solicitor warning Mrs Latham that she was creating a public nuisance. The others were in the same vein except for the last and most recent one, which was hand-written in capitals.

YOU CRAZY DAFT OLD BITCH, GET THEM CATS OUT OF THERE OR WE'LL HAVE YOU COMMITTED TO A MENTAL HOSPITAL WHERE YOU BELONG. THIS IS YOUR FINAL WARNING.

Needless to say, it wasn't signed.

The place reeked of rotten cat food, a nasty cheap fishy smell that made me want to gag. It must percolate through to the shop below.

When I looked round the room it was like one of those puzzle drawings where you have to count how many hidden animals you can see. I saw more and more cats everywhere I looked. There were cats all over the place: cats in the wardrobe, cats on top of the wardrobe, cats in the kitchen sink. Some of the felines looked moribund, but then one I'd pegged for dead stirred and wandered over to be stroked. The cats mostly seemed to be in better condition than Mrs Latham.

'Shocking what they do to animals,' she said when I asked her if she'd seen an ambulance.

'I'm not an investigator from the sanitation department. I'm trying to check up on an ambulance that was parked just outside your window.'

This produced a look of beady-eyed cunning.

'What are you investigating then?' she asked.

I gave her the story from the top again.

'Proper bastard, he was,' she said when I'd finished. I thought she was back on about the furniture restorer. As I looked a black cat flea landed on the back of her hand. She flicked it away with a reflex gesture. I was ready to go.

'He was rough with that girl,' she continued, 'but he wasn't a proper ambulance man.'

I perched on the arm of a chair opposite her. A fat Angora cat occupied the heavily stained seat.

'I could tell it wasn't a proper ambulance. They have numbers painted on the top but this one didn't. It had a flashing light and a siren, frightened the moggies it did, but

I knew it wasn't right. It was just one of them white vans with a sticker on it saying "Ambulance".'

Another half-hour of patient probing produced a vague description of the big bloke who'd bundled Naomi into the back of the van. He was bigger than I was and aged about thirty.

She thought he was black because although he had a clown's mask over his face and gloves on his hands she could see the back of his neck and his hair.

'Why the hair? What was unusual about it?' I asked. 'Was it corn-rows, dreads, fuzzy Afro or what?'

She didn't know what I was talking about.

I tried drawing different 'dos' in my notebook.

'It was something like that,' she agreed when I drew mini-dreads, 'but it was more spiky, like when you beat egg whites to make meringue, you know thick and stiff.'

I didn't know and must have looked mystified because she took the Angora cat off the chair and put it on her knee. 'It was like this,' she said, twining the animal's fur into short upright prickles or spikes. 'Nasty piece of work he was, like a porcupine with that hairdo. They put that girl and the pushchair in the back and then they just set off. There wasn't no siren or anything like they had coming. They just drove off.'

That was as far as I got. More important than the physical description, the van had only been parked for three minutes before Naomi was grabbed. Mrs Latham knew that because she thought it had been summoned by the furniture restorer to have her committed. She'd just had time to get up and put her coat on. Then when she came back to the window she saw Naomi disappearing into the van which was similar to the one owned by the restorer. A glance through the window revealed an old Ford Transit parked further up the street.

There was a telephone on a side table but I didn't bother to ask her why she hadn't phoned the police. I was beginning to get an uncomfortable itching sensation. Before I left I gave her ten pounds: 'For the cats.' She looked at the note suspiciously.

When I left by the front door of the flat I was halted by the occupant of the furniture shop. He was a tall, thin young man with a hollow face, prominent nose and waxed hair. He was wearing faded pink jeans, a dirty T-shirt from a 1995 Lindisfarne concert and three rings in each ear.

'What's it this time,' he said nastily, 'is the old biddy still trying to get Age Concern on her side?' He made the mistake of poking me on the shoulder with his bony finger.

I snatched his hand away and put him a wristlock.

'Here, what the hell are you playing at?' he whined as I applied a little pressure.

'I don't know about Age Concern but if you don't leave Mrs Latham alone you'll need help from Knobhead Concern. I'm going to come back and break your leg if I hear you've been bothering her again.'

'There's no call for that,' he gasped indignantly. 'What are you, a relative? Just come in my shop. All you can smell is cat shit coming from upstairs. I've got a government grant to run this shop, how can I get started with this stench hanging over the place?'

I pushed him back into his doorway. There was a penetrating reek of marijuana from within.

'It's tough about the cats, sunshine,' I growled, 'but judging by the stink of grass in here, you have your ways of coping with the odour problem. Leave Mrs Latham alone or I'm going to the police.'

'It's not fair,' he snarled when I released him, 'bringing heavies in.'

'Next time you feel like writing a letter, try Social Services instead,' I advised.

I left him rubbing his wrist and muttering to himself.

For the second time I crossed Wilmslow centre and the A34 going towards Wilmslow Green. When I reached the spot where I'd found the ash and cigarette ends I stopped and looked around for anything I'd missed.

Diaries? Address books? Convenient books of matches with the name of an exclusive nightclub? No.

I was interrupted in my search by a voice: 'Have you lost something valuable?' a white-haired pensioner asked. He was an erect figure, smartly turned out in well-creased grey trousers, collar and tie, and an expensive-looking sports jacket. He could have been anything from a retired general to a High Court judge. A bull mastiff bitch strained at the leash in his hand.

'Yes, sir,' I answered politely, deciding that something closely linked to the truth might be the best policy with him. Two intelligent blue eyes were examining me closely. 'I'm trying to reconstruct an event which occurred near here where a young woman was involved in an unpleasant incident . . .'

'Police?'

'No, I'm a private investigator.'

I showed him my ID.

'The family would like to get to the bottom of this incident but they'd prefer to keep it out of the public eye.'

'I don't blame them. These newspapers just live for scandal and dirt and the police seem to feed their appetite for it at times.'

'Yes, sir, that's it. They want it kept quiet. I don't suppose you saw anything unusual round here last week?'

'I did, as a matter of fact. I often walk young Gip here along this street and there was a white van parked just where you were looking. What is it? Did someone expose themselves? They'd have been birched for that in my young day, but now all they get is words of comfort from a counsellor.'

'If you don't mind I'd rather not say what it was, but the girl's had a nasty fright and her family want to make sure it doesn't happen to another youngster.'

'Yes, I saw a white van. It was one of those Vauxhall things, you know, very small.' He demonstrated a narrow width with his arms.

'A Vauxhall Rascal?'

'That's it. I can see those very words written across the back of the van in my mind's eye.'

'Did you see the driver?'

'Sorry, I did look and perhaps that's what made me remember the van. The driver dodged down each time I looked. The van was here last Tuesday, Wednesday and Thursday, but I was later on the Friday and it wasn't here and I forgot all about it until you asked.'

'Anything else? Registration? Writing on the side of it? Anything?'

'Sorry, memory's going,' he said with a tap on his forehead. 'It was quite old though. Appropriate really when you think about it.'

'How do you mean, sir?'

'A Rascal van for a rascal man! Now I must bid you good day, sir. Gip's getting a bit restless.'

While we watched the dog peed against the fence I'd just been examining. When she'd finished creating a small steaming lake the gent strode on his way with a friendly nod.

I returned to my inch by inch search of the immediate area.

I was still absorbed in this useless attempt twenty minutes later when someone padding along the pavement behind me broke my concentration. It was a young woman in jogging kit.

I let her go past then shouted, 'Excuse me, can you help me?'

She turned round with a furious glare on her face. Small, bespectacled and intense, with raven black hair tied up in a bun, her grey tracksuit vest was plastered to her chest by a deep vee of sweat.

'I'm expected at Wilmslow Green High School in two minutes,' she coldly. 'People will be out here after me if I'm delayed.'

I waved my clipboard.

'I'm an enquiry agent,' I explained. 'I'm looking for these two.' I held the board up and she peered at it from three yards away.

'Nope! I've never seen them,' she said and turned to go.

'You didn't notice anybody parked here in the last few days, did you?' I shouted. 'A white Vauxhall Rascal van?'

She turned again and jogged back towards me. Like some wary herbivore, she left herself a safe distance for a getaway.

'Now you mention it, there was a small van parked there all last week. The man said he was doing a traffic census for a new road but with the bypass already being here I couldn't quite work out what he meant.'

'Really?' I said eagerly. 'Can you give me a description . . . the van, the man?'

'Ummmh, it was like you said. The van was one of those Rascal things . . . little . . . white. The man, I didn't really notice, nondescript, young . . . also white.'

With that she turned and was off like a hare.

I dropped my clipboard and set off after her.

'Please, spare me a minute,' I begged when I drew level.

'If this is some kind of crazy come-on, you're wasting your time.'

'It could be a matter of life and death,' I gasped. We hadn't run far but already I was wheezing. It had been weeks since I took a training ride on my mountain bike. She ran on without comment and we crossed a kerb.

The next thing I was aware of was a tremendous blast from the horn of a heavy goods vehicle. Brakes screamed and the lorry slid towards us. She grabbed my coat and pulled me forward and I tripped and measured my length on the pavement. The lorry driver wound his window down and for a second the air was blue with curses.

'Persistent, aren't you?' the jogger said. 'Phone the school and ask for Miss Pietrangeli.' Then, nimble as before, she was on her way. I watched her recede down the lane.

7

I took my coat off and slung it over my shoulder. It had borne the brunt of my collision with the street. I wasn't much damaged. My hands were grazed. I was shaken but not stirred. I decided to carry on rather than retreat and lick my wounds.

Back at the car, I got behind the wheel and drove the few miles out to Alderley Edge. From the A34 I caught a glimpse of the Edge lying like a great grey barrier across the fields to my left. A mass of clouds was banked up behind it. There's something mysterious about the outcropping. It rises straight up from the plain like a heavily wooded version of Ayers Rock.

My clients had been told to park at a lay-by on the Macclesfield Road. I checked the spot. Heavy rain had wiped out any footprints on the path. I drove a little further up to the 'Wizard', which is an authentic old inn on the route over the Edge. All round the area people have tried to cash in on the legend of the Wizard of Alderley who gave a farmer a pot of gold to buy a horse for one of King Arthur's knights sleeping in a cave under the hill. There are Wizard chip shops and Merlin pubs and King Arthur takeaways.

Somebody driving by to check that the brothers were in place might well have stopped here.

I drove into the car park. Appetising aromas drifted from the pub and I suddenly felt weak for want of nourishment. I looked at my watch. It was after one. I got out of the car and slammed the door. They weren't doing much trade when I reached the bar of the Wizard but the lunches were still on.

The man behind the bar was friendly enough.

I told him I was hoping to meet a friend for lunch, a black man with an unusual spiky haircut. He'd been in before and recommended the place . . . 'I haven't seen your friend. It's funny you should mention it but we don't get many black people in here. The odd footballer now and then but that's about it. I'd have remembered him if he'd been in recently. Are you sure it was this pub? We're the genuine article but almost every pub in Alderley's cashing in on the legend of the Wizard.'

'Oh,' I said. 'Never mind, I'll order now.'

I asked for chips with a double portion of Cumberland sausage and a pint of bitter to wash it down.

'Feeling a bit peckish, eh?' the grey-haired landlord said. 'It'll be about ten minutes.' He relayed the order to the kitchen and then drew the pint. He hovered nearby but possibly because I was frowning as I considered my present state he didn't initiate a conversation. I took a long swallow of the beer and decided to calm down.

'Get many people round here in the evenings?' I asked, trying to mould my features into a pleasant smile.

'Yes, we have quite a good passing trade. Picks up in summer, of course,' he replied. 'We get people coming out from Manchester, from the Potteries, even Birmingham.'

'I suppose the magic of the Wizard draws them?'

'Don't talk about that! We get all kinds of weirdos.' He surveyed my business suit with a smile, as much as to say that, like him, I wasn't weird. 'Yes, we have all these would-be wizards and witches up here. Whole covens of them go prancing about on the Edge in the buff, especially at Hallowe'en and other dates in their witches' calendar.'

'It's all a recent invention, that stuff, isn't it?' I said, trying to match his sceptical expression.

'There's a dark side to it, though. They call it Wicca, you know. Some funny folk are attracted by it. Sacrificing virgins under the full moon . . . Hah! I used to think it was all a way of spicing up a spot of outdoor shagging, if you'll pardon my French, but now I'm not so sure. Deadly serious some of these people, they can't keep them off the Edge. They claim it's a sacred site.'

'Sacred to what?'

'It's hard to say, but it's no joke to them. The National Trust have a hell of a time with them prowling round up here in the dark.'

At that moment my meal arrived and I retreated to a side table to eat it. As I sliced up the Cumberland sausage I recalled what a friend from the University had told me about the Edge. Delise Delaney was an archaeologist I'd lived with for several years until she forsook both science and me at the same time and got a job as a TV news presenter. About four thousand years ago when the Cheshire Plain would have been covered by a dense forest of oak, birch and elm, impenetrable as any jungle – the Boreal Climax vegetation – prospectors had arrived looking for copper ore. The economy of the period depended on bronze, used for axes, swords and daggers. Copper, one of the ingredients, was in short supply throughout Europe and that's what those early miners were scouring the forests and hills for.

They found the green malachite ores on the Edge and set to work. It's continued off and on ever since. The Edge is honeycombed with mine shafts. Delise had a theory that the legend of the sleeping King Arthur had come about because some medieval copper miner had come across a shaft full of ancient remains, perhaps even well-preserved corpses.

That brought me back to the events of last Saturday evening. The kidnappers had insisted that the brothers remain in their car on the road for a full hour.

Why?

A drive-by would have established that Lee and Jamie were sitting in their car like good little boys. Maybe the crims drove up and down several times to make sure the police weren't in attendance, though too many trips could have been dangerous. But did this watching take an hour? And weren't they confident that Lee wasn't going to involve the police?

So what were they doing?

Answer: they were up to something on the Edge, preparing the method they used to snatch the cash. They couldn't do that too much in advance because, as mine host of the Wizard said, there were always odd characters wandering about communing with the earth spirits.

I finished my meal in record time and then walked over to the bar with my empty pint glass in my hand.

'Refill?' the landlord asked.

I nodded.

He bent to fill the glass.

'You've whetted my appetite for this Edge, you know. I've an hour or two to spare, I think I'll have a walk up there.'

'There won't be any naked virgins hanging around today,' he joked. 'It's too cold and wet.' He handed me the glass.

I took a good swallow.

'Good pint, that. I've got an hour or two before my next appointment. How do you get up there?' I nodded in the direction of the great outdoors.

'There's a path round the back but you'll not want to go in your best clothes and shoes. It's been raining for days.'

In the end he lent me a pair of old over-trousers and green wellies, which I promised to return. He was right about the conditions. The soft, loamy soil beneath the towering beech trees was like treacle. I squelched my way onwards, following the meandering path between smooth grey trunks. I'd have been sunk in ordinary shoes.

83

Conveniently for the kidnappers, rain had been continuous since Saturday evening, blurring their traces. There were tracks all over the place but without forensic resources there was nothing I could do. The wood was eerily quiet, apart from the wind rustling through bare branches. At the pinnacle, with its view over the Plain, the only people in sight were a couple of female dog walkers.

I investigated the 'Devil's Grave', which isn't a grave and has nothing to do with the Devil. It's just a cleft in the rock.

The place where the brothers had stood was just forward of the cleft, looking out over the void below. The stone that had been used to weigh down the luminous sacks was still there. I walked forward to the edge of the cliff, checking for marks where the money had been pulled over. If they'd ever existed the rain had smoothed them away.

The cliff itself was no more a cliff than the grave was a grave. It was a very steep, eroded hillside with many precariously balanced rocks resting on nothing firmer than mud. Some of the boulders were poised to slide. Standing at the bottom tugging a rope seemed to be a good way to end up buried under a landslide.

I pondered the idea of a pulley rigged up between the trees.

It wasn't possible.

I just couldn't see how they'd shifted the money as Lee had described. Difficulties abounded. Pulling two hundred thousand pounds at the end of a rope hundreds of yards long wasn't a practical proposition, and if I'd learned anything about these guys it was that they were practical.

I went back and stood on the sandstone outcrop. The brothers were definite that the money had been wrenched out of their hands at the end of a strong cord. But how?

Maybe Merlin himself gave me inspiration because what happened next looked like magic – a genuine vanishing act.

I could hear a dog yipping. I looked to my right and saw a middle-aged lady in wellies and waterproofs walking towards me. Her Yorkie was off the lead, dashing about from tree to tree. She was on a path slightly closer to the dangerous slope than I was.

In the next instant the terrier ran over the edge and vanished from sight but not from earshot and then its owner disappeared after it. My heart missed a beat. For a second I thought she'd dived down the slope but a moment later she came back into sight, this time with the dog on a lead. I walked up to the 'cliff' edge again.

What I'd taken for the edge as seen from the Devil's Grave was really a 'false' crest.

The lady and the terrier had been walking along another narrow path just feet from where the tumble-down rocks and boulders began. There were young pine trees there, which might have given cover to a lurking kidnapper.

Choosing my footing carefully, I scrambled down to see. There were so many footprints and paw prints in the soft soil that anyone could have been there. I started back but then my eye was drawn by a piece of plastic flapping in the breeze. A black bin liner was tucked behind one of the pines. Someone had tied it to a branch. The grass nearby was flattened, as if a heavy person had been lying there recently.

I studied the marks on the soft earth. There were indentations made by the man's toes and I could also see where his knee had pivoted. He must have been lying face down ready to heave on the cord. Not being an Aboriginal tracker, the only thing I learned was that the subject was tall and heavy. Could it be my masked man from the ambulance?

Hauling myself back up the slope to the Devil's Grave I worked out what had happened. I was now thirty yards from the hiding place. A man would be able to pull a bag from there without getting it snagged. There were no loose rocks to entangle it. They'd demanded two parcels simply to minimise the weight and reduce the noise as they dragged them across the intervening distance. If the sound had stopped too abruptly Lee might have guessed that his money hadn't gone all the way down the slope. A lighter load would just fly over the ground if you jerked it hard enough.

They'd probably rehearsed the whole thing, checked the weights and everything.

To the brothers at the Grave it would seem that their money had disappeared all the way down to the bottom, hundreds of yards below, where they had no chance of recovering it.

Looking at the bin bag again gave me another idea. Black bin bags were used to conceal the luminous postal sacks that would have otherwise been plainly visible in the moonlight. It was a conjuring trick. Now you see it, now you don't. Bright bag disappears into dark bag.

One thing stood out. This had all happened before. Probably not here at Alderley Edge, but there were other 'cliffs', natural and man-made. Oh, yes, only someone who'd done this before would think of luminous sacks. They were easy to find if they went astray. It was easy to make them 'vanish'.

There would be spare bin bags handy in case the man on the rope fumbled and missed getting the sack into one, or maybe the remaining bag was one he'd lain on and carelessly cast aside.

I paced my way to the edge again. My theory had a flaw. How would somebody hiding down the slope out of sight of the top know when to pull on the ropes? If he was invisible to the pair on top, they were equally invisible to him.

I went back down to the trees and looked at the bin bag. There was no one watching me to report curious behaviour so I stretched it out and lay down where the bagman had lain. The Devil's Grave was invisible from here but those tall Scots pines on the crest to the left of the Grave weren't. Their bluish-green branches waved in the breeze far above my head. There must have been two men; one was here waiting to pull when he got a signal and to bag up the money. The other was hidden behind the Scots pines keeping the Grave in sight. They'd said they had night glasses but that would hardly be necessary on a moonlit night like Saturday. The mention of night vision aids was to make the brothers think they were much further away than they really were.

It meant taking a risk but how else could they have done it? The land around the Devil's Grave and Stormy Point was heavily wooded. The only way to see what was happening among the pine and birch trees was to be an owl flying above.

Beneath Stormy Point there was only space and distant fields. From down there on the Plain it would have been near impossible to see what the brothers were doing, however powerful the binoculars. No, these customers were close by during the money transfer.

I went up the slope and strode over to the Scots pines. There were footmarks behind the thickest trunk. There was something else too. Someone had stubbed a cigarette out on the trunk and pressed the butt into a crack in the orange-red bark. I pried it out with a pencil. The brand was Silk Cut. I studied the footprints. There were only heel prints, and not very big. Someone, possibly my smoker from the Vauxhall Rascal, had leaned backwards against the tree and dug his heels into the turf. He'd been desperate enough for a smoke to risk giving away his position. But had there been much risk? They'd made the brothers wait for an hour on the Macclesfield Road. Plenty of time for a quick smoke once he was in position. Perhaps he treated himself to a fag after he made the call to Jamie on his mobile, knowing it would take the brothers at least half an hour to reach him.

And that was another thing. There were several ways to

87

reach Stormy Point and the Devil's Grave. One was the easy route I'd taken from the Wizard car park. That was a farm road for part of the way, muddy but firm going and level. The other was the footpath up from Macclesfield Road that was the more difficult route they'd made Jamie and Lee use coming and going.

It was uphill, along a winding, muddy path through the trees.

Well, they would do that . . . reserve the best access and escape route for themselves. It was practical, and these were practical men. Also the Silk Cut smoker would have been able to see the pair making their way towards him in the moonlight.

What about the signal to pull the cord?

No great problem there. They couldn't use the phone if they were in earshot but a quick flash of a shielded torch would have been easy. Then they'd have to wait until they were sure that Lee and Jamie were heading for the Volvo. That explained why there was no phone call for a long time after the money drop.

Leaning back against the tree I took another look around. Behind a tussock of grass there was an empty Coke can. It might have just been casual litter, although the Trust kept the area clean, but if my man was prepared to risk a quick smoke on the job, why not a drink while he was waiting? I picked up the can and carefully wrapped it in a handkerchief and put it in my coat pocket. DNA testing wasn't readily available to a private detective but fingerprinting certainly was.

Satisfied that I'd reconstructed the crime to the best of my ability, I took a glance over the Plain. In the distance to the north-west I could see the hangars at Manchester Airport. My heart took a lurch. It was quarter-past three and I was due at the airport by four! I hurried away down the muddy path to the Wizard pub. Even jogging part of the way it took me twenty minutes.

I left the boots and trousers on the back doorstep of the pub and headed for the airport. There was no point in getting arrested for speeding and anyway the traffic was busy as usual round the airport so I couldn't go too fast. Clint would just have to wait for me at the meeting point.

One thing about Clint, you can't miss him in a crowd. When I finally reached the airport he was standing under the information screens, solitary and forlorn. His hair was close-cropped and his face shaved and shiny. His eyes lit up when he saw me.

'Dave! Dave!' he shouted, and then he picked me up and squeezed the breath out of me.

'Dear God!' I gasped. 'Put me down!' He dropped me from a height of two feet. I staggered but before I could say anything my attention was diverted by the label that had been pinned to the collar of his coat.

It read, 'Mr C. Lane, to be met by Mr D. Cunane of Manchester'. It was the only thing about Clint that marked him out as different from anyone else. I snatched it off him wondering whether it was the airline or Bob's Dutch friends who'd labelled him in this way.

It was the airline, I discovered when a uniformed male attendant came over.

'Are you Mr Cunane?' the man asked grumpily. 'We've been waiting over half an hour.' He didn't seem to want me to confirm my identity, taking Clint's ecstatic greetings as all the proof he needed.

'Sorry, traffic,' I muttered.

'His luggage is there,' he said, indicating a trolley containing two very large suitcases, and then he turned swiftly and was gone.

Clint's shadow hadn't grown any less since the last time I'd seen him. If anything he seemed larger than ever, more muscular, and his face had filled out. Grinning madly now, you couldn't have mistaken him for someone who was completely normal but before he'd seen me, with his face at rest and anxious, only his unusual size marked him out as different. He was wearing a long, loose stone-coloured coat over farm overalls and a livid red and blue plaid shirt.

Whoever had dispatched him from Schipol hadn't kitted him out very well for the journey.

I looked him over again. There was something different about him, something intangible. He smiled and laughed at me, overjoyed to see me again – or was it just any familiar face? I puzzled over what the difference in him was. He was as solid as ever. You could have mistaken him for a lighthouse. How was I going to entertain him for . . . what? . . . several weeks.

He effortlessly picked up the two massive cases, hardly even flexing biceps that were broader than my thighs, and we walked towards the exit. I asked him about his flight and whether he'd had anything to eat. Food plays a major part in Clint's life and he needs a lot of it.

'I'm hungry, Dave,' he announced so I steered him back to the restaurant at the corner of the concourse. It took a few trips to the counter to satisfy him. I must say I was torn. I wanted to pay a visit to Lee Parkes. He'd demanded progress reports and I needed to clarify some details. I managed to curb my impatience while Clint ploughed his way through several meals and then we were on our way back to Wilmslow Green. Even with the passenger seat pushed all the way back Clint was cramped in the front of my Mondeo. He was as uncomplaining as usual and kept giving me admiring glances as I did difficult things like changing gear or braking. All along the road he gave a commentary about the shops and houses he saw.

'Quiet now for a minute, me old china,' I said when his chatter began to grate a little. I needed to concentrate on finding the right road. Clint's reaction surprised me. He went all serious and shut up completely. That was new. Before, you could tell him something and the command

90

would stick for a few minutes and then he would forget again. We drove along the suburban lanes between the airport and Wilmslow in complete silence. I didn't need to repeat my request. There was nothing unpleasant about Clint's silence. He had a warm and friendly smile on his face.

'You can talk if you like,' I said when we reached Wilmslow. I was nervous in case he'd taken offence as a 'normal' person might.

Clint started up his commentary again as if nothing had happened. There was no trace of resentment. I was puzzled. He'd never had that much self-control before. Not that he was ever out of control either. He was handicapped in his understanding, that was all, never insane or suffering from a mental illness. His sheer size made people nervous. Clint would always obey Bob, or anyone else such as myself who he'd come to trust. That had been his brother's great fear . . . that some wicked person would harness Clint's strength and willingness for their own evil purposes. There were one or two occasions when he was a child when that had happened. His mother and brother had never gone into any detail but that was why they'd kept him in seclusion.

According to Bob, Clint had an understanding of right and wrong equivalent to that of a small child. Many educational and developmental psychologists had examined him. Some had held out hope that he would develop an improved awareness as he grew older. It looked very much as if he had.

A chilling thought struck me next. What if Clint developed criminal tendencies of his own volition? We stopped at traffic lights and I looked at him nervously. He shot me a beatific smile.

When we reached Lee Parkes's house I was in a dilemma. I couldn't leave Clint cramped up in the car so I told him to get out and fasten his coat up so that Lee wouldn't be able to see the farm clothes underneath. I couldn't go round with someone looking as if he'd strolled off a *Beverly Hillbillies* set.

'We're going to meet a man now, Clint,' I explained. 'He isn't a very nice man. Sometimes he says wrong words and gets angry.'

'Yes, Dave,' he replied pleasantly, 'there are people like that at my farm but I don't say anything to them when they say bad words to me. I just smile.'

'That's right, Clint,' I said, again agreeably surprised. 'You've just to say hello to this man and then keep very quiet. Do you understand?'

'Oh, yes, Dave, I'm used to that. Dirk tells me to do that when he takes me round town.'

Well done, Dirk, I thought.

We heard the door open and Lee Parkes appeared. Clean-shaven and lacking yesterday's alcoholic fuzziness, he looked almost normal. Only the dark shadows under his eyes gave him away. He was wearing a green polo shirt and jeans.

'Who's this?' he said. 'For your sake, Cunane, he'd better be someone who can keep his fucking mouth shut.'

The suspicion of a frown crossed Clint's open face as he registered the bad language, then he said 'Hello' and held his hand out. There was a smile on his face.

Lee looked at him suspiciously for a moment then shook the hand that was offered.

8

I told Lee what I'd found.

'Are you saying there were three of them?' he asked. 'One to look after Cheyenne and the two who collected the money?'

'I can't say that for certain, I'll know more when I start circulating the pictures. It looks as it there was an older man, the one who spoke to Naomi in the street. He may be the schemer and the same one who spoke to you in an educated voice . . .'

'Educated! I'll educate the bastard . . .'

As he spoke Lee looked at Clint who was sitting very quietly. Clint smiled at him again.

'Christ, what is he, Cunane? He looks like a bloody Terminator out of one of those films. What is he, your minder?'

'He's just an associate, helping me with the investigation,' I said lamely.

Clint nodded vigorously and smiled again. In this context his innocent expression could only be described as highly sinister.

'Listen,' Lee expostulated, 'I don't like you bringing along some hired muscle into this. You on your own, that was the deal.' He looked extremely nervous. He licked his lips and stared at Clint who smiled back unflinchingly.

'Can he go in the kitchen and get something to eat?' I asked.

Lee nodded.

Clint didn't need to be told twice. Large though he was, he nimbly left the room and found the kitchen.

'Jesus! Where did you find him? He scares the crap out of me.'

'He's a very old friend of mine and he's completely harmless as long as no one messes with him,' I said truthfully.

I could see that Lee Parkes didn't believe a word but we got down to business. I told him about the schemer, the Silk Cut smoker and the black guy. I told him about Naomi's forthcoming session with the artist . . . he seemed impatient.

'Mr Parkes, if you'd wanted quick results you should have gone to the police on Saturday. This is going to take time and money.'

'Yeah,' he drawled. 'I know about that, the money bit especially. It's just that I can't seem to settle to my life while this is going on. I'll be at the hospital with Cheyenne all day tomorrow. A specialist is going to give me the results of her tests.'

The fire seemed to have gone out of him and I began to feel a little more sympathetic.

'I need to know everything about your background,' I said, taking out a notebook. 'We can start with your friend Keeley.'

'What is it with you, Cunane? You come on at me like some old-fashioned school ma'am. "Your friend Keeley" . . . you couldn't sound more disapproving if you tried. Well, Keeley's husband is Kimball Smathers. He's my friend and don't turn your nose up at his name. His grandfather was called the same. Kimball's a fellow sportsman.'

'I need to know everything about you. This wasn't some accident like a street mugger who got lucky. You were targeted.'

'Yeah, yeah, OK. You don't need to make a meal out of it. Kimball Smathers used to carry my money for me.

He's done six years in the Royal Marines and he knows how to handle himself. You can't go on to a racecourse with twenty grand in your pocket without taking a risk. Kimball helped me to cut down on that risk. He's an East End lad like me and we got along fine but lately he's started gambling on his own account. I warned him that he'd burn his fingers but he wouldn't listen.'

'Is there any chance he might be involved?'

'Forget it. Kimball's very straight and, like I said, he's a mate.'

'But his wife . . .'

'Don't remind me. She's mad! When Mel was killed naturally we had the funeral and everything, but Keeley wanted to stay and look after me. I told her then I didn't need help but she insisted and she's been coming round here at all hours since. I'm only flesh and blood after all and she's an attractive woman.'

'Does Kimball know? I mean, it might affect his attitude.'

'That has been known,' he said with a thin smile. 'I don't think Kimball knows, but what he guesses . . .' He shrugged his shoulders. 'The first and last time Keeley and I got it together was last weekend. Cheyenne cried throughout the night and in the morning I told Keeley it wasn't going to happen again. If you must know I've been expecting him round to straighten things out. He's not likely to have arranged the kidnap, is he? I mean . . . Keeley was here before but there was nothing going on. I wasn't feeling . . . oh, hell! Why should I tell you this?'

'All right,' I said. 'I'll cross the Smathers family off my list. But somebody has a pretty intimate knowledge of your business. What about your Malaysian Chinese friends?'

His face darkened. 'They're no friends of mine,' he snarled.

I didn't say anything.

'I'm a fool. I play the horses and mostly I've made

money at it, though there've been downturns, but there was a period in my life when I couldn't stay out of casinos. It's stupid. With the horses you can look at the form, play the odds, pay the right people for whispers and there's some rational system to it. With a roulette wheel you know the odds are always in favour of the house, but I couldn't stay away from one particular club.'

He stopped talking and moodily studied the bar. I noticed that there was a full brandy bottle there.

'Go on,' I prompted.

'Right, well, it's the old story, you know?'

'I can guess but I'd prefer you to tell me.'

'I was down for more than I could possibly pay. Stupid really. I was at the point where they come to break your legs. It doesn't excuse what I did. But hellfire, when the pressure's on, you do what you have to do, don't you?'

I shrugged.

'So I told them that Jamie Piercy is my brother. Next thing I know there's these Malaysians coming to see me . . . legs not to be broken just yet. Oh, very polite they were. They've bought my debts from the casino. *Can I just ask Jamie a few questions? Who does he know who's hard up? Who does he know who might be interested in a bit of cash on the side?'*

'Couldn't Jamie have paid your gambling debts?'

'He could, but you don't understand. I can't be beholden to my little brother and these aren't nice people. They didn't want to be paid, they wanted me to squeeze Jamie for information. Bastards!'

'Do you think these Malaysian Chinese have something to do with what happened to Cheyenne?'

'No, I'm the goose that lays the golden eggs. They've made millions and been generous. They want to keep me happy. They wouldn't have done this.'

'Somebody's done it. Somebody who knew that you weren't *just* a professional gambler. After all, gambling's not illegal. What's the name of this casino?'

'It's a private gaming club in London. But listen, Cunane, the guy I spoke to . . . the owner . . . he died last year. There's no way anything would have come out through him. All he was interested in was getting his money and now he's snuffed it anyway. You'd know his name. He was a well-known guy. A gentleman, not low born like you and me.'

'Thanks,' I murmured with a smile and for the first time since I'd met Lee Parkes the sneer on his face was replaced by a smile.

'I take it you're not going to tell me who he was?'

'It'd be no use to you, and if you go sniffing round at the Smathers', Kimball knows that Jamie's my brother but Keeley doesn't.'

'You *think* she doesn't.'

'I know.'

'Is there anyone else who might have known what you were up to?'

'No, only Jamie, and he's not likely to have told anyone, is he?'

There was no answer to that, apart from checking out Jamie's contacts. That might prove a little difficult. For all I knew there was a network of corruption all the way through the game. There was no way of knowing whether Lee and Jamie were the only ones involved or the first of many.

It was my turn to smile.

'Problems, eh?' Lee said. 'Do you want a drink?'

'That's not the solution,' I said sharply.

'Go on, Cunane. You're no prude, I can tell that, you're just posing as a polite businessman. You're as rough as old boots really.'

'It's no skin off my nose if you want to drink yourself stupid every day, but when I get a result I want to be able to communicate with you, not siphon you up off the floor.'

'Result? What result?' he muttered, heading for the bar. 'I feel like getting pissed. I held on till you came but what have you got to tell me? Three blokes or two, what does it matter?'

'We're getting descriptions,' I said patiently. 'With a face, or maybe two faces, we'll have names. When we get names, this will soon be sorted.'

I spoke more optimistically than I felt. I didn't much like Lee Parkes but he had suffered and I had a certain sympathy for him. When my wife died I drank myself stupid for months. There's a certain attraction about looking at the world through the end of a bottle when your world's gone crazy anyway.

Lee paused in his progress to alcoholic oblivion.

'Are you sure?' he asked. Hope and a kind of wolfishness flickered across his face.

'We'll get a result. It'll take time, that's all.'

He ran his hands over his head. 'Is there anything I can do to help?'

'Not really,' I said, 'but did you phone your fellow high-winning gamblers and put the word out like I suggested yesterday?'

'Subtle, aren't you? I like that. Get the client's mind off his troubles, eh?' He gave me a crooked grin. 'I phoned round and, for your information, not all my friends are gamblers. There's a fair number in that other business where you don't talk about how you make your dosh.'

'Oh,' I muttered, and wondered what I'd got myself into. I might be bored with working for insurance companies but at least their fundraising activities are legal.

'The buzz is that your little friend Lane's on the lam.'

'Bob's current problem isn't to do with drugs, unless you call tobacco a drug.'

'No, pure as driven snow, isn't he, especially as he's a friend of yours?' Lee commented with a certain smugness.

'OK,' I said mildly, 'point taken. I shall want to know more about your background, though. After all, you did tell me that you knew the boys from Vallance Road.'

98

'I didn't,' he said indignantly. 'I said I knew *about* them. We lived off the Bethnal Green Road in Whitechapel for a while. You couldn't help knowing about the Krays. That doesn't mean . . . oh, hell, listen to me! My father was a perfectly respectable man. I grew up knowing which of the lads I was at school with were a bit on the moody side but most of the big career crims didn't send their kids to state schools like I went to. They're all out in Essex or Kent, them lot, on private estates with their kids in posh schools.'

I didn't point out that Lee was now living on a private estate himself.

'Right, well, we'll have a trawl through their names tomorrow,' I said. 'You never know, some of your old school chums might have become extortionists.'

He smacked his forehead with the palm of his hand.

'Extortionists! Bloody barrow boys, most of 'em.'

He moved away from the bar and sat down. He grinned at me. It wasn't a pretty sight.

'Oh, I see. Very clever, Cunane! You think I'll sit up all night drinking black coffee while I try to remember which of my friends might be in on this.'

'You could do worse.'

'I told you before, you're in the wrong job. You should have become a social worker.'

I flashed him a thin smile.

'Listen, social worker, do you think Cheyenne would have been delivered to my door safely if I'd given them the five hundred K?'

'It's possible but what I've seen so far is that these guys went in for careful planning.'

'So?'

'So they never gave a thought about whether Cheyenne lived or died. If they had done they'd have made plans to keep her warm and fed. I think what happened was always on the cards.'

Lee sighed deeply and then said, 'I thought it was something like that.'

I headed for the kitchen to round up Clint. Lee followed me. When I opened the door I found that Clint had washed the dirty pots. He was seated at the table buttering several very thick slices of bread. He had strawberry jam on the table. The only unusual aspect of this scene was that he'd cut the loaf up longwise. I'd never seen such big slices of bread before. He'd made a neat job of it but then his hobby used to be model-making.

Before I could speak Lee intervened. 'What the fuck are you playing at, you big bastard?' he snapped. 'That loaf would have lasted me for the rest of the week.'

Clint's face registered a very faint expression of disapproval, then he looked at the knife in his hand. A bread knife, it looked very small in those big fingers. He laid it on the table and smiled at Lee. I knew his smile was completely innocent but Lee didn't.

'Here, keep him away from me,' he said quickly. He moved out of the kitchen.

'Come on, Clint. We've got to go,' I said.

Obediently, Clint followed me out to the car but not before he'd made the loaf into two enormous sandwiches.

'He's not a very nice man, is he, Dave?' he asked as we drove away.

'No,' I agreed.

'Is he a bad man?'

'I don't think so, not a very bad man. He's just a man who wants more than he earns, like the rest of us.'

Clint's brow furrowed at this but then he remembered the jam sandwiches. He began eating, quite noisily and with an expression of utter concentration. I looked at my watch. It was half-five.

I didn't feel hungry myself and I didn't intend to go home. I was pleasantly tired but there was still a lot to do. The weather had improved to the extent that the rain had stopped. I decided to drive on into central Manchester. The A34 and the Parkway were quiet. Most of the traffic was going the other way.

When I got into town I took the car to a multi-storey at the back of Deansgate. Even at this time of night the traffic wardens were likely to be out in force and it goes against the grain to keep forking out parking fines, even if I could charge them as expenses. I led Clint to the Black and Blue Club just off King Street South.

There were still people on the street but not crowds. Late shoppers were heading for the car parks burdened with bags and heavy clothing against the sharp wind. Young service workers were making for the bus stops along Deansgate. Some of these were impervious to the chill evening air, or so their lack of warm clothing suggested.

The club was approached through a narrow cul-de-sac behind a big store. There was a jumble of doorways and frontages offering all kinds of obscure services. They seem to be different every time you go down that impermanent street but Charlie Costello's club has been a fixture for ever. It was hard to guess the original purpose of the building which now housed the club except that it had been nothing to do with pleasure or alcohol. Only a discreet sign announced its present purpose. The Black and Blue Club didn't need barkers out on the street or big posters to drum up trade.

It was early but I hoped that Charlie Costello would be there already. Charlie, who must have been over seventy, had worked in the pubs and clubs of Manchester since leaving school at fourteen. He usually worked late but there was just a chance that he might have been in for the happy hour when the club tries to snare the homebound office workers. Since prices at the Black and Blue were high anyway, happy hour wasn't what you could call a total success with hardened drinkers who were looking for a bigger bang for their buck.

101

Charlie was an old friend of my father's. In a past that's receding more quickly than I care to think, Charlie was a leading informer when Dad ran the CID in the city centre. Never a true copper's nark because he wasn't in it just for the money, Charlie was valuable because he always knew who was 'at it'. My dad used to call him Mr Whisper because Charlie prefaced his information by saying 'There's been a whisper about so-and-so'. The other name Dad had for him was 'Chuckling Charlie'. This was because Charlie's capacity to laugh or even smile is very limited. He has a deadpan face with a long upper lip. There's plenty going on behind that face but Charlie's one of those people who likes to take more from a conversation than he gives, which, I suppose, is why my father found him so useful.

When we reached the club there were few customers but Charlie was there. He was instructing a shaven-headed lad of about eighteen in the finer arts of barmanship. The place was dark and to my relief there was no music thumping out. The Black and Blue is a fairly adult place. The prices tend to keep the teenies out. The name Black and Blue Club is a joke. Originally it was called that because it was patronised by lawyers and coppers, the black-robed and the blue. They didn't really have bare-knuckle fights in a back room as the fanciful still maintain although there have been a few famous tussles there.

'Drink?' said Charlie.

There wasn't a flicker of recognition in his face but he sent the young skin-head off to collect glasses. Charlie was one of those rare old people who don't look their age, thin without looking withered. I've known him since I started as a detective. My archaeological girlfriend, Delise Delaney, used to say that he looked like one of these bodies dug out of bogs in Denmark and England. Charlie's skin was tanned like soft leather and maybe that's why he seemed ageless.

'A whisky for me and a pint of orange juice for my friend,' I said.

'You don't get concessionary prices, Mr Cunane. Happy hour's off when you're around.'

I laughed at this and Clint, much more sensitive to the emotions of those around him than I'd ever known him, laughed as well. Charlie showed no reaction.

When Chuckling Charlie had put the drinks down he started polishing the burnished copper counter. He studied Clint briefly. I took Clint's drink and led him to a side table, telling him to stay put. When I got back to the bar I took out my wallet and began counting twenty-pound notes on to the counter.

'What's this?' Charlie said when I'd reached two hundred. He put his hand down on the money.

'You know what it is. I want some faces recognised,' I said quietly.

'Whose?' he replied impassively.

'Three men, one white aged about thirty, one black possibly a rough guy, one white aged nearer fifty than forty, maybe an educated man.'

'I have people answering those descriptions in here every night.'

'Do you have people in here who have two hundred grand to spend?'

'Sometimes. What have they done? Blagged money off one of your precious insurance companies?'

'Extortion. They took a guy's baby and wanted half a million to give her back. He gave them two hundred grand and they gave him back his baby, only now she's in intensive care in hospital.'

Charlie remained as boot-faced as before at this news.

'Keep counting,' he grunted. 'Revenge comes expensive.'

I counted out five hundred and he motioned me to stop.

'A monkey should be right for starters,' he said. 'I take it that the upset daddy hasn't been to the law?'

I nodded.

He returned my look unflinchingly. For all the expression there was on his face he might have been one of the metal fixtures on the bar.

'You want to watch it,' he said finally. 'These revenge jobs have a nasty way of going sour.'

'Thanks for the warning,' I muttered.

A ghastly grin creased Charlie's leathery mug for a second. If I'd blinked I'd have missed it.

'You're just like your old man – stubborn and stupid. He'd have been Chief Constable if he'd learned to bend with the breeze. I told him, I see it all from here, but he wouldn't listen either.'

I made no reply.

'A drug dealer is he, this distraught daddy?'

I shook my head. This method of communication can get tedious but it's how Charlie likes to play it.

'But he has to be into something seriously bent. You'll get your fingers burnt, I'm telling you. Someone always does on these jobs. I'll put the word out but it would help if you had a picture.'

'I'm getting one. I'll bring it when I have it. Meanwhile, these people are pros. The job was slick . . .' I told him everything, except the names of Lee and Jamie.

'So they've done this before,' he commented. 'You might be wasting your time asking me. These customers don't sound like the sort who go bragging in back-street pubs.'

'Maybe not. I came here because they must be well informed about who has money but can't declare it.'

'So?'

'You hear plenty. All these lawyers and coppers who come in here must let things slip occasionally and you're in a position to find out if anyone has been making discreet enquiries about high-level crooks.'

'You're not saying I've turned to crime in my old age, are you?'

'No, but you must have a fair idea who the potential targets are, and if you hear a whisper that someone's sniffing round I want to know about it.'

'They do say that if you sup with the devil you need a long spoon. I'm not sure if I should take your money now.'

'Why not? All I want is information.'

'But so do they, and if they see I'm after the same thing they might jump to a hasty conclusion.'

'Oh come on, Charlie. You're fireproof.'

'As there's a kiddie involved I'll put the word out in the right places but I'm not promising miracles, mind.'

He took one of the tenners and turned to the till. He rang up the drinks.

'Keep the change, shall I?' he said.

When I looked at the bar the pile of notes had gone.

9

It was just after seven when I reached my flat. I let Clint in and as we went down the hall past the guest bedroom I noted that there were wood shavings on the floor. I tried the door but it was locked and not with the old lock that a child could have picked with a hairpin. A shiny new brass lock gleamed on the woodwork. I told Clint to make himself comfortable in the kitchen and headed next door.

'What's going on?' I asked when I reached the living room. Lloyd was lying prone in front of the television. He didn't respond.

'What are you watching?' I asked. 'The news?'

'*Rugrats*,' he growled without taking his eyes off the screen.

'You'll turn into a Rugrat one of these days.'

'I can't turn into one,' he said irritably. 'They're children and I'm a child already.'

'Just checking that your brain's still switched on,' I said cheerfully.

'Oh, Dave!' said my partner. 'You're just in time to get changed.'

'Changed for what?' I snapped. It had been a long day and I was looking forward to a long hot soak in the bath.

'Don't say you've forgotten? We've had the tickets for weeks . . . Ibsen at the Royal Exchange? *Ghosts?*'

'Oh, God!' I muttered, dismayed. Then I remembered why I'd come in here hotfoot. 'The bedroom door . . .'

'Yes, Naomi thought she'd be more comfortable with

a door she can really lock so I got a locksmith in to fit one.'

'Cosy,' I said in a tone that was meant to be scornful. I was about to say a whole lot more but Naomi herself appeared at the kitchen door and Janine put a finger discreetly to her lips. A fugitive smile crossed the girl's face when she saw me but she didn't speak. I was uncomfortable at being cast in the role of predatory male.

'Come on, Dave,' Janine chivvied, 'hurry up and change into something more comfortable than that suit. Naomi's going to be looking after Jenny and Lloyd and we can catch the Metro from Stretford if you hurry.'

'I've got somebody with me next door.'

'Well, he'll just have to go. We've no time for entertaining.' With that she showed me to the door. 'Hurry,' she ordered. 'No more than five minutes.'

When I reached my own living room Clint was sprawled on the sofa. Well, 'sprawled' doesn't really cover it. His head and shoulders were on the sofa while his hips and legs dangled off the end. He looked about as comfortable as an adult in a child's play house. He'd found a Gameboy that Lloyd had left behind and was staring intently at the tiny screen.

'I love this, Dave,' he said with deep sincerity.

I looked over his shoulder at the game he was playing: Tetris. It seemed hardly possibly that those thick fingers could work the tiny buttons but they did.

'Clint, er, will you be all right on your own for a few hours? There's food in the kitchen and you can watch the telly but don't go out.'

'It's all right, Dave,' he said abstractedly, his entire concentration focused on the tiny screen.

I dashed into my bedroom and did a speed change into comfortable olive slacks and a green blouson and was at the door by the time Janine tapped on it.

'My friend's going to stay and watch the telly for a few hours. Will you let Naomi know?'

107

'That's all right,' she said briskly. 'Naomi won't be leaving my flat until we get back.'

As we were late Janine drove us into town in her VW Golf GTI. I said nothing about the new domestic arrangements. If Janine wanted to be economical in her explanations about how long Naomi would be staying in my flat I could be equally economical about Clint. There'd be time enough for chat when we got home.

We parked opposite the cathedral.

During the play I struggled to stay awake. I told myself it wasn't because I was bored by Scandinavian drama but because of my earlier excursions in the woods and by-ways of Cheshire. The seats at the Royal Exchange are designed for midgets. At least the discomfort helped to keep me semi-conscious. Ghosts of dead ideas flitted through my mind.

'Dave, I wish I had a photo of your face,' Janine said as we filed out of the theatre. 'You look as if you've just been to a public hanging.'

'No, I enjoyed the play,' I protested.

'Hmmmph! I bet you'd have enjoyed it more if it had been something by Agatha Christie. Face it, Dave, detection's what you do during the day. In the evening you've got to switch on to something different or your mind will start to stagnate.'

Agreement seemed about the wisest thing I could do.

We went to a Thai restaurant on Tibb Street. I didn't enjoy the meal. On the way home Janine quizzed me about where the investigation was going and I told her everything I'd found. The basis of my relationship with Janine is that I have no secrets from her. She's never revealed anything I've wanted kept quiet. She told me Granville Courteney had spent two hours with Naomi sketching every tiny detail she could remember. The finished picture would be available in the morning.

'I found another witness. A jogger called Pietrangeli saw

the lookout parked in a van near the Wilmslow Green private estate.'

'Male or female jogger, Dave?'

'Female.'

'Young or old, ugly or attractive?'

'Young and quite attractive, but you know joggers . . .'

'I should do. I live with one.'

'Hey, Mrs Alving! I ride a bike in case you haven't noticed . . .'

'Same difference, Pastor Manders.'

'. . . and I haven't been out for weeks. I was saying she's one of these fanatics. I practically ended up under a lorry trying to get her story.'

'As long as you didn't end up under her, Dave, that's all right.'

'This woman's a perfectly respectable schoolteacher and I'm going to try and get her to do a picture with Granville Courteney.'

'No expense spared, eh?' she commented. Granville doesn't come cheap but then he's the best. Police photofits all seem to be of the same square-headed man.

Before we got home Janine made it clear in various subtle ways that the lock on Naomi's door, for which she didn't offer me a key, meant that we could go back to normal weekday separate rules as far as sleeping arrangements went.

Naomi was wide awake and watching *Ally McBeal* when we arrived in the White family's living room.

'I'll go next door then,' she said. 'I've got a telly in my bedroom.'

'Right,' Janine agreed.

'There's just a tiny snag,' I said. 'My friend's there and he'll be staying a few days. He'll be sleeping in my bed while I sleep on the sofa.'

'Oh,' Janine said. She was uncertain whether I was making some kind of indirect comment.

I watched her computing the various solutions to this dilemma.

'My friend is called Clint Lane,' I added.

Light dawned on Janine's face. She knows Clint well enough.

'I'd better come through with you, Naomi,' she said. I smiled at her gratefully. The problem wasn't with Clint, but in how Naomi might react to him.

When we entered my living room Clint was still sprawled over the sofa in the same uncomfortable position I'd left him in and was still riveted to the Gameboy. Clint's very dependable in that way.

'Clint, this is Naomi,' I said. He rose from the sofa to his full seven foot. While he was standing up he couldn't quite take his eyes away from the Gameboy. 'Clint,' I repeated. He then focused on Naomi and the Gameboy was immediately ancient history. He shyly extended his hand to shake hers but seemed to have forgotten the words to go with the gesture. I realised he was too tongue-tied to speak.

This was another change from the Clint I was used to.

Naomi's first reaction was to be startled by the sheer physical bulk of the man. I wasn't surprised when she instinctively drew back. Then, to her credit, she shook the offered hand. Like the rest of us, she found taking a grip on Clint's hand something of a problem. She ended up grasping two of his fingers.

'Hello, Clint,' she said in a friendly voice. I'm not sure whether she could see that Clint is educationally challenged or whether she recognised it instinctively, but whatever the process was, her tone and smile and body language were exactly right.

Clint's smile spread round his face until it almost reached his ears. 'Hello, Naomi,' he said slowly. 'Pleased to meet you.'

Janine came over and gave him a kiss and a hug.

'Hello, Clint,' she said warmly. Then she turned to Naomi. 'You're missing *Ally McBeal*.'

Naomi took her cue and disappeared to her room. Clint watched her go. The expression on his face was hard to decipher.

We both looked at him and then Janine took my arm and walked me to the door of the flat.

'What's all this?' she said in whisper. 'Why's he here? I thought you were supposed to be visiting him, not the other way round? You should have told me he was here before we went to the play. We could have stayed and helped him to settle in. It was unfair springing him on Naomi like that.'

'She handled it.'

'Yes, I'm forming a favourable impression of her, but why's he here?'

'Bob's having a spot of bother with Customs . . .'

'Will I be reading about this on the crime pages?'

'You might.'

'Then don't tell me any more. When you said you had a guest I was thinking about saying you could come and share my bed, but in the circumstances it might be better if you sleep on the sofa.'

'What circumstances?'

'You know very well. Clint's eyes almost popped out of his head when he saw Naomi. I think he fancies her. We don't want any problems, do we?'

I shook my head grumpily. After I'd locked my door I realised that she was right. I'd never seen Clint react to the opposite sex before. Emotionally, he'd always been prepubescent, but now?

I returned to the living room and helped him get ready for bed. He was perfectly capable of doing this by himself but I was curious about what he had in those two massive suitcases. It had crossed my mind that Bob's Dutch farmer friends might be growing something other than hay in their fields.

111

There was nothing in the cases apart from a very extensive wardrobe of outsize clothes purchased from a specialist shop in Amsterdam. Shoes you could paddle across a lake in, shirts like tents, massive suits in robust tweed — Clint had enough to keep him going sartorially for a very long while. I hung his clothes in my wardrobe while he got into his pyjamas and a violently coloured green and orange dressing gown and went to brush his teeth, a process that took some time.

When he came back he'd retrieved the Gameboy and looked quite composed again. Janine's fears were probably exaggerated.

'All right, Clint?' I asked.

'Dave, I'm worried about Bob,' he said solemnly. 'I'm going to say a prayer for him. Do you want me to say one for you? That man in the big house wasn't nice, was he?'

'No,' I said, 'he wasn't, but maybe you should say a prayer for him as well. Good night, Clint.'

'Good night and God bless, Dave.'

I retreated to the sofa. I could hear the television from Naomi's room. I discarded the idea of banging on her door and struggled to blank out the sound.

Before falling asleep my brain seethed with problems. I could have done without becoming Clint Lane's chaperone. He'd never been known to press his company on anyone but what was I going to do if he decided to get close to Naomi? Clint isn't the sort of person you argue with.

These and other unkind thoughts were tumbling round in my tired mind when the urgent ringing of the phone startled me back to wakefulness.

It was Bob, the man himself.

'Christ, Dave, I'm sorry about landing you with Clint,' he said before I could put words to my feelings. 'I haven't been able to get in touch all day. Is he OK?'

He sounded so harassed that I hesitated to demand that he immediately arrange for Clint's transfer elsewhere.

Bob's a friend and I've few enough of them to risk offending him.

'He's changed a lot. Seems to have grown up a bit, if that's possible.'

'Yes, I've noticed a change, but he's doing what you tell him?'

'No problem, Bob . . . except that he makes the flat look like a Wendy house.'

'I know. I'm going to find a farmhouse with some land when I get myself sorted.'

I didn't ask when that would be.

There was a pause.

'It might be a while before I'm back in Manchester. I'm in France now, but I can send you money if you want to think about finding somewhere where he'll be happy . . .'

My stomach lurched with shame. I felt miserable about wanting to get shot of Clint. Bob had looked after him for years, built his life round his brother really, visited him over in Holland every other week and I was feeling sorry for myself after a day.

'Forget it, Bob,' I said quickly. 'We'll sort something. There's just one tiny thing. I've got a girl staying here . . .'

'You old ram, Dave! I thought you were tight with Janine?'

'I am, I am! This girl's the nanny for the kids.'

'And Janine's worried that Clint will start getting frisky?' he said with a laugh. 'Well, spring is on the way, you know, but just tell him to back off if he starts getting too friendly. All he'll do is follow her round like a sheepdog. There was a girl on the farm in Holland. Nothing happened. I don't think Clint's had sex education. He's quite unspoiled that way. Misses his mum. Needs a female to tell him what to do.'

'Right,' I said slowly.

'Put some bromide in his tea if you're really worried,'

Bob said with a chuckle. 'My bloke'll be in touch. I've got to keep this short.'

'Wait! Are you saying this line might be bugged as well?'

'Dave, if they'll bug your office, they'll bug your home number.'

He rang off.

I went back to the settee. Before sleep finally came I speculated that it probably wasn't just Clint that had drawn Bob to Holland so frequently. Friend or not, he was in the same business that had provided so many no-neck businessmen from the inner city with the funds to build lovely homes out in north Cheshire.

Images of Bob and Lee and Jamie and the Silk Cut smoker and Spike Head all playing football swirled in my mind. The Schemer was the referee and old Mrs Latham and Chuckling Charlie were running the lines. They were all in a game but I didn't know the rules and I couldn't play.

10

I didn't get to sleep with Janine but we did breakfast together. That is, I took Clint round to her place with me and snatched a few hurried words with her. We needed to arrange one or two things. Janine had been handling the Granville Courteney end of my enquiry. She'd taken Naomi into town with her and supervised while the artist sketched to the nanny's instructions. It's not that she works part-time at Pimpernel or anything formal, it's just that we find it convenient to do each other favours. Every so often I pick up the children, occasionally she gives me a hand.

'I'll pick up the picture from Granville this morning,' Janine said. 'He'll want paying.'

'Don't we all?' I grumbled.

'Cash. Three hundred on the nail.'

I forked out the money.

'I'll see you at the office at lunchtime. You can decide what you want to do with the picture then.'

'I'll need to show it to Lee and Jamie before I start flashing it round Manchester.'

'Why?'

'Because . . . I'm not quite sure. There's something very iffy about Lee Parkes. Sometimes he seems like a broken man, at other times he hardly seems to be affected at all by the death of his wife and the bad health of his baby.'

'That's natural, surely? Sometimes he's down and other times he's coping, Admit it, Dave, you don't trust him because he's a Cockney. If he'd been a Mancunian . . .'

115

'You're a Cockney and I trust you.'

'I'm the exception that proves the rule.'

I laughed.

At that moment Jenny came clattering in demanding assistance to pack her schoolbag and Janine went to help her and to get Lloyd dressed.

Seeing her do that reminded me about the new member of staff, the nanny. There was no sign of Naomi.

Meanwhile Clint had made himself at home in the Whites' kitchen and was breakfasting off a whole box of Coco Pops. He was dressed in a tailored tweed suit of unusually heavy material, a grey with red pinstripe. I wasn't sure what the effect was but it was an improvement on the denim overalls he'd been wearing yesterday. He was daintily eating the cereal out of a large glass mixing bowl.

I realised that he'd have to accompany me in whatever I did today. First of all I needed to go to the office.

I looked across at Clint. He smiled back.

'Where's Naomi?' he asked innocently.

'Good question, Clint,' Janine chipped in before I could say anything. 'You and Clint had better go now, Dave, and I'll see about rousing that young lady from her slumbers. It seems that the alarm clock I gave her doesn't work. I want to show her the children's school and introduce her.'

Clint and I set off into town in the Mondeo, he chatting away about his life on the farm. It was a fine day. In the era when my life had been a little less crowded I'd loved getting up early and starting the day with a bike ride along the banks of the Mersey. I still have the bike but not the time.

We were in before Celeste again. That was a record. I'd started on the paperwork when she put her head round my office door. She smiled at me and then took in Clint's giant presence. He'd put three large seats together and was sprawled over them playing with the Gameboy. He had a different game this time, Donkey Kong.

'A client this early, Boss?' she said.

116

I shook my head.

She was wearing the same slate blue jacket and trousers as yesterday but with a different sweater.

'You look almost good enough to eat.'

She grimaced.

Clint looked up from his game. Mention of food always attracts him.

'Clint, meet Celeste,' I said. 'Celeste, this is Clint. He will be with me for some time. It's sort of work experience.' I didn't feel like going through all the whys and wherefores with her. She'd have to work Clint out for herself.

Celeste raised her eyebrows but made no further comment. I told her to ask Peter Snyder, Marvin Desailles and Michael Coe to be free for a briefing session after one.

'Who shall I bill their time to?' she asked, just a hint of rebellion in her voice.

'You know very well – File Red.'

'Going to come expensive,' she said with a smile.

'Oh, and while you're at it. I need a very large-scale map of Wilmslow. Get the A to Z or the Ordnance Survey and enlarge it.'

'How much?'

'I don't know, big. Six foot by six. Really big.'

'Big! The man wants it big,' she said with a glance at Clint, who smiled sweetly at her. Possibly the smart suit made her look older but I didn't detect the same degree of interest that he'd shown in Naomi.

We discussed several appointments which she'd scheduled for me, and spent the better part of an hour deploying the staff on various jobs. Clint took no notice of us. I gave her the Coke can and the black bin liner I'd collected from Alderley Edge and told her to arrange for them to be checked for fingerprints.

At ten I had a session with two investigators who were delving into a complicated insurance fraud on an estate in

Salford. At ten-thirty I left the office for a meeting with Ernie Cunliffe, senior claims executive at Northern Mutual. Clint came with me but I left him in an armchair outside Ernie's office. Ernie, a bald-headed former schoolmate of mine who harbours delusions of grandeur about his executive status, can be difficult. Despite efforts on my part to reduce it his firm is still responsible for about a quarter of my turnover, so I have to keep him sweet.

'Hello, Dave, you're looking well,' he started.

I couldn't return the compliment. Ernie's complexion was ghastly. His skin looked transparent and he had several pimples on his face. The few wispy strands of hair he'd combed over failed to conceal unpleasant scratch marks on his head. He was wearing a beautiful Italian suit in an expensive charcoal material so, fleshly signs to the contrary, he wasn't a candidate for Skid Row yet.

He must have mistaken my musing for concern. 'I've had one dose of flu after another recently,' he explained. 'I don't get out in the fresh air like you do. God, man, you look as if you've just strolled out of a health spa. What do you use on your hair? It is dyed, isn't it?'

The last comment was made in a roguish 'all lads together' sort of tone.

'Janine has me over the sink every morning getting it to the right shade,' I lied.

He smiled in pleasure at this. His right hand explored his own deforested scalp in an involuntary gesture. I was waiting for the day when he asked me to recommend a good wig-maker.

We reviewed several current cases and set up a timetable for results on some pending investigations. There's a point in any job where the cost of carrying on begins to outweigh what the company might lose by conceding the claim.

'Well, that all seems very satisfactory, Dave. How's Janine? My wife loves reading her pieces in the paper.'

'Flourishing as ever,' I commented. Janine loathes to be thought of as a women's journalist.

'You and she must come out for a meal sometime.'

'I'd love that, Ernie, but she works such odd hours, it's hard to pin her down to a time.' In fact, wild horses wouldn't have dragged Janine out to his pillared and porticoed residence in Mottram St Andrew's.

He let the matter drop with a genial shrug. I seemed to have caught Ernie Cunliffe on one of his better days.

'There's a little problem I'm having,' I said as dismissively as I could, 'and I wondered if you could help me with it?'

'You know me, Dave, anything to help an old school pal.'

I did know him and I knew he'd never hesitated to do me a bad turn when it suited him but the thought had occurred and I wouldn't be happy unless I asked him . . .

'I'm interested in some statistics – young people from wealthy families who've died suddenly or had accidents.'

'We've got lots of them, Dave,' he said with an effort at a sad smile. 'Unfortunately these wealthy folks will buy their sons and daughters powerful cars.'

'No, hear me out, Ernie. It's not those. It's families which appear to be very wealthy, with nice homes in exclusive areas, then one of their children or the wife or whoever has this accident or dies and suddenly they're not wealthy any more. They can't pay their insurance premiums, for example. Have to cash in their assets suddenly.'

'What would the purpose of this enquiry be?' His narrow little eyes were filled with suspicion.

'OK, to be perfectly frank, I've got this wild theory that someone's going round extorting money from families who have come by their wealth illegally. Only instead of returning the victim safe and sound, they don't much care what happens.'

'You mean, they kill them?'

'No, or at least I don't think so. Just give the victim a

119

hard time. The family can't complain about the extortion because . . .'

'Because their money's dirty?' The suspicion in his eyes was replaced by a shrewd look. 'Mmmm, that's an interesting one, Dave. From the company's point of view we would be losing premiums from Grade A clients. I take it you're investigating such an event?'

'I might be,' I said cagily.

'In other words, you are. Okey-dokey, I'll get one of our analysts to spend half a day or so on it. The company's nothing to lose.'

'Thanks, Ernie.'

'Think nothing of it, Dave,' he said expansively. 'I'll be in touch if we get any results. I'll tell the analyst it's a purely theoretical study.'

It was lunchtime when Clint and I got back to the office. We walked through the centre of Manchester looking like Little and Large – or was it Cannon and Ball? – one of those double acts, but I wasn't self-conscious. The streets are filled with curiosities these days and I don't think we attracted a second glance. Or not until I was turning off Deansgate towards the office when a man tapped me on the shoulder.

'You Bob's friend?' he said. The words were indistinct, his accent was so adenoidal.

I looked at him. A thin-lipped, bloodless-looking man of about thirty, he was shaven-headed and wearing only a thin pullover over a T-shirt and jeans although it was a cold day. His face had received hostile attention from somebody's boot at an earlier stage of his life, the wreckage of his nose pressed flat into his face. The menacing appearance was spoiled by the man's lack of inches. He was only about five foot three.

'I could be,' I said cautiously.

For all I knew he could be a customs officer or a

120

copper. I believe a criminal front is much in favour with the undercover branches.

'Here, don't fuck me about,' he snapped, and shoved a roll of notes fastened with an elastic band into my hand. 'Bob sent you this. Said to tell you he's in Germany now. He'll be in touch but it'll be next week.'

With that he looked over his shoulder then walked out into the road, slipping through the traffic like an eel. I tucked the money into my trouser pocket. Clint didn't say a word.

Back at Pimpernel Janine was waiting for us in my room which was now dominated by an immense map of Wilmslow. She occasionally attends these sessions as an unpaid helper and prisoner's friend. The others accept her presence. Celeste had blown up the A to Z in sections on A3 paper and pasted them together on a large sheet of hardboard. On the bottom right-hand corner she'd stencilled the words 'FILE RED INVESTIGATION'.

'Bit obvious, isn't it, Dave?' Janine asked.

'Certain things have to be kept confidential but for others I need help,' I said. 'Why should I keep a pack of dogs and do all the barking myself?'

'Very droll,' she commented.

Feeding Clint was the next problem. He requires something more substantial than a sandwich and a packet of crisps, my usual fare. In the end we bought him several rounds of sandwiches which he devoured uncomplainingly. Celeste joined us for lunch. I amused myself by making a sketch map of the Alderley Edge area while Janine made conversation with Clint.

Peter Snyder, who came into my room just before one, is the senior investigator in the firm after myself. A tall, black man who previously worked for a rival detective agency, Peter bears a slight resemblance to the actor Denzel Washington and is always being told he should look for work in television.

He receives this advice with a grave smile. Peter wanted to be a copper but he failed the health test because he has a mild heart murmur. He's a man with a mission, is Peter. He resents talk of the 'black community' or any suggestions that 'inner city' attitudes are shared by all black people. Naturally, this sets him at odds with Marvin Desailles who sees himself as a potential 'inner city' spokesman.

When Marvin learned of Peter's original career choice he was very scornful but Peter returns any barbed words with interest. He comes from a well-to-do family. His father was a doctor and Peter went to a fee-paying school in Hampshire. His current employment as a private detective causes heartache in his family but his prospects are bright. He shows far greater managerial potential than I do.

Michael Coe, a ginger-haired bachelor from London, came in next. Michael's an expert in all forms of electronic surveillance, an expertise he came by during military service in Northern Ireland. He was a member of a special section of Army Intelligence which he isn't allowed to discuss with us. Michael was wearing his usual black leather jacket and cord trousers. He also sports a pair of granny glasses which make him look a bit like Leon Trotsky, particularly as he wears his hair long. Although Michael's getting a bit long in the tooth for it now, he keeps us in touch with the club culture which still bumps along in the city despite its recent decline.

Both he and Peter studied the map and took no notice of Clint. Celeste must have told them about the work experience.

'Is the implication of this map that you're finally considering a relocation to the wealthy suburbs?' Peter said eventually. He always talks like a management manual.

I explained that I was doing a special investigation of a kidnapping and as I spoke felt the level of interest rise. Marvin came in while I was explaining the background.

He sat in a corner. I gave a full run-down of the story but made no mention of names.

'And the client's name?' demanded Marvin.

'Later, that comes later. I'm nervous about mentioning it.'

Peter and Michael exchanged glances.

'Mr Cunane,' Marvin piped up from his corner, 'what happens when you catch these dudes?' He was wearing an outrageous purple tracksuit and a large black and yellow tam over his abundant locks, set off by wrap-around reflective shades. By a curious quirk, the further Marvin advances in the legal profession the stronger his attachment to 'street garb' becomes. The police find it very irritating, particularly as he can recite whole sections of the McPherson Report by heart. It certainly comes as a shock to obstreperous coppers when this Rasta-looking individual starts spouting legal jargon instead of lighting a spliff.

If Peter is the opposite of the black stereotype, Marvin does his best to compete with the caricatures of Lenny Henry and Ali G. Sadly, though, he's entirely serious. Middle-class *Guardian*-reading members of the public find him difficult to cope with. They think he's joking, sending up the idea of a 'stage Afro-Caribbean', but he isn't. He makes no concessions to 'niceness' and rejoices in embarrassing the well-intentioned.

'Not our problem,' I said confidently. 'I'm just hired to identify them.'

'Hey! It'll be your problem if anything drastic happens to them. Accessory before and after the fact is what those mothers at the Crown Prosecution Service will say.'

'Yeah, Marv,' Michael drawled, 'but that's assuming what Dave's client does to the bastards ever comes to light.'

'You're cynical, man!' Marvin replied. 'You're outrageous! As a legal man it might be better if I withdraw from this discussion.'

123

'No!' I said sharply. 'I'm not condoning violence. The client's agreed that he only wants to identify them.'

'You's better get that in writing, brother Cunane.' Marvin lessened the impact of his dissent by speaking in an American black accent. 'Better leave it alone is my advice.'

'Cut the crap, Marvin!' Celeste said angrily. 'This is a baby we're talking about.'

'I'm only being righteous . . .' he said, waving his hands in the air like a preacher.

'Can we get on?' Janine said crossly. 'I've got to be back at the paper soon.'

I traced the route Naomi had taken and explained what I'd found yesterday by showing them the map of Alderley Edge.

'The ambulance siren's significant,' Peter said after a long silence from the group.

'How?' I asked.

'It's like the dog that didn't bark in the night. You know, in the Sherlock Holmes story?'

This produced a groan from the others.

'No, really,' he insisted. 'The siren was blasting away when it went down the street and pulled up outside the unfortunate Mrs Latham's address. Frightened the cats, didn't it? So it was loud. That's when the dear old ailurophile . . .'

'What o-phile?' demanded Marvin.

'Cat lover, to the uninitiated. From the Greek.'

'All right! We believe you!'

'. . . dragged herself to the window and more or less observed the whole kidnapping.'

'Right,' I muttered.

'Then the perpetrators drove away quietly, without a siren.'

'Yes,' I agreed.

'So they didn't want anyone to know where they were

going. That's because they were going somewhere local, maybe only a few streets away, to park up. They needed to get the baby out, transfer the nanny to a car and drive to Cheadle Hulme to dump her while she was still unconscious. So what you've got to do is find the garage, or lock-up, or whatever, where they did the transfer. It's bound to be close to where they picked her up.'

'Bravo, Peter,' said Janine.

'Sounds reasonable to me,' I admitted. 'We know they had two vehicles, the white Vauxhall Rascal and the Ford Transit, so they'd need somewhere to keep them.'

'It would have to be somewhere where they were pretty confident no one would notice an ambulance pulling in,' Michael added. 'Since we're into literary detection, does anybody know where the nearest hospital or old folks' home is in relation to Hawthorn Lane?'

He got up to look at the map more closely.

'Why?' I asked, just to humour him.

'G.K. Chesterton, the Father Brown stories? Where would you hide a leaf but in a tree? You know, the story about the invisible postman? So where best to hide an ambulance . . .'

'OK, good idea. I'll check it out.'

'Do you want me to pull people off other work?' Celeste asked urgently. 'We can find this place in no time.'

'Sorry, Celeste,' I said. 'I know you're enthusiastic but this case has to go at its own pace. We'll have briefing sessions like this but speed isn't an issue. I'll do the investigating on my own.'

This produced frowns and not just from Celeste.

'I'm the only one who won't be missed from a current assignment,' I said. 'You all know I'm dispensable, not to say disposable.'

'That's enough false modesty, Dave,' my dear partner said dismissively. 'You're going to need all the help you can get on this and as usual you've forgotten the most important

125

piece of information.' She slipped a roll of paper out of a cardboard tube and with the help of Peter pinned it on to the map board. I hadn't in fact forgotten the picture but I'd thought I'd keep it to myself.

'This is the man the nanny described to Granville Courteney,' she announced, 'the bogus ambulance driver.'

Among the people assembled in that room there was a fair amount of knowledge of the local criminal 'faces' but this man was new to them. As drawn by Courteney, he had a look of refinement in a thin, ascetic-seeming face. There was a high forehead framed by thick black curly hair, finely chiselled features, a dimple on the chin. Courteney had indicated colouring with skilful shading and the man looked fresh-faced, an outdoor type, although the heavy black-framed glasses might have indicated a sedentary occupation. You could have taken him for a member of any of the middle-class professions but never for a kidnapper. The mouth was interesting. Narrow lips were partly obscured by a droopy black moustache, which could be false. It was hard to be certain what his age might be.

'No one I know,' Peter said with a sigh.

'Me neither,' Michael agreed.

'And he certainly ain't one of the brothers,' Marvin said with a degree of satisfaction.

'His helper is,' I said quickly.

I described the other man's spiky 'do'.

Marvin gave Celeste a slightly mystified look and shrugged his shoulders.

'Latex,' she explained. 'They put this latex rubber in their damned hair to get the permanent spiky look. I've seen it advertised at an Afro-Caribbean hairdresser's on Ayres Road. The fools' heads look like great big gooseberries and I should think they have about as many brains inside them.'

'Can't all be upwardly mobile, coz,' Marvin said acidly.

'How many Afro-Caribbean hairdressers are we looking at in Greater Manchester?' Michael asked.

126

'Hundreds,' Peter snapped, 'not to speak of people who do hairdressing at home.'

'Right, everybody, thanks!' I said, standing up to conclude the meeting.

'Wait a minute, Mr Cunane,' Peter interrupted. 'Are you just leaving it there? We all go off to our other jobs like good little boys?'

'That's right,' Marvin chipped in. 'You've involved us. Suppose this goes pear-shaped? Suppose your super-secret client *does* riddle these kidnappers with bullets? I mean, it happens, doesn't it? What are we going to do then? We'll be involved in a criminal conspiracy just like you.'

'And another thing,' Michael Coe said, 'why do you need a minder?' He nodded in the direction of Clint. 'We've been able to look after you in the past. Don't you trust us any more?'

I sat down, with a helpless glance at Janine.

'They're right, Dave,' she said. 'It's not as if they're casual employees. If Pimpernel Investigations is to thrive you've got to trust somebody. You can't hope to keep it all close to your chest.'

'I give in. Peter, you can cover the Wilmslow end but you'll have to keep up with current work as well. The insurance work is our money spinner . . .'

'I know that, but well, this kind of work engages one's intellect . . . and I'll do it in the evenings and mornings. And another thing – I could work out the M.O.'

I looked mystified.

'You know, tabulate the modus operandi?'

'Oh, that,' I said.

'What about me?' Michael demanded.

'All right, children,' I said calmly. 'Stay in your places and I'll give out some homework for everybody.'

I gave Michael the name and birth date of Lee Parkes: 3 January 1972.

127

'And the mysterious brother?' Celeste queried. 'He is a footballer, isn't he?

'Jamie Piercy.'

'Shee-it!' breathed Marvin. The others looked equally impressed.

'Michael confine yourself to Lee for now. I'm not absolutely certain he's who he says he is. He claims his parents were killed in a car crash when he was five and that he was adopted by a family who lived in Whitechapel. I want his background checked six ways to Sunday. It's just possible the baby was kidnapped by people who know him really well and that he's just drawn me into the case to be his fall guy. It wouldn't be the first time that's happened.'

'Right, Boss, shall I get off to London straight away?' Michael asked. 'I can get the three-thirty train from Piccadilly, assuming they're still running.'

'I suppose so, if you clear your desk first. It might be better to do that and go in the morning.'

Michael and Peter stood up to go.

'Can I just say one thing,' I added. 'We aren't the police. We're not looking for evidence. All we want are the names.'

'Yes, the names in the frames,' Marvin repeated, 'but don't do anything illegal.'

'Another thing,' Celeste said, always one to have the last word, 'if any of you needs to mention this job and there are other people around, just say it's File Red business.'

The three men exchanged pleased smiles at this touch of cloak and dagger.

'Dave,' Celeste urged when they'd gone, 'the dude with the spiky do . . .'

'Say that again, Celeste,' I joked.

'The man with the funny haircut. Can I have a crack at trying to find him? I know a lot of hairdressers.'

'Come one, come all,' I said, throwing my hands up.

11

By three-thirty that afternoon I was parked outside Wilmslow Green High School waiting for Miss Pietrangeli to come out. The children had gone, the buses had departed. I left Clint in the Mondeo and stood where I had a good view of the car park.

I wanted Pietrangeli to do a session with Granville Courteney. He was expensive but if I could come up with all three faces then there was a much better chance of identifying the crew. She'd said she was going to the school and I'd assumed that meant she was one of the teaching staff. As it happened, I was in for a long wait. Clint fell asleep and it was a full forty minutes after the last child had emerged that the teachers came out in a body. Miss Pietrangeli was easy to spot. Not only was she one of the better favoured of the female staff, she was in a white Adidas tracksuit.

She was accompanied by a very tall, thin man also in a white tracksuit. With his fair hair, prominent features and blue eyes, he looked as if he'd just stepped out of a laxative promotion . . . 'Mr Health and Regularity'. He was carrying an outsized sports bag slung over his shoulder and was ushering my witness towards a battered old green MG.

'Miss Pietrangeli!' I yelled, dashing through the school gates.

My target turned to see who was causing the commotion, as did half a dozen others.

'Miss Pietrangeli, can I speak to you?' I said when I reached the couple.

'School day's over,' the tall guy said. 'Make an appointment.'

'It's about what you saw.' I said, ignoring him. 'You remember? The white Rascal van and the man taking the traffic census.'

'It's that enquiry agent I told you about,' Pietrangeli informed her companion, 'the one who made me five minutes late from my lunchtime run yesterday.'

'Can you just spare me a few minutes?' I pleaded.

'Look, the lady's just sat through a boring staff meeting. She doesn't need some slimy enquiry agent wasting her time. Clear off, you creep!' Health and Regularity unslung the bag from his brawny shoulder and dumped it on the ground near the car with a heavy thump. Then he took a step forward.

I stayed put.

'Down, boy!' Pietrangeli said in an amused tone.

'Some people don't listen,' he said menacingly. He took another step in my direction, then suddenly stopped. His eyes were focused not on me but on the school gates. I swivelled round to look. Clint was out of the car. He waved to me. I waved back. Fortunately, he stayed put.

I turned back to my little confrontation. Health and Regularity's face had lost the look of resolute peevishness it had held before.

I flashed my Pimpernel Investigations ID at them.

'I'm only trying to trace a witness. If you could give me a more thorough description I might be able to trace the driver of that Rascal van you saw.'

Miss Pietrangeli studied my ID. I noted that she wasn't wearing glasses today. Probably using contacts. Then she whipped out her mobile phone and dialled the number of Pimpernel Investigations. She asked if I was employed by them and gave a description: 'Quite tall, dark curly hair

130

and a ruddy complexion, twisted nose and wearing a dark blue suit.'

'Not very flattering,' I muttered.

'They've asked me to say: "What's your father's first name?"'

'Paddy.'

'He's who he says he is,' Pietrangeli told her protector.

Health and Regularity's enthusiasm for a quarrel was now entirely gone. A surly expression appeared on his overly symmetrical features. He put the bag into the back of his car.

'Down to you, Anna, but I don't like the look of him or his mate,' he commented before squeezing himself into the tiny car.

'It's all right, Geoff,' Pietrangeli said firmly, 'you can go. I don't need a lift. I can catch the bus.'

He then drove away. The MG's exhaust was blown and the small car roared like a tank. Geoff put his foot down near the school gates and narrowly missed Clint, who gave him a friendly wave.

'Thanks, Mr Cunane,' she said, handing me back my ID. 'That pillock thinks he owns me. He's my head of department. I see enough of him all day without him telling me to whom I can speak after school. He just wants to use me as an assistant mechanic. You've saved me from a couple of hours of passing tools while he plays with his car.'

'I'll be honest . . .'

'Aren't you always?' she asked with a warm smile.

'I want to steal a couple of hours of your time, too. I want you to work with an artist to make a picture of the man who spoke to you about the traffic census.'

'It sounds interesting, but what's it all in aid of? You're not the police, are you?'

I scratched my head while I tried to think which of the various cover stories I'd dreamed up would be most

131

acceptable to her. In her neat tracksuit and trainers, she didn't look the romantic type, more a practical, down-to-earth sort.

'It's complicated,' I said truthfully. 'It involves a kid-napping.'

She raised her eyebrows at this.

'You know these arranged marriages in Asian families? There are unscrupulous people who'll stop at nothing to prevent the girl from backing out of the match she's been forced into.'

She considered this for a moment.

'But how do I know you're not trying to get this girl back where she doesn't want to go? The man I saw was white.'

'Oh, I'm one of the good guys,' I said with a smile. 'Can't you see that?'

'What exactly is it you want me to do?' she asked cautiously.

'There's this artist, Granville Courteney, you'll have seen his stuff on television. He works for the local paper in Manchester. He'll talk to you, help you to relax and get you to remember details you think you've forgotten.'

'I see,' she said doubtfully. 'And that'll help this girl?'

I nodded.

'It's all perfectly above board. He won't try to hypnotise you or anything.'

She was hooked.

I drove her into town in the back of the Mondeo with Clint in the front. He'd come over all shy and his silence was welcome. I phoned Janine and she promised to ferry Courteney round to the Pimpernel offices and meet us there. The artist was keen enough on the idea of another three hundred tax-free smackers.

Celeste was still on duty when I reached Pimpernel Investigations at about quarter to six.

'Coffee, Boss?' she said as Anna Pietrangeli, Clint and I trooped in.

'Yes, please,' I said, looking at my watch. 'I'm sorry, Miss Pietrangeli. I bet you're hungry and I've dragged you away from your evening meal.' A session with Granville Courteney can last anything up to three hours but I didn't want to tell her that.

Clint gave me a very soulful stare. Mention of food had touched his button again.

'No,' Anna Pietrangeli said eagerly, 'I'm quite looking forward to this. These bastard arranged marriages should be stopped.'

Celeste stared at her oddly but kept her tongue still.

'Coffee will be fine,' the PE teacher continued. 'I don't usually eat till late.'

I showed her into my room and left her there for a moment while I went out to make sure that Courteney was sober enough to do the job.

Granville Courteney's a burly, fat guy, over sixty and bald on top but with dark hair brushed back at the sides. He stands five foot two inches in his socks and when he's wearing his artist's apron, as he now was, you might take him for a pork butcher except that the stains down his front are of paint and charcoal, not blood. He wears glasses and has a little goatee beard which makes him look French.

The large map of Wilmslow we'd used earlier was turned to the wall, which was just as well, and Courteney had pinned several sheets of paper on to the reverse side. There was also a flip chart on a stand. He'd spread his drawing kit, sticks of charcoal, pencils, crayons and watercolours all over the top of my desk.

I introduced him and he started chatting easily with Anna.

Wilmslow? . . . He knew Wilmslow.

School? . . . He'd worked in them for years before getting his break on TV.

PE? . . . He enjoyed exercise.

The man was a polished chat-up merchant. In no time at all Anna Pietrangeli was leaning back in the armchair he'd positioned for her and her face had lost its wary expression.

This charming interlude was punctuated by the loud rumbling of Clint Lane's stomach.

'Ouch! Someone sounds hungry,' Granville Courteney joked.

Clint looked at me, his expression anguished.

'If you're all right, is it OK if I leave you now and come back later?' I asked the teacher.

'She'll be fine with me,' Granville assured us.

Anna nodded and I led Clint out without another word.

Celeste was still at her desk.

'Put three hundred notes in a plain envelope,' I said, 'leave them in your desk drawer and then you can go.'

'File Red money?' she asked, jotting the figure down in a notebook. 'Michael went to London, Boss. He was all fired up to go clubbing.'

I waited until Celeste had gone before shutting up the office and then Clint and I made our way to the car.

There was something faintly ridiculous about my progress through the late evening streets with Clint at my heels. He cast pathetic glances at each of the myriad of food outlets we passed. I coaxed him along with promises of a swift journey to our own kitchen. When we joined the dense traffic heading along Deansgate I knew that I had lied.

At least the slow progress gave me time to think about how the search for the kidnappers was going. Peter's comments about the implications of the ambulance siren were particularly acute. The kidnappers were clever but they'd made a bad mistake by parking outside Mrs Latham's flat. Their error gave me the chance to identify the spiky-haired Afro-Caribbean. With another Granville sketch in production my chances of identifying the third member also were good. The whole case was going well. Ernie Cunliffe's computers might throw out a lead and a close search of Wilmslow might be productive.

So why did I feel uneasy?

Lee Parkes was one reason. He was so unwilling to give information. Usually someone in his position would be falling over himself to help. The gang had known his movements and his business. The informant had to be some-one close. Perhaps Lee's tight-lipped attitude was associated with his East End origins but it was also curious. I could only hope Michael Coe would find some pointer in Lee's background but my suspicion was that the match-fixing scandal ran much deeper than either of the brothers had cared to admit.

Were they trying to walk a tightrope? Feeding me enough information to lead them to the abusers of poor little Cheyenne, while holding back on anything that might implicate themselves in the gambling scandal? Jamie was a professional footballer. He must know that the penalty for his offence was more than a rap across the knuckles. Might his ever-so-shy manner be hiding a much deeper involvement than he was prepared to admit?

Then there was role of Clyde Harrow, the man with more ham in him than a Spam factory. Clyde had more than an inkling of what Jamie had been up to. He'd hinted that the player was involved in something that could wreck the whole game and then muscled his way into my office to collect footage of the investigation.

It was a mistake to ignore Clyde's newshound instincts. He gleaned information from many obscure fields and had built his career on swift responses to trivial clues. If there was blood in the water, then Clyde was already gliding towards the potential victim, jaws agape. His protestations of affection for Jamie Piercy and concern for the future

135

of the English game were typical hyperbole. Heaven help Jamie and his career if they stood between Clyde Harrow and a major story.

Back in Chorlton I led Clint into my kitchen and got busy. I had a packet of fresh pasta in the fridge and some tomatoes and cheese. It didn't take long to put a heaped plateful in front of the hungry Clint. He began shovelling it into his mouth. There was nothing savage about it, no unseemly slurpings and sloppings. Just the rapid ingestion of a very large quantity of food.

He was methodically polishing off a bowl of fruit and I was calculating when I could fit in my second grocery shopping expedition of the week when Naomi came into the flat.

She stood hesitantly at the kitchen door for a minute.

'I was going to listen to some music in my room,' she said. 'Is that all right, Mr Cunane?'

'Great, make yourself at home,' I offered. There was no hint of sarcasm in my voice, nor was any intended. Naomi turned with a grateful smile, ready to take me at my word. I followed her out into the hallway while she fished out her room key.

'Naomi, I've been meaning to ask you,' I said.

She looked at me expectantly. 'Yes, Mr Cunane?'

'When you were in that ambulance . . . stop me if this is too painful.'

'No, it's better out than in,' she said, biting her lip.

'When you were there, were you conscious at all?'

'Sort of,' she said hesitantly. 'That big ape sprayed some stuff in my mouth. I don't think it was anything poisonous. I think it was hair spray.'

'Hair spray?' I repeated incredulously.

'Yes, I know because kids used to do it at school and when I got time to think I recognised the taste. Anyway, I must have fainted when they sprayed me and grabbed me.'

She seemed reluctant to go on.

'Yes,' I prompted.

'It wasn't my fault,' she said guiltily. 'You've been so kind and Janine's so understanding . . .'

'Come on,' I coaxed.

'I fainted but it wasn't for long. Only a few seconds. I know I should have fought and kicked and screamed but I didn't. Maybe it would have turned out differently if I had, but I kept my eyes tight shut and lay on the floor of the ambulance hardly daring to breathe. My dad once told me that if you see kidnappers' faces they kill you.'

Tears were starting in her eyes.

'Anyone might have done that. It was very sensible of you,' I said, trying to reassure her. 'But you did see one of them, the driver?' I asked. I felt a twinge of doubt. Had she just imagined her description of the driver?

'Yes, I saw him but only for a moment. It was the other man who scared me, the big man in that stupid mask. He was so strong. I thought he might break my neck with a twist of his wrist.'

The tears were running down her plump cheeks now but I'd no option but to go on.

'So you were on the floor, pretending to be out of it. Was the journey very long?'

'No, it was only a couple of minutes, I think, or maybe longer. It was hard to tell. It felt like a long journey but it can't have been because the ride to where they left me in Cheadle Hulme was much longer. I was terrified.'

'Good,' I said, patting her arm. 'I mean, it's not good that you were terrified, but that you can remember what happened. Every detail helps.'

It sounded as if Peter Snyder's theory was correct.

'The ambulance stopped and I thought . . . Oh! I don't like to say.'

'Go on, nobody's blaming you.'

'I thought I was going to wet myself because that's when

137

they'd kill me. When they stopped, I mean. Kill me and throw me out into the street.'

'But they didn't.'

'No. They stuck a bag over my head and dragged me into a car and after a short drive I was in the Baptist Church car park at Cheadle Hulme.'

'Do you think they knew you were conscious? Did they carry you to the car?'

'The big man was so strong. I wasn't resisting but I think they must have guessed. I wasn't like a dead weight.'

'When you say "they", were there two men at the church car park?'

'I only felt there was one, but there must have been two, mustn't there?'

I shrugged. It sounded likely. I tried another tack.

'When they were driving you to the place where they put you in the car, did you feel anything?'

'Like what, Mr Cunane?'

'Were you on smooth roads, or were there traffic-calming bumps? You know, sleeping policemen? Were there any sudden stops, or pelican crossings with beepers?'

She smiled.

'I think there were a couple of bumps towards the end of the journey because they went slow and I felt the ambulance go up and down and then they turned and I felt that we were going over cobblestones, all bumpy again like. I don't think there were any traffic lights because they didn't stop at all.'

'That's really good,' I said. She looked pleased.

'Can you think of anything about the car?'

'It was big and the upholstery was leather. It felt cold to my hands. You know, one of those really big cars with a wide, deep seat in the back. They threw me on that and covered me with a blanket and then I heard all the doors shut at once.'

'Central locking,' I said. She looked at me blankly.

'Oh, and it was very comfortable,' she added, 'very

smooth.' She was speaking eagerly now, memory in full flood. 'I think we went over the same cobbles and bumps as before but I hardly felt them.'

'Was there anything else about the car? Was it an automatic?'

'What's that?'

'A car where you don't have to change gears. Did you feel the gears being changed?'

'I don't know,' she said wearily.

'You're doing very well, Naomi. There are just one or two more little things I need to get clear in my mind. When they changed vehicles, were you inside somewhere? You know, like a big garage or a covered space.'

She was silent for a moment, concentrating.

'I think so. It was dark, but then it was a dark morning to be sent out walking the streets. I did notice that the wind had stopped.'

'So you were under cover?'

'I think so.'

'During the whole journey, transferring you and everything, did either of them speak at all?'

She put a hand to her mouth. Then she said, 'No, not a word, that was what was so scary.'

The girl looked white and drained. I'd about done with her but I could tell there was something else.

'What else happened?' I demanded bluntly.

For the first time she looked away from me. She didn't want to meet my eyes.

'The baby,' she gasped. 'I didn't tell Mr Parkes this.'

'What?'

'When they put her in that ambulance she woke up. Cheyenne's always been a light sleeper and I think she's cutting a tooth. She started crying. She didn't stop the whole time. She was really loud. It went on and on.'

Sobbing now, Naomi put her head in her hands. Her whole body was wracked by sobs.

139

'Go on,' I said sternly.

'When they got us to that place, that garage like you said . . .'

I nodded and smiled to encourage her.

'They didn't touch me again at all. They took Cheyenne out of the ambulance. I could hear her little cries going further and further away. Then I heard something slam shut and I couldn't hear it, the noise of her crying.'

'Was it a door slamming?' I suggested.

'I think it was. A room door, not a car door. It was after that they came back and moved me.'

I said nothing. I patted her shoulder again and gradually the sobbing subsided. She took out her handkerchief and dried her eyes. Then she gave me a brave smile and turned her key in the lock. Before she went in she fired a parting shot. 'What I've told you is true. I hope you catch them. I'd like to watch them being castrated.'

'Castrated?' I repeated. 'Did you feel there was anything sexual going on?'

'I don't want to say,' she said like a frightened little girl again, biting her lip.

'You must,' I said firmly. 'Look, come in the lounge for a minute. I'll tell Clint to go to bed. I have to know exactly what went on.'

'No,' she said quietly.

Then she closed her door.

I stood where I was and a few minutes later the mechanical harmonies of Boyzone came throbbing out into the hallway at max volume.

I couldn't leave things like this. If we'd been the police they'd have had her in a special suite of rooms with sympathetic female officers close to her in age trying to draw her out. But this was Pimpernel Investigations, proprietor D. Cunane, and I was all we had. I scratched my head and wondered what to try next.

I tapped on the door very gently.

140

'Naomi, would you like a drink?' I asked.

Nothing happened, the music throbbed out. Then there was a slight diminution in volume. I tried again.

'I wouldn't mind a cup of drinking chocolate,' she said timidly through the closed door. I could hardly make out the words.

'Why don't you come in the kitchen while I make it?' I coaxed.

She opened the door. I had to go to the White residence to get the drinking chocolate from Janine and when I came back Naomi was in the kitchen.

It was some time since I'd made drinking chocolate. I read the instructions on the tin. Naomi took it out of my hand.

'I'll do it,' she said. 'I know just how I like it.'

She went to the fridge, took out the milk and poured some into a saucepan. Then she measured out three heaped tablespoons of the chocolate and whisked it into the milk, while warming it slowly. Naomi seemed to draw confidence from the familiar actions.

I watched the process without speaking. Eventually the pan came to the boil and she poured it out into a cup. Smiling to herself, she reached for the sugar, put three heaped teaspoonfuls of that into the drink and stirred.

'You like it sweet?' I asked.

'Sweeter the better.'

She sat on one of the kitchen chairs.

'When I was in that ambulance the first thing that went through my mind wasn't that they were kidnapping Cheyenne – I thought they were after me.'

'That's only natural,' I said.

'I know I'm stupid, thick as the Great Wall of China – my mum used to tell me that twenty times a day – but I thought they wanted to rape me. One of them, I don't know which, felt me up. You know, put his hand up my knickers. I kept my mouth shut and my eyes closed. I

141

was lying face down and I was too terrified to turn and look at him.'

Naomi said all this in the most straightforward way possible and I suddenly discovered why the modern police employ women to do this kind of interview. I wanted to be ten miles away. My face felt as if it was on fire. I turned away from her for a moment.

'It's all right, I'm not embarrassed,' she said.

'What happened?'

'He might have done something but the ambulance stopped. It was only a short journey. That's when I thought they were going to rape me and kill me. I wasn't thinking about Cheyenne at all.'

'It must have been an ordeal.'

She took a swig of the drinking chocolate. A brown moustache appeared on her lip.

'When the man was bent over me, to touch me like, something slipped out of his pocket. I could see it out of the corner of my eye. It was like a big calculator or a mobile phone only it was different. It had two spikes coming out of the end. One man said, "Shall I give her a shot?" but the other said, "No, Naomi's being a good girl," and that's when they put the bag over my head.'

'I think I almost fainted then because they knew who I was. They had my name. Do you think they were going to shoot me or inject me with something?'

'No,' I said quickly. 'You may have misheard. Perhaps he said, "Shall I give her a shove?"'

She nodded and seemed willing to accept this interpretation, but it sounded to me as if the big man had had an electronic stunner. I didn't like to tell her that if she hadn't been cooperative they'd have given her a ten-thousand-volt shock.

'I could hear Cheyenne wailing and that's when the penny dropped that it wasn't me they were after but her. I could hear it like I told you before.'

'Can you remember anything about the voices?' I asked eagerly. She didn't seem too upset now.

'The one who wanted to give me a shove, the man that touched me, he sounded Australian or Cockney – it was hard to say. Not from round here anyway. He only said a few words. The other one was definitely English. His voice was quite educated, posh, you know, like a doctor.'

'Have you remembered anything else about their descriptions?'

Witnesses can often add an extra detail or two after a session with the artist.

'The one I thought was the driver? He must have been quite tall but didn't seem so because the other was so big. He was huge.'

'The driver was tall?'

'And thin as well.'

I paused to think of something else to ask but she forestalled me: 'Can I go to bed now?' she asked. 'I'm exhausted.' I stood aside to let her out of the kitchen. In a moment the music started up again.

Whatever Naomi felt, and I didn't underestimate the buoyancy of youth, I felt rotten.

I checked that Clint was all right. He was stretched out on the sofa snoring loudly. Then I went next door to see Janine.

The scene that met me there brought a lump to my throat. Janine, Jenny and Lloyd were seated round the table playing Junior Scrabble. Seeing them like that after hearing what had happened to Naomi and Cheyenne just affected me for a moment. I felt as if someone had walked over my grave. I've come across more than my fair share of the world's horrors but cases involving children and animals are the worst.

'Dave, whatever's the matter?' Janine asked. 'Is it Clint? Is he all right?'

'No, Clint's fine. I can't tell you now, I'll speak to you

143

later. I just called in to say that I'm going out again. Naomi's in her room and Clint's passed out on the sofa. I think I've worn him out.'

'Are you worried about him being alone with Naomi?'

I shook my head but Janine chose not to believe me.

'Honestly, Dave, you're like a mother hen clucking over Clint. Naomi will be fine. She's very level-headed.'

'I'm going out again. I need to pay Courteney and take this schoolteacher home.'

'I'll pop in and see that Clint and Naomi are behaving themselves after I put these two to bed.'

'Mum!' growled Lloyd.

On my way back into the city centre I reflected on how clever Janine was at transference. She was the one who'd put the big brass lock on Naomi's door but according to her I was the one who was worried about what Clint might get up to. Surely she hadn't insisted on the lock to keep *me* out of Naomi's room?

Go figure, as our Yankee cousins say.

12

Granville Courteney hadn't finished with Anna Pietrangeli when I arrived. My office was in semi-darkness with just a desk light shining on the picture Granville was drawing. The floor was littered with charcoal sketches he'd scribbled on to the flip chart and then discarded.

'We're just getting the eyes right,' he said. 'Miss Pietrangeli's being very cooperative, but the eyes are so important. I think that's where the police slip up with their computers. "The eyes are the windows of the soul", eh?'

I nodded to Anna and went and sat in a darkened corner. I needed to get my nerve back. A lot of my work has involved rough men knocking nine bells out of each other and occasionally out of me. I haven't had many dealings with child abductors. I produced Clyde Harrow's sixteen-year-old Lagavulin. Granville looked up when he heard the sound of the cap being unscrewed.

'I wouldn't say no to a taste of that,' he commented, peering at me through the semi-darkness. I poured each of them a glass.

'You don't stint yourself, Mr Cunane,' Anna observed.

'It's Dave, please,' I muttered before lapsing back into silence.

Watching Granville at work was intensely reassuring. He would quickly sketch out a feature and place it against the background of the whole face then ask Anna to compare it with her memory. Slight alterations would be made with remarkable speed.

'I think that's enough of pinning the tail on the donkey for tonight,' he said eventually. 'Consider your memory well dredged, miss. I've got enough here to complete a reasonable picture for tomorrow.' He started gathering his fair copies into a folder and dumping the rest in my waste bin.

As he worked I knew I'd have to dump something else in the bin – my theory that there were three men involved. I'd only viewed his partial reconstruction of the man Anna Pietrangeli had seen but unless he was a twin, it was obvious that he was the same man who'd stopped Naomi. He had the same curly black hair and glasses, the same moustache. Anna's man looked younger than Naomi's but that could be explained because she'd seen him under bright daylight rather than on an overcast morning. The likeness testified to the accuracy of Granville's drawing.

I went to let him out and gave him half the money out of the envelope that Celeste had left in her drawer.

'The rest on completion,' I said.

'Businesslike as ever, Mr Cunane,' he said with a smile. We both knew that Granville had a well-deserved reputation for pissing away all his money against the wall of the nearest pub when the mood was on him.

'Janine will give you the rest tomorrow.'

I turned and almost tripped over Anna. I noticed that she'd taken her tracksuit top off and that she was wearing a T-shirt with an unusual logo. It showed the head of a Greek god inside a golden solar disc. The words 'Phoebus Club' were written underneath.

'I thought you weren't just admiring the view the other day,' she said and slipped her hand in mine.

It was like an electric shock went up my arm. I didn't wrench my hand away and say, 'Unhand me, Madam!' but it was a surprise because for once sex was the very last thing on my mind.

I started to say that I'd only been looking at the logo but

146

realised that might sound rather discourteous after she'd spent most of the evening doing me a favour. She had a very neat figure.

She took her hand away.

'You're a married man, aren't you?' she asked. 'I can always tell. I wish someone would tell me why all the decent blokes have to be married. You should wear a ring.'

'I'm not married.'

'You're not gay, are you?'

'No, I have a partner, a girlfriend.'

'I don't suppose you'd consider giving someone else an audition for that part?'

I shook my head.

'Oh, well, back to good old Geoff and his oily rags,' she said cheerfully. 'You can't blame a girl for trying.'

She started to leave.

'Wait a minute. Don't be in such a hurry. At least let me buy you a meal and give you a lift back to Wilmslow.'

'And that's all that's on offer?'

'I'm afraid so.'

'All right, you can come to my club and buy me a meal.'

'And where's that?' I asked.

'Right here in the centre of Manchester, the Phoebus Club. The one you seemed so interested in a few minutes ago.'

'Not one I've heard of,' I said.

'It's fairly new. It's a fitness club. There's a pool in the basement, gyms on three different floors and a restaurant on the top floor. I go there a lot.'

It turned out that the Phoebus was only a short walk from my office. It was in a converted insurance company building near the law courts. The club turned out to be far ritzier and glitzier than I'd imagined. Anna signed me in and showed me through the building. The pool alone must have cost a fortune. The entire basement area had been remodelled and the pillars which supported the building now rose from the waters of the pool. If there was any kind of fitness or health equipment that had been left out I couldn't see it.

The restaurant was equally plush and all non-smoking waiter service, not a utilitarian cafeteria, the menu expensive to match. There were health foods and an extensive vegetarian menu but also Aberdeen Angus steak. I had a steak while Anna stuck to the nut cutlets.

We talked about Geoff. He was divorced with two sons and would like Anna to move in with him.

'It's so unfair,' she said. 'Geoff would like me to help support him while he pays maintenance to his wife and child support for his kids. I ask you, is that right?'

'No,' I murmured soothingly.

'I'm only thirty. I'd like the chance to have a life of my own before it's too late.'

'Why don't you give old Geoff the elbow?'

'I've tried to but he's so clingy. You saw what he was like this afternoon.'

'Still . . .'

'I'd have to get a new job and they're not so easy to find in nice schools. In the first place I taught in you practically needed to carry firearms before the kids would let you teach them. I've never met such hatred.'

I was anxious to change the subject from her single status but before I could a genial red-faced man attired in matching Phoebus top and bottoms arrived at our table.

'Anna, my love!' he shouted. It was definitely a shout. It rang round the dining room. Other diners looked up but then went on with their meals. I decided that he was some sort of licensed jester. He was in his mid-fifties, a fit-looking geezer as Michael Coe would say, definitely 'larger than life', and his hair would have produced a flush of envy in Ernie Cunliffe. The brown hair wasn't just thick, it was denser than that of many a teenage lad, and it was all his own, you could see that. He had a clownish face, with a large, slightly curved nose and matching chin which gave him a passing resemblance to Mr Punch. I learned later that the red face came from laughing at his own jokes.

'Ah, the beautiful Italian,' he said. '*Bella figura*, eh? What a looker! If I was twenty years younger I'd sweep you off the shelf, you lovely creature. What are you eating, olive oil and Mediterranean veg? Live to be a hundred, won't you?'

'Dave, this is Judder Crockett. He owns the club,' Anna said when the torrent of words slackened. 'Dave has his own business too. He runs a detective agency.'

I was shrewdly scanned by a pair of grey-green eyes.

The word 'detective' seemed to spark Crockett off. Perhaps it didn't need much. He started on the police.

'But they *know* who the criminals are,' he said, addressing the whole restaurant like an audience. 'If there's a crime tonight, a robbery, the police will *know* it can only be one or two individuals. They have the names of all the criminals written down in a great big book. No, I tell a lie, it's one of those electric typewriter things. What are they called?'

He scratched his head comically.

'Computers,' someone supplied.

'That's it. They press a button and out comes the answer. Who does burglaries in these streets? Who does them in those? Who likes hitting old ladies and grabbing their pension books? They *know* who all these people are. Most of them have been at it since they were tiny tots. We watch these television *detectives*, Frost and Taggart and that gallery, spending weeks finding a killer. It's all crap! The police pay people to tell them whodunit and then they have to go through a pantomime of finding the evidence or manufacturing it to bang the villains up. Of course, they rarely succeed, the lawyers see to that. It isn't a system, it's a joke.'

I thought he was getting hysterical but Anna put her hand on mine to restrain me when I thought I might intervene.

149

'He's always like this,' she whispered. 'The customers love it.'

'I know there are lawyers here,' Crockett said with another dramatic flourish. There were titters in various corners. He heard Anna whispering. 'You aren't all raggedy-arsed schoolteachers . . .'

'Watch it, Judder!' she shouted.

'Your lovely arse could never be described as raggedy, my love,' he said. 'I'm sure those delicious cheeks are clad in the finest silken underwear.'

This produced a round of clapping from the far side of the room and a blush from Anna. Encouraged, he carried on. 'But there's another example of the same thing: education. Millions on millions spent pretending to educate kids who don't give a damn. What was the finest and most effective education that was ever given in this country?'

He was holding the floor now.

'You tell us, Judder,' a man bawled from the back.

'He's going to, don't worry,' someone else yelled.

'I'll tell you. It was the Army when I did my National Service.'

This produced angry groans.

'No, listen,' he said in a softer tone. 'I'll tell you what they did. They needed people to learn Russian. We were supposed to be getting ready to fight the Russkies then. You young folks won't remember that. So you take the men who are learning Russian out of their nasty cold barracks where there are sergeant majors to wake them up in the morning with two hours square-bashing . . . *left, right, left, right, get that hair cut, you 'orrible little man!* . . . and you put them in a nice clean classroom and give them a nice bedroom with sheets on the bed instead of bare blankets, and every Friday you test them. If they fail, they're RTU'd the next day, returned to unit. My God, there weren't many of us who didn't learn our irregular Russian verbs! Fourteen hours a day in the classroom with perfect discipline. Result? Hundreds of skilful linguists.

'What do we get today? The kids are taking over and they've made the exams so easy that a low-grade moron could sail through with half an hour's honest revision. And what happens? Chaos, that's what.'

He was still hovering near our table when this monologue came to its conclusion and I signalled to him. He turned a chair round and sat with us, picking a chip off my plate as he did so.

'Good chips, these, if I say so as shouldn't,' he commented, helping himself to another.

I smiled at him.

'Mr Crockett, are you sure you're old enough to have done National Service? You look too young.'

'Judder, dear boy, rhymes with rudder, or George if you want to be formal.'

'Judder, you must be too young.'

'Well, I can accept a compliment as well as the next man. Good diet and fitness training, that's what keeps me young and healthy-looking.'

'But what age are you?' I persisted. There was something about the man's playing to the gallery that niggled. It was all too pat. I remembered being told about barracks life by a cousin who'd done National Service. He was well over sixty now and had been unlucky enough to be among the last men called up. He'd hated it. Two years painting kerb stones white, was how he described it.

Crockett frowned. 'I can see that you're a persistent sleuth, Mr Cunane. Take my word for it, that's how it was.'

I nodded and took another bite of my steak. My father says it takes a chancer to know a chancer.

'Now, Anna,' said Crockett, changing the subject, 'how have you come by this hunk of male pulchritude?'

'He's not mine. I'm afraid he's spoken for, Judder.'

'Nonsense! Never say die. Wiggle those pretty buns of yours at him. Pry him loose from his attachments.'

'Judder, stop! I'll choke on my food,' Anna said, coughing. Crockett leaped from his seat and performed an elaborate mime of patting her on the back. Then he walked over to the serving area and quickly came back with a bottle of wine and one of his Phoebus Club T-shirts in his hand.

'Accept the T-shirt as a token of my respect for all those who detect,' he said, offering it to me. 'The wine's to make up for upsetting the beautiful Italian. You could go further and fare worse than with her, my lad. Put the girl out of her misery. Eat, drink and fornicate, for tomorrow – the knacker's yard for all of us.'

With that and the swirl of an imaginary cape he departed and swiftly disappeared behind the scenes.

'A bit OTT, isn't he?' I commented mildly. A waiter hurried over to uncork the wine. It was an expensive red.

'Judder's always OTT. He was quite restrained tonight actually but I'm so embarrassed I don't know where to put myself.'

'Don't worry. We can eat and drink but forget about the rest of his advice. I'm afraid it's as phoney as he is.'

'Phoney? What do you mean? Judder's parties are legendary. He has some of the best connected people in Manchester here. TV people, soap opera stars, footballers, club owners, top lawyers, you name it. They all come running when Judder Crockett throws a party.'

'He's never invited me.'

'He has invited me and perhaps he'll invite you now he knows you. You could come with me,' she added coyly.

'A bit political, isn't he?' I said. My turn now to change the subject.

Anna smiled winsomely.

'Oh, nobody minds about that. His heart's in the right place. A lot of his parties are for charity.'

I finished my meal. I've eaten better steak but at least the floor show was lively. Afterwards we walked back towards Deansgate and the multi-storey car park behind Kendal's. I was feeling quite mellow but told myself that my life was complicated enough without feeling sorry for Miss Lonely Heart.

It turned out that she lived in a flat over a Spar grocer's in Heald Green. I drove her there and walked her to the doorway.

'Come in?' she suggested with the hint of a smile.

'Sorry, there are things I must do in Manchester. I have to get back.'

'Let me know how you get on with the Asian girl.'

I looked at her with a bemused expression, struggling to work out what she was talking about.

'Give me your phone number then, and I'll call you.'

My hand moved slowly to my wallet and I extracted a business card. My fingers seemed to be paralysed.

'You never know, I might remember something else about that man in the Rascal van. I've got a feeling I've seen him somewhere before. Here's my number in case you change your mind.'

She snatched the card from my reluctant fingers, gave me her number written on a scrap of exercise paper, and then bent forward. I gave her a very fleeting peck and she was gone. I stood for a moment and watched the lights come on upstairs. Should I rush up and prove my virility?

No, I decided. I tucked her number into a flap of my wallet.

Driving back to town I suddenly remembered that I hadn't been in touch with Lee Parkes. I looked at my watch. Was it too late? Half-ten. I decided that a sporting man like him would still be up to receiving visitors.

I turned the car round and headed out to Wilmslow. He was paying me enough to learn what I'd found out directly.

The Maranello was parked outside his house when I arrived.

'Oh, it's you,' Lee said unwelcomingly when he opened the door. 'You've not brought your gorilla with you, have you?'

I shook my head, though I was annoyed by his description of Clint.

'I suppose you'd better come in.'

Lee led me into the lounge. Jamie was sprawled on one of the low-slung sofas. He lifted his head and waved three fingers when he saw me.

'It's been a hell of a day, so you'd better make this quick, Cunane.'

'Lay off him, Lee,' Jamie chided. 'You've been grumbling all day that he wasn't here. Listen to what he has to say now.'

'Shut up!' Lee said coldly. 'I've heard just about enough of the wit and wisdom of the great Jamie Piercy to last me a lifetime. Not that that's likely to be long, the way I feel.'

'I'm sorry, Mr Cunane,' Jamie said in his peculiar accent. 'We've been to see Cheyenne. She's really poorly. I can't stop him saying that it's all his fault.' He propped himself up on one arm.

'Lee reckons that Cheyenne would have been delivered back safe and well if he'd given them the five hundred K. I keep telling him it's nonsense.'

He lapsed into silence for a moment. Lee cradled his head in his arms. He really did look like a man at the end of his tether. He was clearly past the stage where he thought drinking would bring oblivion.

'I heard her crying over the phone,' he told us, his face still covered.

'I'm sending people out tomorrow to search for the place where they took her in the ambulance,' I told him.

'You've not let his name slip into this, have you?' Lee looked up and jerked his thumb in the direction of Jamie.

'Absolutely not!'

The brothers exchanged a glance of relief.

'Maybe you're not as big a prat as I thought,' Lee said graciously.

'Maybe not,' I agreed. I took out a photocopy of Naomi's picture.

'Have you seen this face? It's the ambulance driver.'

Lee turned all the lights on and Jamie got up. They spent several minutes scrutinising the picture intently.

'The same man may have had this house under observation last week. He was in a white Rascal van.'

'I've never seen him,' Lee said at last. I searched his face for any sign of deception. It was impossible to be sure with such an inward man but I was fairly certain that was the truth. 'I may have seen that van, though. I've a vague memory of a little white van. I thought it was something to do with the milk delivery.'

'Can I keep this picture?' Jamie asked. 'I can show it to club security and say it's someone who threatened me. They check for known troublemakers on the security cameras at every match. You never know.'

'Hold it, bro,' Lee cautioned. 'What are you going to do if they spot him? You can't say what you really want him for.'

'We don't want him tipped off before we're ready to make a move,' I warned.

'Yeah, I hadn't thought of that,' the footballer said, flapping his hands in that irritating helpless gesture of his. I felt like telling him to put them in his pockets.

'Keep the picture anyway,' I said. 'Say he's someone you owe money to. You know, you scratched his car or something. That way, on the off chance that they spot him, they'll tell you before they tackle him. We might be able to trace him if he's a season ticket holder or a known hooligan or something.'

'Yeah,' Jamie said in relief.

155

'The picture's going to be circulated in the right places and we'll get a name. Believe me, some of these people will shop their own relations for a reward.'

Lee smiled thinly at that. 'That's right,' he said bitterly, 'some of these people will.'

I took that to refer to his match-fixing activities and so did Jamie. He came over and gave Lee a footballer's hug, so that was all right. I decided there and then that Jamie must tell me all the details of the scam. The extortion had to be linked to it in some way. They say a clever criminal is only caught when he gets too confident. The 'smooth' extortionist had been overconfident twice. The first time was when he parked below Mrs Latham's window and the second when he let on to Lee that he knew who his brother was. He hadn't been able to resist putting Lee in his place.

'It may not be my fault that Cheyenne's so ill,' Lee muttered, 'but it is my fault that they knew I daren't go to the police. She'd have had a chance if I'd got the police after them right away.'

'It's chicken and egg, Lee. They wouldn't have targeted you if they hadn't known you couldn't go to the police. There's no point in dwelling on it,' I said sharply. 'That's all water under the bridge now. We've got to concentrate on catching them and I need to get back. I've got an early start tomorrow.'

'Right, sir!' he snapped, making a mock salute in my direction.

I left soon after that.

When I returned to the flat Clint was still snoring loudly but he was now stretched out over my bed. Janine must have chivvied him into his jim-jams. There was music coming out of Naomi's room. Robbie Williams. I was about to fling myself on the sofa when I noticed a note pinned to a cushion.

'Come and sleep next door, J,' it read.

13

Sleeping with Janine was something I could take up on a regular basis with very little effort. I say sleeping because that's exactly what happened, at least on her part. I slipped into her warm bed. She gave me a hug and then rolled over, back into a deep sleep. I lay there listening to the steady cadence of her breathing. A mental image of that baby being shut in a car boot stayed with me a long time.

Then my thoughts drifted to my other troubles. What was I going to do with Clint if Bob was arrested and locked up? It was one thing looking after him for a few days. He was biddable while everything was still new and fresh, but Clint has a will of his own. That's why Bob was happy when he settled down on the Dutch farm. What was I going to do if Clint threw a wobbler, perhaps even in Janine's home? I'd just have to keep him amused and distracted and hope for the best. Meanwhile, I was supposed to be catching skilful kidnappers and running a business. Child's play really.

I made a resolution to call Peter first thing in the morning and start my day out in Wilmslow with him. The longer I could keep Clint strolling round in the open air the better everything would be. Even driving him in the Mondeo wasn't too clever. Clint gets irritated and unpredictable after being cramped up for too long.

Should I get a bigger car? A four-wheel-drive big enough for him to stretch in?

Why, oh, why, Bob? I thought. Why had he gone into the wholesale cannabis business? He isn't a particularly

greedy man. Before sleep claimed me I guessed that it
was because the illegal trade was so pervasive. With Bob's
contacts it must have been hard to avoid being drawn in.
Well, he hadn't avoided it and now I was stuck with the
consequences.

I woke up suddenly. Janine was shaking me by the
shoulders.

'Wake up, Dave,' she shouted. 'Wake up!'

I was groggy. What finally restored me to full consciousness was the sight of Clint looming over her shoulder. He
was in his pyjamas. I sat up suddenly with my fists clenched.
I don't know why that happened but it did.

'Is everything all right?' I croaked.

'Calm down,' Janine said reassuringly. 'The flat isn't
on fire.'

'Clint?' I said anxiously.

'Clint's being lovely and helpful.' She turned to the giant.
He seemed to fill half the space in that small bedroom. It
was as if the ceiling rested on his shoulders — Atlas Lane.
She stroked his arm.

'I'm being good, Dave. It's Naomi,' he said.

His words didn't reassure me.

My eyes must have been wild because Janine leaned
over and kissed me. 'Calm down, Dave. You're so tense.
You've been tossing and turning all night. Maybe you should
think of looking for a less demanding job — school crossing
warden or something.'

'Maybe I should, but what's happened to Naomi?'

My eyes remained focused on Clint's moonlike face. He
gave me a friendly wink.

'Nothing's happened to her. She's just run off, that's
all. She woke Clint at six this morning, didn't she?'

'She did,' he said, his tone quite indignant.

'It seems she knows how to work an alarm clock
after all.'

'I heard it ring,' Clint confirmed proudly.

'Then she came looking for you and only found Clint and told him she was off to Scunthorpe. Clint didn't know what to do for a while but after he'd had a think he came and woke me up. Isn't that clever of him?'

Clint looked as if he'd just won first prize in a raffle. The expression on his face made me feel even more cantankerous. Janine seemed to have the trick of soothing him. Why didn't I? No good at handing out praise, that's the reason.

'Yes, Clint's very clever,' I echoed woodenly.

His smile broadened.

'How long ago was this?' I asked.

'About half an hour,' Janine said. 'Get up and get after her.'

'Good,' Clint said enthusiastically. 'I like Naomi.'

'Why bother?' I asked.

'Don't be stupid, Dave. The girl's distressed. We don't want her doing anything silly.'

I hopped out of bed and started jamming on the clothes I'd worn last night. They felt clammy and rancid. Janine left but Clint remained in the room watching my performance with delight. I raced out of the flat with him padding along behind me like a shadow. I wasn't sure that bringing him along was a good idea but it didn't seem that I had any other option. He put his overcoat on over his pyjamas.

I started the car and tried to think where Naomi would be. She had money. She could hire a taxi to take her all the way to Scunthorpe if necessary but I guessed that wouldn't occur to her. The roads were empty as I headed towards Chorlton Street bus station in the centre of town.

We arrived at the corner of Portland Street just as a service bus decanted Naomi on to the pavement. I felt a surge of relief. The girl was looking for a bus to Scunthorpe, not for some secret confederate. She spotted me right away. She was red-eyed and worn-out-looking, as if she'd been

159

crying all night, and was carrying a small rucksack on her back. I gave a toot on the horn. I don't know what I'd have done if she'd legged it but fortunately she came over.

'I'm just a nuisance to everyone,' were her first words as she poked her head into the car window. 'I've let Cheyenne down.' With that she started wailing, a deep, full-throated cry. There weren't many people about to observe but there soon would be if this went on. I jumped out and opened the back of the car.

'Get in, love,' I said with as much sympathy as I could muster. It was a struggle. My sympathy glands were almost squeezed dry. 'We can talk better in the car.'

She nodded and did as she was told. I felt another big surge of relief. The kidnappers had employed a muscleman to get her into the back of that ambulance. At seven in the morning I didn't have the strength or inclination to force the matter. It took me five minutes of ladling out sympathy with a big spoon before she finally agreed to come back to the flat. I made it clear that she was free to go but understood that this drama was her way of seeking absolution for allowing the abduction. It didn't make sense to me but then I'm not a teenage girl reared on a diet of soap operas.

When we got back to Janine's flat I was able to relax for a few minutes while she took charge. The exhausted girl was calmed and sent back to bed with instructions not to emerge before one. I envied her that, at least. Janine had also thought about breakfast which was just as well because I hadn't made any preparations and Clint's stomach was rumbling all the way back from town like a small volcano about to become active.

He consumed six sausage sandwiches, each consisting of three sausages sliced in half lengthways and positioned between thick pieces of farmhouse loaf. There was something Homeric about the spectacle which was noticed by Lloyd and Jenny as well as by me. They were both too polite to comment as the big man chomped but their awed expressions spoke for them.

'Is Clint stronger than you, Dave?' Lloyd asked.

'He could be,' I said cautiously. Clint revelled in being the object of their attention.

'Would you try arm-wrestling with him?' Jenny demanded. Like mother like daughter, it was hard to fob her off with a diplomatic answer.

'I don't think so. I'm sure he'd win,' I whispered.

'The girl's fast asleep again, Dave,' Janine said when she came back in. I stepped out into the hallway to confer while the kids got on with breakfast. 'She's worn herself out with worrying.'

'Why, though?' I asked. 'Guilt?'

Janine looked shocked at this suggestion.

'Men!' she said. 'For that girl Cheyenne is like her own child. How can you be so hard-hearted?'

'Because if I get any more touchy-feely I'll start growing tentacles.'

'Macho posturing!'

'As far as I'm concerned Naomi's still in the frame, and as for being hard-hearted, I've been there and got the T-shirt. Some hard things have been happening, in case you haven't noticed.'

'What an ugly thing to say!'

'If you want ugly, try this: someone, who may or may not have been known to Naomi, slammed a sick baby into the boot of a car!' I bellowed. 'Take a good look at that girl before you start dishing out the sympathy. Do you think you could sling her in the back of an ambulance if she didn't want to go?'

She shook her head but didn't have anything more to say. I regretted blowing up, but Janine's sympathy for the girl was clouding her judgement.

'I'm going to make an early start in Wilmslow with Peter Snyder,' I announced. 'So get your clothes on, Clint.'

161

He looked bewildered but hastened to obey.

'No, stay where you are, Clint,' Janine said imperiously. 'I'm not going in to work today. I've got a day off in lieu of overtime. Clint can spend the day with me. He's obviously just another encumbrance as far you're concerned, Dave.'

I looked at my watch. I hadn't really time for argument. It was one of those days. If I carried on, we'd end up arguing about what colour socks I ought to be wearing.

'Will you be all right with Janine?' I asked Clint.

'Yes, Dave. I'd like that. Can we go to the shops?'

'And vice versa?' I asked my partner.

'What sort of sensitive plant do you take me for?' she exclaimed.

'A prolific weed you couldn't kill with pure Paraquat.'

'Hmmmh,' she snorted, a hint of a smile on her face.

'Here, plant,' I said, tossing her the roll of money I'd received from Bob's minion yesterday. 'Go on a spending spree. Get some more sausages, lots of them.'

Janine caught the money. She didn't say anything. The children looked from me to her. She didn't throw the money back.

I was on the A34 heading for Wilmslow with my mobile in my hand ten minutes later. Peter was in and he agreed to meet me at the leisure centre car park in Wilmslow.

Although he was nearer to Wilmslow than me, Peter was later arriving and the car park was already beginning to fill up with early shoppers and business people when he appeared.

'Sorry, Boss,' he said as he rushed over and got in my car. 'It took me a few minutes to gather up my stuff when you phoned.'

'Peter, what do I call you?'

'You call me slave or servant,' he said with a chuckle.

'Seriously.'

'Peter.'

'Well, will you stop calling me Boss? Celeste does it

and now everyone's started. I'm sick of being the boss. Call me, Dave, or "you stupid fool", or whatever you want, but not Boss.'

'Yes, Boss,' he said.

I punched his arm, hard.

'All right, Dave it is.'

A few minutes later we were at the corner of the Grove Street pedestrian precinct and Hawthorn Lane.

'I can't see it, you know, that kidnapping,' he said. 'There are so many things that could go wrong trying to pick someone up off the street. Look at it now.'

Hawthorn Lane was busy. There was a post office not far from where Naomi had been abducted. Bambino's was attracting customers. There were even people looking in at the furniture restorer's although there was a sign saying Closed Until Further Notice in the window.

'What if she'd put up a fight? A crowd might have gathered.'

'And then we might have had a dead nanny on our hands,' I said. 'I don't know, Janine thinks I'm being too hard on the girl. The hairspray down her throat must have been a heck of a shock and the guy with the spiky do was very strong.'

'Second thoughts, Dave?'

'It was all over in seconds.'

'It would be quick if she was helping them?'

'OK,' I conceded. 'When Michael gets back from London he can check out her background if we haven't got another lead by then. Meanwhile . . .'

'Meanwhile, we look for the transfer point and try to put the girl in the clear. Has it crossed your mind that we look like a pair of Jehovah's Witnesses going door-knocking? One black, one white?'

'Peter, if you're sensitive I can black my face up.'

'Just saying,' he snorted. 'Anyway, which way are we going? The ambulance wouldn't have turned right.

According to our unimpeachable witness there were no traffic lights or pelican crossings en route but if you go right there's at least three in each direction.'

We went left, past a by-way called Dungeon Walk. We walked for about ten minutes. There were no traffic-calming bumps and no large garages.

'I know this road, Boss. I mean, Dave. It goes past the women's prison at Styal. Kind of appropriate.'

'This was your idea, remember?' I intended to walk the streets until lunchtime if necessary.

We walked on. There were houses on either side with open land behind the ones on our left. When we were almost at the end of the houses we reached an overgrown garden. There was a brick wall surmounted by a wooden fence and behind that an immense overgrown privet hedge. The Evergreens, a peeling sign proclaimed. A Registered Nursing Home for the Elderly.

'Evergreens is the right name for this place,' Peter complained. He tried to scramble up on the wall and peep over the fence. Dense vegetation obscured the view. 'There's barbed wire behind the fence,' he said disgustedly. 'It's more like a prison than a rest home.'

'There is a gate,' I observed.

We walked a little further to a pair of massive wrought-iron gates. They were fastened together with a rusty chain.

'No one's been in here for some time,' Peter exclaimed.

'Look,' I said.

Beyond the gate there was a well-worn gravel path with tyre marks on it. From where we stood it was impossible to tell if they were fresh. Even more interesting, though, there were concrete speed bumps laid over the gravel, hefty ones painted yellow, obviously designed to protect the Evergreen residents. We couldn't see the house because the gravel path curved sharply to our left and there was a mass of holly bushes intervening.

164

Peter rattled the gates.

'Can't get in there, love,' a middle-aged lady said. She was pushing a pram along the narrow pavement. 'It's been shut for years, the Evergreens. A doctor and his wife had it. She was had up for being cruel to the old folk and they shut it down. A proper eyesore it is now.'

'Someone's been in,' Peter replied. He pointed to the padlock and chain. Though rusty they'd both recently been sprayed with WD40. His hands were stained with the rust liberated by the penetrating oil.

'Must be them,' the woman said. She pointed to a placard on a post just inside the gates. For Sale – Rush, Showers, & Co., Estate Agents, Alderley Road, Wilmslow, it read.

While we looked at each other, both surprised by our poor observational skills, the lady pressed on up the road without a backward glance.

'I bet she thinks we're Jehovah's,' Peter commented.

'To hell with that,' I grunted, 'give me a hand up here.' I struggled to get my foot into the first cross member of the gate. Peter put his shoulder behind me and with a heave I was up. Rusty paint came off in my hand. I swung myself up and over the top of the gate, ignoring the dangerous creaking sounds as my weight tested the strength of the hinges. In my eagerness I jumped from the top. There was a rending sound.

'That's torn it, Dave,' Peter commented cheerily.

My pants pocket had caught on a projecting knob on top of the gate and my trousers were ripped from the pocket down to the knee. All my change and keys spilled on to the path.

'Shit!' I muttered. Then I laughed. Peter looked at me as if I was mad.

'I reckon to lose at least one suit on every serious investigation,' I explained, 'and if this is it, it's fine by me. Usually they're ripped off my back by some tearaway or other.'

'What am I going to do?' he asked when I subsided. He was looking down at his own immaculate grey suit.

'Come on, improvise,' I said impatiently.

He looked at the gates again and shook his head.

'I'll do better than that,' he promised. 'I'll go to Rush & Showers and get the key. See you in half an hour.'

He set off back to Wilmslow. As I watched him go, it occurred to me that I'd always thought Denzel Washington was a fancy pants actor, not half as tough as Samuel L. Jackson. I turned back to the path though the overgrown bushes and walked forward.

A large, crumbling detached house was now visible. I'd have said it was Victorian. There were two Tudor-style wings framing a recessed and pillared entrance area in an H shape. Once grand, with three floors and servants' quarters on top, the place now teetered on the edge of ruin. Guttering hung loose here and there. Seedlings sprouted from the roofline. Half-timbered panels were sagging and the doors, ground-floor and first-floor windows had been boarded up. The whole building exuded a smell of mildew. There was a twisted garland of razor-wire running all the round the house like a tide mark and lots of big red notices saying, Security Alarms – No Unauthorised Access.

I looked up and noticed a movement sensor pointing directly at me. It was possible that an alarm bell was ringing in Wilmslow police station. Oh, well, I'd just have to take my chances. Trespass is a civil offence and an occupational hazard in my work.

More interesting to me than the house was the path. A gravelled carriage drive swung in front of the house in a great loop but to the far side there was a cobbled section leading round the back. Holding my trousers together with one hand, I followed it.

The cobbles widened into an open area surrounded by brick outbuildings, stables and storerooms. I went up to one of the windows and rubbed the glass clean. Inside,

I could make out a heap of rusting wheelchairs and Zimmer frames.

All of the outbuildings except one were the same age as the house. The exception was a large corrugated-iron structure standing on a concrete base. It was perhaps twenty years old and the iron was rusting. A strong wind had loosened a sheet off the side. If this had been a farm I'd have said it was a barn but its purpose here puzzled me until I saw the benches that had been piled up against the back. One side stood open, facing what had once been a lawn or a bowling green but was now a wilderness of tall meadow grass. I realised that it must have been an outdoor shelter for the oldies. Some of them could sit on the benches watching the others play bowls.

Whatever lingering doubts I'd had that this was the place now vanished.

There were no cars or vans here now, though.

I did a meticulous grid search of the concrete area. It was big. Too big for a summer house or pavilion. There was a connecting door to the house, now boarded up. Maybe the cruel doctor's wife used to feed the old folk out here, or have them stretched out on beds. It must have been chilly for about ten months of the year, but probably saved wear and tear on the carpets.

Whatever the ancient history was, I soon found recent oil stains. The Rascal van had been here, I guessed. Tracks suggested a narrow wheel base and tyres. There were tyre prints of at least four other vehicles also.

With a full forensics team I could probably have identified them all but I was working by guess and by God. My guess was Rascal, Skoda, Transit, one luxury wide-bodied saloon – Mercedes or that ilk – and one other smaller car.

Irritatingly, the whole area seemed to have been recently swept. There wasn't a single discarded cigarette end. Not even any of the wind-blown leaves which you might have expected. These people were too professional, too alert to the possibility of leaving a tiny shred of evidence. But they had to make a mistake sometime.

Eventually I found it.

In a corner against a wall where it had rolled when unknowingly kicked aside there was a baby's dummy or comforter. It was made of green transparent plastic and the teat bit was pink. I wrapped it in my handkerchief like a precious treasure.

I continued searching until my attention was distracted by the sound of a car horn. I ran round to the front. Peter was there in his Astra. He waved the key at me as he swung one of the wrought-iron gates shut. It moved easily on its recently greased hinges.

'How did you get on?' I asked eagerly.

'He thought I wanted the place for architectural salvage at first, so he was a bit awkward. Apparently it's a listed building and they've had trouble with travellers. But when I told him I was looking to develop it as retirement flats he nearly bit my arm off. He's let me have the key but said not to go near the house because it'll set the alarm off. I said I'd concentrate on the grounds first — two and a half acres apparently.'

'I've been near and nothing's happened so far.'

'That's what he told me. He's going to join me and turn the alarms off when he's free.'

'Did he say anything about someone else being interested?'

'A surveyor from Manchester checked the place out two weeks ago on behalf of a property developer who was interested in turning the place into a health and fitness complex.'

'Any names?'

'He wouldn't tell me but the file was open on his desk and I saw something about Phoebus Leisure Services.'

I felt my throat constrict. Like policeman and detectives

everywhere I don't believe in coincidences. They're the dogs that bark in the night. All sorts of suspicions about Anna Pietrangeli began churning through my mind.

'Phoebus?' I repeated.

'Are you all right, Boss? Er, Dave?'

'Yes, fine. You've done well,' I commented, trying to keep any excitement out of my voice. The Phoebus group had a perfectly legitimate interest in developing suburban health clubs and there was no reason to go jumping to conclusions. Picking locks isn't exactly unheard of either. There wasn't necessarily any connection between the Phoebus people and the group of kidnappers but the time frame was right.

'Dave, you look as if you've seen a ghost,' Peter said. 'Has something happened?'

I took my handkerchief out and showed him the dummy.

'She was here then?'

I nodded.

'Can you find out more about the Phoebus interest? I want to follow that up.'

'Do you think they're connected to the kidnapping?'

'Unlikely, but stranger things have happened and this is the first lead we've got which might give us a name. So we have to check it out.'

'The bloke from Rush & Showers is coming soon, remember. Or shall we skip it?'

'No. Run me back to my car now and then get yourself back here and pump him for every bit of information you can squeeze out of him.'

'Right, er . . . Dave. I don't know much about this property lark.'

'You don't have to. He's trying to sell the dump to you. Let him do the talking.'

Back at the car park I found an old hundred yard tape in a leather case in the boot of my car. I gave it to Peter.

'Make him help you check the measurements,' I said, 'but see if you can dig some names out of him.'

I headed back to my flat in Chorlton. The ripped trousers made it a necessity. Apart from that, the day was starting well. It didn't last. It had been a bright sunny morning when I'd arrived in Wilmslow. Now the sky had darkened to the extent that people were driving with sidelights. A downpour was on the way.

I raced the rain to Chorlton and changed my suit at the flat. Janine wasn't there. I felt a touch of relief. I didn't want to have to apologise for being wrong about Naomi. There was no sound coming from her room. I debated leaving her to her slumbers but the information I wanted was more important than a teenager's rest.

I knocked on the door, gently at first and then more loudly until I was really banging.

No response.

'Naomi!' I yelled.

'Yes!' she screamed. 'I'm trying to sleep. Go away!'

The door remained shut.

I addressed the woodwork: 'Did Cheyenne have a dummy with her on Saturday?'

'Oh, for God's sake! Of course she did.'

'What colour was it?'

'Mmmm, I don't know. I can't remember.'

'Was it green?'

This produced silence and then after a moment the door was flung open. She was still in her outdoor clothes.

'Was this it?' I demanded, showing it to her.

She put her hand to her mouth and then nodded.

'Sure?'

She nodded again.

I didn't know what to do. Tears couldn't be far away.

'Thanks,' I said. 'I had to be certain.'

I turned on my heel and left the flat. Hard-hearted man

I may be, but I felt satisfied that I was at last getting some results.

That was the last satisfaction I got out of this case for some time.

At the office Celeste reported that the bin liner and the Coke can from Alderley Edge had come up negative. There were traces of gloved hands but no prints. Also Michael had phoned to say that he'd need to stay several days to trace contacts of Jamie and Lee in the East End of London.

'I need him now,' I said. 'I want him to put the entrance of the Phoebus Club under electronic surveillance.'

'There you are,' Celeste said, her eyes gleaming. 'What did I tell you? The man's having a long weekend in London at the firm's expense. He thinks you're a soft touch, Boss. You'll see, he'll come back on Tuesday or Wednesday and say he couldn't find anything.'

I was irritated. Michael's expertise is in planting tiny cameras in public places and that was just what I needed at the moment. A camera outside the Phoebus Club might reveal if my three suspects were among its clientele.

Celeste's suspicions can be prophetic but today she was obviously madly jealous because she wasn't out investigating.

'Have you come up with anything on the dude with the spiky do?' I asked.

She looked crestfallen. I reminded myself that she wasn't much older than Naomi.

'I've asked around. It's quite a popular hairdo. There's white boys have it done as well as blacks.'

'No names?'

'There's so many . . .'

'OK,' I relented.

'There's another spot of detection you can do,' I said. 'Check out a company called Phoebus Leisure.'

I gave her the details.

'Yes, Boss,' she drawled, the embodiment of impersonal efficiency in her navy blue trouser suit. 'They have that big health club on Dock Street, don't they?'

I nodded.

'I could go there and check the place out for the dude, if you want. I need to join a health club.'

'Celeste, your figure's perfect. The last thing you need is a health club. Nor do I want you sniffing round there. This guy is dangerous.'

'I can handle him.'

'I admire your intelligence in coming up with the connection between the case and the club but we're talking serious criminal here. He threw Naomi Carter into that ambulance with one arm. I don't want to have to explain to your mother that you've disappeared.'

She looked disappointed but offered no further argument.

'Your wino friend Courteney brought the picture round. He insisted that I give him the rest of the money. The man could hardly stand up at ten o'clock in the morning.'

'Did you pay him?'

'Yes, it was that or call the po-lice. It's on your desk.'

I hurried into the office. Granville Courteney may be a lush but the picture was beautifully finished. I pinned it next to the one of Naomi's man. There were two possibilities. They could be the same man or two individuals who were related. There were already brothers in this case, so why not another pair? Or maybe a father and son. At my request Courteney had also included a sketch of a black male with spiky hair. There was less definition in that picture but the other two were of photographic quality.

I went out to a print shop on Deansgate. After reducing the pictures in size and cutting out the three heads I placed them side by side on a single postcard. They agreed to

172

print five hundred copies. On the back of the card I put the number of an answerphone in my office and the figure £3000.

They would be ready by five.

Then I walked further down Deansgate for the exercise and started looking for somewhere to buy lunch. There are now more wine bars in this corner of Manchester than in the whole of Madrid but I found a sandwich place. I bought a Stilton cheese and crispy bacon sandwich and a bottle of still mineral water to wash it down with, and sat myself on a high stool. I needed the time to think. I was in two minds about going back to the print shop and changing the £3000 to £500, but in the end I decided to let the big reward stand.

I needed those names. I needed to wrap this job up quickly.

Back at the office there was plenty of admin to get on with: time sheets of investigators to be studied, case notes to be read, expenses claims to be verified. I settled down for the afternoon. It was best to get as much out of the way as possible before the weekend.

I was well into the boring routine when the call from Clyde Harrow came.

'Pimpo Boy!' he began.

'You can drop that straight away, Clyde,' I snapped. 'Another word after your trick on Wednesday and I put the phone down.'

'Very well, my prince,' he cackled, completely unconcerned. '"What news on the Rialto?"'

'None for you, Clyde. You know very well I can't say anything.'

'Just the merest suspicion of a hint for an old friend? Jamie's playing against Chelsea tomorrow. There's a strong feeling in certain quarters that he'll need to redeem his blunders on Monday with a stunning performance.'

'I'm sure,' I said thoughtfully. My central processing

unit had come up with the idea that Clyde might be a
source of information about Phoebus. However, to find
out more from him than he found out from me required
a delicate touch.

'Well, can you say if you've resolved his problem? Is he
going to have his mind on the match?'

'Don't I remember you telling me that Jamie's brains
are in his feet? So where does his mind come into it?'

'Come on, Dave, you know what I mean. Will he be
able to give his all?'

'For what they're paying him, he should be.'

'Can't I tempt the slightest indiscretion out of you?'

'His problems are well on the way to being sorted,' I
lied.

'Were they of a sexual nature?' Clyde enquired coyly.

'Not, er . . . necessarily.'

'Hmmm . . . how elucidatory! But his troubles are being
sped towards their resolution by your skilful hand?'

'You could put it that way.'

'Damn it, Dave! I put you on to this. If it's not sex, is
it drugs?'

'Does it have to be either?'

'I can see you're determined not to be my ray of
sunshine.'

'That's right.'

'Would you like to come to the match tomorrow? We're
going to clobber Chelsea. I have a ticket to spare.'

I didn't have to be a genius to guess that it was my
information not my company that was required, but two
can play at that game.

'Sounds good, Clyde,' I said without a trace of enthusiasm, 'but I may be doing something with Janine.'

'Not another play? I heard you were at the Royal
Exchange the other night.'

I grunted ruefully. The man had his spies everywhere.

'You're in danger of becoming cultured, Dave,' he

sneered. 'Shall I ask Madam White if she'll let you out to play with the lads?'

'I'll come. Shall I pick you up?'

'How enthusiastic you sound! I know folk who'd gladly sell their grey-haired granny's virtue for a ticket to this match. But then, soccer isn't your game, is it? No, dear boy, I believe you're more a devotee of bedroom sports.'

'No, that's you, Clyde. I'm on the straight and narrow.'

'Whatever you say. I'll call for you as your love nest is on my route, but it'll be about two hours before kick-off.'

'That's fine.'

'Good, we'll have a chat then.'

I'd hardly resumed my paper-shuffling before Peter put his head round the door.

'I got soaked checking out the Evergreens,' he complained. 'The estate agent had me down by the bottom fence when there was a cloudburst. Trying to get under cover was more like swimming than walking. Some of those weeds are six feet high. Anyway, Dave, I had to go home and dry off.'

'That's OK. You don't need to explain.'

He still looked anxious.

'My wife made a meal and I stayed longer than I should.'

'Peter, will you stop this? Do you really think my middle name's Simon Legree?'

He thought about this for a minute. 'Oh, the slave-driver in *Uncle Tom's Cabin*. It's just that . . .'

'Forget it. You did well today. We'd never have found that place if it hadn't been for your idea. The boy done good, OK?'

'If you say so.'

'I do say so. Did you find out any more about Phoebus?'

'Damn all. The man kept talking about a large Manchester company seeking a development opportunity. Oh, and he

175

was really pissed off about them when he got out there. He said they must have left the alarm switched off although they'd assured him that they'd switched it on before they left. The agent obviously thought he was going to have two bidders battling for the old pile. He was very cagey about who the opposition were but he did let slip that the place was surveyed by a firm called David Ridley & Partners. I checked the Yellow Pages. They're in Fountain Street.'

'Good,' I said. 'Now all you have to do is get David Ridley & Partners to tell you how they let a gang of kidnappers have a borrow of the keys.'

Peter's face fell.

'Only joking,' I said.

'No, Boss, there's got to be a way.'

He left before I could say another word.

Celeste finishes early on Fridays but I hung on in the office. The postcards came from the printer at five-fifteen. I studied them admiringly. Apart from what I'd found at the Evergreens they represented the fruits of the best part of a week's work.

On my way home I dropped in at the Black and Blue Club. Chuckling Charlie Costello was presiding as usual. I handed him one of the cards.

He studied the faces and then shook his head. 'Not my customers anyway.' Then he turned the card over and looked at the back. He whistled. 'Three grand, eh? What are you trying to do, Mr Cunane? Start a treasure hunt? For that kind of money you'll be offered all kinds of lookalikes. They'll be coming at you like rats to a cheese factory.'

'I don't know about that. You wanted a monkey just to make a start and you've come up with nothing, have you?'

'Impatient sod, aren't you? Your old man was just the same. Give me a chance. You didn't give me much to go on. And for your information, I have heard a whisper.'

'What about?' I said eagerly.

He turned away from me to the optics stand behind and adjusted one of the bottles. Then he measured out a shot of the amber liquid and lifted it to the light.

'Checking for short measure, or making sure you're not giving too much away?' I asked.

'Both,' he said laconically. He put the whisky down in front of me and pushed it towards me. 'I always give a fair measure. I've heard that there's a certain amount of unrecorded extortion going on but I need to confirm the story over the weekend. Call in on Monday and I'll let you know what I've found.'

14

When I got home that evening Janine was giving Clint a reading lesson. I goggled. He was sitting at the dining room table with her at his side. Lloyd was flat on his stomach on the table, poring over the same book as the big man who had a look of total absorption on his face. He didn't look up when I entered the room.

Nor did anyone else. Jenny was drawing a picture in an exercise book.

'I'm sorry. Shall I go out and come in again?' I joked.

Janine gestured for silence.

'Sit down and be quiet,' she whispered. She carried on pointing to words with her finger. There were pictures on the page opposite. Clint's eyes flicked from the words to the pictures.

'Ball,' he said triumphantly, 'the boy has the ball.'

'Good, Clint!' she exclaimed. Lloyd clapped his hands.

Then Janine turned to me. 'We had a Chinese. We got some for you. You can put it in the microwave if you want.'

'Where's Naomi?' I asked cautiously.

'In your flat listening to music. She seems a lot happier with herself.'

A powerful argument against going there and preparing a meal. I hauled myself up and headed out to Janine's kitchen. The piles of metal cartons heaped up by the bin suggested that feeding Clint had required the usual gargantuan quantities.

My food was in the oven. It was still warm. I heaped fried rice, crispy duck, deep-fried seaweed and cashew nuts on to a plate and tucked in.

After a few minutes Janine came in. 'That lad's not as handicapped as you make out. I could have him reading in a few weeks. His mind's like an unploughed field. No one's ever made the effort with him before.'

'His mother had him all over the place looking for help,' I said defensively, remembering what Bob had told me.

'Dave, you don't need to be so protective of the Lane family. They probably got palmed off with long-winded medical explanations and simply gave up.'

'Possibly.'

'You look exhausted. I'll tell you what, we're going to use some of that money you gave me and have a nice relaxing weekend, just the six of us.'

'Six?' I echoed.

'You, me and the kids, Clint and Naomi. We can't leave her out.'

'No, I suppose not.'

It turned out that Janine's idea of a nice relaxing weekend was joining a reclamation team on the Rochdale Canal. Volunteers were needed to dredge it clear of a century's worth of old bedsteads and prams. As far as I was concerned it was conservationism gone mad.

'Why don't they give the work to unemployed teen-agers?' I demanded peevishly. 'There's plenty of them round here.'

'It's voluntary,' she exclaimed. 'Come on, Dave, you know you'll love it. You've been overtaxing that tiny brain of yours too much recently.'

'I can't go tomorrow. Clyde Harrow's taking me to watch Jamie Piercy do his stuff.'

'Clyde Harrow! That monster? He's not calling here, is he?'

179

'I live next door, actually,' I said as calmly as I could manage.

'How can you bear to speak to him after what he did to my children?' Last year Clyde had assisted Henry Talbot, Janine's ex, in an attempt to smuggle the children out to America.

'I loathe the man as much as you do but he might have some information I need.'

'Information!' she exploded. 'What information could he have that justifies your being in the same room as him?'

'Do you approve of all the people you interview? I don't know what information he has, that's why I need to talk to him.'

I explained about the dummy at the Evergreens and the Phoebus connection.

She subsided after that.

'All right, Dave, you go to your precious football match with that lecherous toad. But don't expect me to be around tomorrow.'

In the end we reached a compromise. She'd go labouring with the gang tomorrow and I'd join in on Sunday. I say a compromise, but there was no internal compromise. My mind seethed for the rest of that evening. We both avoided further argument.

I asked myself why I was compromising my relationship with Janine for the sake of one tiny piece of the jigsaw puzzle surrounding Cheyenne Parkes. The only answer I could come up with is that I'm an obsessive personality . . . whatever that means.

Whatever perverse trick my mind was playing on me, I slept better that night than I had all week.

Next morning saw the canal clean-up expedition move off. Masterful though she can be, Janine found even her powers stretched by her generous decision to include Naomi in the family arrangements. I've seen criminals receiving a sentence of life imprisonment who were more cheerful than Naomi on being coaxed to join the White family's day out. Clint was very puzzled by her reluctance to join the labouring masses. It sounded like really good fun to him. Digging, lifting things, it was just up his street. In the end I think it was only the prospect of having to stay at the flat with me that persuaded Naomi to go.

'If we find any dead bodies . . .'

'What!'

'If we find any corpses in the canal I'll leave them for good old Dave Cunane to investigate,' Janine joked as she left.

'Only if they're guaranteed organic,' I replied. 'I can't cope with genetically modified stuff.'

'Ugh, skelingtons!' said Lloyd.

Jenny merely gave me a reproving look.

I was in a pensive mood when Harrow pulled into the car park at one p.m. in his massive long wheel base Toyota Land Cruiser. Like so much else about the man it was excessive. All that polished chrome and steel and horsepower just to transport one person!

He started on Jamie Piercy's troubles as soon as I climbed aboard.

'If it's not sex or drugs, what is it?'

'You know I can't tell you,' I said cheerfully.

His face was a study in frustration.

Clyde worked his way through the entire lexicon of human folly from acedia to zoophilia while we crawled the short distance to the Theatre of Dreams. The one thing that didn't occur to him was that one of the highest paid players in the game was the linkman to a corrupt gang of match fixers. But then, it was pretty incredible. I'd so far refused to believe that Jamie had actually 'thrown' matches himself but once he'd crossed the line by furnishing information who was to know what else he'd done? There were naughty boys in cricket, so

181

why not soccer? Were Monday's penalties given away deliberately?

I'd looked up reports on match-fixing. There isn't much literature. It isn't exactly the kind of topic lovers of the game choose to dwell on. It seems to be generally accepted that a lot of funny stuff went on in the early days. In 1965, for instance, ten players were sent to prison for match-fixing. The ringleader got four years. Another big trial in the 1990s failed to convict anyone. There were subsequently attempts to sabotage matches by blacking out the floodlights, which would tend to suggest that it's easier to nobble the equipment than the players. Still, when you consider the amount of money washing round the Far Eastern bookies on the results of English Premiership matches, the possibility has got to be there.

When we reached the ground there was special parking for bigwigs like Clyde. We were shown to a reserved space and entered the ground up carpeted stairs through a special door. The fixed grins on the supporters' faces, the undertone of excitement, left me cold. I like football but I'm not a fan. I felt as if I was in the executive suite under false pretences.

Clyde wasn't commenting on today's game so he had the opportunity to pester me for the whole time before the match. He only shut up when Jamie and his mates trotted out on to the rich green turf. A deep-throated chanting and roaring started that would normally have raised the hairs on the back of my neck, but not this time.

My feeling of being an agnostic in this temple of true believers didn't get any better when the game started. I began to understand that if it became general knowledge that results were decided before the match was played it could kill soccer stone dead. I watched in silence as others groaned and howled around me.

At half-time the home team were three goals down. Jamie hadn't touched the ball. He seemed to be completely out of the game. The sea of red supporters was quiet while the blue section erupted in raucous chants of premature triumph. I looked at the men around me. Heads were being shaken gloomily. The prospect of a second home defeat in a single week was almost too much for some of them to bear. It crossed my mind that Jamie was being paid to fix this match, but then he'd hardly touched the ball so far.

When they came back on Jamie scored three times and his side eventually won 5–3. It was a sensational turnaround. Even my cool blood quickened a little. Men dodged the stewards and ran on to the pitch to hug the redeemed hero. How long would it take them to bay for the golden boy's blood if the truth came out? I wondered.

If there'd been an undertone of excitement before the game, undiluted euphoria hung over the stadium now. Even Clyde seemed to forget why he'd invited me.

'What's the matter with you?' he finally asked when he noticed my less than joyful expression. 'It's something really gross, isn't it? The lad's killed someone, hasn't he?'

'It's nothing like that,' I said sharply. 'Will you get off the subject? There are reporters all round. The last thing we need are rumours in the tabloids.'

Clyde passed his hand slowly over his face and changed his expression from clownish joy to judge-like sobriety.

'You're an idiot, Harrow,' I told him. 'You know, I'm in danger of falling out with Janine just by being here with you. She doesn't have my forgiving nature where you're concerned.'

'Hah-hah! Now I smell a very large rodent, Mr No-Smiles Detective. Why did you agree to come here if your keeper is so opposed to me?'

'I just wanted to ask a few questions about something quite unrelated to this business with Jamie. When all's said and done, you're pretty well informed about the local scene.'

'Oooh, flatterer!' he said loudly, sucking his cheeks in

and making a face. 'Beware, Harrow! "A thousand flatterers sit within thy crown, whose compass is no bigger than thy head" . . . *Richard II*, Act Two, Scene One.'

In the general hubbub this went unnoticed.

'Have you ever heard of Judder Crockett?' I asked casually.

'Who hasn't?' Clyde muttered. 'I can't make out what side of the street that man walks on. He comes on at you as if he's as gay as all get out and then you hear that he's got a string of pretty young ladies. Why do you ask?'

'Oh, I was speaking to him the other night.'

'Just speaking, eh? Well, it won't have been about Jamie because the man despises footballers. Not that they need to patronise health and fitness clubs.'

'Oh?' I said. This sounded interesting.

'Yes, he doesn't make any secret of it. Crockett's a class one poser and before you speak, I admit it . . . it takes one to know one. But that fellow's a virtual fascist. He holds the attention of a crowd of sycophants by reinforcing their provincial prejudices.'

'That sounds about right,' I agreed, 'but it was more his business than his politics I was interested in. He seems to be expanding very fast.'

'Now what does my sensitive proboscis detect? Corruption? . . . Criminality? . . . You think he's dealing his cards from the bottom of the deck?'

'He could be. How long has he been operating? And where did he find the money to convert that insurance building?'

'So many questions, young Dave, but not one answer have I had from you.'

'And you're not going to, either.'

'Very well, I'll say only this about the man — there's base metal there, so you be careful. I don't trust a health centre owner who keeps a Rottweiler as his lapdog.'

'I saw no Rottweiler.'

'A metaphorical Rottweiler, you untutored fool! The man has a minder, a zombie-like, slab-faced myrmidon who closely resembles the three murderers in the Scottish tragedy all rolled up into one vile parcel. "As hounds and greyhounds, mongrels, spaniels, curs, shoughs, water-rugs, and demi-wolves . . ."'

'Steady, Clyde,' I muttered as his eyes rolled up into his head. I was alarmed that he was about to climb on to a table to finish his peroration.

'". . . are clept all by the name of dogs" . . . the Scottish play, Act Three, Scene One . . . so this insolent encourager of muscular development keeps a man, and I use the term in its widest connotation, a man, by the name of Thompson . . .'

'Clyde,' I said. 'I never know whether to bring the *Collected Works of Shakespeare* or the *Oxford English Dictionary* along when I have a chat with you. What's this Thompson done to get up your nose?'

'Accurately, if somewhat vulgarly put, to those of us with the benefit of a literary education. Why, the said Crockett turned this brutish Thompson on to me when I tried to interview him about his cellulite-reducing racket. He threw me and my whole crew on to the street and that is treatment that Clyde Harrow does not respond kindly to.'

'Let's have the truth, Clyde. You were doing one of your piss-taking pieces on him and Crockett twigged and took the hump, right?'

He raised his eyes heavenwards, which I took for assent.

'So what's with this Thompson?'

'He's some species of South Sea Islander of the most frightful demeanour. You don't want to meet him twice, I'll tell you.'

'Not a black man with spiky hair?' I asked eagerly.

'Not . . . No, Pimpo-lad, fair exchange is no robbery. Tell me what Jamie's trouble is and I'll describe this creature's tigerish aspect down to the colour of his liver spots.'

'You know I can't,' I said. It was on the tip of my tongue to lie but I realised that even a lie might be grist to Clyde's mill. He's made more bricks without straw than any enslaved Israelite.

That seemed to close the interesting part of our discussion. Clyde shrugged expressively and I wasn't about to beg. The crowds had left the stadium and we got up to go. He made one last effort before he dropped me outside Thornleigh Court. 'Dave. They say discretion is the soul of wit but you're only a halfwit, so won't you give me a clue as to how Jamie's transgressed?'

'What makes you think *he* has?' I said. 'And that is a clue!'

When I went into Janine's flat a spirit of the most profound exhaustion pervaded the place. The residents were all slumped over various pieces of furniture. The children were asleep. Naomi was leaning on Clint's shoulder. She was completely out of it and Clint looked as if he'd done fifteen rounds of mud wrestling.

'Had a fun day?' I enquired.

'Don't start,' Janine said feebly.

It was lunchtime on Sunday before normal service was resumed. Nobody mentioned the plan for a second day of canal delving and I kept my mouth firmly shut.

I was itching to head down to the Phoebus Club to check out Crockett's henchman but from what Clyde had said observation from a distance might be the best course. There were no Pimpernel employees I could send at the weekend. Peter would probably have been willing but I felt it would be unkind to deprive his wife and four children of his company.

So Sunday was a slow day at the White/Cunane establishment. I wasn't exactly biting my nails. Clint and I went for a walk on our own down by the river. After the heavy

186

rain the Mersey was high and water was spilling out into the overflow scheme. There were little floating islands of yellow and brown foam spattering the banks. We stood watching ducks battle upstream for ages and then finished up in the restaurant at Sale Water Park. Janine needed a break from cooking for Clint and so did I. He had double steak and chips which I hoped would hold him until breakfast.

It was quite dark when we got back to my flat. Clint had found a new game for the Gameboy and I went in the kitchen to wash up the pots from lunch and turned on the radio. I was tuned to the local BBC station:

Police in Manchester have released the identity of the elderly man found battered to death in the entrance of a drinking club off Deansgate in the early hours of this morning. He was Mr Charles Costello, a resident of the Ordsall district of Salford, aged seventy-eight. Despite his advanced age, Mr Costello worked as a barman at the drinking club where he was found and was a well-known local character. There is as yet no description of individuals sought in connection with the incident. Detective Chief Inspector Brendan Cullen characterised the killing as a cowardly attack on an elderly man and stated that the police will spare no effort to apprehend the perpetrators. It is believed that Mr Costello may have been carrying a large amount of money with him when he was killed. Mr Cullen appealed for witnesses to come forward . . .

The plate I was holding fell from my nerveless fingers and smashed on the tiled floor. Clint poked his face round the door, smiled at me and then retreated to the living room. I came back to reality with a jolt. There was no way this was another coincidence. The Whisper Man had been checking up on his facts and he'd found that they

187

were accurate. My impatience may have cost him his life. He must have discovered the identity of my three villains. Unfortunately, it looked as if they'd also discovered his.

I phoned Peter and asked him to come round right away. He agreed even though I didn't explain the circumstances. After Bob's warnings I couldn't say anything over the phone anyway. I tried to tell myself that Chuckling Charlie's death was unrelated but I couldn't get past that old nagging feeling about coincidence. If only Charlie had given me a name or something to go on, but there was no way I was going to find out now who he'd suspected.

'I told Levonne that I'm working overtime,' Peter said when I let him in. 'She doesn't like me doing any out-of-hours work so I can't stay long. I was out most of yesterday as well.'

'Yesterday?' I said vaguely. Peter's domestic arrangements didn't seem very important at the moment. No more than my own did. Clint was sprawled over the sofa intent on his Gameboy but greeted Peter politely enough. I wondered what to do with him. Next door was out of the question. Janine was still shattered by her navvying experiences. I wondered how much Clint understood of what was discussed in front of him. However much it was, I decided not to risk it. I took Peter into the kitchen. I switched the radio on and turned the music up loud. If Clint did put his ear to the door he wouldn't pick up much.

Peter looked at me, obviously worried.

'Are you all right, Boss? If you don't mind me saying it, you look as white as a sheet.'

'I'm not all right but what's this about yesterday? Levonne's unhappy?'

'David Ridley & Partners . . . you know, Fountain Street.'

I looked at him blankly.

'The surveyors. I phoned on Friday afternoon and tried for an appointment, but the girl on the switchboard said none of the partners could see me until this Tuesday. Anyway, I went round to their offices on Saturday morning. There were only a couple of kids there, filing reports and stuff. I told them I wanted the Evergreens surveyed on behalf of the Moss Side Elderly Residents' Association . . .'

'Is there such a thing?'

'I don't know, but one of the kids, a girl . . . well, actually she was a black girl . . . took me on one side. Her granny lives in Moss Side. She said they'd already done a survey on that place but that the partners would charge me an arm and a leg to do exactly the same again, and all to find out that the place is no good. To cut a long story short, she showed me the file. Two surveyors and an assistant went out there three weeks ago last Monday. They spent three days on the job. It's a big place. They found wet rot, dry rot, rising damp, structural problems: you name it, that place has got it. It'll cost millions to put right.'

'Peter, please . . .' I said impatiently.

'The surveyors passed on the keys and the code for the alarm system to a Mr Thompson, a representative of the client, Phoebus Leisure Services of Manchester, who wanted a look round on behalf of his firm. They didn't see the man personally. The keys were delivered to him by motorcycle messenger and replaced in the firm's letterbox the following morning. It's all there in their report notes.'

'So this Thompson could have had copies made . . .'

'Easy, they were just standard keys, and he would have known the alarm code. It's up to the estate agent to change it after each visit but I don't think Rush & Showers had. Now, if you don't mind, Dave, I'd like to be getting back.' Peter seemed pleased with himself as he had every right to be but I didn't.

My throat had gone very dry.

'Just a minute, Peter. Er . . . would you like a drink?'

189

'That's a problem, Dave. Normally I wouldn't say no, but Levonne's mum's with us for a few days. She's an Adventist and I'd never hear the end of it if she smelled the demon drink on my breath.'

'Sit down for a minute,' I ordered.

He sat. I remembered his joke about what I called him: slave or servant. God! True words spoken in jest.

I told him what had happened to Charlie Costello. It didn't seem right to call the old man Chuckling Charlie or the Whisper Man now. Peter's eyes widened and he swallowed once or twice when I told him what Clyde had said about Thompson.

'So in the circumstances if you'd like to transfer to other work that's fine by me,' I finished. 'It's just not worth the risk. You could even take an early holiday if you want.'

He frowned as he took in my suggestion.

'I can't believe what I'm hearing,' he said angrily. 'The case gets dangerous and you want me off it? Why? Don't you believe a black guy can handle it?'

'It's nothing like that, Peter, and you know it. I just don't want it on my conscience . . .'

'I don't believe this! You've no proof that Costello's death is connected with what he was doing for you. It could be just a simple mugging.'

'It's too much of a coincidence. Costello survived for seventy-odd years without getting mugged until I gave him the job of finding those names. I sorry, Peter, but I'll be happier with you off the case.'

'No, I won't go! Why should I? Do you think Janine will be any the less upset if something happens to you than Levonne will be if it's me? You're thoroughly rattled, that's what the trouble is! I could get run over crossing the road tomorrow. This is the job we do and these are the risks we take.'

'Then don't say I didn't try to warn you.'

'I don't need any further warnings, I'm not some

190

illiterate hobbledehoy from the slums of Kingston. Just tell me what you want done next. Do you want me to go round to the Phoebus Club and see this Thompson?'

'The last thing we want is someone barging in there. If Thompson and Crockett are involved we'll have to go softly, softly.'

That sounded like a feeble excuse for doing nothing. Peter thought I was rattled and he was right. It gets harder to risk losing everything when you finally have something.

'Dave,' he asked earnestly, 'what did you think you were getting into here? Did you think we'd find a couple of minor thugs? And what did you expect would happen when we found them?'

'I don't know,' I said angrily. I wasn't ready with any explanations. He was the last one I could tell that I'd drifted into an impossible situation because I was bored with running Pimpernel Investigations.

'Tell me what to do?' he urged.

I went into the living room and brought a stack of the postcards with the three faces on them.

'Phone Andy Gilby when you get home tonight,' I said, naming a hard case ex-copper we employ part-time. 'His number's in the book, he lives out Sale Moor way.'

'Right!' Peter said eagerly.

'Then tomorrow you and he can work the streets with these.' I passed about half of the cards over. 'He doesn't need to know why we're after them. Tell him it's white collar crime, computer fraud or something. Work nine to five and if you get any bad reaction back off fast. This isn't a hospital job, do you understand? You stick with Gilby and stay alert. I'm not paying you enough for you to risk your skin.'

'Agreed!' he joked.

When he'd gone I wondered if I'd done the right thing but decided that it was past the time for second thoughts.

It had already been past that time when I'd accepted Lee Parkes's challenge last Tuesday.

I looked at my watch. Incredibly, it was still only six in the evening. I ought to do something myself, but what? I thought of phoning Anna Pietrangeli. Took the scrap of paper bearing her number out of my wallet. Then I put it back. I'd remembered Anna's membership of the Phoebus Club.

Suppose she'd actually been in that white Vauxhall Rascal van with the Silk Cut smoker? Suppose she'd been asked to go along with me while Crockett took a gander at who he was up against? Suppose . . . There were too many supposes to phone her.

I went into the living room and poured myself a drink.

Anyway, I was kidding myself. Where did I think I was going with Clint in tow? I couldn't dump him on Janine again and it wasn't fair to expose him to danger. I spent the evening watching television. They were showing an *Inspector Morse* repeat . . . a really relaxing way to round off the weekend. Naomi let herself into the flat at nine. She nodded at us but didn't say a word. She went into the kitchen, fixed herself a snack and then went to her room.

Presently the strains of Travis coming from the bedroom mingled with the Wagnerian chords beloved of the great Oxford detective. Watching the sad-faced actor make his moves I gradually began to feel more cheerful. I understood that he was sad because of all the horrible crime he'd seen. I've seen my share too but it hasn't left me like that. I felt alive and ready for anything. I'm the contrary sort.

At ten-thirty I encouraged Clint to go to bed and then the phone rang.

It was Janine.

'Eeeh oop, lad,' she said in a poor imitation of northern dialect. 'What ails thee, then? I thowt thee'd have gotten

thy backside round here hours since. Don't say thou art
sulking?'

'I'm just getting Clint to bed.'

'Well, lad, get thyself round here and I shall tuck thee
oop wi' me. It's still the weekend, big boy!'

15

Next morning the bright Italian red of Jamie Piercy's Maranello hit me straight between the eyes as I turned the corner from the flat to collect my car from the garage. Its owner was sitting in it.

He opened the passenger door and I got in.

'I thought I'd come and find out how you're getting on,' he said nervously. Once again it was hard to connect that scratchy London voice of his with the dominating figure I'd seen playing on Saturday.

I gave him the edited highlights, told him about the postcards and Charlie Costello's murder.

'This is much worse than I thought it would be,' he said sadly. 'It's all going to come out, isn't it, about me and Lee? If only I'd told him to piss off when he started pestering me.'

'What exactly did he want to know?'

'Inside stuff, things the clubs keep out of the papers: problems with booze and drugs, wife trouble. You know, anything that makes a player ready to accept help from the likes of Lee. I'm not proud of this, Mr Cunane.'

'No, I can see that.'

'When I started in football they told me that in the old days they used to shove the bribes into a player's boot, but these days we're all too big for our boots. A bung could be anything they wanted. Lee would fix it for them . . . houses, cars, women, even advertising deals. Oh, you have to give him credit for that. He really grafted for his split.'

This was the most I'd ever heard Jamie Piercy say at one sitting. I waited for the punchline.

'I've never thrown a match myself. I couldn't.'

'What about those two penalties?'

'That was stupid. I seemed to have my feet on the wrong legs that day. No one told me to do that. Lee was in no position to. He was terrible that day. Drunk. I was just stressed out.'

I nodded. It sounded believable.

'There's more, though, isn't there?' I insisted.

'You've got to believe me, I've never thrown a match,' he emphasised.

'But you tell your brother who will throw one, don't you?'

'That's not the same as actually doing it.'

'What about gambling? I expect Lee was able to make a fair packet gambling on his own account.'

'That's down to him. I've never bet on the result of a game I've played in.'

'All right,' I growled. 'Be more specific. How did Lee do the dirty deed?'

He started that irritating hand-flapping again.

This time I couldn't restrain myself. I leaned over and took hold of his hands and then clamped them to the steering wheel.

'I can't help you unless you talk,' I said.

'Oh, shit!' he muttered. 'It's not every game they're interested in.'

'They being Lee's Malaysian Chinese friends?'

'Yeah, that's right. Certain matches that can affect the outcome of the Premiership – top games, you know what I mean? – they're the ones that attract the real gambling. Sometimes Lee would know what they wanted doing well in advance. Sometimes it was a right scramble for him.'

Jamie seemed to think that was sufficient explanation.

'Go on!' I urged.

'Lee did it, not me! I know a lot of players from being in the England squad. He approached them. He paid them. They did it, not me.'

We sat in silence for a while. I couldn't grasp the actual mechanics of bringing about the desired result. Still, if the players involved matched Jamie intellectually it couldn't be anything too complicated.

'OK,' I said gently, 'it wasn't a bung in the boot and you personally never threw a match, but how did Lee do it?'

He started squirming with embarrassment. I waited for him to subside. He'd be lucky to escape lynching if the tabloids got hold of this.

'People think that all we do is train and play, and that we stick with our own team all the time, but we don't.'

'Go on,' I coaxed. This was worse than getting Lloyd to eat his vegetables.

'We play golf together. We have businesses. We have parties. I arranged for Lee to be involved and then it was up to him. Golf courses were his favourite places.'

'Does anyone know he's your brother?'

'Do you think I'm stupid?' he yelped.

'Keep your cool,' I said with a smile. 'I'm not a Premiership referee.'

He laughed nervously.

'Let's come at it another way. Lee's given them the bung, whatever it is. Then does he ask them to turn in a result to order? You know, does he ask for an actual score?'

'No, you can't do it like that. You'd need too many players, some on both teams.'

I nodded. That sounded true.

'You can make your own team lose, like by giving away a penalty in the last minute,' Jamie explained sadly, 'but it's a lot harder to make your team win against the odds.'

'Like you did on Saturday?'

'That was a one-off. I was playing out of my skull. I had to prove something.'

'Prove to yourself that you're not bent, you mean?'

'Yeah, all that codswallop!' he snarled. 'But my team never win against the odds because the odds are always on us to win.'

'So the big money's in helping them to lose?'

'I swear on my mother's grave, I've never done that. I couldn't. You can check the results of every match I've played in. I've always played well.'

'Except last Monday.'

'That was Cheyenne!' he snapped.

There must have been something in my expression, perhaps disgust that the poor baby was getting the blame, because he responded angrily.

'I'm not a marble statue! Even a stone would weep at what they did to her but I can't show any feeling because no one has to know that her daddy is my brother. If other players have a tragedy in the family the manager rests them for a game, but I can't say a word. I love that baby. It was horrible seeing her like that.'

'It must have been,' I agreed.

'Listen, I'm telling you, aren't I? It's only certain games that attract the really big money . . .'

'. . . and Lee fixed it so that a team would lose. But how, if he only bribed one man? Surely the manager would substitute that player if he was playing badly?'

'You don't know football, do you?'

'Rugby was my game.'

'You think Lee bribed them and then they went and kicked the ball in their own goal or gave away a couple of penalties?'

I shrugged. 'It happens.'

'It's not dead obvious like that. For instance, you can spoil your own side's rhythm by getting yourself and maybe one of your mates sent off. They blame the ref then. Oh, there's dozens of ways and they wouldn't think it was you unless someone told them. We all have off days.'

'So how many has Lee nobbled?'

'Seven or eight. Do you want their names?'

It wasn't just Jamie's hands that were shaking now. His face was alive with tension. The man was coming to pieces in front of me.

I thought for minute. What were we looking at? Four or five years in jail for Jamie and Lee and their friends, assuming anything could be proved. Jamie was singing like the proverbial canary now but it could be a very different story in six months time in front of a judge and jury. They'd all lie their heads off then with Lee and Jamie in the forefront. Even if there was a successful trial, what next? The total ruin of Clyde Harrow's Beautiful Game?

I felt sick. Lee Parkes had already paid a very big price for his crime, and there was someone else out there capable of far worse than match-fixing. It would be time to think about reckoning up the score when I found the abductor of Cheyenne Parkes and the slayer of Charlie Costello.

'I don't want names. You and your brother hired me to find out who kidnapped Cheyenne, not to clean up football. That's down to you.'

'But how?' he whined pathetically.

'I don't imagine you want the public to know what you've just told me.'

'I can't go public. I'm just reaching the peak of my career. I couldn't stand it if I didn't have the game any more.'

'Pass the message that it's over to your mates. They're in it as deeply as you, worse even. They won't speak.'

'But what about Lee?'

'I think we can both help him to see the error of his ways, don't you?'

'I suppose so,' Jamie agreed. 'Do you think if they find this old man's killers . . . I mean, will it come out then?'

'I don't know. You tell me. Is there any way that the extortionists . . . killers as they are now . . . could be linked with Lee's Malaysian Chinese friends? It would all come out then.'

'I've thought about that a lot. Neither they nor Lee would have had anything to gain from talking about me and Lee to anyone else. I know I've told no one. My dad . . . I mean Jack Piercy, not my biological father . . . has always warned me to keep quiet about Lee. If there is a connection, I don't know what it is.'

I looked him in the eye. There was obviously more to be said on the score of his 'biological father', etc. The fact that he'd used the esoteric term suggested he was brooding about the matter. But I'd been engaged to help him, not to drive him into some clinic. I decided to pursue my own enquiries, as we say in the trade.

'Well, nothing'll come out through me,' I said confidently, 'but you must have always known there was a risk of exposure. Is it possible that Lee's Oriental associates have any actual physical evidence: videotapes, recorded phone taps, photographs?'

He shook his head. 'I don't think so. Once they got him started Lee was in it for the money. They didn't need to blackmail him and he was always very careful. He knows about evidence and that kind of thing.'

'Well, then, it's your word against theirs. You'll just have to brazen it out. If they try any rough stuff, I can supply you with all the minders you'll need.'

'Thanks, Mr Cunane,' he said, looking the way he'd looked on Saturday when they were carrying him off the pitch in triumph. I restrained myself from giving him a footballer's hug.

'I'm seeing some of my mates this morning,' he continued. 'We're doing this film for the government, an advert like, for teenage boys. We're encouraging them to study and behave. It's part of a government programme for excluded lads.'

'Role models?'

199

'That's it.'

I looked him straight in the eye again. Jamie stared back at me unflinchingly, not the least bit uncomfortable with being a role model.

There was a protracted silence.

He scrutinised me expectantly. I wondered what I'd left unsaid. The colour had come back into his face.

'Did you see us hammer Chelsea on Saturday?'

'Yes,' I said. The Sunday papers had been full of his wonderful performance.

He waited for me to say more.

'OK,' I said resignedly. 'You were great. Now can I ask you some questions about something else? Have you ever heard of a health club called the Phoebus Club?'

'No, never heard of it.'

'It's a massive place in town with a swimming pool, restaurant and everything.'

'I told you before, I don't go out in Manchester much.'

'They have this logo, the head of a Greek god inside the disc of the sun with rays coming out of it.'

I took an envelope out of my pocket and sketched it for him.

'I've seen that somewhere,' he mumbled. 'Yeah, but where?' He scratched his head.

'Oh, I know,' the role model exclaimed eventually. 'That piece that tried to get off with Lee . . . what's her name? It's something to do with her husband.'

'Smathers,' I prompted. 'Kimball Smathers.' How anyone could forget a name like that was beyond me, but then Jamie's brains are in his feet, aren't they?

'Yeah, that's him. Old friend of Lee's from London. He was trying to get Lee to put money into this health place but that was months ago, way back before Mel was killed. Lee wasn't interested.'

'Do you know where Smathers lives?'

'Shouldn't you ask Lee?'

I didn't say anything.

'Oh, you don't want him to know?' Jamie scratched his head again.

'Yeah,' he said after a long pause. 'I've played golf with him and Lee at his club. It's in Mollingtree, right over the other side of Cheshire. It's handy for the races at Chester and Heydock and Aintree. He lives right there in Mollingtree.'

'Fine,' I said.

'Do you mind if I ask you something, Mr Cunane? How long do you reckon all this is likely to go on for? I only ask because we're still in with a shot at the Treble. To be honest with you, the next few months are going to be tough and I'd like this business sorted.'

'Oh, it'll be sorted, mate, and soon,' I said confidently.

'Great! Would you like a couple of tickets for the next home game? We're playing Liverpool.'

'Thanks, Jamie,' I said.

'The tickets'll be in the post.'

He switched the Ferrari engine on and I got out. He touched the throttle, the mighty 485 b.h.p. engine gave a subdued roar and he was off. Forty-eight valves in twelve cylinders playing a symphony can't be described as quiet, but Jamie slipped out of the car park and vanished into the morning traffic like a shark sliding into a school of minnows.

I scratched my head. His gesture was catching.

What was all that about? I wondered.

It was clear to me where I figured in the Jamie Piercy scheme of things. He wanted his mess clearing ASAP. 'Dave, Dave, the footballer's slave,' I hummed to myself tunelessly.

Jamie wasn't guilty of anything. According to him it was all down to Lee.

Hah! Jamie's one-sided, self-serving story made me unexpectedly sympathetic to his brother. I wondered what he was doing now? It might be very convenient for some people if Lee got his head bashed in like poor old Charlie Costello. Then we could all get on with our football matches and our role-modelling with minimum fuss.

I took out my mobile and called him.

He answered immediately and sounded alert.

'Lee, Cunane here. Don't speak, just listen. I know you don't rate me highly.'

'Who the fuck told you that?'

'You did, but just listen for once. Things are getting heavy. Switch on the local news and you'll hear that an old man was killed in central Manchester. He was helping me and I think he was killed because he stumbled on the names of our three friends with the ambulance.'

'Christ! I'll come down there and help you get the bastards.'

'That's exactly what I don't want. You might be next on their list. I want you to take a long holiday abroad.'

There was a pause.

'I don't let anyone chase me out of the country.'

'Shut up and listen or you'll be six feet under the country! Somebody knows everything about you, Lee. Who's to say they don't know you're trying to hunt them down? Get out while you can.'

'I've got to be here for Cheyenne. Let them try it with me. They'll find I'm tougher than a baby or an old man.'

'Very macho, Lee, but aren't you supposed to be the one with the brains in your family?'

He grunted affirmatively so I continued, 'Cheyenne's got doctors and nurses to look after her. Tell them you've been unavoidably called abroad. They'll be sympathetic. It's a private hospital after all. You can't be the first dad to be called away.'

'It's possible,' he agreed grudgingly.

'If you go you'll be helping Jamie.'

'Say that again?'

'I've seen him this morning. With you out of the picture he has a chance to pull himself out of the mess he's in. He claims he's never got his own hands dirty. Give him a chance, Lee.'

There was a lengthy pause.

'Little Brother, Little Brother, eh?'

'Come on,' I muttered.

'I'm thinking.'

'You owe him a chance.'

'Yeah, I could go to . . .'

'No, don't tell me. Don't tell a living soul, just get out of the country.'

'This isn't a ploy to make sure I'm out of the way when you find that scum, is it?'

'I should be so devious, Lee.'

'Hang on, Cunane, does this mean you're jacking the job?'

It was my turn to pause and think for a moment. Charlie Costello wasn't a relation and he did what he did for money but should I just let his killers walk free? Prudence said yes, but when have I been prudent?

'No,' I snapped. 'I've taken it on and I'll finish it. Now go!'

At the office there was the usual dull routine. Celeste was on her best behaviour. I told her to charge Peter's and Gilby's work for the next week to File Red. I had several prospective new clients to interview and lunchtime came round very quickly. I was acutely aware that there should be surveillance of the Phoebus Club but there was nothing I could do about it. I was the only one free and I'd already decided not to send Celeste, willing though she might be.

On the way back to Chorlton I listened to local radio. There was no progress in finding the killer of Charlie Costello. Murders in the inner city tend to fall into certain broad categories as far as the media are concerned. There are drug-related shootings, which get the breathless treatment. There are those which result from meaningless fights among tanked-up young men, which attract a more cursory handling. Then there are the killings of the old, battered in their beds for a handful of change. They provoke maximum indignation.

Charlie's killing was a bit of a puzzler. It didn't fit neatly into the category of old-age pensioner battering. He was reported as working, for one thing. Why was a seventy-eight-year-old working, and reportedly carrying large amounts of money around with him? The subtext of the report was that Charlie had only himself to blame.

I realised that subconsciously I was blaming him too.

Charlie Costello was too fond of preserving his trade secrets. He loved to be the conjuror lifting the rabbit out of the hat. It was possible that he'd known who was involved right from the moment I first spoke to him. He'd been indignant that I was offering three thousand pounds as a reward but that wasn't why he was killed. News about that would only be percolating through to the criminal fraternity from today onwards as Peter and Andy did their rounds. Did the large sum nudge him into acting with a little less caution than usual? If so I shouldn't blame myself.

Charlie Costello was a veteran. He must have been more than capable of assessing the risks. At the back of my mind was the idea that someone he'd trusted had let him down. For a start the killing was on his own doorstep. Whoever had had information for him must have been bringing it to the Black and Blue Club.

Solving his murder wasn't my job, but I couldn't dispel the thought of that indomitable old man lying in the gutter with his skull stoved in.

Back at the flat, Naomi had got Clint ready for his afternoon outing. He was wearing leather trousers in a kind of shimmery metallic finish and a long black leather

204

jacket. His crew-cut hair had been freshly shampooed. On his feet he had heavy black work-boots with steel toecaps. The effect could only be described as distinctive.

'Come on, me old china,' I said genially. 'We're off on our travels.'

'Good, Dave. When am I going to see Bob?'

'Not today. He's thinking about you but some men want to see him and he doesn't want to see them, so he's had to go away.'

That was the wrong thing to say. A spasm of annoyance crossed his normally bland features.

'These men, Dave? Who are they?' he asked, his fists clenched.

'Don't worry, they're a long way away. They won't hurt him if they find him. They only want to speak to him.'

His face lost that faint air of menace and the frown gradually faded. But as he calmed down I found I was growing angrier myself. I don't know if it had anything to do with Clint but a thought had occurred. It was more a series of jumps to conclusions than a logical deduction. Suppose Charlie Costello's death was due to something he'd learned about the Phoebus Club? The health club itself was only a short walk down Deansgate from the Black and Blue. Charlie probably passed it several times a day.

There were two leads to the health club: somebody from Phoebus could have had access to the Evergreens at the critical time and Kimball Smathers had been trying to involve Lee in a business deal with Phoebus Leisure. Nothing was substantiated, but then this was probably as good as my evidence was ever going to get. I don't have squadrons of detectives and teams of forensic scientists churning out clues for me.

But my mounting anger wasn't due to any conclusion I'd leaped to – it was about Clyde Harrow.

Judder Crockett wasn't your run-of-the-mill business-man. He employed a minder. Why did he need one? Not to protect him from overweight ladies who hadn't lost cellulite as promised, surely? The minder could be my porcupine-headed suspect. Clyde described him as a menacing South Sea Islander, and some South Sea Islanders are dark-skinned Melanesians. The more I ran it over in my mind the more convinced I became that Thompson was Porcupine Head.

If only that fool Harrow had told me more I could have warned Charlie to stay away from the Phoebus Club. If only I'd insisted. I should have realised at the football match that I was playing in a game without rules and made the fat fraud tell me exactly what he knew.

I decided to have it out with Harrow rather than take Clint on a tour of the pubs and clubs handing out cards.

So I drove to Clyde's office. The glory that is Clyde Harrow has long departed the showily carpeted corridors of Alhambra TV. As an independent producing his own quirky little local news show he now occupies a suite in an old shared office in Knott Mill near the Mancunian Way. There's a lot of dust and noise from traffic but it's cheap, which suits Clyde very well. As usual there was no parking within about half a mile of the place. I finally left the car near a railway arch and set off with Clint easily keeping up with me. With every step I could feel my temper worsening.

By the time I reached the office building, called St Sebastian House, of all things, I'd stoked up a fine head of fury. Clyde Harrow would be lucky to avoid being studded with arrows like a pincushion.

I scanned the board at the entrance. There were lots of companies but no Harrow. I eventually decided that CHTV on the fourth floor was him and set off. The lifts didn't work. That didn't slow me down. Clint and I arrived in front of a door with a neat brass plate saying

Clyde Harrow
Managing Director
CHTV

206

I pushed the door open. A startled young woman in tight sweater and jeans stared up at me.

'Are you lost?' she asked timidly. She didn't look like a proper secretary, more like one of the 'media studies' graduates gaining work experience that Clyde used as a source of cheap labour. The way she was pecking at the word processor suggested she was in no danger of getting repetitive strain injury.

'I've come to see Harrow,' I said. 'Dave Cunane.' Then I took a resolute step towards the inner door.

'No, he's busy,' she squawked.

I went in. Where I led Clint followed.

Behind the inner door there was a short corridor with four more rooms leading off. Sounds of female laughter came from behind the end door.

Past caring about niceties, I flung it open. The scene was more or less what I'd expected. Clyde was at his desk, a semi-clad young woman draped over him. He never rests in his pursuit of new perspectives.

'I need a word,' I said.

'How about bastard!' he snapped back. 'Does that suit you, matey!'

The girl heaved herself up and set about fastening her blouse over her prominent assets. She gaped at Clyde indignantly. Clint's eyes bulged as he took in the view.

'Is he a bad man, Dave?' he whispered anxiously. 'Was he hurting that lady?'

'No, he's not hurting her. Just stand by the door, Clint.'

The effect of this little conference on Clyde was dramatic. He jumped and legged it for the door. He may have thought I was arranging for his legs to be broken. He reached the door at the same time as Clint, who filled the whole doorway. Clyde tried to wriggle round but Clint extended his elbows. Clyde did a little dance of frustration.

'Guilty conscience, Clyde? And spare me the Shakespearean quotes.'

'What is this?' he said angrily.

'You feel free to come into my office whenever you like. I'm just returning the favour.'

'Why?'

'I need to hear exactly what you know about Judder Crockett and his man Thompson. I have the unpleasant feeling that someone I know may have met with an accident at their hands.'

'Evidence?'

'None whatever.'

'Hmm, that's often the best sort. But I told you before: no tickee, no washee! You tell me what Jamie's been up to and I tell you what I know.'

I felt a surge of fierce anger. I wanted to get him by his fat neck and shake the truth out of him. He could see it in my face.

'All right!' he muttered, retreating behind his desk. 'Just keep your pet away from me and tell me about our footballing friend.'

'What do you think Jamie's been up to? What is it footballers do?' I asked sarcastically.

'You'd better go, Stacey,' Clyde said to the young woman.

She darted to the doorway. Clint beamed warmly at her and made no attempt to block her path. 'Shall I get the police?' she shouted as soon as she was safely out of Clint's reach.

'That won't be necessary,' Clyde said with a sigh.

'Sit down there,' I said to Clint, indicating the rumpled day bed in the corner. 'Your casting couch, Clyde?'

'These young dears come here expecting a spot of gentle shagging. To tell you the truth, Dave, I find living up to their expectations can become rather onerous.'

'Oh, dear. They say cod liver oil is good for vitality.'

'Enough chit-chat,' he countered with an aloof smile. 'I do have work to do. In what precise manner has young Jamie erred?'

'He hasn't, but he knows people who have. Clyde, I can't tell you any more '

'Criminal connections. Is that it?'

'It could be something like that. I can't tell you because I don't know myself.'

Light dawned on Clyde's plump face. He took his glasses off and mopped his brow. Then his face darkened.

'What are you saying? That he's fixed matches? . . . Oh, those two penalties! The little shit! And to think I wanted to help him.'

'Are you crazy? Jamie's earning enough to pay off the National Debt of a small country.'

'Since when has that stopped people being greedy for more?'

'It's not that. There are some things in Jamie's background that he doesn't fully understand himself. That's why he needs me to investigate.'

'What though? What are you investigating? Something that makes him play like a crippled duck and give away two penalties?'

'Something or somebody did upset him and that's why I need your discretion.'

'You're extracting him from the mire?'

'Hopefully.'

'Isn't this wonderful? I uncover the football story of the year,' Clyde said gloomily, 'a story that could restore my failing fortunes and have every branch of the media eating out of my hand and the man I trusted to share the information clams up on me.'

'I never promised to share anything with you.'

'It was implicit in our understanding. However, Clyde

Harrow does not stoop to beg. If your lips are sealed about Jamie tell me about the old man who was mugged.'

'Murdered.'

'It wasn't Charlie Costello, was it?'

I nodded.

'Everyone knows his reputation. It's a marvel he survived this long.'

I felt my anger surging back.

'He was seventy-eight years of age, Clyde. He lived so long because he was extremely cautious. I think he put out a feeler to someone connected to the Phoebus Club and you said . . .'

'. . . that Thompson's certainly capable of murder. He's a Fijian citizen of mixed Indian and Fijian blood which means he's had both races on his own island on his back since birth. He's a very mean customer and I've heard he's wanted in Fiji for murder.'

'So what's he doing in Manchester?'

'He's claiming political asylum. Naturally he won't be listing his own crimes on the application. Apparently he knew Crockett before he arrived in Britain.'

I put the postcard of the three villains down in front of Clyde.

'Is he here?'

He squinted through his glasses and surveyed the trio. My heart was in my mouth.

'No, none of those. He's dark but he has long wavy hair, nothing like that one there.'

Clyde looked up.

'Physically I'd say he's almost a match for your play-mate here, but he's ferociously ugly. Once seen, never forgotten.'

My disappointment must have shown on my face.

'Another theory comes crashing to the ground, eh?' he said with a smirk. 'Sorry, Pimpo Boy, but Thompson's not your man.'

I wasn't ready to abandon my suspicions completely.

'How did you find out all this about Thompson and Crockett? It's not the sort of thing they put on the club's handouts.'

'My young ladies, Dave. Fiona and Stacey, the . . . er . . . nymphet who just dashed out, practically live at the Phoebus Club. I believe it's a favourite pick-up spot for our gilded youth. I also hear on the grapevine that Crockett's overextended himself with that club. They say he's looking for a partner to inject some cash into the business.'

That gave me hope. Maybe Crockett had found a way to inject cash into his business without the need for a go-between.

'I believe that was the cause of my own little altercation with Mr Crockett. He agreed to do the interview thinking he might sweet-talk me into parting with some of my mazuma.'

'He's insane then!'

'Yes, we both know the state of my finances, Dave. However, this gentleman was ever so obliging while he had his hopes up, but then when he realised with whom he was dealing he revealed his true nature. "One may smile, and smile, and be a villain . . ." *Hamlet*, Act One, Scene Five.'

'Cut the educational stuff, Clyde!' I barked.

'I'm ever hopeful where you're concerned, Dave, but often disappointed.'

'Here's a valuable piece of education for you: don't go shoving your snout into this Jamie business. It's cost Charlie Costello his life and he was a hundred times more streetwise than you are.'

'A valuable lesson indeed and may I offer the same to you? Your muscular friend over there may not be able to protect you either.'

Clint beamed at us both.

'That smile of his is truly chilling,' Clyde said. 'I hope he's not a villain too?'

I didn't attempt to enlighten him about Clint. We left quickly and the walk back to the car seemed twice as long as it had coming. When I got to the spot where I'd left it I found it had been towed away by the hyper-active firm who now control our streets.

Retrieving the car and paying the fine took me most of the rest of the day.

16

You win some, you lose some, I thought bitterly as I drove the Mondeo away from the car pound. I wasn't thinking about the car.

Did the fact that Thompson wasn't Porcupine Head mean that Judder Crockett was off the hook? No way, Jose!

My brain seethed with alternative scenarios.

Lee Parkes had spoken of Kimball Smathers with a certain condescension. The ex-Royal Marine was a mere money carrier. He'd tried making money at gambling just like clever Lee, and he'd had his fingers burnt for his trouble. Then Lee had given his loving wife Keeley a poke. When did that start? I only had Lee's word that it was a one-off. An affair could have been going on for months, possibly the cause of the late Mel's decision to charge off on a winter's evening in a high-performance sports car she didn't know how to handle. According to Lee, Kimball might or might not have known that Lee was having casual sex with his wife.

He seemed to think the matter was unimportant because Kimball was an old school mate. As if that made any difference to the price of eggs!

Kimball had joined the Royal Marines and saluted the flag morning and evening for six years. There was every chance that loyalty meant something quite different to him than it did to a crafty lad like Lee. He had made a good living by taking the risk out of gambling while

Kimball had spent a hard life in the Marines going to whatever rough spot in the world the Queen sent him to.

Big-heads like Lee are always the last to know what their mates really think about them.

So Kimball gets a chance to make some money by investing in the rapidly expanding field of health clubs. How did that come about?

I cudgelled my brain to come up with an answer. Nothing stirred.

In the seat beside me Clint was gently humming to himself as we negotiated the blocked roundabout at the end of Deansgate. I smiled at him. Clint leads an uncomplicated life. His loyalties are straightforward.

There I go! I thought.

I was doing a Lee Parkes, taking someone for granted.

Clint isn't a pet dog, whatever Clyde Harrow might have implied. He was born handicapped, which doesn't put him off the scale of humanity. He'd been sheltered by his devoted mother and brother for the first thirty years of his life. Then his mother, the beginning and ending of everything for him, died. Bob, his elder brother, tried to keep him in the same routine that their mother had. But the life he led was unsuitable for Clint. Men came into Bob's office and threatened him with death, not on a daily basis but there was a constant stream of them: head bangers, hard men on the way up.

Bob Lane knew how to handle them, but Clint didn't.

His feelings towards his brother were so protective that Bob was terrified Clint would kill one of these casual operators. There'd been a time when everyone, including the Greater Manchester police, was convinced that Clint *had* topped someone. I was able to help them sort that out and soon afterwards Bob shipped his brother off to the Dutch farm.

Bob was entitled. He'd had no relief for years and was

still committed to Clint but Dutch farms weren't the solution for his brother.

'How are you doing, Clint?' I asked.

'Fine, Dave. I like being in Manchester and seeing all the people. Everyone's so busy.'

'You see more people than you did on the farm, eh?'

'Oh, yes, Dave. There was only Dirk and Margarethe and a few other people there.'

'Would you like to go back to Holland?'

'No, Dave! Don't send me back. I love Manchester.'

The change in him was startling. His face was suddenly the picture of misery.

'What's the matter?' I asked. 'Were they unkind to you there?'

'No, Dirk and Margarethe are kind, good people but I can't speak to anyone. I don't know their words and they keep away from me. They say things about me that I don't understand. They take their children away when I come near, not like Janine. She's very good, Dave. I want to stay near her.'

'So do I, Clint. I think she's very good too.'

'Naomi's nice as well,' he added. I caught a wistful note in his words.

'Yes, she is,' I agreed. 'But she might not be staying with us for long.'

'Oh, yes, Dave,' he said firmly. 'She's staying. Janine wants her to look after Jenny and Lloyd and she's said she will for at least six months. Janine's going to give her a very lot of money.'

'Well, ask a question and you learn something,' I said in surprise. Nothing had been said to me about six months. Six months of listening to Boyzone and Robbie Williams and Travis!

'Yes, Dave, I do that,' Clint agreed gravely. 'Janine's going to teach me to read books then I can learn even more things.'

'Clint, by the time you've finished you're going to be so clever!'

'I am,' he said proudly.

'I wish you could tell me how Kimball Smathers linked up with Judder Crockett.'

'I don't know that, Dave,' he said after a moment of consideration.

It could have been through an advert in a trade paper but I suspected that Judder Crockett would prefer a personal approach. So do I, but I could hardly go and ask Smathers what his connection with the Phoebus boss was. Or could I? Why not? The direct approach had paid off with Clyde Harrow. I'd nothing to lose. If he was hand in glove with the people who'd kidnapped Cheyenne he must already know that it was my firm that was on their trail . . . they'd have seen the postcards with my phone number on the back by now or soon would.

When I got back to the flat that evening the Whites and Naomi were out. There was a note under my door: 'All gone to Pizza Hut and film at Trafford Centre, Love, Janine'.

Clint settled in front of the television and I took advantage of the unusual silence to continue my cogitations in the kitchen while I prepared Clint's dinner. That involved peeling lots of potatoes since we'd discovered that he liked huge amounts of well-buttered mash.

I decided that the investigation was still moving ahead. We might come up with a name through the postcards. Although not massive compared with the rewards for naming a bank robber, three thousand pounds was enough to jog somebody's memory. Or Michael might find out something in London. I served Clint a vast meal of stew and mashed potatoes and as I did so the red mist that had descended earlier in the day returned.

Who did these people think they were? Casually crushing poor old Charlie Costello as if he was a bug. I couldn't wait for the slow process of discovery to turn up names. I wanted action now. I don't know whether I was actually grinding my teeth at this stage but Clint looked up in alarm.

'Am I doing something wrong?' he asked. He looked like a frightened child.

'No, I am,' I said. 'Don't you worry, Clint.'

I went into the living room and got the Smathers' phone number from directory enquiries.

'Mr Smathers,' I said when a male voice answered, 'my name's Cunane, I'm a private enquiry agent.' I tried to stifle the fury I felt and be as smooth as possible.

'Are you really?' he asked in a mocking way. 'Makes a change from double glazing.'

'Yes, I'm making some enquiries on behalf of Mr Lee Parkes.'

'You don't say?' he replied, the tone more guarded this time.

'I wonder if I can come and speak to you tonight?'

'I don't know about that. What's it in connection with? It's nothing to do with my wife, is it?'

'No,' I said quickly, grateful that he'd confirmed he had suspicions. 'It's nothing to do with your wife except that she was the baby's mother's best friend. Lee's baby daughter's ill . . .'

'I know that. Been weak since being born, hasn't she?'

'Sorry, sir, it's difficult over the phone but there's been a complication.'

'Am I a quack? It's very sad about Cheyenne and all that palaver, but I haven't been able to speak to Lee for the last week. What's going on?'

I could feel my temper rising. I struggled to keep a grip.

'Obviously you don't know anything directly relating to Cheyenne's recent turn but I thought as Mr Parkes's oldest friend you might be able to fill in some background.'

'Sorry, cocker, no can do,' he said bluntly. 'I know

217

nothing about Cheyenne's state of health, and the way that I've stayed friends with Lee is by keeping my mouth shut about his business, so I'm not about to start rabbiting about him to some total stranger.'

'I'm sure Mr Parkes would appreciate your discretion but he needs all the help his friends can give him now.'

I looked at the hallway and the locked door of Naomi's room and improvised desperately.

'The child's nanny's made allegations. There's a question of neglect, with Mr Parkes being a single parent. The nanny says that your friend didn't take the child to the doctor for days when she needed treatment and now Mr Parkes has got to prove that he didn't ignore her condition. Just a simple statement from you as his oldest friend and possibly another from your wife . . .'

'So Lee's finally come unstuck, has he? Child neglect's the last thing I'd thought he'd get done for.' It was hard to say what Smathers's reaction was. 'You say it's the nanny who's trying to stitch him up?'

'Yes.'

There was a barking sound in the background that could have been a laugh, could have been a dog, but Smathers certainly wasn't overcome with concern for his friend. As I'd thought before, people like Lee don't have friends.

'Statements from you and Mrs Smathers might make all the difference,' I coaxed.

'All right. I suppose I can do that much,' he agreed. 'I can see you tomorrow.'

'I'm sorry, sir, but this is urgent. I need the statements for tomorrow morning.'

'Hellfire! I suppose you'd better come out then, but I want to see proof that you're who you say you are and not some termite working for the *News of the World*.'

'I'll bring a copy of Mr Parkes's contract with me,' I said, and that seemed to reassure him. He gave me directions on how to reach him in Mollingtree.

I went back in the kitchen where Clint was systematically demolishing the heaped plateful I'd put in front of him. I watched with mounting frustration as each forkload went down his throat. At last he finished, but then he reached for a thick slice of bread and began polishing his plate.

'Are you still hungry, mate?' I asked.

He looked at me soulfully.

I looked round the kitchen. I made him a super-sized jam sandwich and passed him two bananas.

'Bring them with you,' I ordered.

On the way out I left a note under Janine's door: 'Investigating in West Cheshire with Clint, back late, Dave'.

I timed the journey to Mollingtree. It took us thirty minutes on the M56 and the extension that led into the Wirral. Not a journey that would put someone who saw opportunity for profit in Manchester to much trouble.

The Smathers residence turned out to be a large semi on the main road through the village. There were no fences, the lawn was open to the street. We passed the golf course on the way there.

I was met at the door by both of them. Mrs Smathers looked extremely stressed. A bottle blonde, not very tall and in a tight blue low-cut dress that looked as it she'd been poured into it, she was sweating freely although it wasn't particularly warm inside the house or outside. Under the bright light of the porch lamp, Keeley had very white skin. She was on the fleshy side and her bra was too small judging by the way her cleavage kept trying to jump out of the dress. Although she was struggling to smile at me, I could see she wasn't finding it easy. There was a livid purple bruise on the soft muscle of her upper right arm.

'Fell over on the golf course,' she said when she noticed me eyeing the mark.

'Drunk as usual,' her husband said unpleasantly. She

turned to him. 'Only joking, love!' he cackled, with a barking laugh. She delivered a mock blow from which he recoiled.

Looking at them I realised that, though this pair might have their differences, they were still batting on the same side.

Smathers smiled at me but there was no humour in his face. Tension oozed out of him. He was a tall, dark, hatchet-faced character with eyes like shiny black pebbles. Surprisingly for an ex-Marine, he wore his hair long. His face was bony, with prominent cheekbones and a black moustache. The teeth were white and regular and I guessed there was Hispanic or Romany blood somewhere in his family tree in the not too distant past.

Beauty and the Beast, Keeley and Kimball, except that he wasn't a beast, far from it, but could have earned a living as a male model. He had that long lean shape on which any clothing hangs well, in this case new white trainers, designer jeans and a white T-shirt. His feet were touching the ground like anyone else's but he gave the impression of being 'on his toes' to the extent that he was almost floating. His body was in motion the whole time, weight shifting from foot to foot as if he was dancing to music the rest of us couldn't hear.

He ran his thumbs under his belt as if he needed to anchor his arms somewhere. They were brawny and tattooed, I noticed.

'Come in, Mr Cunane. We're not always this comical,' he said. 'Must be having a private eye here. It's set her off.'

'Go on!' Keeley muttered.

'A private dick, eh? Keeley, what's he going to tell us?'

'Stop it, Kim!'

'It don't need much to set my wife off, Mr Cunane. She's a right little firecracker, in't she?'

220

'Stop teasing the man, Kim!' she urged. 'He's not interested in our carryings on, are you, Mr Cunane?'

'No,' I said, looking her in the eye. She flinched slightly.

'So that bloody nanny's landed Lee in it, has she?' Keeley said in a high-pitched, anxious voice. 'The two-faced bitch! I told Lee and Mel they should never have taken the little cow on. Her father's in prison . . .'

'That's all right, love,' Kimball interrupted. He touched his wife's arm and she shut up instantly. 'Our visitor isn't here for a character reference on the girl, are you?' he asked. He took a grip on my arm and led me back towards the car. I thought I was getting the bum's rush before I'd had the chance even to open my mouth.

If Keeley Smathers was slightly past her sell-by date and almost exactly as I'd imagined her from Naomi's account, Kimball was a surprise. He reminded me more of an attack-dog than a bodyguard.

'Just taking a look at who you've got with you,' he said genially when I stiffened up. 'You should never go into action without a recon, should you?' He let my arm go and we walked to the end of the lawn.

'Did Lee send him with you?' he asked, nodding his head at the darkened form of Clint which we could make out under the dim street lights. He walked up to the window and rapped on the glass. Clint looked up from his Gameboy and smiled right back at him.

'Not one of his usual team,' said Kimball.

'He's with me, a friend,' I explained.

'Ask him to come in.'

'No, he's all right there. He's nothing to do with this enquiry.'

I looked at him and he nodded as though he didn't believe a word I'd said.

'Show me your ID,' he ordered. I passed him the impressive-looking Pimpernel Investigations ID and also

221

the contract that Lee and Jamie had signed. He peered at them under the dim street light and then tossed them back at me. He turned and walked back to his house in three or four quick strides. It wasn't difficult to believe that he'd been trained to make amphibious attacks.

'Come in then,' he said over his shoulder, 'and this had better be good.'

The temperature had suddenly changed from chilly to sub-zero.

We went into a lounge dominated by a television so large that the other fixtures and fittings in the room seemed inconsequential. The curtains weren't drawn and I noticed that Smathers took a seat from which he could keep Clint under observation.

'OK, Knobhead,' he said, 'let's have your cards on the table. Who really sent you?'

'I'm working for Lee Parkes.'

'That sounds unlikely. Lee can pick up a phone and speak to me any time he wants. He doesn't need to send a private detective.'

'I am working for him. I showed you the contract.'

'So what's he thinking of?'

'Leave it, Kim,' Keeley gasped. Her alabaster skin had turned a deathly shade of white in the harsh lighting. 'We can phone the police.'

'No,' he snapped. 'I want to know why a fucking bloke who claims to be my fucking friend sends two fucking hard cases out to see me.' He started fingering a heavy Maglite torch which he picked up from the side of the chair. 'If I'm supposed to be fucking frightened you can tell Lee it hasn't fucking worked. I'll send the fucking pair of you back to him in fucking plaster if you don't fucking talk!'

I could see he was working himself up into a lethal frenzy. The repetitious swearing had a dehumanising effect, as if he'd become a machine. It was aggression and rage that had brought me here from Manchester but I could feel that

222

draining away now. It wasn't so much fear that replaced them as embarrassment. This meeting was not going as planned.

'I'm not a hard case,' I said coolly. 'I'm a private detective and I'm investigating the brutal kidnapping of Cheyenne Parkes. She was snatched and left to die by two or possibly three men who knew every detail of Lee's routine . . .'

This information had a shattering effect on Keeley Smathers. She went into a fit. Started screaming in short bursts at the top of her voice, then pulling her hair, gasping, and crying. Kimball leaped from his chair and grabbed her just as she started rolling on the floor. Her dress slid up her legs as she struggled with him.

As a display of hysteria it was more than impressive, it was stupefying. The volume of sound Keeley was emitting made my ears ache. It went on and on, note rising on note, and was far more frightening than Kimball's threats.

'You bastard!' he shouted at me above the din. 'You're making this up.'

'If I'm making it up, ask your wife where she was a week last Friday,' I roared. I could feel the veins standing out on my neck.

By this time Keeley was making a kind of unearthly whooping sound, over and over, like some broken machine.

'Shut it, you fucking cunt!' the ex-Marine said gallantly. He then gave his wife, prone on the floor at his feet, a crack across the face that must have been audible a hundred yards away.

She did shut it. The noise stopped as suddenly as if someone had turned a switch. Keeley looked up at her husband like a frightened rabbit watching a snake.

'So where was she then?' he demanded.

'She was in Wilmslow with Lee, and on the Saturday morning Cheyenne was kidnapped and somebody in this room knows all about it.'

223

'I'm going to break your fucking neck for you anyway, Cunane, but how do you work that one out?' He sounded genuinely puzzled.

'You, or Keeley, but I think it was you, told someone that Lee has a safe full of money he can't account for.'

'You've got some bottle coming in here and telling me that.'

'Are you denying that Lee wouldn't invest in a business you wanted him to put money in?'

'That was months ago.'

'But when he wouldn't give you the money you told them his little secret, didn't you? About him and Jamie!'

'What if I did? The shit was asking for it. Did he think I'm some kind of fucking Eskimo that'd let him share my wife every time that whey-faced bitch he was married to wouldn't open her legs to order?'

'It's not true!' Keeley wailed.

'Oh, give it a rest. You never were any good at amateur theatricals. I've watched you making cow eyes at Lee for months. Do you think Mel didn't notice too? Where the hell do you think she was going that night in the fucking Porsche? She phoned me before she set off. She was coming here to have it out with you.'

'No, no, no!' Keeley insisted, beating the carpet with her fists.

'Who did you tell about the money?' I demanded. For my own satisfaction I had to hear him say that it was Judder Crockett. Neither Kimball nor I took any notice of Keeley's histrionics.

'Oh, so you don't know everything, Mr Clever Dick!' Kimball's eyes glittered with malicious pleasure. 'Well, fucking find out yourself because I'm not saying another fucking word.'

It's always a mistake to ignore an enraged woman. I think it's listed as error number three in the private detective's handbook and I'd just made it.

While Kimball and I were squaring up to each other Keeley rolled away from under her husband's feet and out of the room. She came back a second later with a golf club in her hand. It looked like a one wood and she took a swing with it that would have made work for the embalmer if she'd connected. I dodged her as she wound her arm back for another swing.

'Grab him!' she screamed at Kimball. 'He's a filthy liar! I'll beat the truth out of him.'

Kimball obliged.

While my attention was distracted he slipped behind me and grabbed me in a double-nelson. I tried to scrape his instep with the side of my leather shoe but he was ready for that and jerked his leg away. Keeley took another swing that would have seen me six feet under if I hadn't jumped backwards. She wasn't playing either. Despite her words, the only thing she was trying to beat out of me was my brains, such as they were. I used all the strength in my upper body to lever Kimball off the floor and stop him breaking my neck as he'd promised. I did a sort of crazy dance round the room with him attached while my attacker tried to line my head up for a three-hundred-yard tee-shot.

The driver whistled past the end of my nose. I was tiring fast when I saw Clint's face pressed against the window. He didn't hesitate. He picked up an ornamental wrought-iron bench and put it through the frame and then himself through after it. Glass and wood showered into the room. Sophistication isn't Clint's strong point. He fended Keeley off with one open hand while prising Kimball's fingers from the back of my neck. He was an adult dealing with children. There was no violence on Clint's part, just a lot more grunting and swearing from the Smathers as the wedded pair were deprived of their prey.

I jumped out through the window, heading for the car with Clint a step behind.

Kimball's Marine training must have helped him because

he recovered quickly and launched a counter-attack. He came after us like a rocket. Clint body-checked him, caught him and sort of folded him up. It was creepy watching the display of strength. Clint had turned the struggling Kimball in the direction of the gaping hole in the living room window when Keeley came out of the front door screeching like a fire engine under full emergency acceleration.

Gently, as if the ex-Marine was as light as a feather, Clint pushed Kimball towards the onrushing Keeley. They collided in mid-air with a crisp slapping sound and fell on to the lawn with a thump. Behind me I could hear ironic cheers from a group of neighbours gathered several doors away. I didn't wait to take a bow. The next sound I expected to hear was the wail of a police siren.

As soon as Clint was seated beside me we roared off into the night. A glance in the rear-view mirror revealed Kimball and Keeley feebly struggling to get up. They weren't dead then.

I slowed down as soon as I got round the corner. There was no point in being picked up for speeding. We cruised along in silence for a while until we reached the Pemberton district of Chester. I drove around aimlessly and finally we ended up in the car park of Chester City Football Club.

'I like football,' Clint announced.

I stopped the car and got out. I needed a moment of stillness while my heart stopped banging away in my chest.

Clint joined me.

'That man was a bad man, wasn't he?' he said.

'Quite a bad man.'

'He swears a lot, doesn't he? All those people in the street could hear him!'

'That was very wrong of him,' I agreed.

'I saw him hit the lady and then you started playing with them. I thought it was a game until I saw that your face had gone all red.'

'Thanks, Clint,' I said.

I patted myself down, allowing myself a silent moment of congratulation. For once I'd achieved a piece of rough-house detection without having the suit ripped off my back. Clint watched me checking myself out with a grave expression on his moonlike face.

'Shaken, but not shredded,' I announced.

Clint laughed until his sides shook.

'That's funny, Dave. "Shaken, but not shredded." I love Shredded Wheat.'

17

Janine was not amused.

Next morning we held a conference on the future of Clint.

'Dave, I don't know what you and he were up to last night and I don't think I want to know but Clint's wild with excitement. He keeps going on about bad men.'

'What could I do?' I asked lamely. 'I couldn't leave him here on his own, and as it happened he more or less saved my life.'

'No, Dave,' Janine said severely. 'He didn't more or less save your life, you put yourself into a dangerous position where Clint had no option but to help you. If you hadn't had him with you, you wouldn't have gone rushing into danger quite so quickly.'

I had no answer to that.

'The sad thing is, if Clint does someone a real mischief *you'll* probably get off with a caution while *he'll* end up somewhere like Broadmoor or Ashworth. Did you think of that?'

'It wasn't like that,' I protested. 'He was in the car outside . . .'

'Where he could see and hear everything this "bad man" was doing to you. Dave, it won't wash. We've either got to tell Bob Lane to come and collect him . . .'

'He hasn't been in touch.'

'. . . or find some other way of dealing with him.'

'Such as?'

'I've a friend on the paper who's part-owner of a stables out at Carrington. She can find a job for Clint as a labourer.'

'But that's what he was doing in Holland and he hated it.'

'He didn't. He liked the farm and the animals. He keeps talking about them.'

'Not to me.'

'That's because you don't listen. At least the inhabitants of Carrington speak English and Jane says the people at the stables are used to working with the handicapped. Clint might fit in well there and it'll certainly be better for him than us sitting round here wondering if the police are going to come and march the pair of you off in handcuffs.'

'That's not fair. The Smathers attacked me.'

'That's what all these rough boys say. Don't forget I've done court reporting, Dave. You get up in the dock and say that, and the first questions the prosecution will ask is what were you doing in their living room and why did you bring a twenty-two-stone, seven-foot man with you?'

'You're right,' I admitted grudgingly. 'I think your idea of the stables is OK but I'm only prepared to go along with it if Clint agrees. There's been enough shoving him into places where he didn't want to go. If he doesn't like the stables I'll have to take time off work and look after him here until Bob gets in touch.'

In the end we arranged for Naomi to take the children to school while Janine and I took Clint down to Carrington. There were two men playing football on a piece of land next to the stables when we got there and I think that swung it for Clint. He watched them, as fascinated as if they were a Premier League team. By the time we left he was getting instructions for his day's work, looking happy and relaxed.

'There, that wasn't too hard, was it?' the omnicompetent woman in my life asked when we parked her car in

229

Manchester. 'It might not be for long. I haven't heard any news about Bob on the grapevine, no starring role on *Crimewatch UK* or anything.'

'I haven't either,' I agreed. 'It's all a bit mystifying. I am sure he'll turn up smiling eventually.'

'Oh, so am I. All you big boys enjoy your games. I just think it's up to me to see that no one else gets hurt while you're having your fun.'

She gave me a warm kiss that cut off any thought of argument. We had a quick mutual grope and then went our separate ways.

Even so, I wasn't in the best of moods when I arrived at the office. There was nothing to report on File Red. There'd been several callers but just from people who wanted to know why I was after the trio, no one offering to supply information. I knew it might take weeks. That was where the late Charlie Costello had come in so useful as a short cut.

Back at the flat that night a thought did occur.

I'd cleared most of the stuff out of the small room I use as a home office and put a camp bed in there. There was no point in trying to put Clint on a camp bed. There isn't one big enough. At any rate, I was putting the camp bed up for myself. Before I fell precariously asleep thoughts of Charlie Costello returned to plague me. I imagined him setting off for home every night. He garaged his car in the sub-basement of an office near the Phoebus Club. Must have walked close to it every night. Then, I thought, suppose he spotted one of the three abductors by pure accident? Suppose discovery wasn't the result of Charlie's long acquaintance with the criminal underworld but just pure, or in this case bad, luck?

Porcupine Head was still my favourite to be picked out because before Charlie received a copy of Granville's pictures the most graphic description was of him. The other two were just nondescript white males. If he'd seen

Porcupine heading into the club it wouldn't have taken him long to find out who such a character was. Charlie was well connected with all bar and restaurant staff in central Manchester. But suppose whoever he spoke to let Porcupine know or maybe arranged to meet Charlie later.

That was what I told myself. The other possibilities were that Charlie's death was indeed a random mugging, and that my obsession with the Phoebus Club was all part of my own 'big boy's game'.

I woke early, my body as stiff and sore as if I'd slept on the bare ground. There was a groove in my head where the iron bar at the top of the bed had left its mark. Iron was entering my soul. Thunderous snores rattled out of the master bedroom as Clint slept on undisturbed while I put on a tracksuit. I slipped downstairs and got my mountain bike out of the garage and pedalled on to the Meadows.

It was dark and misty and damp along the Mersey which just suited my mood. If I was right about old Charlie sniffing round the Phoebus Club and being killed for it then my involving him in the investigation had cost him his life, but I had a lead. If I was wrong, and his death was just everyday random violence, then I had no lead. Gradually, as I worked up a sweat, I became more certain of myself. Of course I was right! Smathers hadn't admitted that he'd told Crockett about Lee Parkes's big secret but he wouldn't, would he? Jamie had let that cat out of the bag. He'd remembered Smathers trying to sell the health club deal to Lee.

When I got back to my flat everybody was in motion. Clint was dressed in his overalls. Naomi, bleary-eyed with sleep, had nevertheless fed him quantities of toast and cereals. I was superfluous to the domestic scene so quickly showered and dressed. The new arrangement was that a taxi would arrive to take Clint off to the stables so Janine and I were free to start our own morning's work. We went about our appointed tasks.

At the office the first thing I did was to check the answerphone. Again, there were only queries from the deranged, no one offering an identification. I'd been so certain I'd get a quick result with that.

Peter looked in. He was setting off for Gorton and points east with his pictures.

'You know, Boss . . . er, Dave . . . they say Moss Side is the criminal heartland of Manchester, but it isn't. Maybe a lot of dealers live there but there's a lot more violent crime up Cheetham Hill and Broughton and Gorton.'

'I did know that, Peter. So just make sure no one kicks your face in when you go up there.'

'No danger of that when I'm with Andy Gilby. He knows a lot of the crooked element. He's banged up most of them up at one time or another.'

'Stick to him like glue,' I ordered. 'There's a meeting this afternoon at three. Michael will be back from London and he's going to fill us in on what he's found out about the brothers.'

'Andy's been telling me a lot about the job.'

'You have a job with me.'

'No, about the police. I'm thinking of having another medical examination. The heart murmur might have improved.'

'The institutional racism doesn't put you off, then? You still want to be one of the boys in blue?'

'Don't get me wrong, Dave. I love this job. It's just that some weeks I spend hours proving that some silly fool's trying to con the insurance company and then I go home and I think, why shouldn't he? A bloke who'll hobble round on crutches for eight months when there's nothing wrong with his legs deserves some sort of reward.'

'You do lots of other things. Like today, for instance. Or I could put you on to more admin work. Levonne likes you home at night. She won't get that if you're a constable. You know the arguments about so-called victimless crimes. I think we're doing some good by making insurance fraud more of a challenge for these hobbling bozos.'

'OK, Boss, back here at three,' Peter said as he left. He didn't sound convinced.

At three Michael, Celeste, Marvin and Peter but not Janine assembled in my room.

'Where's the lovely Janine?' Marvin asked. 'Has she got a pressing engagement?'

'Very funny, Marvin,' Celeste replied. 'She phoned to say that the paper's sent her to Ashton-under-Lyne to interview members of the Gujarati community and she won't be back until late.'

I put up the board with the pictures on. Celeste had pinned a picture of Jamie to one corner. I started by going through everything I'd found out. It didn't take me very long.

Then Michael Coe began speaking.

'I did find out quite a bit,' he began, with a defensive glance at Celeste. 'I found their birth certificates and I found their parents' marriage certificate to start with.'

He put the copies on my desk.

'So we know they're not a pair of bastards,' Marvin commented with a smile. 'Legally speaking, that is.'

Celeste nudged him sharply in the ribs.

'You'll see the father's occupation is listed as club manager. I tracked down the name of the club. It was the Old Bow Bells Sporting Club, actually in Hackney not Bow.'

'So?' Peter asked. 'Hackney . . . Bow . . . what difference does it make?'

'None,' Michael said quickly, 'except that the money to open a lot of these clubs in that part of London came from the crime scene. Heavyweight crims hired more or less straight faces as fronts. They had to, couldn't get a licence otherwise.'

'Not the good old Krays?' Marvin asked.

I was thinking exactly the same thing.

'There were lots of criminal firms in that part of London. Still are. We're talking about the early seventies when Reggie and Ronnie had already been banged up for the "Jack the Hat" McVittie killing. I've no evidence that Mr Parkes Senior, middle name Antonio by the way, was anything other than legit as a club manager.'

'Wait a minute,' I said. 'What was the father's name?'

'Dennis Antonio Parkes.'

'But why did you make a point about the Antonio?'

Michael sighed wearily. 'I was in intelligence work in the Army, Dave, remember? Maybe I was only an electronics tech but it was still intelligence.'

I nodded.

'First thing you do when you're vetting someone is check up on their parents' background. It's not very politically correct these days but I shouldn't think you'd get past the initial interview at Century House if even one of your parents or grandparents comes from a target country.'

'What you saying, man?' Marvin said forcefully. 'Cut to the chase.'

'The point is that according to the death notice in the local paper Dennis Antonio Parkes was known as "Dino". I was only saying that seeing the name Antonio on the marriage certificate alerted me to go through the local papers and find out more about the father.'

'What's wrong with Dino, then?' Celeste asked. 'Probably he was nicknamed Dinosaur.'

'No,' Michael said patiently. 'He was probably of Italian extraction, and in case you don't know it organised crime in London was dominated by families of Italian extraction for the earlier part of the twentieth century every bit as much as it was in New York, if not more so.'

Marvin gave an excited laugh at this.

Celeste began humming the theme music from *The Godfather*.

'Can it,' Marvin said. 'I love that film and *Godfather II*. Marlon Brando, Robert DeNiro . . . *Goodfellas*. I've got all those videos. This is great, Mickey! If only it was true.'

'What do you mean?' Michael exploded. 'Have you never heard of the Sabinis? They ran crime in the south of England until well after the Second World War. It's just that we never had Prohibition in this country like they did in the States. It was Prohibition that turned those Italian American crime families into billion-dollar businesses. Before that they just ran protection rackets like the ones in England.'

'All right, calm down,' I entreated. 'I can accept that Lee and Jamie's dad may have been on the fringes of organised crime but where does that take us?'

'I haven't finished yet. Dennis Antonio Parkes and his wife Julia were killed in 1979 in a car crash – except it wasn't a simple car crash. The brakes of their car had been tampered with and they went smack into the front of a lorry in the Blackwall Tunnel. Now, I haven't got access to police archives but there are lots of true crime books and one of them, called *London Crime Gangs* by John Merton, has this to say about the accident.'

He took a photocopied page out of his file and read aloud.

'"Police investigation into the death of Dino Parkes and his wife was cursory to say the least. A theory circulated that Dino Parkes was trying his luck in the one-armed bandit business south of the river at the time of his death, which may have been due to an intended spot of 'discouragement' that misfired. Parkes, who is widely held to have had undercover connections with a well-known East London gang, was certainly an unwelcome visitor south of the Thames where coin-in-the-slot gambling was a jealously guarded monopoly of certain south London firms. Parkes's death was investigated by police who stated that the damage to the brakes of his Jaguar car could have been due to

235

faulty maintenance rather than deliberate interference. The coroner directed the jury to return a verdict of death by misadventure at the inquest but Dino Parkes's friend, Jack Piercy, insisted there'd been a cover up. For several months he tried to stir up a campaign in the press to have the case reinvestigated by an outside police force. Piercy insisted that Parkes loved the Jag and had it serviced regularly."'

'Jack Piercy?'

'Yes, the same. He adopted Jamie and brought him up as his own, but for some reason I haven't been able to find yet, he and his wife didn't adopt Lee.'

'Perhaps they didn't like him,' Celeste said. 'He was older.'

'Whatever,' agreed Michael. 'Lee was placed in a local authority children's home. He was then fostered by Henry John Binns, a bakery van man, and his wife Maureen, and later legally adopted by them.'

'This is fascinating stuff,' Marvin said. 'Does it mean that Jamie Piercy, the football hero who scored against Italy, should have been playing for them and not England? Just goes to show, doesn't it?'

'Show what?' I growled irritably. I was getting tired of Marvin's commentary.

'Hey, man! We all live up to our stereotypes. That's what it shows,' he said. 'Lee and Jamie, they is really Eyeties – into conspiracy, but real good at football. Dave here, de master, he's really a Paddy – into bombs and secret shootings. Michael – well, he's an empire builder. He'll discover somewhere or annex a small country soon.'

'And what about you, fool?' Celeste demanded. 'Where do you fit in?'

Marvin started doing a soft-shoe shuffle.

'Why, Celeste, don't you know? You, me and good old Peter in his nice suit, we're the clowns of the world, put here to spread smiles and sunshine wherever we go.'

I was feeling a bit sick at all this. Not at Marvin's little piece of entertainment but at the revelation that Jamie's adoptive relatives might well have their own criminal connections. Suppose he had let slip to one of them that Lee had something in his safe worth extracting? A horrible prospect of investigation on top of investigation opened up before me. I'd be lucky to wrap this one up before I became entitled to an OAP's bus pass.

'Sorry, Dave! Only joking!' Marvin said when he saw my expression.

'No, it's not you, though there's many a true word and all that. What I want you to tell me is this. Is it worthwhile maintaining a watch on the Phoebus Club or going on distributing those pictures? For all we know the three men we're after might be in London or Essex by now.'

'Dave, those pictures cost six hundred pounds,' Celeste said.

'Water under the bridge. I gave Charlie Costello five hundred.'

'They're local, Dave,' Peter argued. 'How would they know about Alderley Edge otherwise? And don't forget the Evergreens. Someone from Phoebus could easily have had the key to that place. Going in and out with a key would have attracted a lot less attention for the kidnappers than just smashing their way in. Don't forget the alarms had to be switched off.'

'If they're so local why haven't you and Gilby turned up something by now?'

'Give us a chance. We've only been at it for three days.'

'Sorry,' I muttered. 'I sometimes let my enthusiasm get the better of me. But we haven't got the resources of the police force. If we don't start making a few more connections by next week we're going to have to give this up.'

I arranged for Michael to fix electronic surveillance of the Phoebus Club entrance as soon as he could.

At home that night I discussed the gloomy outlook with Janine. We were washing the pots after the evening meal. She doesn't approve of dishwashers on ecological grounds.

'It could be a London firm that kidnapped Cheyenne,' I concluded. 'We'll never find them now.'

'What's got into you, Dave? You never used to be like this. Is it because I stopped you using Clint?'

'Of course not!'

'You've had a long face on you since yesterday.'

'You were right about Clint.'

'I don't think you're sleeping properly. You'd better give the camp bed a miss tonight.'

'Is that meant as a romantic invitation?'

'Take it any way you like,' she said with a pout and a laugh.

Just then Lloyd came into the kitchen. He must have heard the mention of Clint. 'Dave, is Clint the strongest man in England?' he asked.

'I don't know. Why do you ask?'

'Naomi says he can pick up a pony under each arm. Can you do that, Dave?'

'Of course Dave can't,' Janine said quickly.

'I've never even tried it. I might manage two very, very small ponies.'

'Like Shetland ponies?' Lloyd asked. He sounded disappointed.

'Could be.'

'Clint's told Naomi that he picked up two proper-sized ponies today.'

Boasting was not one of Clint's failings. I looked at Janine. She shrugged her shoulders.

'If he says he did it we've got to believe him,' I told Lloyd.

'So he is the strongest man in England?'

'Well, in Chorlton cum Hardy at least,' I conceded.

When we were in bed together Janine said, 'Dave, I know you took this case because of what happened to that baby . . .'

'I took the case because I was bored.'

'You took it because of the baby. I know you better than you know yourself, Cunane.'

'OK. It's just that the thought of someone slamming that car boot down on a sick child then getting away with it is a bit much.'

'Yes, it is. Keep plugging away for a bit longer. Something's bound to turn up.'

18

The break didn't come that week or the week after.

I got a phone call from Anna Pietrangeli after two weeks of useless checking of phone calls and staring at blurry video images of short black men, fat black men, tall thin black men, tall muscular black men, but not at spiky-headed black men. Ninety per cent of our callers revealed themselves to be nuts as soon as they opened their mouths. The ones who did give us something to check were either fraudulent or deceived. Anna rang just as I was leaving the office on a Tuesday evening. I'd also had half the Pimpernel staff including myself out scanning the streets near the health club. Again, result nil. There was all the other work of the firm piling up on top of this and I was beginning to feel frayed around the edges.

'Dave, have you found that girl yet?' Anna asked.

It took me a moment to remember what she was talking about.

'You said you'd keep in touch and I've been expecting a call. You know, I did that drawing for you?'

'Sorry, Anna. I was miles away. I'm just finishing up at work.'

'Another day's detecting done, eh?'

'Something like that. We still haven't been able to identify that guy you described for Granville Courteney.'

'Well, that's not my fault. That drawing he did was as good as a photograph. Is that why you haven't called?'

'No,' I mumbled. 'I've been busy.'

'You know what they say about all work and no play, don't you Dave?' She gave a tinkling little laugh. 'I only mention it because I've got an invitation to a party at the Phoebus Club. It's one of Judder's special parties. The invitation's for two.'

'Oh, yes?'

'I've finished with Geoff Smith. You know, my divorced head of department? The school head's warned him to stop harassing me. He only communicates by note now.' She gave her tinkling laugh again. 'That was down to you really, Dave. The way you stood up to him and told me to give him the elbow was just the push I needed. I saw him for what he was.'

'Always ready to help a lady.'

'Are you? Well, in that case I'm going to be a bit pushier. Would you like to come to this party with me? I mean, it *is* a new millennium and a girl's allowed to ask. You can only say no. It's not as if you're a married man or anything. I mean, you're far too determined to let me snatch you away from your lovely partner, aren't you?'

'Whoah!' I said. 'Yes, a girl's allowed to ask and a man's allowed to answer.'

'Right.'

'When is this party?'

'It's this Friday,' she said breathlessly.

'What time shall I pick you up?'

When I put the phone down I recalled Michael's suspicions about Italian connections but dismissed them. While it might be true that some Italians had been involved in organised crime in England that was surely only the tiniest of tiny minorities? In the period he was talking about crime had been at an all-time low anyway. Events that wouldn't even rate a line in a national paper now would have earned screaming headlines in the thirties. Anna Pietrangeli didn't sound as if she was trying to involve me in organised crime, she sounded as if she wished to involve herself in

241

a conspiracy of two — her and me. As for Marvin Desailles, well, he would pick up racist overtones after a day on retreat in a Trappist monastery. The man was obsessed.

I left the office. It was my turn to spend an hour trudging the highways and by-ways near the Phoebus Club in the hope of spotting someone. As usual, it was a waste of shoe leather although I was beginning to recognise the faces of the people moving around the streets at that time. I tried to remember stories my father had told me about protracted stakeouts that had eventually paid off. There weren't any. It was hard not to be discouraged.

The invitation from Anna couldn't have come at a better time. Janine had booked into a hotel at Alton Towers for a two-night stay starting this coming Friday. She was taking Clint and Naomi as well. I'd cried off at an early stage in the arrangements. I can't stand all the queuing at these theme parks. So whatever Ms Pietrangeli had in mind for Friday evening I was up for it.

I finished work early on Friday to give Janine a hand with packing everyone into the car. They were taking my Mondeo. I told myself that the appointment with Anna was just an innocent work-related detail that Janine didn't need to know about. Things had been going well between us and I didn't want any strife.

'You seem very keen to see the back of us,' she commented as I secured her case to the roof rack. Although they were only going for two days they had so many cases that a pick-up truck would have been more suitable than a family car. Eventually, I got it stowed. Janine gave me a warm kiss.

'You're up to something Dave, I know you,' she said. 'Behave yourself until we get back.' She patted my cheek.

Clint finds it incredibly funny to see me being chided by her.

'Behave yourself, Dave,' he repeated, laughing out loud. The children joined in.

Even Naomi managed a smile.

Not for the first time I thought about my domestic situation as the car disappeared down the road. If I've asked Janine to marry me once I've asked her a hundred times. It's always the same answer. She doesn't want to commit herself to a permanent relationship. I do, that's the trouble. So whatever Janine thinks about commitment to me, I regard myself as committed to her. If Ms Pietrangeli had anything more than partying on her mind she was going to be disappointed.

I arrived at her home at nine. She was wearing a long black self-patterned dress with a beautiful light blue pashmina over her shoulders. A single pearl hung on a golden chain round her neck. She looked stunning. She bent forward and I delivered a chaste kiss on her cheek. Her perfume was something fragrant and expensive that I didn't recognise. I felt a little surge of familiar excitement. Then I remembered my obligations.

'Won't you come in? I like to have a drink before I go to these things,' she said.

'Dutch courage?'

'No, Judder's parties are great. I just like to feel a little high before I go in. He keeps you on your toes with all those questions of his.'

She led me up the stairs to a lounge. An Ikea sofa and armchair, coffee table, a gate-leg table and two dining chairs by the window were comfortably spaced in a quite large area. Everything looked new. There was a bookcase with a lot of books about running and computer science but no television. A stereo system was mounted on one wall. These were painted a warm shade of terracotta and there were several abstract pictures. The floor was sanded and polished wood.

'What do you think?' she asked. 'Cosy, isn't it? Geoff was mad to think I'd want to move into his junkyard.'

'This is certainly shipshape. I live on my own but I seem

to be accumulating non-paying guests and their luggage at the moment.'

'Oh, I thought you said you have a partner?' she said quickly.

'I do. She lives in the next-door flat with her two children.'

'Yours?'

'Unfortunately not. They're Janine's by a previous marriage. At the moment I'm accommodating her nanny and a handicapped young man who's the brother of a friend of mine.'

She went to the gate-leg table where she had several bottles and glasses arranged on a mat and offered me a drink. I took a small whisky and she had a large Martini. She smiled at me. Her eyes had a lustrous quality. I smiled back.

'Well, Cinders, has she given you a time to be home by?' she said sadly.

'Janine's away this weekend.'

She coloured slightly.

'Would you like the full guided tour?' she asked, and without waiting for a reply showed me the bedroom, dominated by a four-poster bed covered in a hand-embroidered quilt, the kitchen, which was where she kept the television, and the bathroom. Everything was catalogue fresh and smelled new. The only jarring note was a full ashtray under the kitchen sink.

'A friend smokes. I hate to flush the butts down the toilet,' she explained.

I made no comment as she emptied them into a pedal bin.

'Small and neat but my own.'

'Neat and perfect, like its owner.'

'Why did you come?' she demanded bluntly.

'You invited me.'

'That wasn't true about the arranged marriage, was it?

I could tell by your voice on the phone. You couldn't remember what you'd said.'

'It's true a girl was kidnapped,' I admitted. 'I'm sorry for lying. The case I'm on is confidential and if I told the truth people would immediately get in touch with the police which would defeat the whole object of the exercise.'

'Have you found the girl?'

'Yes.'

'But there's something more, isn't there?'

'A child was involved. I'm sorry but I can't say more.'

'Judder Crockett's mixed up in it in some way, isn't he? You were so eager when I told you about the party. I thought it was because you wanted to see me but it's something to do with him, isn't it?'

'Are you always this perceptive?' I asked. 'You shouldn't sell yourself short, you're a very beautiful woman and I'm flattered that you invited me.'

'Except you're already spoken for and you thought you'd have a bit of fun this weekend while your partner's away.'

I looked into her face. She was serious now. Her face was lively and intelligent, dark eyes positively glowing with insight. I wondered if I could trust her and then decided I would. My investigation was going nowhere fast anyway.

'The case I'm on involves a clever villain extorting money from very rich people who daren't go to the police because then they'd have to explain how they came by that money.'

'You're so clever, Mr Cunane . . .'

'Dave, please.'

'Dave. I don't know whether to believe you. Presumably the money's drug money or proceeds of some other crime?'

'Not drugs in this particular case . . . a sort of white-collar crime. But whatever the parents have done, their children are completely innocent.'

245

She thought about this for a moment.

'I think I trust you,' she said. 'You seemed so genuine that day you ran after me and nearly ended up under the lorry. How is Judder involved?'

'That's what I'm hoping to find out. One lead goes to him.'

'And you thought you'd go to his party with me as camouflage? What are you going to do, turn the place over for clues while you're there?'

'No,' I said with a laugh. 'My plans aren't finalised. Listen, have you seen a man called Thompson? I hear he's Judder's minder.'

'I don't know about minder. Aaron Thompson's a friend of Judder's. He's always working at the weights. I don't know why, he's massively built already.'

'What does he look like?'

'He's very dark, about six foot four, and he isn't very pretty.'

'What about his hair?'

'What is this, Dave? I think he was close-cropped the last time I saw him.'

'Close-cropped!' I exploded.

'What have I said?' she retorted in alarm.

I sat back and didn't feel too pleased with myself. Why had I assumed that the man with the spiky haircut would keep it that way indefinitely?

'Tell,' she said.

I took out one of my postcards.

'These are the three men who carried out the abduction. There's your man. I think this one is Aaron Thompson. There's no face shown, just the haircut which was all I had on him. Have you ever seen him with spiky hair like this?'

'I don't live in the Phoebus Club, you know, and I don't see Thompson every time I go. But I think I'd have noticed hair like that.'

246

'I've been a complete fool. I kept getting these descriptions of a powerful-looking black man but I discounted Thompson because someone told me he had long straight hair.'

'Cropped when I saw him, but then there are such things as wigs.'

'There are,' I admitted.

'This is really interesting. What are you going to do if you find that Thompson is the one?'

'Nothing, I need to find evidence to link him to the other two and then somehow prove they were responsible.'

'Let's get going then,' she said. 'I haven't been so excited since my form won the school netball trophy.'

We drove into town on the A34 and parked in a multi-storey near the Crown Courts. As we crossed the road to the club I was startled to see that the party was much more of a happening than I'd anticipated. There were two policemen on the pavement for a start and people were being dropped off by limousines. Bystanders had gathered to gawp.

I was puzzled that the whole phenomenon of Judder and his parties had somehow passed me by. My existence must be more cloistered and routine than I'd appreciated. Janine and I should obviously have been down here living it up among the real swingers instead of sampling Victorian taverns and lottery-funded theatres.

Anna handed me the tickets. We entered the Phoebus Club to find the foyer decked out in brightly lit solar emblems in honour of the sun god, Phoebus Apollo. Arrows and rays were everywhere. Young women in classical Greek costume, clutching lyres and pan pipes, inspected our tickets and ushered us to a special lift which took us to the fourth floor. Here we reached a closed-off area where more white-robed females pinned large solar discs with our names on to us and issued us with curious party hats in the shape of a flaming solar disc.

Sheepish-looking youths in white tunics with ivy leaves twined in their hair and silly-looking sandals on their feet offered us a choice of Buck's Fizz or cheap bubbly.

There was a frenetic atmosphere of noise and excitement as people milled around. Upper-class tones mingled with flat local accents. Drink flowed freely as the ivy-wreathed waiters replenished empty glasses. If you'd wanted you could have downed a pint of champagne in as many seconds as it took the waiters to pour it. From the way the volume of sound began to rise several citizens were trying to do just that. Anna looked delighted with it all but I found it hard to work up any feeling apart from wariness. Scanning the room, I didn't see anyone I knew. No one resembling the trio on my postcard. Then I spotted the combed-over dome of Ernie Cunliffe through the alcoholic haze. He was with his wife, short, plump and sweating, to whom I'd been introduced but whose name I'd forgotten.

'Turn round,' I said to Anna. 'There's someone over there I don't want to meet.'

'Friend of your partner's?' she enquired, raising her pretty dark eyebrows.

'No, nothing like that, just the biggest bore in Manchester, that's all.'

We joined a long procession of people lined up behind a rope.

'Didn't I tell you Judder knows how to throw a party?' Anna asked.

'This is going to be a unique experience,' I said. I kept peering round hoping to spot Thompson. There was no sign of him but I found it difficult to switch off after three weeks of searching.

'Relax, you're making me nervous,' Anna whispered.

In the large party area created by closing off the restaurant the classical theme was continued with weird Apollonian music and other effects. Spotlights illustrating large pictures of Greek gods provided what little light there was. The bar area was disguised as a temple complete with Ionic columns. In a corner an artificial cave had been created and a female grappled with what appeared to be a very large python in the smoke rising from a three-legged burner. As we inched closer I could see that the python was actually made of rubber but the illusion was convincing enough. The woman was chanting something and I could have sworn I detected a whiff of the dreaded weed among the fumes she was dispersing into the room.

'What's that supposed to be?'

'She's the Oracle at Delphi,' Anna explained. 'She'll tell our fortunes later.'

'Weird,' I said. 'This is Weirdsville, Oklahoma.'

'Weirdsville, Oklahoma!' she exploded. 'If you think this is Weirdsville you must lead a sheltered life.'

'Just a turn of phrase.'

'Why in the Gay Village . . .'

'Sorry . . . Normalville, Normalchester. Is that OK?'

'Just enjoy it,' she said, putting her finger to her lips as we neared the presentation area. Here we found Judder Crockett himself, dressed as Phoebus in a white robe with a crown of sun rays on his head, greeting his guests from a seat in a four-horse chariot. The horses were half-sized and made of polystyrene and Crockett, with his stiff brushed-forward hair and ageing face, looked anything but godlike, but again he was going to a lot of trouble to create an illusion.

As well as himself, Crockett's chariot contained a large, spiky flashing sun about five feet in diameter from which rays seemed to shoot out over the whole room. I didn't know how it was done but it was clever.

In front of his chariot there was a smaller two-horse replica containing an almost naked young woman with the name 'Eos the Dawn' pinned to the scanty fragment of scarlet material that revealed more of her chest than it concealed.

We waited patiently in line to be greeted by our host. He had something to say to each couple. It was like a Royal Command Performance. There was no sign of Thompson.

'The delightful Miss Anna,' Crockett gushed when we reached him. He shook my hand limply, 'and the detective of her choice. Didn't I tell you to persist with him, my dear? Greetings, greetings.' One of his attendant nymphs checked the names on our solar tags, ticked us off a list and sorted through a large quiver full of golden arrows before handing Crockett two with Anna's name on. He passed them to us with a flourish. 'These are your admission to the cave of the oracle, don't lose them,' he said. 'You must meet my companion, Eos the Dawn. She rides before me.'

Eos the Dawn turned and flashed an insipid smile at us.

'Give these two extra petals, they're friends of mine,' he instructed her.

He waved us on with a flourish of his arm. I thought Crockett's memory was fairly impressive considering that I'd only met him for five minutes three weeks previously.

'How well do you know the old Sun god?' I asked as we shuffled forward to be greeted by Eos the Dawn.

'Shush! He might hear us,' she whispered.

The Dawn's plump bare arms were plastered with real rose petals. With a simpering smile she graciously handed us each a paper replica. Her hands were dyed scarlet. Then, remembering the Sun god's order, she gave us two more petals.

'Keep those,' Anna instructed me. 'They entitle us to free drinks at the bar.'

'Do you mean, we have to pay otherwise?' I asked.

'The food and wine are free and you get one free drink at the bar for a rose petal.'

'Not so godlike with his favours then, old Phoebus.'

'He is,' she insisted. 'When I first joined the club Judder

was very good to me. I was coming out of an unhappy relationship.'

'Geoff?'

'No, it was before him. Anyway, Judder looked after me for a long time and got me back on my feet again.'

'Did he?'

'Don't look like that! Physical therapy, running, swimming. It helps you to get back your balance. I'm telling you, Judder's a very kind man. Whatever Thompson may have done, I'm sure Judder knows nothing about it. There's nothing weird about him really.'

I had to be content with that. We found seats and waited as the room gradually filled up with the noisy crowd from the entrance area. We traded our petals for drinks and waited for something to happen. The Apollonian music gave way to throbbing techno and some couples started dancing. I felt stupid standing there clutching an arrow.

We went over to the oracle, now seated inside her cave. I was ninety per cent certain that it was marijuana that she'd been burning, that or some other classified herb. For want of something else to do we joined the queue for fortune-telling. The glazed-looking priestess was seated on a three-legged stool when we entered her den, rubber python dumped in a corner. Close up, the oracle was almost elderly. When we entered she focused on us and peered unsteadily into a crystal ball mounted on a pedestal beside her.

She took Anna's hand in hers. Anna passed over her golden arrow and to my surprise the woman held it close to her eyes and read the name on it.

'You have made an important decision and freed yourself from something that was holding you back,' she announced. 'Beware, though, the future is clouded. Ahhhh! I see one path now. It is bright and sunny. There is an older, wiser companion leading you to happiness. Now there is another

251

path but it is clouded and dark. Make a wise decision again, my dear.'

Then she dipped her hand into a bag at her feet, rummaged around and came up with a small gift which she pressed into Anna's hand.

For me she prophesied 'many changes, much prosperity'.

My gift was a pen.

'Cheeky slut!' Anna said when we came out. She unwrapped her gift, a small box.

'Like Santa's Grotto,' I suggested. The box appeared to be gold.

'Not at all,' she muttered angrily. 'Judder tells her what to say to people, that's why she has to know your name. He sends you a message through her.'

'What's yours?'

'Why, don't you know?' she said, opening the box and dangling the keys it contained. 'Judder wants me to move in with him. *These* are the keys to his penthouse.'

'The randy old goat!' I commented.

'He isn't. He's bisexual or something. I've never established quite what his preferences are. He likes to fondle women but that's about as far as he goes! I'd sooner live on candyfloss for a month than move in with him.'

She stamped her foot.

'Maybe you're right. This is Weirdsville.'

I smiled.

'Shut up,' she snapped, fighting back tears. 'I'm fed up of being used.'

'I didn't speak,' I protested.

'No, but you were going to.'

I laughed and as I did we were plunged into darkness. Anna jumped forward and we embraced.

There was a fanfare and then a single spotlight picked out Judder Crockett. The white-kilted wine waiters were dragging his chariot, horses and all, along a curving route into the centre of the room. As he came on he flung out

252

handfuls of gifts to right and left. I caught one, a small packet of Belgian chocolates. Anna picked up another, a tiny bottle of scent.

'He usually puts a few fifty-pound notes in with these,' she said, as we watched dinner-jacketed men get down on the floor and scramble for the packets. 'Even holidays on health farms.'

'How generous,' I muttered. I'd no intention of getting down on my hands and knees in front of Judder Crockett.

When he reached the centre of the room he hung the solar disc on a hook and shouted, 'Let there be light!' The spotlight moved from him to the disc which reflected beams all over the room and gradually the main lights came back up. In spite of myself I found the effect striking.

A floor show started with nymphs and shepherds performing complicated gyrations around Phoebus Crockett.

'Come on, this is our chance!' I said. I pulled Anna out of the room to the entrance area. It was deserted now.

'What are you doing?' she said indignantly.

'Looking for Thompson.'

'Are you mad?'

'Yes,' I replied, 'but I've only just started. I'll get really mad in a few minutes.'

She looked confused, uncertain whether to laugh or summon psychiatric assistance. I smiled, and she came over and took my hand.

'He's very strong, you know,' she warned.

I shrugged.

In front of us there were two large lift entrances, one for the 'private' lift we'd arrived in and another which was in ordinary use. The indicator was showing that it was in motion. There was no security camera.

'You can't get off this floor except by the fire escape,' she said, 'and that only takes you out to the street, not to the other floors. The public lift will go no higher than the third floor tonight and you need a special key for the one we came in.'

'Where does that door lead to?' I asked, pointing to a silvery metal doorway alongside the lift doors. There was a handle and a lock and it was also secured with a padlock.

'That goes up to the penthouse. Judder lives up there with his women.'

'Needs to feel secure, does he? He has all his guests corralled on to one floor while his own quarters are locked and padlocked, yet you think he's just a benevolent old poof.'

I looked around. There was a massive fire hose in a red cylinder and secured above that a fire axe behind a sheet of glass. I whipped my shoe off and smashed the glass. Behind me, Anna looked shocked. I took out a pair of rubber gloves and put them on. The axe was the genuine article, a massive heavy head with a hook as well as a blade. I whacked the padlock with all my strength.

The axe bounced back at me. In the confined area where we stood the sound was overwhelming. I thought I could feel the steel frame of the building vibrate.

Anna Pietrangeli stared at me open-mouthed. I was surprised at myself. Shame at my own stupidity in not realising that Porcupine Head would have changed his appearance was what drove me on. He must have passed me in the street during my surveillance walks outside the club.

'But these are the keys,' she said.

'And if we use them he'll know it was you who entered his private quarters,' I said. 'In for a penny, in for a pound,' I muttered. The noise from the party continued unabated.

I laid into the padlock with every ounce of strength. It took me at least twenty blows. I had to lever the securing bolts out of the door. The door had sprung from its frame and was jammed. There was no movement in either direction.

Determined not to be defeated by inanimate objects I kept on swinging and levering. My hands felt incandescent inside the rubber gloves. I wrapped the axe handle in a handkerchief. The more the door resisted, the madder I got. Eventually, with great sounds of metal grating on metal, I levered it open.

'You crazy idiot!' Anna gasped. 'It opens the other way!'

I laughed. She must have thought I really was crazy – Mad Dave the Axeman. She caught my mood and giggled.

'Have you been up here before?' I asked as we went up the stairs to the penthouse.

'No,' she said quickly. 'Well, just once,' she corrected.

The penthouse was exactly that – a house set up on the roof as an afterthought, not part of the original building. Of modular construction, it was big. I found it hard to estimate how much space it occupied in relation to the floor space of the club. At a guess, at least half. The smoked-glass walls were positioned well back from the edge of the building on all sides. Those parts of the roof which the structure didn't occupy were covered by a Japanese-style garden with brushed gravel, hanging lanterns, miniature pagodas and plants in oriental tubs. There was even a raised pond with koi carp swimming under an anti-bird netting. The reflected lights of Manchester gleamed on the surface of the pool.

I advanced on the smoked-glass door with my axe at the ready. It had an opulent look to it. A chrome lock and handle were set into the glass.

'No need for that,' Anna said as I raised the axe, 'it's never locked.' She turned the door handle and pushed the door open. Using the handkerchief from the axe I wiped the door where she'd touched it and gave her a pair of rubber gloves. Shaking her head doubtfully, she put them on.

There were no visible cameras or alarms. Judder must have decided that the only way an uninvited guest was

255

going to get on the roof was via a helicopter and even that would be quite a trick with all the irregular-sized buildings rubbing shoulders with this one.

Inside the glass door there was a large central lounge sunk about three feet below the roof level. A raised mezzanine ran all the way around. Circular stairs set diagonally opposite each other led upwards from the mezzanine floor to a balcony running round the whole room. I put my hand on a dimmer switch set in the wall beside me and turned it on. An immense modern crystal chandelier in the shape of a Winged Victory shed light over the whole huge room. There was enough space there for a full-sized basketball court, I thought inconsequentially.

'Some pad!' I exclaimed.

'We shouldn't be here,' Anna whispered.

The floor was cluttered. There were heavy metal and leather sofas, chairs, an electrically operated recliner, a table tennis table, throw rugs, a bar football game, an exercise bike, several old-fashioned coin-in-the-slot pinball machines, a small church organ, tables, a cooking area with ovens and utilities set in a screened-off alcove, and a dining table with six place settings. A cunningly lit bronze statue of a Greek god formed the centrepiece.

Cumulatively it was overwhelming. Here at last was a living room that would dwarf Clint Lane.

Around the walls there were niches containing classical statues, vases on pedestals, large photographs of Greek temples, and reproductions of the horses and warriors from the Parthenon frieze. Dramatic lighting revealed that the niche walls were decorated with obscene Pompeii-style paintings showing naked gods and goddesses in interesting postures. All tastefully done in 'antiqued' colours, mind you. The entire length of one wall was occupied by a bookcase crammed with all kinds of books, small objects, videos and CD cassettes.

I ran towards the tall bookcase, rocked it forward to the

point of overbalancing and then pushed the whole thing over. It collapsed against one of the sofas sending a cascade of debris across the entire floor area.

'What are you doing!' Anna screamed.

There was no secret compartment behind the bookcase. I ran round the room tipping up chairs, throwing cushions about, overturning tables and generally wrecking the place.

'This is a casual robbery!' I said to Anna.

She looked at me in fearful horror, biting the joint of her forefinger through the rubber glove.

'It's got to look that way,' I explained. 'Help me!'

I headed up the nearest circular stair to the other rooms. The master bedroom was very plain, the only frivolous touches being a mirrored ceiling and a huge projection television facing the emperor-sized bed.

I hurriedly emptied the drawers and discovered that Crockett had an extensive collection of thongs as well as every designer label on the market. Calvin and Tommy and Yves and Giorgio and Hugo had all made their contributions. Gee, the gang's all here, I thought as I flung everything into a heap on the floor.

I hit pay dirt in the bottom of a wardrobe. There was a cardboard box containing hundreds of pictures of Crockett on beaches with much younger men in bathing costumes. All races were represented, a true United Nations. One from near the top showed him with his arm round a muscular brown-skinned man with a villainously ugly face. The man's head, clean-shaven and oiled, gleamed like the rising sun. There were palm trees and a deep blue sea in the background. It had to be Thompson on his native isle.

'That's him,' Anna confirmed over my shoulder.

There were several more pictures of Thompson in various poses. I folded one inside my jacket pocket. A second wardrobe contained a comprehensive selection of bondage gear, whips, manacles, shackles, oddly shaped electrical implements and various rubber goods. I threw them down on to the pile of clothes. My mother's jumble sale collections were never like this.

'I'd no idea he went in for all this,' Anna breathed.

'This was a treat in store for you, then,' I said. 'Do you want to change your mind?'

She shook her head, numbed by the sheer amount of material the man kept in his bedroom.

Three of the other rooms were obviously women's bedrooms. A picture in one of them showed Crockett with his heavenly friend 'Eos the Dawn'. They were both naked. Another showed him in a jacuzzi with the Dawn and two other naked, or at least topless, young women, all blondes. Not a single bare boob in Judder's bedroom but here six at once. What was he trying to prove?

Thompson's bedroom was more interesting. There were Fijian carvings, some showing little bent human figures doing nasty things to each other. There was a stone club hanging by a cord on the wall behind the bed. It wasn't a museum piece. There was a sinister brown stain on it. It was similar in shape to a rounders bat, about seventeen inches long with a thickened end and a thinner handle. The cord, made from some rough hemp-like string, was threaded through a hole in the handle. The weapon itself had been manufactured from green-coloured stone.

I took it off the wall and weighed it in my hand. Were the stains poor Charlie's blood? I wondered. An object of sentimental value? Disgusted, I tossed it down on the bed. Useless as evidence if I took it, it had to remain in the room. I tipped the bed over. Tucked in the mattress there was a Fijian passport showing the now familiar ugly face only in this one the features were in repose. The surname given was Singh and the forename something polysyllabic. I threw it down.

There was no bundle of notes.

'We must go!' Anna urged when I came out of that

room but there were others to investigate. I rushed round the balcony trying doors. Only one was locked. I kicked it open. There was a computer, a desk and three large filing cabinets. The cabinets, a special security make in heavy rolled steel, were all locked. I looked at the drawer labelled P and considered the axe. There wasn't time. I'd never get into it without an angle grinder. On the desk were some papers.

I snatched a hurried look. At first I thought it was a play script. There were personal names and then sentences. I threw it down. We were on the staircase on our way out when I realised what it was. The transcript of a recorded conversation.

'What are we going to do?' Anna gasped as we made our way back to the fourth floor. There was no sign that my vandalism had been discovered. Party noises were still echoing. I threw the axe into a corner and pulled off the rubber gloves. Anna seemed to be paralysed. I took her gloves off and stuffed them in my pockets.

'We're going to go and enjoy the rest of Judder Crockett's marvellous party,' I said.

19

Anna Pietrangeli was a cool customer. She showed no sign of nerves when we returned to the darkened restaurant. The floor show was still on. Incredibly we'd only been away for ten minutes. Judder was just announcing that food would be served shortly. There was no way of knowing if we'd been missed but as there were more than two hundred people in a darkened room, I didn't see how it was possible.

Waiters dressed in ordinary black and white rig erected tables along one side of the room then speedily brought food from the kitchens. We took our places in the queue, grateful for the diversion. I was hungry. There's nothing like axe-work to sharpen one's appetite. The buffet itself wasn't exceptional, no quails' eggs in aspic or caviar, but it was good and substantial and nicely presented. Ham, chicken, beef, pork pies, potatoes, rice, salad, coleslaw – I crammed my plate.

'How can you eat all that?' Anna whispered. Her vegetarian alternative selection consisted of a couple of onion bhajis, vegetable samosas, crisps and a nut cutlet. The noise level around us was considerable.

'No one's going to overhear us, you know,' I said.

'Overhear what, Dave?' Ernie Cunliffe asked, tapping me on the shoulder.

I nearly tipped my dinner over the floor.

'Ernie!' I said delightedly. 'What a surprise!'

'What have you been plotting?' he asked archly. From

260

the flushed state of his face I think he'd traded more than a few rose petals. 'I know you, Dave! You're always up to something. Ha, ha!' he cackled. 'I know what it is. This isn't your usual young lady, is it?'

'Ernest, will you stop showing us up!' his wife hissed. Every word was like an edged weapon. 'You're embarrassing us all.'

'Don't fuss, Cynthia,' he chortled. 'This is Dave Cunane, he does a lot of work for me. You're not going to take offence are you, Dave?'

'Of course not, mate,' I said.

'That idea of yours about the blackmail didn't work out. I think I ought to knock something off your next cheque. My analyst wasted a full day on it.'

'Never mind, all part of life's rich pattern, isn't it?'

Cynthia's dragon smile widened to encompass me as well as her mate.

I introduced Anna and Ernie introduced Cynthia, a woman with a surprisingly strong grip, then towed us off to a table in the corner.

It was just as well. I could hardly have found better camouflage than an insurance executive.

Like the first little flurries of snow on a clear slope that signal an impending avalanche suggestions of disturbance were few but highly indicative.

First Judder himself appeared dressed in a dinner jacket, not in his divine robes. He must have discovered that he'd had visitors as soon as he went to change into mortal garb. He walked around the room several times, apparently agitated, although only Anna and I knew why. We watched him brushing people off as they approached for a friendly word.

Next he turned and dashed out and came back a moment later with the female acolyte who'd ticked our names off on the list. She had it with her again. They seemed to be frantically trying to count and check all the names and faces in the room. After much head-shaking he gave that up as a hopeless task. People were moving around the whole time. Some were dancing. There was a five-piece band playing Beatles and Abba selections.

Ernie waved and signalled across the room to Judder as one notable to another. Judder gave him a stony-faced smile and then went out again.

Ten minutes later the security staff arrived. The lights went up. Very discreetly, staff quartered the room looking for intruders. They checked high and low, searching under tables, in dark corners and behind curtains. Eventually, they retreated empty-handed.

'I think he's lost Eos the Dawn,' Ernie suggested. 'Do you think we're going to be stuck here in an endless night?'

That was rather good coming from Ernie, I thought.

After several hours, though, his comments began to get a little repetitive. He insisted on taking turns to buy rounds of drinks, and tried to supply me with whisky despite being told I wanted orange juice. He had a chauffeur to take him home. I pushed the glasses towards him and he polished them off along with his own.

'Cream of Manchester here,' he said, 'accountants, lawyers, computer programmers, systems analysts, executives. This is the future here, Dave, not those stale politicians in the Town Hall or the stately home snobs out in Cheshire. Did I tell you I met Christine Hamilton? Some guts that woman . . .'

'You did tell us, Ernest, several times already,' his wife protested unavailingly.

I danced with Anna and even a little with Cynthia. Ernie was far too wobbly to dance by that time.

'I've had Christine Hamilton and her guts until I'm sick of them. I don't know what he's trying to communicate but I wish he'd come to the point,' Cynthia commented waspishly. 'According to Ernest, the woman's innards would stretch from here to Macclesfield.'

As it happened we didn't have much more gore from Ernie. He passed out. Soon after, precisely on the stroke of one, Judder popped up on the stage to wish us good night and to tell us that to make the party even more thrilling for us we were all to receive gifts as we left. All we needed to do was to show our tickets. The serial numbers would be checked and one lucky person would find that he or she had won a full, all expenses paid, week for self and partner at a nationally famous fat farm. This announcement produced an orgy of delving into pockets and searching of waste bins.

I took our tickets out of my inside pocket and winked at Anna.

Cynthia discovered hers in her purse and I manfully offered my shoulder to the insurance executive.

When we arrived in the lift area it was obvious that extra security staff had been brought in. They all had flaming disc party hats on their heads and fixed expressions on their faces but some were in uniform, not ancient Greek costume. Smiling like a Scot with a grievance, Judder himself presided over the scene. All the glass and wreckage had been cleared and a large piece of silvery cardboard was taped over the ruined penthouse entrance. Few commented on it. I noticed that the axe was back in its case behind an unbroken sheet of glass. As we pressed forward there was delay. Our tickets were being minutely scrutinised and matched to faces as names were ticked off lists.

Two lines formed for each lift, each discreetly guarded by half a dozen security bodies. I struggled across to the line on the left with Ernie. Suddenly Anna stepped forward in front of me.

I thought she was about to tell all to Crockett and my stomach plummeted the whole four floors to the basement pool.

Instead she turned and gave me a very public kiss, even running her hand round my neck. 'There's a piece of glass stuck in your hair!' she whispered frantically.

263

I hung on to Ernie while she extracted it.

'Oh, darling, that was a wonderful evening,' she cooed.

Judder gave her a frosty glare but was obviously unwilling to be distracted from checking for gatecrashers. A number of red-faced couples who'd lost their tickets were arguing with the guards and showing ID. I proffered our tickets. Cynthia showed hers. We all got a prize, but not the trip to the farm. Mine was a rather handy little Swiss Army multi-tool in the form of a card with all sorts of attachments.

We had to wait for a while until Ernie's limo arrived. I poured him into the back. Cynthia got in the front with the driver. She offered me no thanks for the safe delivery of her husband, only a sour smile.

'He'd have spotted it as soon as you went by him,' Anna explained as we walked towards the car park. She held the piece of glass in her hand. The fragment was clearly marked with part of a red letter from the axe case. She threw the glass in the gutter and I took her hand in mine. I could feel the blood coursing through my veins and felt more alive than I had in weeks. There was no proof but I knew I was right about Judder and the still unseen Thompson.

'I can't believe what I did in there,' Anna said when were in the Golf GTI. 'Do you think he'll involve the police? I'll lose my job if I get arrested.'

'Don't worry, Mr Crockett has far more to hide than we do. There's no way he'll find out who turned over his little love nest.'

She started laughing in relief. She went on and on, until tears streamed down her face.

'I don't think I've enjoyed a night out so much since I was a teenager,' she said. 'Did you see his face when he came into the room after he'd found out? He was puckered up with rage – and after he'd enjoyed himself so much playing at being God. It was so funny. I wanted to shout something out to him.'

'Anna, you must promise me you'll never go back to the Phoebus Club. Even if he invites you or phones you must never set foot in there again.'

'You needn't be so serious, I'm not attracted to bondage,' she said with a warm smile. 'I like normal men.'

'It's not that. I'm certain that Thompson, or Singh, or whatever his name is, is a killer. You don't play games with people like that.'

We drove in silence for some time.

'Are you going to tell me who he killed?' she asked eventually.

'It's better you don't know, but stay away from Thompson and Crockett.'

'And if I don't, what'll happen?' she said sharply. 'Will you come and hack my door down with an axe?'

That took my breath away for a minute.

'Are you crazy?' I asked eventually.

'Are you?' she snapped. 'You were the one who went mad with the axe. Tell me what those two are supposed to have done or . . .'

'Or what?'

'I'm not certain. I *am* certain that you're going to drop me at my front door and toddle off back to your bachelor flat. You've made it pretty plain all evening that you aren't interested in me as a woman.'

'For God's sake, you invited me to Crockett's party, not for an affair!'

'Dave Cunane, I think you're a bit more grown up than you sound. I know how you looked at me that first night you brought me back to my flat.'

'Anna, I find you very attractive, but as you said yourself I'm spoken for.'

'Yet your girlfriend clears off for the weekend and leaves you on your own. What sort of relationship is that?'

'One that I won't have at all if I pop into bed with another woman as soon as her back's turned.'

'When did I say I wanted that?' she demanded hotly.

'Isn't that what this is all about?'

'Don't flatter yourself. That's the trouble with men. I want a relationship. I want to be involved. This isn't about sex. I want to know what Thompson's supposed to have done. I won't allow anyone to use me.'

'I didn't attempt to use you! You invited me to a do at the residence of my major suspect. Naturally I was interested.'

'That's what I'm saying – you used me! You should have told me what you were up to, not involved me in breaking into Judder's penthouse. Maybe he is kinky, but he's entitled to his privacy.'

We arrived outside the Spar store in Heald Green and sat in the car arguing the toss for another half an hour. In the end it got so cold that I agreed to adjourn the discussion to her flat.

Inside we argued up hill and down dale for another half-hour at the end of which she agreed to stay away from the Phoebus Club. We discussed Geoff Smith, and then her previous boyfriend, an Indian doctor with whom she'd lived for three years. To my mind that explained her bitterness about arranged marriages. He was a high-caste Brahmin and his parents had arranged for him to marry a girl of similar background. The guy didn't dump Anna, he offered her the chance to be his mistress.

I cursed the coincidence that had led me to make up the one story which would appeal so much to this particular woman.

My head was spinning as I drove back to Chorlton. I couldn't work out whether she wanted to share my investigation, make a stand for female rights, strike a blow against arranged marriages, or what. I still hadn't told her what Thompson and Crockett were up to. Back on my own turf, I'd hardly turned the key in the lock of my flat before the phone rang. It was Anna again, phoning to tell

266

me that she was so unhappy she was about to kill herself. People who phone you like that never carry out the threat, but I didn't feel like taking the risk.

I shot off back to Heald Green, doing well over ninety on the fifty-limit section of the A34, and pounded up the stairs to her flat. I found her lying naked on the four-poster bed with two open bottles of paracetamol on the quilt next to her.

I leaped across the room and grabbed her by the arms.

'How many have you taken?' I demanded.

'What do you care?' she mumbled. Her eyes had an unfocused look.

'How many?'

'Will you throw me over your shoulder and haul me off to Casualty if I tell you?'

The woman was infuriating.

'Yes!' I bellowed.

'I haven't taken any.'

I sat on the quilt and counted. She started running her hand up my back. There were thirty-two pills in each bottle. I could see black dots in front of my eyes. I looked at her again. That unfocused look was due to the removal of her contact lenses, not creeping narcosis. They were on the bedside table. I was so angry I wanted to smack her face. Instead, I tried deep breathing.

'Stay with me,' she said.

I stayed.

I slept under the quilt fully clothed and she got into bed alongside me.

The morning was well advanced before bright sun streaming on to my face woke me. I turned and experienced a weird feeling of disorientation when I saw a head of raven black hair on the pillow next to me instead of Janine's mousy brown. Memory and sensation returned together with an unpleasant wrench. I groaned.

Anna stirred when I woke, turned to me and kissed me

full on the lips. She sat up, stroked my face. Her breath smelled of tobacco.

My body felt clammy and grubby after a night spent clothed. Anna was a beautiful woman but if she'd been Helen of Troy and an Onassis heiress rolled into one she'd have been hard-pressed to stir my libido.

I got out of bed and reached for my jacket.

She lay back on the pillow, bright sun illuminating her small perfect breasts to advantage.

'I suppose I've blown it,' she said. 'Oh, well, a girl has to try. I didn't think private detectives were supposed to be this chaste. What does she do? Put something in your tea?'

I stopped myself grinding my teeth and reached for my shoes. I said nothing. I saw the two paracetamol bottles on the bedside table, took my time tying my shoelaces then said, 'You've given me one hell of a headache, lady. I'm taking these with me.'

I put the bottles in my pocket.

She let out that tinkling laugh of hers and that was the last sound I heard from her as I left the flat.

Back in Chorlton I lay around doing nothing in particular until one o'clock. My brain felt detached from my body. I listened to rather than watched the sport on television.

I was still in this spaced-out, dreamy mood when the doorbell rang. I hauled myself over to the intercom expecting to hear Anna but it was the clipped Manchester accent of DCI Brendan Cullen that greeted my ears.

'To what do I owe this pleasure?' I queried cautiously as he crossed my threshold. Although Bren is my oldest friend in the police force, almost my only friend in the police force since Assistant Chief Constable 'Archie' Sinclair retired to his cottage on the banks of Loch Lomond, he is a man who always puts duty before friendship. I speculated on which crime he wished to lay at my door.

'Dave, old cock, do I need an excuse to call on you?'

'Yes,' I said flatly. 'I've had no social calls from you since you made Chief Inspector.'

'Am I that obvious?' he asked with a sad shake of his head. He tumbled on to the sofa I'd just vacated. 'I'm absolutely knackered,' he muttered. 'Is it all right if I hide in here for a few hours? I accidentally left my mobile and pager in the office and they're hardly likely to think I've come here.'

I went to the drinks cupboard and poured him a stiff one.

'Have you got Canada Dry?' he asked. 'I'm trying to water my drinks.'

'Whatever next? You'll be turning teetotal soon.'

'Not impossible,' he murmured as I fished a stale bottle of ginger out of the back of the cupboard.

'Here,' I said, 'do you want a straw with that?'

'Leave it, mate,' he muttered. He looked quite out of sorts with himself. His face was tired and drawn, hair slightly rumpled, greying at the temples. Otherwise he was well turned out in a neat blue suit, crisp white shirt and tie, polished black shoes; he looked every inch the senior copper that he now was. The days when he used to buy his suits at a second-hand store behind Kendal's are long gone. He's still a roly-poly figure but the suits fit better.

'So, why are your fellow bluebottles so unlikely to think you'd be here with me?'

'Technically speaking, you're not exactly flavour of the month down at Bootle Street, Dave, particularly since you set yourself up as a rival police force and started circulating pictures of villains.'

'What villains?' I asked innocently. 'We trace lots of missing persons.'

'Don't try and con a con-artist, Dave,' he said, fishing the triple-headed postcard out of his pocket. 'We found one of these in Charlie Costello's room.'

'You don't say! I'm amazed you didn't arrest me immediately.'

269

He held up his hand.

'That's exactly what half my squad wanted me to do. Some of the younger guys hate your guts. What are you paying your investigators these days?'

'Classified information.'

'Oh, come on.'

'They get a retainer then a percentage of what the insurance company saves.'

'Practically speaking, what does your best man get? Twenty, twenty-five thou' tops?'

'It's nearer forty than thirty, mate. With the business we're pulling in this year, it could be nearer fifty.'

'God almighty! Do they do overtime?'

'They're on flexitime. They sort a case out as and how they can.'

There was a long silence. He started drumming the side of the coffee table with his fingers. I thought he was going to announce that I was under arrest, but it wasn't that.

'I'm thinking of putting my papers in,' he said. 'I started at seventeen, you know. I'll have done twenty-five years soon.'

'What's brought this on? I thought you were happy since you got promoted.'

'I am, but it's not the same job I started in. All this political correctness . . . institutional racism, huh! I still don't know what it means and I've been on the course.'

'This isn't like you, Bren. You've got strong roots, bend with the breeze and stick it out. The fashion will change, it always does. I need you to become Chief Constable.'

'It's all right for you to say that, Dave. Somebody comes and spouts a load of bollocks at you and you throw them out of your office. No comeback. But me, I've got to smile and say, "Yes, sir, no, sir, three bags full, sir."'

I laughed at Bren's idyllic picture of life in the private sector.

'I have to put up with idiots too!'

270

'It's not the same.'

'Same difference. It's life, Bren. Don't resign. I can remember when you were on the point of being kicked out and you hated that idea.'

He grimaced but said nothing.

'Listen,' I argued, 'I've got this guy Peter, Afro-Caribbean as it happens, one of my highest earners. And do you know what he said to me? He wants to join your lot because he don't get no satisfaction nailing insurance frauds! He's been doing the rounds with Andy Gilby.'

'Good-looking guy? Like that American film actor?'

'Yes.'

'A dickhead DI of mine had a tail on your man and Gilby for three days. Thought they were a gang-related protection racket tied up with the Costello killing.'

This time I didn't laugh. I took a swallow of my whisky and then topped up my glass. Brendan topped up his drink with ginger.

'Gilby came over to him on the third day and said, "I don't mind helping to train you lads in surveillance techniques but you're starting to get underfoot." He'd made them from day one.'

Bren now had that sad, rather wistful expression on his face which told me he expected some sort of confession from me at this stage. If 'my' man, Peter Snyder looks like Denzel Washington then Brendan Cullen is a ringer for the late Pat O'Brien, star of forties 'priest films'. When he stares at you manfully with that noble look on his clock you have the choice James Cagney had when facing the electric chair: to die bravely and give a bad example to the lads or go out like a coward and please Father Pat.

I said nothing.

'What's the matter, Dave, cat got your tongue?' he asked eventually.

I shrugged and remained silent.

'I see,' he said with a smile, 'going to be like that, is it?'

271

'Like what?'

'Like, are you going to tell me why you're offering three grand for these geezers, or do I have to get the thumbscrews out?'

'They're three naughty lads, but what they've done is my business and my client's.'

'Wrong answer! Any crime in this town is *my* business.'

'Good, we'll have a walk round the streets, shall we? You can go into all the houses where we smell cannabis and arrest the culprits.'

'There's a difference between a minor offence and murder.'

'So you're saying that I got Charlie Costello murdered?'

'Could be, Dave. We've run through everything else and you know what they say: when you've eliminated all probable causes and only the improbable remains then you're stuck with that.'

'Don't you think I'd have told you if I knew why Charlie Costello was murdered?' I asked angrily. 'He was one of my father's oldest informants.'

'He was everybody's oldest informant. I couldn't believe it when they said he was seventy-eight. . . . He knew the people who did him, you know. He had the keys of the club in his hand and the door unlocked behind him. He must have come out to speak to someone and you're not telling me that such a sly old bird as him would have stepped out to have a chat with a couple of potential muggers?'

'There were two of them?'

'Yes, forensics reckon one held him while the other brained the old coot. The killer did the job with a single massive blow struck from the front. There were no defence injuries. It was an execution.'

'Oh,' I muttered. An unpleasant image of Charlie watching that stone club descend fluttered in the corner of my mind like a trapped bird.

272

'Dave, Charlie's trainee barman, says he saw a man answering your description pass Charlie a considerable number of notes the week before. You were with an unusually sized individual who sounds remarkably like your old friend Clint Lane. You're working for Bob Lane, aren't you? Has he hired you to find out who's been stitching him up?'

'I didn't even know anyone was trying to stitch Bob up. I'm looking after his brother and I should think that after what happened last time you lot tried to fit Clint up you'd be walking on eggs where he's concerned.'

'Precisely, Dave. Just what I told my DI when he wanted to arrest the pair of you.'

'I am not working for Bob. There's nothing illegal about offering a reward for information and according to my solicitor I'm not bound to break a client's confidence unless there's actual evidence that he intends wrong doing himself.'

'Can an old friend tell you something, Dave?'

'Yes, as long as it's not that I'm aiding and abetting a drug dealer.'

'Why else do people get killed in this town? But that's not what I want to say. You sound just a little too strident, Dave. You sound as if you're trying to convince yourself that you didn't get Charlie killed.'

'I *didn't* get Charlie killed. At seventy-eight he didn't need a nursemaid. I paid him for information but he always had more than one iron in the fire. I've no way of knowing . . .'

'I've got the message!' snapped Brendan. 'Have you found these three yet?' he asked, tapping the postcard.

'No,' I admitted.

'So what have they done?'

'That's what I can't tell you.'

'I've had the faces circulated. No one knows who they are. Were they done by Granville Courteney?'

'Yes.'

'He's good but too expensive for us. Which tells me that there's heavy money involved in this.'

I shrugged.

'The ethnic guy's just an impression. Was he wearing a mask?'

I tried to avoid saying or signalling anything but Bren's just too clever. He stared at me like a mind-reader and did what a mind-reader does.

'He was wearing a mask,' he continued, with smile. 'Which tells me that this wasn't a white-collar crime. There's been no robbery reported so we're talking about someone's home being turned over, unlikely as your other two faces look like bank managers more than blaggers, or else we're talking extortion. Am I right?'

'I'm saying nothing.'

I went in the kitchen and found a couple of Marks & Spencer's cottage pies. Clint copes with three at a time but I asked Bren if he wanted one and we ate in meditative silence for a while.

'It's unusual to see an extortionist's face like this, you know,' he said at last between forkfuls. 'Particularly two faces. They're rarely eyeballed before they're caught. Like timid woodland creatures they are. Actually, this pair look like the same man seen by different witnesses.'

I knew he was trying to goad me into dropping the vital bit of information that would eventually send him round to Jamie's or Lee's door, but determined though I was to give nothing away, Bren was holding my complete attention.

'Why is it unusual?'

'Profiling indicates that extortionists and blackmailers are usually criminals who haven't got the balls for face-to-face crime.'

'That lets Charlie's killers out then.'

'They're not necessarily nicer criminals. Just a bit leery

274

about bursting into a bank or a building society with a shooter in their hands.'

'Or in this case a club,' I said unguardedly.

'How did you know that?' he snapped.

'You said Charlie was killed with a single massive blow.'

'I didn't say *club*. It could have been a chair leg, iron bar, sock with PP9 batteries in, anything. I didn't say club.'

'Was it a club?'

The expression on Bren's face was extraordinary. He was tired but weariness seemed to be struggling with hope.

'You know, don't you, you bugger? Charlie's skull was smashed like an eggshell. I should take you down to Bootle Street right now and sweat this out of you.'

'You'd have done that already if you weren't scared witless of Marvin Desailles.'

The hope in Bren's face was immediately quenched by gloom.

'How the hell are we supposed to solve any crime?' he asked rhetorically. He sounded so bitter that I almost sympathised that he wasn't able to 'sweat' me.

'Was it a club, a stone club?'

He nodded. 'Microscopic traces of a granite-like, metamorphic rock were found in the skull samples. Gas chromatography shows that the rock was not local to the British Isles, or isn't in the database. The Birmingham lab's still trying for a match but the world's a big place.'

'That doesn't tell you it was a club.'

'Oh, yes, the weapon was smooth-sided, not jagged like a rock. It could have been a large beach or river pebble but there aren't many lying around in Manchester. The pathologist's reconstruction suggests a club and you wouldn't have used that word unless you knew something.'

'I could have. Club, cosh, bludgeon . . . what's the difference?'

'Don't argue, Dave. I know when you're lying.'

'Tell me more about this profiling.'

'Cheeky, aren't you? You want to pick my brain but you won't say a word.'

'When I can, I will. You'll be the first to know but it's more complicated than I can explain.'

'Aren't they always when you're involved?' he muttered with a sigh. 'Right, your career criminal . . . professional bank robber, safe blower, major league burglar, or whatever . . . will know other people in the same line of work. He'll have met them in prison or they may be relatives or the people he worked with on other jobs. He relies on them for help if he's in trouble. Like, he's part of a community as your friend Desailles would say.'

'Leave him out of it, Bren.'

'I'd better. I don't want them putting homophobia on my charge sheet along with institutional racism. OK, your extortionist isn't like that. He's often a mature man who's turned to crime suddenly because of some incident like losing his job or his business folding or whatever, but it comes on sudden. The chap feels the world owes him and one fine day he decides to collect that debt. He plans his crime meticulously, every move thought out well in advance. He's not like your average villain. There's nothing spur of the moment about him. Practically speaking, that's his weakness – he can't improvise. Put him under pressure and he'll screw it up. He's not a pro.'

I poured some more whisky into his glass. I noticed that he didn't ask for Canada Dry this time.

'This is like what that writer fellow, you know . . . Lord Whatsit? The Tory big bug? . . . like what he does. He has these parties and gives out shepherd's pie and they make him Lord Mayor of London or something.'

'Or in his case, don't,' I said with a laugh.

'His books are crap anyway but I know he gives out shepherd's pie and . . .'

'Champagne, Brendan. I'm plying you with Famous

Grouse Scotch, a far better brew than Krug, and if you're interested we could go on to sample some sixteen-year-old single malt after you've finished the pie.'

He was interested.

I'd bought a couple of bottles of Lagavulin, the whisky that Clyde had attempted to bribe me with. I could easily acquire a taste for the smooth, peaty Islay malt, I decided. It didn't take Bren long to finish his pie and Grouse. We went back into the living room where I poured us both a healthy tot of the Caledonian nectar.

'Another thing about these extortionists is they make intricate arrangements to collect the money they've demanded and then often back out if things don't smell right.'

'Intricate arrangements?'

'Yeah, there was one bloke who wanted to collect his ransom out of ATMs anywhere in the country. You know, the magnetic strip in your cash card? This cheeky sod made the victim print tens of thousands of so-called dummy promotional cards. Only they weren't dummies. Each and every one had a pin number, known only to him, so he could draw out money and no one the wiser.'

I almost blew it then. The story of the Alderley Edge transfer was scorching the tip of my tongue but I managed to keep a grip. I got up and turned the television on and we settled down to watch rugby union. I don't have Sky so there's no Saturday afternoon soccer for me. Bren took his coat off and put his feet up. He has a fund of dirty stories but I wasn't particularly in the mood to listen.

We watched and commented and sipped Lagavulin until the soccer scores came on at five. Jamie Piercy had scored twice. The evil thought crossed my mind that someone had been bribed to let him score. Once the scandal was out in the open every soccer result would be under similar suspicion. I kept my gloomy thoughts to myself. In a mellow mood Bren announced that he was going home. He ordered a taxi.

'Bren,' I said, as we stood by the window waiting to see the taxi turn into the car park, 'have you ever come across a case where a heavy gambler or a rich drug baron suddenly lost all his money, and at the same time a member of his family had some sort of accident?'

'Unreported extortion in other words?'

'I can't say.'

'Practically speaking, Dave, you're not clever enough to be cunning. Why don't you come straight out and tell me what all this is about?'

'I can't.'

'Won't, you mean.'

'What about Bob Lane?' I asked.

'Him? Huh! That's no secret. I hear someone's grassed the tricky devil up to put him out of business. Serves him right. Who needs grassing up more than a grass dealer?'

At that moment the taxi hooted from below. Bren punched me on the shoulder and departed. I remained slumped on my sofa in a darkening world. I had a lot to think about.

20

The phone woke me from a heavy sleep. This time it was
Anna Pietrangeli.

'I've got to see you again.'

'We've said everything we have to say to each other.'

'We haven't . . . You don't understand, there's someone who wants to meet you.'

'Who, your mother?'

'No, stupid! Judder Crockett. He wants to talk to
you.'

I stopped breathing for a moment.

'What!'

'Judder wants to talk to you. I told you we were
friends.'

'You implied that was all in the past.'

'You just heard what you wanted to.'

'And he gave you those keys through the oracle and you
just pretended you were insulted?'

'I *was* insulted. Judder plays silly games but I still like
him. Anyway he wants to see you.'

'Why?'

'He's frightened about Aaron. Wants to know what it
is you think Aaron's done. I told him what you said about
murder and he just went absolutely spare. You must tell
him what Aaron's done.'

I didn't speak.

'Do I have to spell it out to you?' she asked impatiently.

'Yes, but not on the phone,' I said.

'Where?'

I tried to think. I needed somewhere public just in case this was a set-up. God, I needed a place where they'd let me wear a steel helmet if Thompson was going to be around.

'Have you still got the mobile?'

She had and she confirmed the number.

'OK, get yourself and Crockett on to Upper Cambridge Street.'

'Upper Cambridge Street,' she repeated woodenly.

'It runs parallel to Oxford Road behind the MMU and the Royal Northern College of Music.'

'We'll come in a taxi.'

'Get yourselves there and then I'll phone and give you the name of a pub where we'll meet.'

'What's all this rigmarole for?'

'I don't want Crockett getting his pal Thompson to arrange some unpleasant surprise for me.'

'Judder's not like that!' she said fiercely. 'He's fallen out with Thompson.'

I didn't argue. I'd done enough of that with her.

I slapped some cold water on my face in the bathroom. What was I getting myself into? I've been beaten to a pulp by men with less justification than Crockett. Still, I couldn't complain. This was a confrontation of my own devising.

There wasn't a steel helmet in my wardrobe but I did have a bullet-proof jacket which I put on under a loose shirt. I also have a certain piece of ironmongery that goes with the jacket – a 9mm Heckler & Koch automatic pistol, a P7. I shoved the gun in my trouser pocket and hurried downstairs.

On my way into town I couldn't help remembering what Bren had said. There was no way that either Crockett or Thompson fitted the profile of an extortionist. Crockett's penthouse was hardly the abode of an embittered failure, while Thompson didn't fit either. He had too much going on in his life and was too young.

My theory that Charlie had spotted a spiky-haired Thompson prowling the streets was clearly wrong. Thompson's head was as bald as the Millennium Dome. He must have been wearing a wig as well as a mask when he flung Naomi Carter into that ambulance. It had to be him, the connection with the Evergreens was a coincidence too far.

Where did that leave me?

It left me with a trail of wild guesses that had led me to a bloody stone club hanging on the wall of Thompson's bedroom. It left me with Crockett, who might or might not be involved but was certainly Thompson's boss, and it left me with my guilt for the death of Charlie Costello.

Charlie had come to his death at the hands of two people, according to Bren. If Thompson was one, who was the other if not Crockett?

Suppose when I'd described the kidnapping the old man had known exactly who I was talking about? Suppose he didn't need pictures or descriptions. Suppose the crime alone was enough. People talk to barmen. Had some embittered middle-aged customer let slip his twisted ambitions one evening? Or had the knowledge percolated to Charlie through the fraternity of city barmen of which he was the senior member? I tried to remember exactly what he had said.

I'd offered him two hundred but he'd insisted on a monkey, as he called it, five hundred. Was the price so high because he wasn't passing on a whisper but direct knowledge? Had he realised immediately what the cost of betrayal might be? Was Thompson's accomplice a regular at the Black and Blue Club? It was possible but unlikely as most of the regulars there are either coppers or lawyers while Charlie had contacts all over Manchester and Salford. If he did have a strong suspicion who the extortionist was it could be anyone from a large list and not just a member of Charlie's own club.

I remembered something my father had said about Charlie, about him hoarding his knowledge about the criminal fraternity as insurance against a rainy day. Never a blabbermouth, information had to be coaxed out of him. Had he, along with his other arcane lore, stockpiled the name of a man who thought it might be a good idea to get rich by squeezing money out of criminals? Was he just biding his time until someone like me came along with an offer of cash for it?

If the extortionist was in fact one of Charlie's customers then the probability that he was either a lawyer or a copper was high. I found that hard to swallow.

I know it's the fashion these cynical days to believe that all coppers and lawyers are ready to take up a career of crime at the drop of a hat, but in reality not many of them do. Most of them are above suspicion. Still, there was a certain twisted logic to the theory that made me reluctant to cast it aside. It might be easy for a villain in the legal hierarchy to select targets. My extortionist was certainly getting his information from somewhere.

Then what if Charlie, knowing the extortionist, had tried a little extortion of his own? At seventy-eight, the prospect of retirement from bar work must have been on his mind. A warden-controlled flat in crime-scarred Ordsall wasn't much for an old man to look forward to. Had the tight-lipped old fool decided to extort a pension fund for himself?

It would have been easy for him to send me on a wild goose chase.

The more I considered, the more horribly possible it all seemed. Charlie had known his man, reckoned he wasn't personally capable of violence but had forgotten Thompson, the slammer of car boots on wailing babies.

So what was I doing driving to a meet with Thompson's

best buddy? I'd only the say-so of Anna Pietrangeli that he and Crockett had fallen out and I'd spent a good part of the previous twenty-four hours discovering just how reliable Ms Pietrangeli was.

I drove through Fallowfield on to Lloyd Street South. Soon I was passing the Manchester City football ground, then the dental hospital. Opportunities to turn back came and went as I crossed each successive junction. I arrived at Upper Cambridge Street. Then I saw the taxi parked near the lights on the corner of Booth Street West and drove past. Apart from the driver, a diminutive Asian, there were only two figures in the car. Anna was talking rapidly to Judder. They didn't look up as I passed. There was nowhere Thompson could have hidden.

I parked and took out my mobile.

'I want you to drive on down Upper Cambridge Street, take the second turn on your right, Boundary Street, and then go into a pub called the Salutation on the corner. I'll be in there a few minutes after you.'

'Dave, this is all so unnecessary. All Judder wants to do is talk.'

'Fine, then do what I say.'

'This spy stuff's ridiculous,' spluttered Anna.

I broke the connection and drove to a spot where I could observe them without being noticed. There was always the chance of Crockett phoning Thompson but I had to gamble. I saw the taxi pull up. They got out. Anna was in tight jeans and a denim jacket. Crockett paid the driver off and they both looked around uneasily for a moment before going into the pub.

I waited five minutes before following them.

The Salutation is a tiny little pub, sole surviving building from a former dense warren of terraces. The streets and the working classes have gone, replaced by university offices, halls of residence and students. There was a varied crowd there on this Saturday evening: cleaners and porters from the university, students and a few locals.

Crockett and Anna were wedged into a corner with glasses in front of them. When he saw me Crockett's face creased into a frown that deserved classification as structural damage. Anna gave an anxious little wave but I was in no hurry to renew her acquaintance. I pushed into the crowd round the bar and ordered a pint of Guinness.

Crockett's scowl deepened when I squeezed on to the stool they'd saved for me. My back was against the wall and I had a good view of the only entrance. I took a long drink of my pint then wiped the foam off my lips. Crockett waited for me to speak but I kept my mouth shut. He'd asked for the meeting.

'Well,' Anna said eventually, 'haven't you something to say to Judder?'

'Such as?'

'You could apologise for smashing his place up for a start.'

'I apologise,' I said, 'but I was looking for a murderer.'

'And you thought it was me?' Crockett asked. His normally ruddy face had turned a deep shade of purple.

'It could have been you.'

'To break my door down like that,' he gasped. 'What kind of a man are you?' He looked ready to cry.

'I found the murderer.'

Crockett began breathing deeply through his curved beak of a nose. I could hear the breath whistling into his lungs. Anna patted his back and he reached inside the old black leather jacket he'd thought appropriate wear for a trawl round the slums. His fingers went nervously from pocket to pocket until they eventually found what they sought. He pulled out a tiny gold box, opened it and slipped a pill under his tongue. The effect was immediate. His breathing became much better. He leaned back with his head against the wall, eyes focused on the ceiling.

'Judder's got angina and if you give him an attack you'll be the murderer,' Anna said fiercely.

'That's all right, my dear,' he said to her. 'Who is this murderer, Mr Detective? Let's have names.'

'It's not Eos the Dawn or one of your other trophy bimbos, is it? It's your boyfriend Thompson, or Singh, or whatever his name is.'

'He's *not* my boyfriend!'

'You looked really cosy together in your holiday snaps.'

'I'm entitled to some relaxation when I go abroad. Who I talk to is my own business, not yours, but I wish to God I'd never met Aaron.'

'Why?'

'I refuse to be cross-examined about my private life.'

'OK, I'll go and drink somewhere else,' I said. I picked up my glass and took a big swallow out of it. I was thirsty, dehydrated by all the whisky-drinking in the afternoon.

'Stay,' Anna said quickly. 'Judder wants to know what you suspect Aaron of.'

'And that was what last night's histrionics were all about? You wanted to find out what I knew. Why didn't you say that you were working for the Greek god here?'

'That was my idea,' Crockett admitted. 'It's not a good idea to let your business rivals know what you've found out about them.'

'Business rival?' I said, with a laugh.

'A girl from David Ridley & Partners, surveyors of Fountain Street, followed a man to your office. You have to get up very early in the morning to get the better of Judder Crockett. If I'm going to sink millions into a development I'm entitled to know . . .'

'I'm not a property speculator.'

'You're in business. Health and fitness clubs are a competitive field. You could be acting for someone.'

'My business in this case is finding murderers.'

'A cheapjack private eye like you!'

285

'First I'm a business rival, now I'm a cheapjack. You don't deny you were making enquiries about the Evergreens then?'

'We're not going ahead with that now.'

'Did you know that the place was used as headquarters for the kidnapping of a child, a sickly little baby who may yet die?'

'Listen to him,' Anna sneered. 'First of all it was an arranged marriage, then it was extortion from rich criminals. He'll say anything.'

'A group of men, one of them answering the description of Thompson, kidnapped a nanny walking a baby in broad daylight. They took the nanny to the Evergreens and then dumped her in Cheadle Hulme. They kept the baby, who they knew was in delicate health, and then abandoned her in the boot of a stolen car before extracting two hundred thousand from her father.'

'More of your lies,' Anna snorted.

'What possible connection has this farrago with Aaron?' Crockett asked. He sounded genuinely puzzled.

'The connection is this,' I said patiently. 'Thompson collected the keys and the alarm code for the Evergreens from David Ridley & Partners and kept them overnight. Did you get up early enough in the morning to learn that?'

'What?' Crockett exclaimed. He seemed to be short of breath again. 'My business with the surveyor was nothing to do with Aaron. He had no right . . .'

'Cunane's lying,' Anna sneered.

'Proper little mother's helper aren't you?' I answered. I turned to Crockett. 'Phone your informant at David Ridley's and ask her. That's what my man went round there to find out. Do you think I really want to buy that old ruin?'

Crockett looked very thoughtful at this. He bit his lip in concentration. Anna started to speak again but he shut her up.

'Go and get us some more drinks, darling,' he ordered. She looked doubtful about leaving him in my company but he pressed a twenty-pound note into her hand and propelled her towards the bar. Judging by the mob struggling there, she'd be gone some time.

'Aaron was blackmailing me, still is, but I expect you've guessed that.'

'I saw the computer with the locked files. And the pictures in your bedroom.'

'This country's disgusting,' Crockett wailed. 'What I do abroad is my own business. It was bad enough Aaron Thompson landing on my doorstep to haunt me. Just a few little lapses but I knew I had to pay for them. Then he discovered what I'd download from the Internet, and now you know too.'

'I'm no blackmailer.'

He took no notice, seemed to be absorbed by a miasma of self-pity.

'I've worked and slaved to build up my business. Years it's taken me, and now he threatens to wipe it out overnight by writing PAEDOPHILE all over the walls outside. Half of my trade's with families. I'd be wiped out overnight. The bastard couldn't even spell the word until I showed him.'

'His other crimes are a little more serious than blackmailing you,' I told him. 'He's a killer.'

'This baby you mentioned, you said she was in delicate health. It's possible that he didn't know . . .'

'He knew all right, and he knew what he was doing three weeks ago when he bashed in an old man's skull.'

Crockett gasped. He'd turned purple again. I honestly thought he was going to pop his clogs right there, but he took another pill and got control of himself.

'Three weeks ago?' he queried. 'I haven't seen him for three weeks. You're not lying, are you?' He looked at me searchingly. 'No, I didn't think you were. You're a prick but not a liar. I could tell that you didn't like me that first night you came in with Anna. What is it? Are you unsure of your own sexual identity? Anna says you have difficulties in that department. I can help, you know. There are therapies.'

I didn't feel like laughing.

'I'm sure there are but don't change the subject, Mr Whiplash. For your information, the reason I didn't like you is that you lied about doing National Service. It ended years before you were eligible.'

'Nit-picking pedantry,' he snorted.

'Were you ever a member of the Black and Blue Club?'

'Why should I join a drinking club when I have my own licensed premises?'

'Was Thompson?'

'I don't know. He went out occasionally. I made it plain that I wasn't going to buy his wretched drug for him.'

'Tell me about him,' I insisted. 'Your only chance to get him off your back is if I can get him for what he did to that child and Charlie Costello.'

'You're a gangster yourself, aren't you?'

'No. Tell me about Thompson.'

'I wish I'd never gone to Fiji. The island's riddled with Methodism but there's a small cruising scene on the north coast. I met Aaron at a beach resort there. I find I can relax with a young man . . . don't look down your nose at me. I only need them for companionship.'

'Just tell me who he is?'

Anna returned at this point and put the drinks on the table. Crockett snatched his pint up and took a long swallow.

'Don't tell him anything,' she advised.

'Shush!' Crockett hissed, sloshing his drink down on the table. 'Aaron's an ex-soldier. He told me a sad story about being persecuted in the Fijian Army because of his mixed race origins and his inclinations. The homophobia on that island has to be seen to be believed. I found out later that he'd been cashiered from the army for something quite different.'

'What?'

'Drugs. Aaron's into cocaine in quite a big way. I didn't know that until later, of course. As I said, he took advantage of my kindly nature by spinning me a tale of woe. I suppose my guard was down and although Aaron wasn't the prettiest fish on the beach, well . . . enough said.'

Anna didn't look overjoyed at this confidence.

'He's quite well educated and he'd actually done all right in their army until they found out about the drugs. His mother was Indian, daughter of a well-respected doctor. The father was from a chiefly family and quite high up in their army. They never married because of opposition from their families but she gave birth to Aaron and then later his father pulled strings to get him into the army. It was quite a scandal when they found out about the drugs apparently. The Fijians do a lot of training with British Special Forces. They're in the Commonwealth, you know. I remember during the war, they put up a hell of a show against the Japs . . .'

'Spare me your phoney reminiscences.'

'I forgot you have this inordinate thirst for accuracy.'

'I do where Thompson's concerned. There might be lives at stake.'

'How melodramatic!'

'Tell me about these Special Forces.'

'A number of Brit troops, SAS, commandos and what not, were drummed out for using the dreaded white powder during their stay on the island. It turned out that Aaron was the one who'd supplied them. It was all hushed up at the time.'

'So he had criminal contacts?'

'I suppose he must have done, but I was there for a holiday, not to investigate him which was a pity in a way.'

'Why?'

'I might have known what he was up to. He was taking notes and spying on one of my little hobbies.'

'Which is?'

'You know. I take one or two harmless entertainment photos to keep with me during the year.'

'Kiddie porn?'

'Leave him alone,' Anna snarled. 'You're supposed to be after Aaron Thompson. Judder's never done any harm to anyone.'

I said nothing and kept my face expressionless.

'Aaron pleaded with me to give him the money to go to the Sydney Mardi Gras event. He said he wanted to come out but I don't think he's really gay at all. It was just a scheme to get money out of me.'

'Go on.'

'I gave him the airfare and spending money. I was generous, thought he just wanted a stake. Naturally I didn't tell him my address in the UK. I got on the plane to fly home expecting that would be the last I saw of him.'

'When was this?'

'It'll be three years ago this summer. I wasn't prepared for what happened next. He turned up at the club. He has a contact near Chester, had been staying with him and then he found out where I was. He came on very heavy with his photos. He wanted money and he wanted shelter. He's an illegal immigrant. I made enquiries through an agency in Suva and found out that he was wanted in Fiji.'

'So what did you do?'

'What could I do? I paid him and I paid him and I paid him. Fortunately he's interested in bodybuilding so that kept him occupied some of the time, but he had to keep a low profile round the club. He came on to me for so much money that in desperation I thought of a way of getting some of it back. I offered him a share in the club if he'd come up with some capital for expansion. He toyed with the idea but of course

290

it was easier for him to sponge off me than to put anything back.'

'Who's the contact near Chester?'

'I don't know. He just mentioned that he had a friend there when he turned up in Manchester.'

'Did he say if this friend was in the Marines?'

'He said nothing about him. The man's a positive Sphinx about his own background. I told you, I had to hire a private detective in Fiji to find out what I know now.'

'Who are his contacts in Manchester?'

'I don't know that either. He goes off for weeks at a time without telling me.'

'Does anybody phone or ask for him?'

'He has an e-mail address on my computer. I can't read his mail though. I don't know his password and the stuff he gets is encrypted.'

'So you've tried.'

'Naturally.'

'What was that script thing on the desk in the computer room?'

'That was something sent to him. He left it there to tantalise me but I could make neither head nor tail of it. There didn't seem to be a story to it at all.'

'It was a transcript of a bugged telephone conversation. It might help me if I could have another look at it.'

'I'll think about it.'

'I wish you'd get serious. There are lives at stake here.'

'You said that before but if it's true why haven't you gone to the police?'

'My client prefers it that way.'

'That's what I told you, Judder,' Anna chipped in. 'He claims to be working for some rich criminal.'

'Not exactly,' I said.

'But what I've told you won't go to the police?' Crockett asked.

I shook my head.

'And you're not trying to blackmail me?'

'No,' I said impatiently. 'This isn't about you.'

'But you thought it was,' Anna chimed in again.

'We all make mistakes. Did Thompson wear a wig like this?'

I showed him the picture of Porcupine Head.

'I've seen that already. Yes, he had a wig like that. His own head's naturally bald and before you say anything, I thought it gave him a certain distinction when I first met him. The planes and stark angles on his face . . . He looked like an Easter Island carving, all dark and muscular and mysterious.'

'He's been described to me as someone you wouldn't want to meet twice.'

'That can have its uses,' Crockett said defensively.

'Do you know either of the other two faces?'

'Never seen them. I have a photographic memory and they've never been in my club. That's definite.'

'Where did Thompson get his cocaine from?'

'I don't know. I told him I wasn't getting it for him. The last thing I need is to get pegged as a drug dealer. He went somewhere for steroids, perhaps he got it there.'

'Where?'

'I don't know. I didn't want to know . . . some gym in Salford, I think. He dropped a receipt once.'

'Think, it could be important.'

'Important to whom? I don't remember.'

'Did Thompson tell you to get in touch with me through Anna?'

'No, that was my idea. I thought you might be setting me up for blackmail. I wanted to be a jump ahead this time.'

I finished the pint Anna had brought. I was roasting in the bullet-proof jacket.

'Right, I'm off,' I announced. 'For your own safety, call me if Thompson turns up again.'

'Suppose I were to tell him about you and your nosy-parker business?'

'You might find that you'd outlived your own usefulness to him in that case. I think Mr Thompson has a very quick way of dealing with nuisances.'

I made a chopping motion with my hand.

I left them both looking suitably frightened, or so I thought.

When I got out into the fresh air I had my hand on the Heckler & Koch but I didn't seriously think they'd laid an ambush or that Crockett was still in league with Thompson. My skull felt secure. I got in the car and drove to Chorlton.

There were no messages on the answerphone when I got into the flat. I stowed away the illegal firearm, feeling slightly deflated. Janine seemed to be getting on very well in my absence. I stripped off and stood under a very hot shower for ten minutes.

It took me that long before I felt clean.

Crockett was certainly an item. He was into everything, an exception to every rule. I wouldn't have been surprised to hear that he was married with a wife and children, maybe more than one wife. Clearly Anna Pietrangeli had enough protective impulses towards him to stock a large shop.

21

It had been a long day and when I hit the sheets I was ready for sleep, a deep dreamless restful sleep. It wasn't to be. I'd just settled when the phone began ringing. I struggled back to consciousness and picked the phone up.

Lee Parkes spoke. 'Hey, Cunane, guess where I'm phoning you from?'

I struggled to strip the layers of weariness away. There was a noise like a thousand hammers battering in the background.

'A factory?'

'No, you berk, listen.'

The hammering noise resolved into a jingling sound. Coins dropping into metal trays.

'Las Vegas,' I said.

'That's good,' he complimented.

'It wasn't hard to guess where a gambler would end up. Are you losing a lot of money?'

'You hope? No, I'm holding my own, winning at poker and losing at blackjack.'

'Lee, I don't know what time it is there but I'm trying to get some sleep. If there's anything you want . . .'

'Yeah, there's something I want. Too fucking right there is. Have you sorted that little bit of business of mine?'

'Sort of,' I said. 'I know who one of the . . . er . . . gentlemen is.'

'"Sort of." What kind of an answer is that? I'm paying you for results, not fucking sort ofs.'

294

'It is a result but you might not like some of the information.'

'I can't do this over the phone. I'm coming home. Have you dug up any reason why I shouldn't? You know, what happened to the old guy, is that likely to happen again?'

'I don't think so.'

'I don't think so? Will you fucking listen to yourself? You sent me halfway round the world. Is it safe to come back? I can't stay here for ever, Cheyenne needs me, and besides the sausages are shit. Everything's bloody burgers here, breakfast, dinner and tea.'

'No jellied eels?'

'Answer the question, damn you.'

'Just a minute, let me think,' I pleaded.

It was hard to answer Lee's question especially as I had to remember that the phone might be bugged. I'd sent him away in a moment of panic after Charlie's murder but that killing now looked rather different. Charlie had known who they were. With him gone they'd probably felt confident I would never trace them.

'Come on,' bawled Lee above the background din.

'They probably think they're safe with Charlie dead but there's always the danger they might feel even safer with you out of the way as well.'

'Sitting on the fence, are you?'

'Just giving my honest opinion.'

'Are you sure you're not bleeding me dry?'

'I told you it would be a long job. You were happy enough . . .'

'Yeah, yeah, you don't need to spell it out in capitals. All right, I'm on my way home. Gambling in Las Vegas is fine but only the house wins in the end. Do you know, they've got used car lots full of Rolls-Royces and Bentleys and top of the range Mercs and Beamers at ridiculous prices because losers trade their wheels in for what cash they can get? Sad, innit? I don't intend to be a loser.'

295

He hung up.

I lay back on the bed feeling drained. Rain was drumming against the windows, real stair-rod stuff.

Would Lee be safe in England? Was I? The only answer to that was to see the extortionist behind bars. How to do that without involving the police and giving away Jamie's secret? There was no way, I concluded gloomily.

Next morning I woke up late and the inside of my mouth felt as if I'd been burning coal in my internal boiler. I climbed out of bed and drew back the curtains. There was no rain but massive purple and black clouds were rolling up from the south-west. Wind-blown leaves were piling up against obstructions. It must have been pouring solidly all night. There were pools in the road where drains had blocked.

Lee Parkes was coming home to this? The thought cheered me.

I busied myself in the kitchen for a couple of hours. We were going to have roast beef and all the trimmings for our evening meal so I got the vegetables ready.

Kitchen work always helps me think and I thought I could see the way ahead now. Thompson had obviously gone to ground somewhere. If I could root the Fijian out of his lair like the eye out of an old potato then surely his extortionist friend would soon be revealed?

I was in the midst of these thoughts when Janine returned with all her party intact.

'It was wonderful,' Lloyd said. 'You should have been with us. Clint went on Oblivion three times and Mum went on Nemesis.'

'Oblivion and Nemesis! That sounds just like what I've been through this weekend!'

'Don't tease him, Dave,' Janine warned. 'They wouldn't let him go on those because he's too little. We've had tears and more tears but he likes the Ghost Train, don't

296

you, Lloyd? I've been on it so often they reserved me a seat.'

'Oblivion's great!' he continued. 'They take you up really high then they drop you into this big dark hole in the ground.'

'Yes, it's good, Dave,' Clint agreed.

'I know. I've had exactly that sensation myself – being dropped into a dark hole.'

'What's the matter with you, Dave? You could have come with us,' Janine said.

'It's been quite a white-knuckle ride here.'

'Come into the hall,' she ordered.

The children turned on the telly, Clint found the Gameboy and Naomi watched us go out with a quizzical expression on her face.

'I really missed you,' Janine said, kissing me fiercely. 'You should have come. You need a break. So what's up?'

'I just found that nearly everything I thought I'd discovered is wrong.'

'Never mind,' she said. 'Think about tonight. You've to make it up to me for missing the weekend.'

Just to leave me in no doubt about what she meant she nibbled my ear.

I served the meal but my mind wasn't on the job. Normally, I enjoy carving the joint like an old-fashioned *pater familias*. Atavism, Janine calls it, but first I forgot the gravy, then the horseradish. I slumped into a corner of the sofa after serving the sweet course.

'Hello, Dave, anyone at home?' Janine enquired, waving her fingers in front of my eyes.

I gave a grunt. She sat down next to me.

'Guess who I met at Alton Towers?'

I shrugged.

'Annette Stedman!' she replied eagerly. The name meant nothing to me.

297

'You know, she has two children at Jenny and Lloyd's school. Anyway, she says the city education department runs special courses called "Readiness for Living" in which they help people with Clint's problems. They have classes in things like counting change and getting on buses, all about leading a normal life. I'm going to find out about it first thing in the morning.'

'Great,' I muttered.

'You're not listening,' she exclaimed angrily and then hit me with a cushion. Fortunately, Naomi and Clint were already doing a spot of 'Readiness for Living' by washing the pots in the kitchen and Jenny and Lloyd were so used to our domestic upsets that they hardly even turned round to look.

'Bloody man!' she whispered. 'You're always saying you want a family and here we are with four of them, if you count Naomi, and what do you do? Switch off, that's what.'

'Naomi!'

'You're old enough to be her father.'

'God help me!' I muttered.

'Don't be so unkind. I'm trying to make arrangements for your friend's brother.'

'I know. You're great. The course sounds wonderful. It's just that I've got a lot on my mind.'

'You want to go out, don't you? What is it? It's not that schoolteacher, Pietrangeli, is it?'

I laughed. For someone who wants to remain unattached, Janine can be very suspicious at times.

'I just want to make a few phone calls,' I said, which was partly true. If I'd been a little less domesticated and a little more alert that weekend when Charlie was killed he might be alive now.

I went into the hall and phoned the Phoebus Club. After listening to the complete works of J. S. Bach I finally got through to Crockett.

'Oh, it's you,' he mumbled.

'Who were you expecting? Your playmate from Fiji?'

'If you just called to be abusive I'm going to hang up,' he said huffily.

'I want that printout you had in your computer room,' I told him.

There was silence for a while.

'If it helps you to put Aaron where he belongs you'd better come and get it, but don't bring your gun this time. We've got a metal detector on the main doorway.'

'What gun?'

'You didn't fool me, Cunane. I may not have done National Service but I know when someone's tooled up.'

'Swiss Army knife, that's all that was,' I lied for the benefit of any other listeners we might have had on the line.

'Meet me on the fourth floor,' he snarled and hung up.

Next I phoned Michael Coe. He wasn't in but I left a him a message telling him to go to London tomorrow and resume his enquiries into Lee and Jamie's background and also Keeley and Kimball Smathers. I'd nothing to tell him about the Smathers that he didn't already know but I knew he'd come up with something.

Finally, I phoned Peter Snyder. I decided I needed someone with me on the second trip to Judder Crockett's den. Safety in numbers, or something.

As Brendan Cullen had reminded me, Peter was earning a lot of money and although Levonne liked him home at weekends she'd just have to share him with me for once. He agreed to meet me outside the flat in twenty minutes, only too eager to quit the happy home in Cheadle Hulme. His mother-in-law was driving him to distraction. 'That's one problem you single men don't have, Dave,' he informed me before hanging up.

'If only,' I murmured to myself.

299

On the way into town I filled him in.

'So you reckon this Anna Pietrangeli is some kind of crazy fantasist? A thrill seeker?' he grumbled.

'I don't know what she is, Peter, except that the word "unreliable" is stamped all the way through her like the letters in a stick of Blackpool rock.'

'So that means this is bloody useless,' he said, extracting one of the cards with the three heads on from of his pocket and ripping it in half. 'I've worn out two pairs of shoes hawking these round Manchester.'

'Your time wasn't wasted,' I said. 'You're the one who's always quoting the great detectives. What does the fact that no one located them for us prove?'

'It proves they don't exist,' he snorted.

'No, we know Thompson exists. We've got his photo now.' I passed him the photo of the bald-headed Fijian. 'We didn't have a face for him before and the spiky hair led us astray.'

'Led you astray, Boss.'

'OK, Peter, but at least I know when there's a tail on me.'

I told him about the two occasions he'd been followed.

'Gilby never said a word!' he fumed.

'They don't,' I remarked. 'The boys in blue stick by their own even when they're out of the job. That's why he's the hired help at Pimpernel and you're my top banana.'

'Don't rub it in,' he exclaimed with a laugh. 'I tried the medical again. They'd be prepared to accept me but Levonne won't hear of me joining the police. Her mother threatened that she'd never cook her jerk chicken for me again.'

'Tough!' I grunted unsympathetically. 'So why haven't we had a nibble for Naomi's guy? Three grand should have had witnesses coming out of the woodwork.'

He rummaged around on the floor of the car for the

half of the picture that he'd dropped. We both looked at the bespectacled, moustachioed face.

'I don't know. Perhaps he doesn't live in Manchester?'

'You went all round the suburbs with those. No, I think he's disguised. Naomi got a look at him but he wasn't worried about letting her go after seeing him and that doesn't fit the pattern of extortionists. They like to kill anyone who can tie them to their crimes.'

'Is she in any danger?'

'I don't think so. This extortionist, let's call him Mr E . . .'

'Mr E . . . mystery. So witty, employer mine!'

'Cut the sarcasm! Mr E lets a witness get away knowing she'll put out a totally false description of him. Double bluff. If Lee had made this official the police would have been just as far up the creek as we are. All we've got now is that according to Naomi he talked "posh" and he was tall and thin. With Naomi Carter, "posh" could fit more or less anyone who speaks Standard English. She told me I talk posh when I asked her.'

'Where does that leave Anna Pietrangeli's description of the same guy watching the Parkes house?'

'Precisely nowhere. I think Anna just took a peek at the original picture of our moustachioed friend, Mr E, that was pinned on the board in my office and fed it back to us. She's mischievous or attention-seeking or something. Needs a psychiatrist.'

I didn't feel like giving him a graphic account of my evening with Anna.

We reached the end of Deansgate and the traffic slowed to a crawl. I parked the car in the multi-storey near the law courts and we walked to the Phoebus Club. The tropical downpour of earlier hadn't deterred the crowds of pleasure seekers heading for the numerous bars and eateries.

A beefy-looking uniformed security guard met us at the

301

portal of the Phoebus Club. He didn't have three heads but his teeth looked pretty sharp.

'You Cunane?' he growled.

I showed ID and he signalled us to enter the private lift to the fourth floor. He was reaching for a phone when the doors closed on us.

When they opened on the fourth floor Judder Crockett was waiting for us. He was wearing a dark suit and stood with his arms folded across his chest as if he was afraid I might try to pick his pocket. There were four massive Afro-Caribbean males accompanying him, all wearing neat grey slacks, black blazers, white shirts and red bow ties. I recognised Leon Williams, Celeste's brother. He gave me a surreptitious wink before searching me for concealed weapons.

The door to the roof had been replaced by a steel hatch which could only have been shifted with a couple of pounds of Semtex. Crockett's eyes narrowed as he saw me examining it.

'You won't get through there with an axe,' he sneered.

'Somehow, I don't think it's me you're trying to keep out,' I replied.

He turned a shade paler, started to say something and then shut up. Going to the door, he shielded it with his body and punched numbers into the lock. After a great deal of whirring and clicking it opened.

Crockett's new minders followed us upstairs. The Japanese garden was still there and the koi carp still gyrated round their pool but everything was different. Bright lights cast harsh shadows. There were footprints all over the gravel and coils of razor wire set back from the edge of the roof as a surprise for anyone mad enough to climb the outside walls. At the penthouse entrance the glass door had been reinforced with steel rods and a security camera had been mounted since my last visit.

'Someone's been busy,' I said conversationally.

'Cunane, I owe you a favour for pointing out how weak my security precautions were but don't push your luck. I might remember how much all this is costing me and decide you ought to pay.'

There were more workmen inside, all clad in red nylon overalls. The words 'Secured Outcomes Inc.' were stencilled across their backs. The cluttered living room floor had been cleared of all the various fun items. In their place there was a low pile of steel components, sheets, beams and rods. Pizza cartons and McDonald's boxes littered the area. Where I'd kicked the door of the computer room in, the whole wall had been taken out. There was no sign now of the computer or the filing cabinets. That room and Thompson's stood exposed and gutted.

'Look away,' one of the workmen warned as he lifted a welding mask to his face. The man spoke with a strong Brooklyn accent and was holding a welding torch in his gloved hand. I shut my eyes as glaring light flooded the room but not before I saw that he was fastening sheet steel to the floor of Aaron Thompson's former room.

'I had to fly these people in from America,' Crockett boasted. 'They're installing a security shelter for me. I couldn't get it done in the UK, of course, everyone's too busy enjoying the weekend, but say what you like about the Yanks, they'll graft for honest cash night, noon, morning or weekend.'

'Nice if you have honest cash to give them,' I agreed. 'But what exactly is a security shelter?'

'Always willing to bring an ignorant man like you up to speed on something,' Crockett said agreeably. I could see he was itching to boast to someone. 'A security shelter or refuge room is what all the top people in the States have next to their bedroom. Sylvester Stallone has this same model. Of course they also have guns but if that isn't enough to deter an unwelcome visitor they can retreat to this room. It's fire-proof, bullet-proof . . .'

'Yeah, you name it, pal,' a foreman chimed in. 'Your room's guaranteed to stay intact whatever happens, up to and including an earthquake above eight on the Richter scale. This whole building could collapse around you but you'd be sitting fresh as a daisy in your room when they dug you out. It's got supplies for eight days, radio, emergency lighting and its own air supply. We're talking security with a capital S, here.'

'It's all right, Arnold,' Crockett said, cutting off the sales pitch. 'I don't think Mr Cunane's in the market for a refuge room. He relies on brute force and stupidity to protect him.'

'Still a lot to be said for them,' the American agreed before returning to his work.

I noticed that Crockett's frown was back. He'd wanted to do his own bragging.

'Here,' he said abruptly. 'This is what you came for.' He pressed an A4 envelope into my hand.

'So where's the computer?' I asked. 'Nervous about what someone might find?'

'You aren't the only one who knows how to use an axe, Cunane. I smashed it up until the pieces were smaller than that.' He held two fingers a couple of inches apart. 'All my pictures and files are shredded so if you're thinking of a spot of blackmail, forget it.'

'Perish the thought,' I said. 'Where's your lovely companion then?'

The frown deepened. I guessed he was working out if I was referring to Thompson or Anna.

'If you're talking about Ms Pietrangeli, she isn't my companion and never has been. She's merely a casual acquaintance who occasionally flits through my life like some beautiful butterfly glimpsed in passing on a summer's day.'

'Poetic, but that's not what it looked like last night. I thought you'd have announced your engagement by now.'

'You've got what you came for, now go,' he snapped. The minders clustered closer, responding to the mounting unpleasantness like a pack of Dobermanns sniffing raw meat.

I decided it was time to leave but not before I had a final word.

'Forget the steel room, Crockett. Phone me if your other buddy shows up. I'll deal with him for nothing.'

'How noble of you, but no thanks,' he said. 'Oh, and Cunane, if you're intending to catch Aaron you'd better be quick. The last thing he said to me was that he was intending to return to Fiji to sort out a few people there.'

'I thought that was all going to get heavy,' Peter said as we rode down in the lift accompanied by a security man to see us off the premises. 'What was that about Anna and him. Is she his partner?'

'If I could tell you what was going on between those two, I'd be a clever man.'

We walked out on to the street and the hydrocarbon-laden air of inner city Manchester smelled clean and welcoming for once. Back in the car we studied the sheet of paper.

Subject (#3/ Am/DPol):	I don't want any accounting done in euros. I tell you that is shit, man. All the accounting's got to be in dollars.
Subject (OO/D/71/NW/Reg):	That gives me a problem, brother, all my business is in sterling.
Subject (#3/ Am/DPol):	Don't try to sell me that. I hear you're buying pure white from the Afghans. They will only accept dollars.
Subject (OO/D/71/NW/Reg):	They accepted my credit, brother. I have relatives there. I can settle in sterling.
Subject (#3/ Am/DPol):	I'm not taking your lousy sterling and less of this brother business.

Subject (OO/D/71/NW/Reg):	In my religion all men are brothers. Are you sure you wouldn't like to do business in guilders?
Subject (#3/ Am/DPol):	Don't get funny, Paki. I've got lots of customers UK side who will trade in dollars.
Subject (OO/D/71/NW/Reg):	(Inaudible expletive) I'm not a Paki! Don't call me that.
Subject (#3/ Am/DPol):	(Laughs) Don't be so touchy. I'm not your brother. Our relationship is strictly business only.
Subject (OO/D/71/NW/Reg):	(Inaudible expletive) Trade in dollars, I can do that as long as you accept payment in sterling, but account in dollars. I'm sitting on a *mountain of cash* here that I can't shift. My customers pay me in pounds not dollars. I'll give you a premium to take sterling.
Subject (#3/ Am/DPol):	That sounds more promising but it leaves me sitting on a heap of sterling. I'm telling you, the banks are getting a lot tighter.
Subject (OO/D/71/NW/Reg):	Could we do a half and half deal again? I could deliver you merchandise worth half the invoice if you'll take the rest in cash.
Subject (#3/ Am/DPol):	The usual merchandise?
Subject (OO/D/71/NW/Reg):	Of course, and don't say you can't get rid of it because I know you can.
Subject (#3/ Am/DPol):	What sort of a premium were you thinking of? I could deliver at 1.20.
Subject (OO/D/71/NW/Reg):	1.20! (Foreign expletive) 1.20 (Repeated expletives). It's not fallen below 1.50 for two years and it's been at 1.60 most of the time.
Subject (#3/ Am/DPol):	I'll go to 1.30 but that's final.
Subject (OO/D/71/NW/Reg):	1.50
Subject (#3/ Am/DPol):	I'll split the difference for goodwill but I want to see you in Amsterdam before the trade goes through.

Subject (OO/D/71/NW/Reg): That's no problem. I can pop over
to Schipol any time. I'm just round
the corner from the airport here
but you're skinning me alive. (Foreign expletive) If I come I'll . . .

The transcript ended there.

'Thompson's highlighted the words "mountain of cash"
so it's extortion,' Peter said after we'd spent some minutes
reading it through.

'Have you ever had that problem? Sitting on a mountain
of cash!'

'Sad, isn't it?'

'It looks as if our tall, thin, well-spoken Mr E is going
to solve his problem for him.'

'Tall, thin, well-spoken, white and English Mr E,' Peter
corrected me.

'Yeah,' I agreed, 'that narrows it down to about twenty
million but it doesn't tell us where, when and who.'

'It might be another of his mind games,' Peter suggested
gloomily. 'After all, leaving it there like that – it's pretty
obvious.'

'It was the muscular South Sea Islander who left it lying
around, not Mr E.'

'Would anyone be that careless?'

'Thompson could be. The club he used to kill Charlie
was hanging over his bed with Charlie's blood and brains
still stuck to it.'

22

Monday morning found me struggling into work alongside the throng of commuters. Unlike many of them I didn't feel bright-eyed and bushy-tailed after my weekend. Even the sight of Jamie Piercy's smiling face staring out of the news-stands and advertising hoardings failed to perk me up.

At the office watching Celeste sort the mail on her desk made me feel exhausted and the day had hardly begun. Michael had departed for the capital after leaving a message on the office answerphone. That didn't suit Celeste who for some reason was insanely jealous of Coe's trips away from her immediate jurisdiction.

I summoned a meeting of the File Red group for ten. If Lee Parkes suddenly arrived on my doorstep I wanted to have all my ammunition prepared in advance.

'I see they won again,' Marvin said when he arrived.

I raised my eyebrows. Marvin Desailles has slightly less interest in football than he has in the literary works of the late Harriet Beecher Stowe.

'Yeah, won away at Leeds, three-one, and your little darling scored the two winning goals. They can't be bribing him to lose,' he continued.

'Marvin,' I reminded, 'Jamie claims he's never been bribed to do anything.'

'And you also believe the police aren't racist,' he said nastily. 'Have you seen the amount of pre-match gambling on football results in every betting shop from Land's End to John O'Groats?'

I gave an affirmative grunt. Much as I wanted to believe in Jamie, Marvin had right on his side.

'Can we get on?' Celeste prompted. 'I've a lot of bills to send out.'

'OK,' I said. 'First, there's a little problem.'

I turned the large sheet of hardboard round so that we could all see the maps and the pictures. I pointed to the photograph of Naomi's kidnapper.

'Do you remember when we had Anna Pietrangeli in here with Granville Courteney? You took her a cup a coffee while I spoke to Granville, remember?'

Celeste nodded her head.

'This board was facing the wall. Was there any chance she might have seen this picture?' I asked, giving it a rap.

Celeste appeared flustered.

'I didn't know what she was supposed to see. She was standing looking at that calendar over there.'

The calendar was on the wall behind the board.

'So she could have had a good old gander,' Peter said. 'It's obvious that's what she did, and I've asked about ten thousand people if they've seen that second man.'

'It's not my fault,' Celeste protested.

'No one's blaming you,' I said.

'Dave,' she replied, 'why would the Pietrangeli woman pretend she'd seen someone?'

'I don't know. Any ideas?'

'She wanted to keep you interested in her?'

'It's possible. I think she's a nutcase but your guess is as good an answer as we're going to get.'

'There's something else, Dave. I forgot this,' Celeste said. She put a parcel on my desk. 'It was propped against the door when I opened up this morning.'

I opened it and there was a photocopied police file inside labelled 'McAteer'. It was stamped 'For police use only, Not to be removed' but somebody had removed it and it didn't require many guesses to work out who that was.

'You can do time for having confidential police files in your possession,' Marvin said.

'Yes, and so can the person who sent us this, so we'd all better keep our lips zipped, hadn't we?'

He gave me a tight smile.

The file related to a traffic accident in Bramhall. It was dated January this year, just two months before the abduction of Cheyenne Parkes.

Summary of Enquiries in the McAteer Case

Eric McAteer(four years three months) was killed in an accident with a white Transit van. The van driver failed to report the accident. Enquiries are continuing as described in the appended report but so far neither the van nor the driver has been traced.

An eyewitness, seventy-two-year-old Dr Norma Grieve (now deceased), who was walking her dog (a West Highland terrier) on the pavement opposite the accident site stated that she saw the whole incident. In her signed statement (ref: SK 17586/AIU attached) she claimed that Eric McAteer *was inside the van before he was killed*. Dr Grieve was attending to her dog's natural functions under a dark tree (referred to as Tree A on attached diagram C) and may not have been visible from the van driver's position.

She noted the van halting sharply a short way beyond where she was standing with the dog (position A on diagram C) but in clear range of her limited eyesight (see attached from Sgt P.Z.Laski) and was surprised to see a little boy being let out on the passenger side.

To her continued surprise the child then set off running frantically along the edge of the pavement towards 110 Mansion Road, Bramhall, SK7 3XW, his parents' address (subsequently determined), screaming his head off, in her words.

310

Dr Grieve further stated that the van then mounted the pavement, raced towards the fleeing child and deliberately swerved into him. The child's body was thrown into the air. The van then drove off without stopping. Although overcome with shock for a moment, Dr Grieve (not a medical doctor) approached the child and saw at once that he was dead.

Dr Grieve summoned emergency services from a public phone box and her call was timed at 10.17 hours.

She told officers attending the incident that the van was driven by two men, one white, and one non-white. Physical description was vague. Men were both 'big'. Dr Grieve failed to note the registration number of the vehicle.

In view of the nature of the child's death as alleged by Dr Grieve a murder inquiry was initiated by Stockport CID reporting to Detective Chief Superintendent Pound. Murder inquiries were suspended by DCS Pound after interviews with the child's parents and further investigation into Dr Grieve's health which revealed that her memory was becoming progressively affected by Alzheimer's disease.

Accident Investigation Unit Report

The AIU established that there were tyre tracks consistent with a Ford Transit van on the pavement at the point where the child was struck. Detailed calculations indicate a speed not greatly in excess of 30 m.p.h. (see attached App.IV)

The boy's mother, Ingrid McAteer (Swedish national), stated that she had missed Eric only moments before the accident was reported at 10.17 a.m. Eric attended a nursery afternoons only and was with her at home. Mrs McAteer received hospital treatment for profound clinical depression after the accident (reported not to

311

have spoken for three weeks) and was not available for further statements after the day of the accident itself.

The father, Howard P. McAteer (occupation not recorded), stated that he works from home. He ran out into the road after hearing the screech of brakes. He saw the white van but his attention was distracted by the accident. He stated that he had an impression of two men and that there was blue lettering on the side of the van.

Mr McAteer stated that he could think of no reason why anyone would have picked the child up in a van. He knew no one who owned a white Transit and he believed that his wife's statement that the child had wandered out of the front gate only seconds before the accident was correct. 'Eric was an adventurous little boy. You had to keep your eye on him or he'd be off.' He firmly stated that the child would not have gone with strangers and that Dr Grieve's account of the accident must be wrong.

Mr McAteer was deeply traumatised by the accident and the subsequent hospitalisation of his wife. He received medical treatment at home (anti-depressants) and in the circumstances further interview was regarded as likely to be unproductive.

Road traffic officers subsequently interviewed two witnesses who claimed that they saw a white van in Mansion Road. Colin Redpath, seventeen years old, of 22 Buccleugh Drive, Wythenshawe, M20 7SJ, employed as a trainee groundsman at Bramhall Park Golf Course, stated that he saw a white van swerve out of the exit of Mansion Road into oncoming traffic on Bramhall Avenue South. Redpath said that the van did not halt at the junction and very narrowly missed an oncoming bus. He believed that he saw the word Stockport on the side of the van and that the year letter of the van was V. He could not identify the make of vehicle nor did he see into the cab.

Mrs Averill Payne, thirty-seven, 43 Mansion Road, Bramhall, SK7 2PW, was pushing a pram containing her nine-month-old infant son in Mansion Road and also saw a white van racing down Mansion Road towards her just seconds after she had crossed the road. The accident site is concealed by a bend in the road from the position where Mrs Payne crossed to gain access to her own address. She heard screaming and believes the van had the words 'Techno-Electric, Stockport' on the side and rear, written in blue stick-on letters.

Stockport CID (Det. Sgt. Hilda Greenwood and DC Anthony Lundy) pursued further inquiries in view of the element of corroboration to Dr Grieve's statement supplied by Mrs Payne. They re-interviewed Dr Grieve in the presence of her daughter. Dr Grieve stated firmly that she had seen the child run screaming and that he had been deliberately run down. However, she was unable to remember other details from her earlier statement such as the colour and make of the van or even whether it was a van or a lorry.

Greenwood and Lundy pursued telephone and personal inquiries into fifty-eight businesses in the SK postcode area which contained variants of the words 'Techno' and 'Electrical' in their titles. They made visits and inspections in a number of cases where firms owned white vehicles. They also contacted CID in similar-sounding Southport, Merseyside and Stockton-on-Tees, Teeside, for reports of hit and run accidents involving white vans and for businesses titled Techno Electrical. To date all inquiries have been fruitless and the incident is being treated as an unresolved hit and run accident. They have issued repeated appeals through the local media for the driver or witnesses to come forward. So far there has been no response.

Inspector Jeremy Goodbody of the Road Traffic

Accident unit has stated that he believes Dr Grieve certainly witnessed the accident but that she reversed the order of events owing to the stress of the occasion. He believes the child was in the road in the path of an oncoming vehicle which may have been speeding. The child screamed and ran for the pavement and the van swerved to avoid him but then the child ran back into the path of the swerving vehicle which may have been out of control at that stage.

Inquiries are continuing on a routine basis.

'Right Peter, guess where we're going?' I said when we'd all read the file. 'Shame the old lady's dead – I for one believe her version – but the parents just might be up to talking now.'

'Don't go saying you're police officers. You can get a long stretch for impersonating a dibble,' Marvin cautioned.

'Marvin, I want you to imitate being a solicitor. I want you to go to places where lawyers and senior coppers hang out. In particular the Black and Blue Club.'

'Why?'

'Because there's just a chance that's where Charlie Costello met his killer.'

'A very slim chance. Are you saying the killer was one of his customers?'

'He could have been, but Charlie might have known about him from somewhere else. I want you to check all the clubs and pubs along Deansgate, John Street, and round the courts where lawyers and coppers hang out.'

'This is needle in a haystack stuff. They wouldn't let me in some of those places.'

'That's why you're going to dress like a nice middle-class solicitor.'

'No way.'

'Marvin, when I come back to this office I want to see you tam-less, lock-less and suited.'

314

'Can't, Boss. It's against my religion.'

'Bollocks!' said Celeste. 'You've never been a Rasta man. They've got standards. They wouldn't let you join.'

'These locks are part of my faith.'

'No, they're not!' Celeste shouted. 'They're part of your excuse for not working properly.' She looked just about ready to knock his glasses off.

'I pay you a retainer to act as a solicitor,' I said. 'Right?' My chest felt tight. I'm much better at arguing with enemies than with employees.

'Right, as a solicitor,' Marvin agreed, 'not as an investigator.'

'Tell me what court would allow you to attend dressed like that?'

'They all would,' he replied calmly.

I could feel my temper sliding towards the edge. He was probably right. Celeste saved me.

'Your contract states that Pimpernel Investigations employs you to act as a retained solicitor,' she said firmly, 'and to undertake "such other related duties as shall be deemed reasonable". Mr Cunane wishes you to work undercover among other solicitors and legal people. That's reasonable. If he asked Peter to dress in Rasta gear he would, so why won't you put a suit on?'

'You should be the solicitor in the family,' Marvin said frostily before walking out.

'He'll be back and he'll be wearing a suit,' Celeste promised.

Gaining access to 110 Mansion Road wasn't easy. A large, modern detached property in about a quarter-acre of ground it was no longer occupied by the McAteer family. A notice in the herbaceous border proclaimed that the premises were protected by North West Security Associates although the high spiked fence all round the perimeter seemed to render their services unnecessary. A letter-box

315

and milk receptacle was built into the outer wall. Communication from the street was via a microphone unless you were prepared to risk climbing the eight-foot-high gate.

I spoke into the mike and explained our mission and gained admittance after considerable explanation, bandying of telephone numbers and brandishing of ID. Electronic gates clicked and slid open. The effect was reminiscent of a maximum security prison.

'I'm sorry about all this,' the young woman who admitted us said apologetically. 'I'm Amy Stott – Mrs Ronald Stott. Perhaps you've heard of my husband's firm? He's building a stadium in Eastlands.'

We both nodded and smiled knowledgeably at this information though I'd never heard of the firm.

'The security stuff came with the house when we bought it and we don't know whether to have it removed or not. My husband says it's like living in Strangeways Prison but I'm here on my own all day.'

Tall, and washed out-looking, with almost transparent skin, Amy Stott looked as if she needed a blood transfusion rather than security devices.

'It's bound to make the criminal fraternity think you've got something worth stealing,' I said.

'That's what my husband says,' she said with a nervous smile, 'but I like it.' I noticed that there was a panic button on the wall behind her.

I asked about the McAteers before she decided to start checking our ID again.

It turned out that she'd only moved in three weeks previously and didn't have the forwarding address for the McAteers. She was leaving mail with an estate agent in Bramhall: Rosewall & Son, just off Bramhall Precinct. We left with the sound of electronic locks snapping into place behind us.

Son Steven, of Rosewall & Son, was willing to talk

316

once he'd established that I was a bona fide insurance investigator. I didn't contradict the impression he formed that money might be going in the direction of Howard McAteer. He listened to my spiel with the careful air of one intent on learning something to his advantage.

'Poor sod, he deserves some luck,' Rosewall said as he retrieved McAteer's address from his computer. 'I told him I could have got him another fifty thousand for that house but he was determined to sell, even at a loss. I suppose losing his wife like that . . .'

'Sorry, we heard it was his son?' I interjected.

'Oh, yes, him as well. His wife went back home to Uppsala, she was Swedish, and took an overdose there. It was terribly sad.'

He pressed a button and a printed label shot out of the computer with the address 16 Bickley Road, Gorton, M12 2SW.

'Sorry, Mr Rosewall, are you sure this is the right address?' I asked. 'There can't be many people moving from Bramhall into Gorton.'

'Yes,' he said with a faint smile. 'That's right. A council property, I believe. Like I said, he was desperate for a quick sale. Money troubles of some sort on top of all his other problems. I never did quite establish what Mr McAteer did for a living. He must have been well off at one time because he owned that property in Mansion Road free of any mortgage. He didn't buy it through us. Still, if you're able to steer some cash his way you can tell him that we have lots of modestly priced property here in Bramhall.'

16 Bickley Road, Gorton was everything the estate agent's mannered little smile had implied it would be – starved-looking dogs, graffiti, broken-down gates, weeds on the pavement and all types of litter in the street. Although it was term time there seemed to be as many children around as during school holidays.

As a dwelling the house was quite reasonable. That is, it

317

was equipped with the usual number of walls, windows, etc, and supplied with everything except a desirable location. The present occupant, the former wealthy suburbanite, was at home and clearly not happy to receive visitors.

Peter banged on the door for almost five minutes before we heard the sound of cursing from within.

Six foot tall, approaching twenty stone, with thin wavy blond hair brushed across a pink scalp, McAteer was an imposing figure. Or at least had been at one time. The flesh seemed to hang loosely on him now, flapping over his belt and the neck of the dirty white T-shirt he was wearing. His face and skin were brick red as if he'd spent the entire day in front of a furnace. He had no trousers on, just underpants. He was about my age, late thirties, but he looked much, much older. The veins were standing out on his face like the willow pattern on a china plate and dark pouches under his eyes gave him the look of an infinitely sad bloodhound.

'What do you want?' he snarled as he inspected us. He stood in the doorway guarding the narrow gap, the door half closed in readiness for a quick slam. There was a sweet smell on his breath which I couldn't quite place. It wasn't wine or spirits.

'We're investigating the circumstances of your son's death,' I said quickly.

'What do you mean "circumstances?" It was a hit and run accident and don't say you've caught the bastard who did it because I know you never will.'

'No, we're investigating how it came to happen.'

'If you're trying to blame my wife or me, forget it.'

'We know who to blame, Mr McAteer,' I said, abandoning caution. 'The people who kidnapped your son. They're the ones who should be blamed.'

He crumpled at this.

'Kidnapped? How do you know . . . Oh, Christ! I've been half hoping that you'd find out. I don't mind

318

going to prison. What have I to lose now? You'd better come in.'

'Before we do, I have to tell you we're not from the police. I'm a private detective investigating a similar case and I received a tip-off that you'd had the same problem. What you've just said makes me believe I'm right.'

'They've done it to someone else? The bastards! Did the kid die?'

'She's really ill.'

'A little girl?'

'A baby.'

'How much did they take?'

'Two hundred thousand.'

'They got a hell of a lot more off me.'

He opened the door and led us into the living room.

A pungent, sickly-sweet aroma of urine hit us in the face. Peter flinched and tried to retreat but I pushed him forward. We were too close to finding a few answers to let minor considerations of hygiene deter us.

There was only one article of furniture in the room. An artificial leather sofa, propped up on bricks at one side, which had obviously arrived in its present location via some rubbish skip, was positioned about three feet from a gas fire that was belting out heat. The fire was the only thing in the room that seemed to be unbroken. Draped with a filthy duvet, the sofa almost resembled a modern art installation. This dreary ensemble was completed by a television with a distorted picture.

McAteer made a gesture as if to invite us to share the sofa with him but then became suspicious. 'How do I know you're not from them? You might be checking up to see if I've . . .'

I gave him my Pimpernel ID.

'That's my name and address on there, and it's a real phone number. You can check me out.'

McAteer studied the ID for a moment with a hopeless expression on his face.

'Sorry,' he muttered as he passed it back. He went into the small adjoining kitchen and returned with a stool on which he perched.

I sat down but Peter, fastidious as ever, preferred to lean against the wall.

I loosened my tie.

'Sorry,' McAteer repeated, and turned the heat down. 'I don't get out much these days and I feel the cold.'

'Any chance of a bit of fresh air in here?' Peter asked. He looked on the point of passing out.

'Sorry,' McAteer said feebly again. 'I don't have many visitors, no family now. Open the window.' He gathered up the old duvet, which incongruously had the face of Eric Cantona on it, and wrapped it round his shoulders.

'Mr McAteer, you don't need to keep apologising. We've come to see if you can help us.'

'I need to keep apologising to someone,' he said, with a spark of anger. 'I've made a total cock-up of my life, haven't I? My son murdered and my wife killing herself . . . that's him.'

He gestured to the gas fire. There was a small metal can on top of it.

Peter's face became perceptibly paler. I said nothing. The gas fire hissed away.

'Sorry,' McAteer mumbled eventually, 'but what will you do if you catch them? Hand them over to the police? I don't think so. If this little girl's father made his living the same way I did that'll be the last thing he wants . . .'

'Can I stop you there?' I interrupted. 'I'm not interested in what you did for a living. Eric was completely innocent, wasn't he?'

McAteer's chest started heaving at this and then tears began to roll down his face, streaking his unwashed cheeks. 'It's all my fault,' he murmured over and over, crooning the words to himself.

'Go and see if you can make a drink or something,' I barked at Peter who went into the kitchen area and started opening cupboards.

A few minutes later he returned. He pressed a mug of tea into McAteer's hand and, more practical than me, handed him a couple of paper tissues from his own pocket. McAteer put the tea down and wiped his face.

'You may think I'm a pretty poor specimen,' he said, 'but I know I am. They wiped me out financially, I had to give them everything I had – half a million near enough – and then I had to sell the house to pay off the people I owed. They're not the sort who let you buy now, pay later. That wouldn't have mattered, I had Ingrid and we could have started again, but then she had to kill herself. She blamed herself worse than I did.'

This recollection seemed to be about to open the flood gates again so I intervened with a question.

'What exactly happened?'

'In the morning Ingrid usually took Eric to the park. I was expecting them back any minute. The phone went and then this rough voice was demanding money. He said they knew how I made my living. I don't mind telling you this . . . what difference can it make now?'

'I don't want to know about your living.'

'Yes, you do. I imported cocaine from Amsterdam but I didn't sell a single ounce in this country. Sweden and Norway were my markets. It started when we were students. I met Ingrid on an exchange scheme, lovely girl, some of her mates wanted charlie and I happened to have some and it started from there. Just a casual thing, doing a favour for a few friends. We used to visit Ingrid's parents in Uppsala four or five times a year and come back with the car stuffed with money.'

'Were you ever under police investigation?'

'Not as far as I know. These are all respectable people I'm talking about. University and professional people in

321

Sweden and Norway – doctors, lawyers, all kinds, even Lutheran priests. We didn't hang around on street corners in the slums. Not that they have any in Sweden. There's no Moss Side there.'

'Moss Side isn't a slum,' Peter put in. 'It's definitely better than your current address.'

'I expect you're right,' McAteer agreed self-deprecatingly. 'Why should I have anything against slums? I've found my level now, haven't I? Actually the neighbours here are all better people than I am. They mostly work for a living. It's their bloody kids I can't stand! Not that I'll be here for much longer. I haven't paid the rent on this dump for weeks.

'Anyway, we never brought any gear into England. We used to drive to Felixstowe and cross to Holland, pick up our cargo and then drive through Germany and Denmark up to Sweden.'

'How did you launder the money?'

'I thought you didn't want to know my business?' he retorted sharply.

'It's relevant. It might help if we can find out how they knew you had a safe stuffed with cash, which presumably you did?'

'Yes,' he admitted, with just the faintest trace of a regretful smile, 'I did.'

He took a long swallow of his tea. As he put it down he exhaled noisily and I finally identified the scent on his breath. It was cider and meths.

'This is what we did. We got Swedish and Norwegian currency and on the way back through the continent we detoured through Germany, Belgium and France and changed enough into dollars to pay our supplier in Amsterdam. He wanted . . .'

'Dollars, not Swedish kroners, I know.'

'Right. Well, the exchange rate was lousy but we didn't care. We were too careful to put anything in a bank

322

account. I was working as a teacher at first, sixth-form college not a comp, but I gave that up the first time a kid threatened to rearrange my features. They were sorry to lose me, my subject was maths.'

You should have stuck to it, I thought.

He must have picked up an inkling of that because he said, 'You're a hard bastard, aren't you? Mr Cunane of Pimpernel Investigations. A bit on the poofy side your firm's name, isn't it? Out of character.'

'A private joke,' I said.

'As you say, but I can see you hate my guts. You're right to. I don't want your pity and I expect you have to be a hard nut to catch up with this bunch. You must be making progress to have come across me.'

'I don't despise you, Mr McAteer, if that's what you mean. I just don't think that you drinking yourself to death is going to make much difference in the scheme of things or make up for what happened to your wife and son. Helping us just might.'

'Leave them out of it!' he snapped. 'It makes a bloody big difference to me. You know Ingrid and me sweated blood to have Eric. She couldn't conceive for years, something was wrong with her tubes. We tried every fertility treatment in the book and then when he came along . . .'

'OK, I get the picture, but I still don't see that you ending up face down in the gutter is going to make anything right. Any tiny detail you can give us may help. Better still, show us.'

In Bramhall he took us through the various moves. The one thing that stood out was that he'd never caught even the slightest glimpse of his son's kidnappers. There had been a white van parked along the road for several days before the kidnap but the only thing that had registered on him was its presence.

When Eric went missing from a play area in the park Ingrid was talking to another mum. One minute the boy

323

was there, the next nowhere to be seen. She ran home, convinced he must have returned there in search of his dad. She arrived back to find Howard already receiving the ransom demand and his instructions. As with Cheyenne, two different voices were used. Unlike Lee, McAteer had complied exactly with their wishes. With the child's distraught mother weeping on his shoulder, there'd been no room to bargain even if he'd been willing to try. Every last note from the safe was loaded into a large Adidas sports bag.

Delivery of the cash followed the 'cautious extortionist' pattern Brendan Cullen had described. McAteer was ordered to park in a Sainsbury's car park adjoining the A34 at Cheadle several miles from his home. The car was to be against the fence and facing the dual carriageway at 11 p.m. He was phoned at intervals and told to flash his headlights. He couldn't see who was observing him. Traffic was light. There was some mist. At midnight he was told to drive slowly along the B5358 Handforth to Prestbury road until he saw two plastic bollards by the kerb side. When he stopped he was instructed to place the sports bag on a white plastic tray. He found the tray on top of the wall of a bridge over the A34 Handforth bypass, deposited his cash and drove off.

McAteer showed us the delivery point. There were still faint marks on the stonework but no physical evidence remained. It wasn't hard to guess that someone had parked on the hard shoulder below long enough to pull the tray and bag off the parapet above by means of a cord.

The parents had been promised that the child would be returned safe and sound between eleven and twelve the next morning so they weren't waiting by the roadside when Eric was dropped at 10.17 and somehow pressured into making his last dash for freedom.

McAteer insisted that he had no friends or relatives who would have done this to him. He had no connections with the criminal underworld apart from in Amsterdam. No reason to think that he'd been under police surveillance in England. The only thing he and Ingrid had done here was to change their remaining Swedish cash into sterling at as many bureaux de change in London as it took. This usually involved stopping there for as long as a week.

Before going back we drove through the lanes round Bramhall Park several times. It was quiet now as it must have been when Eric was lifted.

The simplicity of the snatch implied that the gang hadn't seen the need for the elaborate measures they'd used with Cheyenne, such as taking over the Evergreens. They must always have intended to release Naomi with her misleading description of her kidnappers and hence a secluded transfer point was essential. Also, the decision not to use the same drop point at the bridge on the B5358 was interesting. Had they felt that the A34 was a little too public? Did someone spot them? Or did the fact that they were dealing with two fit young men rather than a bloated drug dealer make them change their plans?

McAteer held up well during all this. When we drove back to Gorton he had some colour in his face. Apart from the bloodshot eyes and worn look he could almost have passed for normal.

'I'm going to pay you for your help,' I told him.

'You don't need to pay me,' he muttered sullenly. 'Just give me a call me when you catch them.'

'I'm not offering cash. We'll pay your back rent and get you some furniture.'

'I don't want charity,' he stammered.

'This isn't charity. I pay for information and you've supplied it.'

We stopped off at the Gorton Neighbourhood Office in Mount Road and paid his back rent. The polite African behind the counter told me where I could get furniture. We drove round to an old warehouse used by a local charity. For a hundred pounds I got a table, chairs, sofa, bed, mattress and some bedding. They would be delivered to 16 Bickley Road before dark. Before dropping McAteer at his address I stopped at a supermarket and bought a mop and bucket, a large-sized bottle of household cleaner and an air freshener, as well as some basic foodstuffs.

We took him to his door.

'This is your low spot, Howard. Pick yourself up from here and I'll get in touch when we find the people who killed your son, but a useless pile of jelly is no good to anyone,' I told him.

He slammed the door shut on me.

23

'Sorry about this,' I said to Peter as we drove back to the office. 'First thing in the morning you're going to come back here and take friend McAteer round the stops in Bramhall again. Ask him some more about the white van. His brain's so soaked in booze there's no saying what he might remember next.'

Peter accepted the inevitable with a brave little smile.

'We haven't done anything about that conversation on Thompson's transcript,' he said, adroitly changing the subject.

'Have you noticed how the A34 figures in everything we've found so far?' I asked.

'Including the pick up of McAteer's money,' Peter agreed.

When we got to the office Celeste was still there. 'He's gone,' she announced with a beaming smile. 'He got a suit and went to that club.'

'Fine,' I muttered, too wrapped up in my thoughts to pay much heed. 'Who's gone?'

'Marvin,' she exclaimed.

'Oh,' I muttered. Then we retreated to my office and worked out a plan on the flipchart . . .

McAteer	Parkes	Unknown victim
Drug dealer	Illegal gambler	Drug dealer/ merchant
2 miles from A34	½ mile from A34	Round corner from airport ???

Cash at home	Cash at home	Mountain of cash
White van	White van	White van ???
Surveillance probably by white van labelled 'Techno Electric'	Surveillance by 'Silk Cut' smoker . . . *no description*	Surveillance ???
Ransom collected on A34 at bridge	Ransom collected at Alderley 2 mls. from A34	In progress now??

'It's not much, is it?' Peter grumbled when we'd finished. 'I mean, if we had five hundred men and we saturated areas "round the corner from the airport" within two miles of the A34, looking for a white van, we'd still have an impossibly large area to search.'

'I'm worried about this Silk Cut smoker,' I said. 'We know there was observation, Lee Parkes spotted a small white van, and there were the cigarette butts, but is it Mr E or someone else?'

'Do you think we should take this to the police?'

It was the question I'd been dreading.

'No,' I said abruptly. 'No police.'

'But they've got the resources.'

'They've also got someone in their ranks who, if not the actual extortionist himself, is passing information to him.'

'You don't know that for certain. That intercept could have come from Customs, from foreign police, even from MI5.'

'Peter, no one respects our blue-suited friends more than I do . . .'

'Get out of it!'

'No, my dad was a senior policeman . . .'

'Who didn't get the promotion he thought he deserved.'

'Steady! You'll be saying he's Mr E next.'

'I didn't mean that but he's never made any secret of the fact that he felt he should have gone further.'

328

'They all do unless they're content to be a constable all their lives.'

'I still think we should tell them. Eric McAteer and Cheyenne Parkes may be just the tip of the iceberg. Then there's this Asian. We don't know who they're planning to kidnap belonging to him.'

'You could be right, but I think we've nearly got enough to catch them at it ourselves.'

'How are we going to find an Asian drug dealer when we don't even know his name? It's hopeless.'

'We could find Thompson, and if we find him we'll find out what they're up to.'

'How?'

'You could go round with his photograph.'

I turned to the map.

'We don't have enough crime sites here but there's a well-established theory that criminals operate at some distance from their home. So if we shade in the areas where there've already been crimes he must live in one of the remaining unshaded areas with easy access to the A34.'

I shaded in Wilmslow, Handforth, Bramhall, Alderley Edge and Cheadle Hulme.

'Still a lot of places left,' Peter grumbled.

'Look at that face,' I said, holding the photo of Thompson in front of him. 'Would you forget that once you'd seen it? This guy likes cocaine and steroids. He'll have to make contact with a dealer.'

'You're assuming he's moved in with Mr E. He might have gone somewhere else.'

'I assume lots of things. We know he's left Crockett and isn't welcome at the Phoebus Club. Who else does he know apart from Mr E and these people in Chester? I'm going to check the Smathers out again tomorrow. I assume this Asian case is the last big score for Thompson if he's heading back to Fiji as Crockett claims.

'And since he killed Charlie Costello, he hasn't been too

trusting of Mr E. I expect the pair of them are watching each other like hawks. Where better to go to ground than with our Mr E?'

'He might be disguised.'

'He might be wearing a turban, a wig, even a beard,' I admitted, 'but that face can't be disguised. As for the fate of our drug dealer's nearest and dearest, I think we've got time. They took three months between the McAteer and the Parkes jobs. Mr E is a careful man. Every detail has to be meticulously planned in advance. I want you to go round Cheadle, Poynton, Woodford, and Heald Green . . . all those places. You know where to look.'

Peter looked at me speculatively for a long time. 'Round the pubs, clubs and dives again with Gilby?'

'No, go upmarket this time. Include gyms, leisure centres and fitness clubs.'

He gave a grunt which I took for assent.

'You can forget about Asians, too,' I added. 'The guy in the transcript was a Muslim but that includes a lot of people. He could be Albanian, Turkish, anything.'

Peter nodded, then grinned and said sarcastically, 'All right, there's also Marvin. You never know, he could get a lead at the Black and Blue Club.'

'That was always a long shot,' I said defensively.

'You said it yourself, Boss. We've no proof that Charlie Costello's murderer ever set foot in the club. Charlie was killed at the front door, not inside. The killer could have been anyone among hundreds of Charlie's acquaintances. There are things called telephones, you know. Charlie could have phoned him that night.'

'All right, don't rub it in. At least we're keeping Marvin out of trouble.'

'Just crossing the Is and dotting the Ts. I'll have the photo copied,' he said, 'and we'll get going tomorrow. Same reward as before?'

I nodded.

Bren Cullen had said that the extortionist wasn't a pro and that he'd make a mistake if he got rattled. I was counting on Peter's expedition to the suburbs and Marvin's visit to the club to give our friend the feeling that someone was hunting him. A careful man like Mr E would have keen instincts for signs of pursuit.

When Peter had left I sat staring at the chart and map. I felt as if someone was twisting a hayfork in my guts. What right did I have to take chances with some unknown individual's life, probably a child's. But it was our best lead, finding this rich drug dealer who lived 'just around the corner from the airport'.

I knew the very best way to do that – ask another drug dealer. I must speak to Bob Lane. To find him I had to locate his battered little henchman with the adenoid problem.

It was five in the evening and the weather was fine when I left the office. Five hours later it was raining steadily and I was in Cheetham Hill entering my twentieth sleazy drinking den of the night. This one was masquerading as a social club on Buckingham Road.

'You a member, pal?' the doorman asked. 'It's a private club.' He was a chunkily built individual about five feet wide across the shoulders, with ginger hair and spade-shaped teeth.

I fumbled through my pockets until I came up with a ten-pound note.

'I'm looking for a mate.'

I put the note down on the counter beside him.

'You sure you're not looking for trouble?' he asked.

I shook my head.

I'd put on an old jacket and trousers before I left the office and now I clearly looked bedraggled enough to pass inspection because the bouncer nodded his head and put his hand down over the money.

'This mate?' he asked, flicking his head interrogatively. They don't waste their words in that part of Manchester, or perhaps he only had a limited vocabulary.

I wasn't stupid enough to mention Bob's name though I knew I was in his general territory.

I mimed a twisted nose and low stature.

'Talks like this,' I said through my nose.

'Short arse?'

'Yeah, shaven head.'

'Your funeral if you mess with him. Tony's in the back room.'

I went into the main bar area. There was a long, poorly lit bar served by a middle-aged woman with a bust like a ship's figurehead, a couple of pool tables, a lot of broken furniture and thick carpet all over the floor. Customers peered at me from darkened recesses like vampire bats appraising their evening meal. They all looked as utterly wrecked as the rest of the place. The carpet squished under my feet. It was soaking. There was a pervasive smell of damp and beer but as I neared the bar another reek hit me in the face: the sweet sickly smell of grass.

I had to wonder why people wanted to pass their evenings in such a place when they could be at home watching soap operas. Perhaps they all wanted to get rheumatism and claim on their insurance.

When I took a step in the direction of the back room the two youths who were playing pool turned towards me, holding their cues at the ready.

'All right, lads,' I said. 'I'm just looking for Tony.'

They looked at me with that ignorant glare I was so used to.

'Fuck you,' one of them muttered under his breath. I strode between them and they moved to one side. When I passed they sniggered. One of them farted, obviously the floor show.

The back room turned out to be no more choice than the main lounge.

Three men were sprawled on chairs round a table improvised from a packing case. They were supposed to be playing cards but were actually high as kites on the spliffs they made no attempt to hide. Bob's henchman was one of them. He seemed to be wearing the same sweater and T-shirt he'd had on when I met him weeks ago and with no intervening washday for himself or the clothes.

'I need a word with you, Tony,' I said. 'I need to get in touch with our mutual friend.'

He looked at me blankly. His eyes had that glazed-over look. I could feel my anger growing.

'Popeye . . . Bob? You know? I need to talk to him.'

Eventually a look of dim comprehension dawned.

'You mustn't say Bob's name, there's been trouble,' he slurred.

'I know that, but there'll be more trouble if he doesn't get in touch with me. Have you got a number for him?'

'Can't say,' he mumbled. His two smoking companions looked equally out of it. If this was the remnant of Bob's merry band of men then it was no surprise he was on the run. But there was no point in getting hard with poor Tony. Life had inflicted enough on him. His face looked as if a horse had trodden on it at one time.

'Step outside for a minute,' I suggested, waving some money at him. The stink of weed was getting on my throat.

It took him some time to make his mind up but at last he came out with me. His habit didn't come cheap.

'What went on here?' I asked as we passed through the wrecked bar.

'Bit of a rumble at the weekend,' he muttered.

Once out in the fresh clean rain we stood under the street light and I asked him again about Bob.

'There must be some way to get in touch with him,' I coaxed.

He lifted his face to look at me and under the sodium light I could see the thin blue lines of old scars under his skin. Rain pelted into his eyes which held nothing but emptiness. Then there was a gradual change. Ferocity crept

333

back into them. They became brighter. It was as if a light had been turned on somewhere.

'You're Bob's friend, aren't you?' he intoned.

'Yes.'

'You've got his brother with you, haven't you?'

'Yes.'

This went on for ten minutes.

I left when he'd finished the litany with some hope that he'd get Bob to phone me. He'd written my number on the back of his hand.

It was after eleven when I returned to my flat in the south of the city. No one was stirring. The steady sound of snoring came from my bedroom so Clint was obviously at peace. I wished I was.

Next day I drove over to Mollingtree. The Smathers' house had been repaired. There was no answer when I knocked. An elderly next-door neighbour came out. 'They're in Spain,' he announced.

'I wish I was with them,' I muttered, more to myself than him but he took it as a general comment on the weather and gave me his views on that.

'They haven't got anyone staying with them?' I asked when he'd finished. 'A big black chap? Face like a train smash.'

He shook his head, and stared at me in owlish surprise, as if the very suggestion that there were big black people in the world was astonishing. From the point of view of an elderly Mollingtree resident maybe it was.

Peter turned up nothing new from Howard McAteer. Michael was still travelling incognito in southern parts, or at least not getting in touch with us in Manchester. I chose to believe he was working. Marvin announced that his infiltration of the Black and Blue Club to sniff out traces of Mr E would take time.

I told him I wasn't holding my breath.

*   *   *

What did take my breath away was a phone call from Jamie Piercy when I got home that evening.

'She's dead,' he gasped.

'Oh, no,' I murmured.

'I was with her, the poor lamb. Respiratory failure, the doctor said. They had her pumped full of antibiotics but her little body couldn't fight off the infection any longer. It was those bastards leaving her in that car that caused this . . .' He struggled against the sobs that threatened to choke him.

'Yes,' I agreed.

'She wasn't a well child but leaving her like that . . .'

'They'll pay for it,' I promised.

He sniffed loudly.

'Are you any closer to catching them?'

'I think so,' I said carefully.

'Tell me!'

'We may soon know who their next intended victim is,' I said hopefully. 'That'll lead us straight to them.' I didn't feel like going into the story of Eric McAteer right now. It would only make Jamie feel worse.

'Well, I want to be there when you find them,' he said heavily. 'Listen, I'm too choked up to go into all this now but the reason I phoned is so you can let Naomi know the bad news. I reckon we owe her that.'

'How about you?' I asked.

There was a long pause.

'Yeah, well, I'm not too good,' he admitted eventually. 'Fortunately, I'm not playing this weekend. Strained ligament in the last game.'

'Right,' I murmured. It wasn't his ligaments I'd been worried about.

'Listen, Mr Cunane, I feel rotten. Sometimes I feel like calling a press conference and admitting everything that's gone on, but I can't. Football's my life. I might as well be dead myself as give up now. The doctors at the hospital know who I am but it's a private place. They let me in through a special entrance and I think they've decided that I was really the kid's father, but they guarantee complete privacy. Not like the NHS where they'd bell the tabloids as soon as I put my nose round the door.'

'I see.'

'Yeah, what I'm saying is that even though the worst has happened it's still important that you keep everything secret at your end. I don't think Cheyenne would have wanted to see her favourite uncle ruined, do you?'

'No.'

'And Naomi, she's probably twigged who I am by now. I know she's thick but she could hardly avoid seeing my picture in the paper.'

'She doesn't read them much.'

'Yeah, but even so . . .'

'OK, say she does know, so what?'

His tone became sharper, altogether more focused. Clearly grief at a child's death was not blinding him to its wider implications.

'Tell her if she keeps quiet there'll be something in it for her when all this is sorted. A token of our appreciation for what she did for Cheyenne, like. Can you do that for me?'

'Yes,' I said slowly.

'Great!' he replied and rang off.

There was a nasty taste in my mouth when I put the phone down. The great soccer player had tied up all the loose ends now, hadn't he? If I could ensure that Naomi kept her mouth shut, that is.

She'd never talked about Jamie and as far as I knew just considered him to be a friend of Lee Parkes's. She'd only seen him at the house a couple of times, had certainly never mentioned that she knew he was a famous footballer.

In his vanity, Jamie had assumed she knew who he was and that she'd be bound to want to score money off him, just like everyone else. I'd agreed to help keep her quiet. Did that make me as corrupt as he was? I had to face it, you can't play with tar and keep your hands clean.

I waited till later in the evening to break the news to Naomi. Janine was with her and they'd just put Lloyd and Jenny to bed.

The mercenary reaction envisaged by Jamie simply didn't happen.

Naomi cried. She wanted to go to the funeral. I told her it would be a private interment and she cried some more. Indirect questioning established that she still didn't know who Jamie was. She had absolutely no knowledge of the big secret.

She still blamed herself for not resisting the kidnappers and cried about that. She was frightened that the police would become involved and accuse her in some way because of her father's record. I told her there would be no police and she cried again.

I hadn't the gall to offer her money for silence.

Jamie would have to do his dirty work himself.

24

They say that if you poke a wasp's nest with a long stick you can expect to get stung. Even so it was Thursday before anything happened.

Lee Parkes turned up at my office that afternoon, jet-lagged and steaming with rage. He expected me to have the heads of the men who had caused Cheyenne's death on a platter.

'I told you it would take time,' I shouted.

'You've already had more than a month!'

'Why this sudden urge to quit?' I demanded. 'Are your Malaysian Chinese friends after more information from you, is that it? You knew it would take time.'

He drew his lips back from his teeth like some feral animal and started toying with the heavy ashtray I keep on my desk. I thought he was going to hit me with it. But just as suddenly as the violent fit had taken him, it began to subside. I prefer to avoid stereotypes but it was hard not to remember what I'd found out about his Italian ancestry. Lee definitely wasn't the phlegmatic Anglo-Saxon type.

'Sorry,' he said grudgingly. 'I get so mad thinking of them leaving Cheyenne in a car boot and taking that money, the bastards!'

I wondered what order his grievances really came in, money or babe? Was the rage contrived for effect?

I recounted the progress that had been made without naming names. Unfortunately that didn't take very long.

I could see the storm clouds gathering over his head again even as I spoke.

Celeste came in then.

'Not now,' I said impatiently.

'You'll want to see this,' she said, giving me a meaningful stare. She laid a fax down on the desk in front of me. 'It's from Michael.'

It was hard to divert my attention from Parkes to the flimsy sheet of paper but when I saw what it was I momentarily forgot about my visitor.

It was a marriage certificate between one James Anthony Parkes, aged sixteen, bachelor of this parish, and Ashleigh Elizabeth Binns, also aged sixteen. Both were listed as unemployed. The marriage was solemnised at a register office in Hackney. James Anthony Parkes's date of birth was all too familiar.

There was further enlightenment on the facsimile of another document. Kimball Smathers had apparently been dishonourably discharged from the Marines in July 1997 following an incident while on a training exercise in Fiji.

My eyes were roving over these details when Lee leaned over and grabbed the paper off me. He must have spotted the name Parkes before I snatched the sheet back off him. It tore in two and I got the larger piece.

'Checking up on me? Bloody cheek!'

'This is Jamie, isn't it? And Binns was your adopted father's name. Who's this Ashleigh Elizabeth Binns then?'

'Who the fuck do you think you are?' he snarled. 'I'm paying you to find Cheyenne's killers, not to dig up this crap.'

'Maybe I'll find her killers this way. Maybe the answer's in London not Manchester. What do you think, Lee? Is there something in your background that might have inspired someone to take revenge on you? Who is this Binns woman?'

'You absolute fucking arsehole!' he said, but the words

339

were uttered diminuendo. He subsided into his chair. 'She's my sister – not my blood sister, but the daughter of Henry and Maureen Binns, the couple who took me in. They thought they couldn't have children but when they adopted me, Mum – Maureen, that is – got pregnant. Apparently it's quite common for childless women to get pregnant that way.'

'Spare me the gynaecology lesson. You were blackmailing Jamie with this, weren't you? There's never been anything in the papers about England's soccer darling having a wife. What are all his young female fans going to think?'

'They'll think he's a right bastard if they ever find out the truth.'

'Which is?'

'He put Ashleigh up the spout. She must have been technically under age at the time. It wasn't all his fault, but she was a damn sight more naïve than him, to say the least. Henry went mad when he found out. He went round to Jack Piercy's place and played merry hell with him. He was an intimidating bloke when he wanted to be, was Henry.'

Lee seemed lost in recollection.

'Go on!' I urged.

'Jack Piercy tried all ways to prevent Jamie from getting married. Ashleigh was just an East End slag to him. They're all the same, his type. They get a bit of money, move out past Chingford and start thinking they're landed gentry. Jamie was already on his way to the Premier League with scouts from three top clubs sniffing round. So Piercy wanted her to have an abortion, or have the kid adopted, anything to stop Jamie tying himself to trash like her. I came in for a lot of stick, too. Jamie wasn't supposed to come sneaking round to see his big brother. Jack Piercy was crazy – still is. He'd been getting coaching and everything for Jamie since the kid was five and now he could see a big pay-off just around the corner. He didn't want Ashleigh wrecking the boy's chances.'

'I don't see how being married would have wrecked anything.'

'You don't know Jack Piercy. He only wanted the best for his lad and Ashleigh wasn't it. Anyway, they did get married. The baby had spina bifida – Jamie walked out on Ashleigh soon after the birth. The kid died and Ashleigh ran off somewhere. We've had no contact with her since. Jamie's still married to her as far as I know. A nice squalid tale for the tabloids about Mr Clean, eh?'

'Were you threatening to reveal all this? Is that why he helped you?'

'Was it fuck! He helped me because he wanted to. Jamie's not so lily-white as you and his ten million adoring fans think.'

'It must have helped you to put pressure on him.'

'There's worse. I haven't told you the half of it. The baby died when she was two. She needed surgery but there was a six-month waiting list with the NHS. She could have had treatment in America if her father had paid like he should have. Jamie was into the big money almost right away and Piercy wasn't short. But Jamie wouldn't pay. He kept avoiding her. That pissed me off something rotten at the time.'

'What about you? Why didn't you pay?'

'Family thing. He was the father. It was down to him to pay and then when I was ready to offer help the baby died and Ashleigh ran off. Like I said, a tragedy from beginning to fucking end. The story won't stop Jamie playing football but it'll kill his reputation.'

I thought about it. It was true that in the hands of a hostile tabloid the desertion of Ashleigh Binns and her handicapped child could be made to seem very messy. *Was* very messy. Even messier if they got Ashleigh to write her exclusive account: **'England soccer star deserted me and our sick child,' says wife.**

341

Another thought occurred.

'Where is Ashleigh now?'

'I told you, I don't know. She never got in touch even when her father was ill. They put messages in the papers for her but there was no answer. My guess is she's got herself another bloke somewhere and doesn't want to disturb her present life by raking up the past. Or maybe she thinks we're all to blame . . . I don't know. Who really understands what goes on in a woman's head? If you're thinking she had anything to do with what happened to Cheyenne, forget it. That wouldn't have been her style. Why should she harm my baby anyway? I've done nothing to her.'

That wasn't entirely true but there didn't seem much point in pressing the matter. The knowledge that Lee could easily ruin him seemed a much better motive for Jamie's wanting to keep him happy, rather than brotherly love which was all I'd been offered before. I looked at Lee and tried to get my head round everything that was going on here.

Jamie recruited me to pursue the killers of his brother's child and to protect the secret that he'd been involved in serious corruption of the national game. At first Lee's only interest had seemed to be vengeance but over the weeks there'd been a shift in focus. Now he was more interested in getting his money back and clearly resented paying for my services. Then there was the Smathers connection . . .

'What are you looking at me like that for?' he blustered, and stood up as if to go.

'Sit down and shut up!' I snapped.

He looked startled but he did sit down.

'Is this how you treat all your clients?' he asked, not unreasonably.

'No, because when my clients have a problem they really want me to help them, they tell me everything I need to know. Why is it that every time I meet you I come away wondering what the agenda really is?'

'Listen to yourself,' he taunted. 'All getting a bit too much for you, is it?'

'It all comes down to motive, Lee: your motive, the kidnapper's, Kimball Smathers's motive.'

'What's he got to do with it?'

'He has a pretty good motive for hating your guts.'

'I told you, Keeley was just a one-night stand. Have you seen the flabby cow? I can do a lot better than that.'

'That's not what Kimball thinks. He believes you and she were an item.'

'Stroll on!'

'He says Mel was going to see him on the night she died. She was sick of you carrying on with his wife.'

'What an imagination he's got! Keeley was Mel's friend.'

'So why did he say that?'

'Because he's a cokehead. If you've met him you must know the guy's wired all the time. Can't sit still for a minute. Even though he was a mate I had to let him go as my minder. He was taking too many liberties.'

'There's more to it than that.'

'Who the fuck do you think you are, Cunane? The Recording Angel? You're supposed to be finding Cheyenne's killers.'

'I'm coming to that but I'll tell you who I think I am first — I'm a private detective you sent off on a cold trail and didn't tell half the story to, and I just wonder why that was? Did you ever seriously intend to catch these extortionists or was it just an expensive gesture to please brother Jamie?'

'What do you mean? I loved Cheyenne.'

'What I mean is you've been more hindrance than help. You didn't tell me that Kimball had asked you to put money into the Phoebus Club.'

'Why should I tell you all my business?'

343

'Because someone connected to the Phoebus Club helped to kidnap Cheyenne.'

'Not that old pouf Crockett? I'll kill him!'

'Not Crockett.'

'Who then?'

'A man called Aaron Thompson.'

I looked at Lee closely. The name produced no reaction. 'A black man, six foot four in his socks, built like a tank with an unforgettably ugly face,' I continued.

'Never seen him,' Lee said with a confident shake of his head.

'He was in the Fijian Army where he met a Brit called Kimball Smathers. They were both kicked out of the military for drugs. They have such a lot in common that Thompson stayed with Kimball when he arrived in the UK just under three years ago.'

There was a reaction from Lee but it was hard to know if it was genuine. He seemed able to turn his emotions on and off at will. This time he started cursing quietly.

'That dirty scumbag! After all I've done for him,' he muttered. 'This is what you were hinting at when I phoned you from Las Vegas, isn't it? Why didn't you tell me straight out? What am I paying you for?'

'You've *never* been straight with me. I have to protect myself. If you'd told me everything you knew about Smathers I might have found Aaron Thompson, and then an old man called Charlie Costello would still be alive. For your information, Mr Moneybags, this case is personal now. I'll go on and find out where Thompson is whether you pay me or not.'

Unpredictable as ever, Lee Parkes threw back his head and roared with laughter at this. 'Feisty bugger, aren't you?' he mocked. He opened his jacket and drew out a thick wad of money which he threw down in front of me.

'Whatever you think, Lee Parkes is a man who never

344

welches. I said I'd pay for this and I will. Here's another five grand on account.'

Then he kicked back his chair and walked out of the office without another word. Grand opera.

No sooner had the front door shut than Celeste was in my room.

'Are you all right?' she asked anxiously. 'I thought there was going to be a fight. There's only me in the office.' She was holding a heavy coat hanger in her hand.

'Thanks, Celeste,' I muttered. 'His bark is worse than his bite — I think.'

She picked up the money off the desk.

'At least he pays well. All this work is costing him a fortune. This makes his account straight.'

She bustled out, leaving me with a lot to think about. Kimball Smathers had betrayed Lee to Thompson, set him up for the kidnapping and extortion. That must explain why he'd made up the story about Lee and Keeley being a long-term item, needing an excuse for his own treachery. I thought about it some more but that explanation didn't seem quite enough somehow.

I tried to remember every word of my two conversations with Smathers. The confrontation that had resulted in Clint's dramatic arrival through the window was most vivid in my mind but I'd spoken to him on the phone as well. He'd known about Cheyenne being ill but not about her being suddenly hospitalised. When I'd spun him a yarn about Naomi making allegations he'd appeared to buy the story.

There was something there, some clue, but what? I scratched my head in frustration.

When I met him in Mollingtree he'd thought Lee had sent me . . . why? To administer punishment? A straightener? 'Two hard cases' was how he'd described myself and Clint. I needed to know more about what had been going on between him and Lee. Then there was Keeley.

345

Her obvious anxiety when I'd arrived on her doorstep could be explained by a guilty conscience over her affair with Lee – or did she think he had sent me to beat up Kimball? Herself maybe? Why would she think that? Then there was the wild hysteria when I'd told her that Cheyenne was kidnapped and left to die. Another guilty reaction?

The more I thought, the more questions I kept coming up with. I walked round the room so many times I was beginning to wear a track in the carpet. I dialled the Smathers' number. Keeley answered. I put the phone down. They were clearly back from Spain.

'I'm off to the wilds of deepest Cheshire,' I told Celeste on my way out. If there was going to be rough stuff I'd have to take my chances.

'Where exactly shall I say you are if Janine phones? I thought it was your turn to pick up Clint from that stable?'

I groaned. I'd forgotten him.

'He only works at the stable, he doesn't live there,' I complained. 'He's not an animal.'

There was no way I could drive to Mollingtree with Clint in the car after the bollocking Janine had given me last time. I wanted to go now, this minute. I knew that I'd lose impetus if I had to go and pick him up, make him a meal and get him settled for the night. I felt peevish about the obligation I'd taken on but I felt a lot worse about feeling like that. Thank you, Bob Lane, I thought.

'He knows me,' Celeste volunteered. 'I could take a taxi down to Carrington and pick him up then take him to your flat.'

'Could you?' I murmured.

I considered the idea. Celeste was my indispensable prop in the office yet she'd never been to my home. Then anxiety swept away all my reservations. I needed to get the truth out of Kimball Smathers and if I had to use bribes, or threats, or whatever, then I was going to do it. I knew that

I couldn't survive another day playing 'piggy in the middle' in some elaborate game involving the Parkes brothers, the Smathers family and Aaron Thompson.

'It's no problem,' Celeste answered in a tone which implied she wouldn't be offended if I decided against the idea.

I swiftly wrote a note authorising her to pick Clint up. It had no legal status. She was no more his guardian than I was but it might help if the people at the stables got difficult with her. At least Clint knew her. She wasn't a total stranger. I gave her my key and directions to the flat.

'Thanks,' I said, leaning forward with my lips ready to bestow the merest peck of gratitude. Instead I found myself firmly gripped, as Celeste returned the embrace with interest, patted me on the back and planted hot lips on my cheek.

I didn't shy away from her but I did put some space between us.

'Don't worry,' she said reassuringly, 'I'll take care of everything.' On my way out I wondered what precise construction she put on the word 'everything'.

Ten minutes later I was inching through traffic on Deansgate and trying to work out the quickest route to Mollingtree. I found my way on to the Parkway and then joined the M56. The congestion was dense all the way to the M6 interchange and then again from Frodsham, three solid lanes of traffic all belting along as fast as it dared go. I was in the fast lane. I hoped I was also in the fast lane for this wretched case. It had gone on long enough.

I followed the signs for Ellesmere Port and the Outlet Village and then plunged into the network of country lanes that took me to Mollingtree. I was keyed up when I approached the village, I don't know what I expected but I was ready for anything except what I saw.

Mollingtree's an odd little village, at least to my townie's eyes. The street threading through it winds and turns and at one section the houses have very high walls round them. Then, coming round the bend from this section, there's the more open, newer part of the village where the houses have unfenced lawns. The Smathers lived in one of these expensive 'executive' homes. I rounded the curve in the road expecting to park and go to their door.

Instead, I found the side of the road I was on closed, only one lane open for traffic. There were at least ten marked and unmarked police vehicles blocking my route. Some were double parked and some were on the pavement.

A motorcycle cop signalled me to stop and allow oncoming vehicles through. The halt gave me a chance to take in what was happening. The area in front of the houses was taped off and a line of coppers were doing a fingertip search. Beyond them there was an even more chilling sight. Screens had been erected in front of the Smathers' house. White-overalled figures were conferring.

I was so absorbed in this spectacle that the traffic cop had to toot his horn to get my attention. He signalled me to move. I drove past the house unable to satisfy my curiosity. I pulled into the wide entrance of the golf club about two hundred yards further down the road. I was taking a risk but I had to know what was happening.

My first guess was that Kimball had done something to Keeley.

There was a crowd of journalists collecting a statement from the self-same gabby old neighbour I'd spoken to yesterday. I pulled out a notebook and pencil and joined them. The old guy was wearing bedroom slippers, threadbare old trousers, a patched fawn cardigan and a wide smile. If the man smiled any more he'd be laughing.

I watched him preening himself under the TV lights, running his fingers through thick grey hair at the sides of his head. He was enjoying his fifteen minutes of fame.

'They didn't have a chance,' he crowed. 'The van pulled on to the pavement at the end of their drive and sounded the horn. Really blasted it, you know. That's why I came to the window of my house. I could see the Smathers looking out. The van driver just kept blaring away on his horn. They both came out and walked down to the van . . .'

'Did you get the impression they knew the people in the van?' the TV reporter asked.

'They must have. Keeley waved to them as if she knew them but I've never seen them before.'

'Sorry, go on, sir.'

'I heard Kimball — that's the husband, daft name if you ask me — say something. Least, I heard the sound but not the words. Swearing most likely, he usually was. Then this enormously ugly Asian woman in a . . . what do you call those things the silly tarts wrap over their faces? Veil, yashmak or something . . . looked like a proper Christmas parcel she did. She listened to Kimball effing and jeffing for a minute then pulled out a gun, cool as you please, a revolver. I don't think he was expecting she'd shoot. He thought it was a joke. He made what you'd have to call a rude gesture . . . then bang. She shot him, clean as a whistle, right between the eyes.'

This graphic detail was too much for some of his questioners.

'We can't put this out on the evening news,' an authoritative-looking young woman announced brusquely. She signalled to her TV crew and a light went out.

'Listen, Mr Burslem,' she said bossily to the old man, 'can you just tell the story straight without all these embellishments about the victim's name or the ugliness of the Asian woman, and cut out the unnecessary gore? There'll be children watching when this goes out. Oh, and try to look shocked and upset.'

Burslem didn't look even slightly abashed by this advice.

'Here, love,' he said, tapping her on the wrist.

The woman bristled. I saw her shoulders stiffen. She moved several paces away from him.

349

This didn't upset him at all.

'I was in the first wave on the Normandy beaches in 1944,' he continued. 'Nobody told us to look shocked and upset then. My best mate caught it smack between the eyes . . . sniper, you know. Stood next to me, he was, poor Herbert, just turned nineteen like me. I went right through to Luneburg Heath without a scratch but Herbert copped it just like Kimball did. Out like a light. Hole in the back of his head you could put your fist in.'

He demonstrated with a clenched fist.

The woman, a producer I guessed, didn't turn a hair at this. Instead she faced the reporter and put her hand to the side of her mouth. Burslem couldn't hear her but what she said was perfectly audible to the rest of us.

'I think veil would be all right, Tim, but I'm not sure they'll allow yashmak. What do you think? Does it sound a bit too colonial, like the old soldier here?'

'Veil's fine,' the reporter assured her. 'I think *chador* is the correct term. I'll steer him through it all again from the top, shall I?'

'No, Tim, I couldn't stand to listen,' she said crisply. 'Just take it from where you were and we'll edit for anything usable.'

She signalled and the light came on again.

'Right, Mr Burslem, sir,' Tim said, 'can we carry on?'

'Wasn't me that wanted to stop,' the old man groused.

I was burning to hear what else he had to say. So was everyone else. They all clustered round. I put my head down and pretended to take notes.

'Well, as soon as I heard a shot I started to hit the deck,' he continued. 'First thing you learn in the army, that.'

'But you saw what happened next?'

'Oh, aye, bruised my elbows going down but I saw what happened to that poor woman.'

Burslem rolled his sleeve up to show a spreading purple bruise on the flesh of his withered old elbow.

'You mean, Mrs Smathers?' the reporter prompted.

'She turned as if to run but didn't get a step, poor wench,' Burslem stated. 'The Asian bint in the van got her before she could even turn round. Just there, side of the forehead,' he said, tapping his own temple. 'Down she dropped like a sack of potatoes. I've seen too many of my mates hit in my time not to know she was as dead as Old Adam. I was down behind my living room wall by then but I heard the van revving so I risked a look. They were getting away. The other Asian bitch, also in a yashmak, was driving. How the blue blazes they do it, I'll never know. Drive, I mean, with those towels over their heads. You could only see her eyes.'

The TV light went out at that but the other reporters began clamouring questions.

'What were they like as neighbours?' one asked.

'They weren't here all that much. I never did find out what he did for a living although he claimed he'd been in the Royal Marines. I'm not sure I believed him.'

'Was there any previous trouble?'

'Oh, aye, lots of that. They'd been having marital problems recently. The wife claims she saw him hit her. That's my wife, that is. Then there was that fight . . .'

'Yes?'

'Yes, a gang came round some time last month. You never saw anything like it. It was like the Wild West out here. This is a quiet village. We've seen nothing like it until now.'

'There was shooting?'

'No, no shooting, but there were about five or six men, big ones, fighting with the Smathers. Some of them used a battering ram to smash the front of the house in. They went right through the window, the whole frame was caved in, and some went through the door, then they drove off.'

'Were they hurt?'

'The Smathers? I reckon they were. They finished up

in a heap on the lawn there. They went off to Spain right after that. No one round here was surprised to see them in trouble. They weren't like ordinary folk.'

'Do you think they were involved in the drug scene?'

'Oh, aye. My son told me that Kimball looked as if he was on charlie all the time. He calls it charlie, my son, but it's really cocaine.'

'Can you tell us any more about the killers?'

The old man considered this gravely.

'Yes, bloody rum do if you ask me. They were in a gas board van. A white van with the words "Gasco of Chester – Your Local Gas Supplier" in big blue letters on the side. You'd have thought somebody would have spotted that. I mean two Asian women in yashmaks driving a gas board van? Bloody rum.'

'You keep on saying they were Asian. How did you know that?'

'They were in their veils, like,' Burslem said tolerantly. 'You don't get many English women in them unless they're nuns, and these weren't, and the one that fired . . . the colour of her skin was as brown as my boots. I didn't get such a close look at the other.'

'Are you sure they were women? Not men in disguise?' a sceptical voice asked from the back.

'Oh, aye, I know a woman when I see one.' He illustrated the concept of breasts with an incongruously roguish smile. 'The one who fired had bosoms on her you could eat your lunch off.'

The words were hardly out of Burslem's mouth before a harassed-looking uniformed inspector rushed up.

'Mr Burslem!' he said sharply. 'This is where you've got to. You were asked to stay in your house until we were ready for your statement.' He put his hand on Burslem's sore elbow.

'Not a police state yet, is it?' the old man yelled, wrenching his arm free. 'I'll go where I please. I'll have you

352

know I went all through the Second World War fighting Hitler, and there were plenty of little Hitlers here at home then too.'

The copper took a step back.

A comely policewoman arrived next and the old soldier looked on her more favourably. He allowed himself to be led off.

The inspector turned to the press and began to shoo them away like a farmer's wife dealing with a gaggle of recalcitrant geese.

'Whatever he's said, ladies and gentlemen, you can't use any of it. There'll be an official statement issued at the village hall in half an hour. I believe the old gentleman's on some sort of medication.'

This produced a general groan followed by a volley of questions and I thought it was time I left.

I whistled through my teeth as I steered round the winding lanes towards the motorway. There was a phone box at the junction of one. I stopped and checked with directory enquiries. As expected there was no 'Gasco of Chester' listed. Medication? There aren't many people in their late seventies or eighties who aren't on some sort of medication, even if it's only aspirin. I'd believed every word Burslem said.

I arrived outside Thornleigh Court without any awareness of how I'd got there. The nights were getting lighter but I peered into every dark corner. There were no lurking assassins and no white vans but I didn't feel completely secure until the door of my flat was locked behind me.

'Hello, Dave,' Clint said cheerily. 'I've got a new friend. Celeste brought me home and made my tea.'

'That's right, Clint,' I said vaguely.

He smiled at me expectantly but I had no time for conversation. He turned back to the television. He was watching The Simpsons and soon I heard him chuckling.

I needed to speak to Michael Coe.

I took out my cell phone and dialled the number of Michael's hotel in London. This was where most of Lee Parkes's money was going. Keeping a full-time investigator in London costs the earth but there was nothing else for it.

As I punched in the numbers I noticed that my hand was trembling. I tried to slow down my breathing and calm myself. This case wasn't getting any easier. Every time I imagined I was close to a solution somebody got killed, first poor Charlie Costello, now the Smathers.

Why them and why now?

'Michael!' I said breathlessly when he came on. 'I'm phoning to thank you for what you've found.'

'Just research, you know,' he said dismissively. 'Easy when you know where to look. They've offered me my own seat at St Catherine's House.'

'It isn't just what you found so much as your timing. I had Lee Parkes with me when I got that fax.'

'What happened?'

'Nothing much. He claims Jamie abandoned his wife.'

'Nice guy! I thought it would be something like that. I can't find any record of a divorce.'

'No, Lee says there wasn't one.'

'Jamie's secret's safe because the tabloids don't know his real name is Parkes. It'll never come out unless someone tells them.'

'We're not going to do that, are we? But it might be helpful if you could find out where Ashleigh Parkes has disappeared to.'

I felt a twinge of guilt. I could be sending Michael into danger.

'Needle in a haystack, Guv!'

'Even so, I'd like it.'

'Finding her will cost. You won't believe this, but I'm missing Manchester.'

'Come back at the weekend if you like but perhaps

you're safer where you are. Listen, Michael, I must tell you that Kimball and Keeley Smathers have both just been shot dead outside their home. Cheyenne's died too. This job's getting hairy and if you want out it won't affect your position in the firm.'

Michael gave an odd laugh. He didn't sound nervous.

'Guv! Do you think I'm some kind of wimp? I served in Northern Ireland for years. We already knew Charlie Costello had been killed and that the child might not make it. The only question is, are you going to involve the police?'

'No,' I said. 'No police. Not yet, anyway.'

'I thought you'd say that. Do you think Jack Piercy may have helped Ashleigh to disappear? Killed her even?'

'It's possible, but I'm also concerned about Lee's wife, Mel. I need to know what was going on between her, Lee, and the late Keeley and Kimball Smathers.'

'Have you got her maiden name?'

'No,' I said.

'Right, back to St Catherine's in the morning then. See you!'

I still had the phone in my hand when Janine appeared at the door. I didn't know how much of my conversation with Michael she'd overheard. Too much, judging by her expression.

'What kind of game are you playing now, Dave?' she demanded.

Sometimes people catch you on a raw edge and this was one such moment for me. I didn't feel like having my conscience unravelled and reknitted again.

'I'm not playing any sort of game,' I rapped back.

'Oh, yes, big boy's games,' she retorted. 'Instead of picking Clint up, I'm told, courtesy of your secretary, that you've gone to Mollingtree. Thanks very much, Dave, and what's wrong with your mobile? And then what do I hear when I switch on the local radio? Only that a couple have been found shot dead on their doorstep in Mollingtree of all places, a sleepy Cheshire backwater. What a world of coincidences we live in.'

'Are you suggesting I did it?'

'No, but we both know that you're capable of violence.'

'No, I'm not!' I shouted. I knew I'd lost it when I raised my voice. Janine gave one of those pleased little smiles she uses for putting down stupid males. My emotions were churning away. I love that bold way she has with her, but I hate being on the receiving end of her tongue. It is usually completely unfair. I clenched my fists in frustration.

'Yes, Dave, you are. You have one of those little boy's toys hidden away in here as well.'

'What are you on about, woman?' I thundered.

'The old shooter, Dave. Where is it? I know you have one, and don't you dare call me woman!'

'Can I play this game?' Clint asked suddenly, his eyes bright with excitement. We'd both forgotten he was present.

'It's all right, Clint,' Janine said soothingly. 'We're just having a frank exchange of opinions.'

'Frank works at the stables,' he agreed, 'but I know this big boy's game. It's like hide and seek.' He went to the bookcase where I'd hidden the gun in a hollowed-out book.

'Here it is,' he said triumphantly, waving the book at us. He must have spotted me hiding it.

'That's not a gun, Clint,' Janine said in the cause of education.

He gave a deep gurgle of laughter. I felt the hairs stand up on the back of my neck.

'This is,' he said, opening the book. He held the weapon in his hand, pointing at us.

'I win the game. Shall I hide it again?'

'No, I'll take it,' Janine said firmly.

356

'For God's sake!' I shouted. Clint looked mystified. He could tell I was angry but not why.

'Give it to me,' I ordered.

Clint looked resentful.

'I won the game,' he insisted. He still had the gun in his hand.

'We're playing a different one now,' I said firmly. 'It's called, "do what you're told". Give me the gun, Clint.'

He handed the gun over but there was a cunning glint in his eye.

'You've got to pay me a forfeit now,' he said. 'I was "it" then and you took my turn.'

'Yes,' Janine agreed. 'We'll play hide and seek again. You go next door and hide something and we'll come and look for it in five minutes.'

Clint's expression was one of pure delight which was more than could be said for Janine's. She sat on the sofa and began crying as soon as he was out of the door.

'You're going to get killed,' she said. 'I know it. And for what? Just so that some selfish, overpaid soccer star's guilty secret can remain hidden.'

I took the magazine out of the pistol and handed them both to her.

'Here, it's safe now. Throw these in the Mersey if it makes you any happier,' I said gloomily.

'Go to the police, Dave. Surely you have enough for them to charge Thompson with by now?'

'Quite apart from me breaking a contract, and the excellent chance that the police would bang me up for something out of pure spite, there's the fact that no one knows where Thompson is. His henchman, the guy who's arranged all these kidnappings and killings, may well be a senior policeman himself. Thompson's perfectly capable of finding me before they find him and I'm certain that it was him who shot the Smathers.'

'If you can prove that . . .'

'I can prove nothing!' I barked. 'The police already think the fact that Clint's living here shows I'm hand in glove with Bob Lane, and I can't *prove* a thing about Thompson. I *know* what he and his friend did but I'm not going round collecting forensic evidence, am I? I'm not trying to win a case in court.'

'Do you think he'll come here?' she asked nervously.

'I've no reason to think he knows where I live. I don't advertise the address.'

'That rotten Piercy knows where you live. I heard you telling Michael you suspect his brother, so he might tell them.'

'Jamie's not part of the gang that caused Cheyenne's death. We've nothing to fear from him.'

'If you say so, but a man who'll cheat the public like he does is capable of anything.'

I shook my head, but there was no point in arguing to protect Jamie's reputation. He had none round here.

'I think it's best if I move out for a while. You're right, I don't want anybody following me here.'

'You're not sulking, are you?' she asked.

'What, me?' I protested with a laugh.

She smiled.

'Promise me that if you sort this and manage to stay out of prison, you'll give up this sort of case?'

'How do I know how a case is going to turn out? This is how I make my living.'

'Living!' she snapped. 'You call this living? Hounded from pillar to post by some thug. Here, take the gun if you need it, but this is all so stupid.'

'I don't think I'm in any danger. Mr E has only killed people who know who he is. I *don't* know who he is and the way things are now I'm never going to find out, so I should be safe.'

'Brilliant logic! Let's hope this extortionist, whoever he is, thinks the same way as you do.'

358

'I think he does.'

'You do know that the only reason I haven't married you is that you won't give up this crazy lifestyle?'

She kissed me. Only reason? I'd been given a thousand different ones.

'Dave, say you'll stick to insurance cases after this?' she pleaded.

'All right,' I growled, 'but there've been some pretty hectic insurance scams.'

'You idiot!' she said, running her hand through my hair. 'I'll look after Clint for the time being but I think we need new arrangements for him. Keep in touch with me every day and don't leave it to Celeste. I think she's got plans for you after the way she looked round this flat. I thought she was going to start measuring the curtains.'

'You're mad!' I laughed. 'She's possessive . . . but me? I don't think so!'

'You'd be the last to know. She studied that wedding picture of you and your first wife for a long time.'

We both glanced at the picture. My one and only wife was an African medical student who died of anaemia. I wondered if Janine's reference to my *first* wife was a Freudian slip? There was clearly hope for us yet.

25

I hadn't been back in my own flat more than a minute before the phone started ringing. It was Clyde Harrow. He demanded to speak to me and when I tried to put him off threatened that he was going to the press with a story about Jamie that would make the headlines in every paper. I agreed to meet him at my office.

If my troubles were personal, Clyde Harrow's were cosmic.

'The whole future of the game, and not just in England but the whole world, Dave. Think of that,' he exclaimed. 'Two hundred million Chinese playing soccer and they all look up to the English Premiership. Jamie Piercy is a god throughout the Orient. Imagine the disillusionment . . . it could even lead to world conflict.'

'Clyde, you're insane,' I snarled.

'No, not at all. A sudden revelation of corruption in a cherished institution can be the single snowflake that starts a mighty avalanche.'

'I don't know what you're talking about,' I protested vainly.

'I think you do, and unless you come clean with what you know about our young friend's misdemeanours I won't be able to protect your name when all this comes out.'

'You're exaggerating as usual,' I snapped. 'A single snowflake? Jamie's been foolish but what he's done doesn't amount to even a single ice crystal.'

'That's not what I hear.'

'You're priceless. You drag me into this case to protect his reputation then you go scavenging for any scrap of malicious gossip that you can find.'

'I've been discreet and what I've heard comes from various sources. I know he approached several people with some very dubious propositions. He's not the only one implicated but his name has come up a few times.'

'Names, dates, places?' I said sceptically.

'You're being naïve, Dave. If the tabloids get even a hint of what I know squadrons of reporters will be out flashing their chequebooks to help people remember.'

'Help people to fantasise, you mean.'

'That too, but it comes to the same thing in the end. Reputations will be ruined, and more. I keep telling you, the whole game will go down the tubes but you won't listen. If you'd ever been interested in soccer you'd know that a massive amount of the money flowing into the game comes from commercial sponsorship. Do you think multinational corporations will carry on paying millions to have their name on Jamie Piercy's shirt when the shit hits the fan? And it's not just the clubs. The Premier League, the Cup, TV rights . . . everything would come crashing down if sponsorship was withdrawn.'

I looked at Clyde carefully. The earnest way he was speaking, the hectic colour in his chubby face, and above all the absence of the normal irritating Shakespearean quotes convinced me he was deadly serious.

Then light dawned.

'This isn't about Jamie, it's about you, isn't it?' I asked. 'If you had the goods on him you wouldn't be round here now. You're panicking about something.'

'What do you mean?' he retorted huffily. 'It's the good name of the sport I love that I'm concerned for. If I die tomorrow they'll find the words "Beautiful Game" inscribed on my heart when they open me up.'

I laughed raucously at this.

'Nice one, Clyde,' I commented. 'You deserve a drink for that, and for introducing me to Lagavulin.' I took out a bottle of the Caledonian nectar from my desk drawer and poured us both a dram.

'I've always tried to improve your education,' he said reflectively as he sipped the whisky.

'Well, educate me further by telling me just how any revelations about Piercy would affect you financially.'

'No, no, no, dear lad! You've got the wrong end of the branch entirely,' he protested.

'Let's see – you run a sleazy little TV company, you do a spot of commentating on commercial radio. Sky Sport is hardly reeling from the threat of competition but there's something, isn't there?'

'"Highly fed and lowly taught", that's you, Dave . . .'

'No, don't tell me,' I groaned.

'. . . *All's Well That End's Well*, Act Two, Scene Two.'

'*You* won't end well, unless you tell me what your angle is. I'll have you investigated by some of my staff. Find out everything you're up to.'

'There's such a thing as freedom of the press. You tell me what you've found out about Jamie or a certain newspaper will hear my suspicions tomorrow.'

'What suspicions?'

'I know the names of the players Jamie has corrupted.'

'He's corrupted no one.'

'How is it then that I was interviewing a certain very talented player, nationally known for his spendthrift habits, boozing and coke snorting, and he let slip that his good friend Jamie Piercy put him in touch with a financial consultant who got his affairs in order for him?'

'What's wrong with that?'

'Nothing, except that on investigation the financial consultant doesn't exist though the money's real enough.'

'You'd have thought nothing of Jamie telling him the name of a consultant if you hadn't been looking for dirt,' I said angrily. This 'consultant' sounded very like Lee Parkes. I tried to think of some way to head Clyde off.

'"Suspicion always haunts the guilty mind; the thief doth fear each bush an officer" – *Henry VI, Part Three*. Not that *my mind* is guilty, but analysis of this spendthrift gentleman's recent games reveals some curious anomalies.'

'Such as?'

'Such as his failure to score easy goals in games where there's been heavy pre-match betting on the result.'

'Everyone has their off days.'

'Blosh Stevenson doesn't have many, especially against opposition from non-league clubs in vital cup matches. No one's asking questions now, but they soon will do if word gets out about his coincidental change of fortune.'

'Why are you interviewing these people? Blosh Stevenson doesn't have any local connections.'

'There's always interest in Blosh.'

I tried to guess what Clyde was up to. Blosh is a national figure, a brilliant footballer, as famous for his antics off the pitch as on it. He isn't highly regarded by the guardians of the nation's moral welfare. There've been divorces, arrests for assaulting police officers, drunk and disorderly convictions, and many more naughty tricks on Blosh's record sheet but so far he's always been forgiven by the fans because of his flashes of genius. He's one of those players people pay good money to watch because there's always the possibility that something special might happen when he's around.

'Who else have you interviewed?' I demanded.

Clyde named half a dozen players, all England internationals playing for clubs in other parts of the country. There was something fishy about all this. Clyde's commentating usually appears late at night on local channels, not on national networks.

'You recorded for television?'

'That's what I do, dear boy.'

'No, you don't,' I muttered. The local channels never feature profile slots on players from other areas such as Blosh Stevenson. The limited air time they have for sport is spent on cultivating a small number of local coaches and players from clubs in the region. When it comes to soccer, local loyalties are everything.

'Very well,' Clyde said irritably. 'I've ventured to expand my horizons a little. So what? My name is not unknown in soccer circles and so I've produced a series of short features on some of our famous players. You won't be seeing them unless you go to South East Asia. The series is dubbed into Oriental languages.'

'Where did you get the money from?' I asked suspiciously. 'These players won't look at a camera without cash in hand.'

'Wrong!' he boasted. 'They were willing to work for a percentage of the gross profit when I told them how often the profiles will be repeated. Don't you know that so many Premiership matches here now start before noon so that they can go out live on Asian television at eight in the evening? The sums at stake are colossal.'

'And you stand to lose if there's bad publicity?'

'We all do. Haven't I explained that?'

'Explain again, I'm thick. How can it be to your advantage to know if Jamie Piercy has been washing his boots in dirty water – not that I'm saying he has, mind you?'

'It's all about rights, dear lad. I can sell the stuff outright for a quick profit now or I can retain the rights for a bigger profit spread over several years. I have to know the truth. Listen, Dave, we've had our ups and downs but I'm prepared to advance you a small ex gratia payment if you can confirm or deny that Jamie Piercy's up to his neck in illegal gambling.'

'No, forget your payments. I've got the picture now. You owe a load of money for this TV production and you've persuaded the blokes you interviewed to accept deferred payment, only now you're scared witless that there won't be any payment because if there's a scandal no one will want the programmes.'

I watched him struggling with my words. His brow furrowed and I guessed he was searching for an apposite Shakespearean quotation but for once the Bard was unable to put words in his mouth. Sweat started on his domed head. He took his glasses off and stared into a corner of the room for a moment. His normally bright eyes looked dull. I wondered if I was going to be on the receiving end of a rare moment of candour from the old TV hack.

'Dave,' he said, when he'd composed himself, 'I know you don't think much of me and your good lady thinks even less, but I'm begging you – I must know the truth before anything breaks in the press. Is Jamie Piercy on the fiddle? Is it all likely to go national? And don't say you don't know anything, it's all round town that you're conducting some kind of heavy investigation and I'm the only one who knows how it started. It's a gambling syndicate, isn't it? They've got their claws into him.'

As he finished speaking he whipped out a large handkerchief and wiped his forehead, then he knocked back the whisky remaining in his glass. He looked like a large spaniel begging to be taken out for a walk.

I poured more whisky into our glasses.

I preferred the arrogant, confident Clyde who liked to swagger into my office and bully me to the nervous, sweating wreck in front of me now. Clyde is perennially strapped for cash. The alimony payments to his many former wives and maintenance for the large brood of children he's fathered are a staggering burden.

It was true that I've never thought much of him but then he was never trying to recruit me to his fan club, and I have known him a long time. My problem now was that he'd somehow gleaned a grain of the truth from his many contacts and in his panic over his own financial plight he might well rush to the press. I guessed that his motive would be to get the best end of the deal for himself.

With totally selfish people like Clyde you always know where you are. That thought led me to a solution.

'Listen, Clyde, Jamie is in trouble but not in the way you think. He's the innocent victim in a chain of circumstances and if things go well I should be able to unwind him from the coils. That was why you originally introduced me to him, remember?'

He grimaced at the recollection.

'I guarantee you that Jamie hasn't made any money out of the game that he shouldn't have but he has been a little indiscreet. Not on his own behalf, mind you.'

'A gambling syndicate?' Clyde asked eagerly.

'No, nothing like that but I'm going to need a little more time to extricate him. If you go to the papers now things could look bad for him. He may have said one or two silly things to the likes of Blosh Stevenson, but then Blosh is hardly an unimpeachable witness himself, is he?'

Clyde nodded, with a grim expression on his face. I realised that Blosh was his sole source of information.

'In a few months' time everything will be sorted. I think it's quite possible then, if everything comes out straight, that young Jamie will want to reward you personally.'

'Money, though always welcome, would only make things worse in this case, Dave,' Clyde said wearily. 'It would look as if he was paying me off.'

'I'm not talking money. You know Jamie's never given an interview on TV?'

'That voice of his . . .'

'But still, there's tremendous interest in him. Suppose he agreed to give your little company the exclusive rights to make, say, an hour-long feature about his personal life? Maybe he could have one or two friends with him . . . take

366

the public behind the scenes of a footballer's life, that kind of thing.'

'Are you sure you weren't thinking of organising this yourself?' Clyde asked suspiciously.

'I run a detective agency. I wouldn't even know where to begin with such a project.'

'No, you wouldn't,' Clyde agreed, brightening considerably. 'Would he give me rights to additional materials? For instance, if I arranged for a biography to be ghosted?'

'You'd have to speak to his agent about that but I'm sure something could be arranged,' I said smoothly. Jamie's unexpurgated biography was turning out to be more exciting than any ghostwriter might imagine. I was sure Clyde was hooked. 'Especially when I tell him how helpful you've been in keeping indiscreet friends like Blosh off his back.'

'I'll speak to Blosh this evening,' Clyde interjected hastily. 'Tell him he's in danger of being dragged through the libel courts if he doesn't button his lip. Another court appearance is the last thing he wants.'

When the TV producer and self-proclaimed football lover had left I exhaled a long, slow sigh. I'd sailed pretty close to the wind in volunteering Jamie Piercy for a TV special but it might be a good thing for him. It would give him the opportunity to release the information about his youthful indiscretions in a controlled way. At any rate, if the promise was successful in keeping Clyde off his back then it was worth making. I'd have to worry about fulfilling it when the time came.

26

I stayed in the office. It felt odd being there late at night. I kept expecting Celeste or Peter to walk in at any moment. Thinking of Peter, I had to recognise that our campaign of showing Thompson's photo round the suburbs was getting nowhere fast. When we'd started, and it felt like years ago, not weeks, it had been reasonable to believe that we were dealing with ordinary criminals who would have contacts ready, willing and able to shop them for three grand.

This lot didn't.

I remembered what Brendan Cullen had said about extortionists: that they were often embittered men who were striking back at society. My guy, Mr E, probably felt he'd come up with the perfect crime: extortion from criminals who daren't reveal his activities. There was obviously an element of spite, too. Why was it necessary to kill Eric McAteer, for instance? It was conceivable that a four-year-old child could identify them . . . but unlikely as they already knew the parents wouldn't be getting in touch with the police.

Why go to the trouble of keeping Eric alive all night and then run him down in sight of his parents' house? That wasn't just spite, it was a powerful message being put out.

There was a likelihood, a strong suspicion at least, that my man was taking revenge for some incident in his past involving the loss of a loved one. That did open up some possibilities. Accidents happen and they get reported in the papers. I could comb the back copies for details of accidents involving children of police or legal officials . . . accidents where the culprit had been under the influence of narcotics.

My other lead was money.

Mr E was into money big time. He'd lifted at least seven hundred thousand pounds that I knew about. Thompson had been in the country almost three years. Assuming he didn't join up with Mr E until he'd been here for, say, six months, and that they only pulled a job once every three months, that gave them a possible ten jobs not counting the one we thought was now in the planning stage.

So Thompson and Mr E were in possession of seven hundred thousand pounds minimum and several million maximum.

Was that possible? What sort of people could come into such large sums without provoking suspicion? Had they spent any money? There'd certainly been no sign of excessive wealth in Thompson's room at Crockett's flat. So my man was either a miser or someone people expected to have sudden wealth, like a lottery winner. I thought about that. Someone claiming to be a lottery winner, not necessarily a big winner, could use that as an excuse for sudden riches. How many people were likely to check up on it? Could you check, or was anonymity of winners protected?

It was.

My mind went back to where I'd started in this case . . . the kidnapping of baby Cheyenne. Lee Parkes wasn't a drug dealer but he did have criminal connections. Had Mr E learned about him through some police surveillance operation as he'd probably learned about McAteer or the mysterious man with the mountain of cash and an address near the airport? It didn't feel right somehow. If a police agency had been keeping Lee and Jamie under watch, why weren't they in jail now?

No, knowledge of Lee Parkes and his wealth must

have come to Mr E's attention via Thompson and the late Kimball Smathers. They hadn't been sure how much money Lee had. They'd accepted a reduced amount from him because they didn't know for certain what his cash flow was.

When you thought about it, targeting a gambler rather than a drug dealer was a clever move, in keeping with the finesse which Mr E had displayed so far. Someone might notice if all the local major drug dealers went belly up one after another. In fact, someone *had* noticed – Brendan had supplied me with the McAteer file. So who else was there besides drug dealers who might be sitting at home with a safe stuffed with illegal cash? Gamblers like Lee, but who else? Corrupt politicians, bent property dealers, pornographers, brothel keepers, major league pimps, criminals of every stamp: they were all out there but how to check if they'd lost money or relatives?

If I gave Brendan another tiny clue about what was going on he'd find Lee Parkes and then Jamie.

So what?

According to my dear friend Clyde Harrow, Jamie was so big that his fall could bring down the whole teetering structure of English soccer. A vision of a deserted, abandoned Theatre of Dreams flashed through my mind: tall rank grass growing on the pitch, the stands rusted, pigeons nesting on the seats, all the fans at home watching rugby on television.

Did I care? Did it matter? Unfortunately I'd given my word and that mattered more to me even than the fate of English soccer. Melodramatic, but true.

I left the office. It was just coming up to eleven p.m.

I drove down the A34 as far as Nether Alderley. The suburbs unfolded in front of me. The road was called Kingsway through Didsbury, East Didsbury and Cheadle, an urban dual carriageway with houses on both sides. Then it became a mini-motorway, following its own embanked

370

route through Heald Green and Cheadle Hulme, bypassing Handforth and Wilmslow town centres. The motorway section ended at Harden Park to become a normal main road passing among the houses of the rich, the famous and the footballers at Alderley Edge before plunging on through open countryside at Nether Alderley.

I had the window open for most of the journey and gradually some of the heat that had been gathering in my brain dissipated into the cold night air.

I was driving back past Wilmslow, feeling thoroughly chilled and sorry for myself, when my mobile rang.

It was Bob Lane.

'Dave, you old fart! Where are you?' he asked.

'In the car. Where are you?'

'At the airport, just got in from . . . well, never you mind where. Do you fancy picking me up seeing as you're mobile?'

'I'm just around the corner from the airport,' I said, then paused and wondered at my own words. Wilmslow *is* just around the corner from the airport. Mr E's next victim had to live somewhere near.

'Go on,' Bob said. 'Has the record stuck or are you drunk or something?'

'No, I'll be with you in ten minutes. Which terminal or is that a state secret too?'

'Three.'

I made it to Terminal Three in less than ten minutes. I didn't break any speed limits either, there was so little traffic and I was so close to start with. Bob was waiting by the pavement with his luggage on a trolley.

'Nothing manky about this, is there?' I asked as I loaded it into my boot.

'Just three kilos of heroin, cocker,' he quipped. Then he saw my expression. 'Only joking Dave! Don't be so serious. I'm out of that now, not that I was ever into heroin.'

'Get in the car,' I said grumpily.

'Are you pissed at me for phoning you so late?' he asked. 'Is that it? I didn't think you'd be in bed by one.'

I looked at him. He was the same old Bob but he seemed to have met a tailor somewhere on his travels; a tailor who'd finally managed to make a suit that fitted him. When his mother was alive all he ever wore were the suits she ordered from expensive catalogues and they never fitted over the massive forearms that had earned him the nickname Popeye. Now he was wearing a suit of some costly-looking shiny material. I couldn't quite determine the colour in the artificial light.

'Come on mate, I'm freezing my butt off here,' he complained.

We got in the car. It was freezing and I turned the heater full on. A powerful reek of expensive aftershave hit me from Bob's side of the car. He has this condition of excessive sweating which means he has to change his clothes and bathe several times a day if he isn't going to lose all his friends. He tries to control the odours with aftershave. The fact that there was no cheesy tang mixed with the aftershave told me he hadn't been on a long-haul flight.

'Have you come far?' I asked.

'What is this, Dave? The third degree? First you meet me looking like an undertaker who's lost his hearse. Then it's questions, questions, and more questions. What happened to "Bob, you're looking great" or "Bob, I like your suit"? Or even, "I'm dead chuffed to see you, mate, and how have you gone on?" I have come a long way as it happens but I broke my journey for a night in Amsterdam. Now if we're playing questions and answers you can tell me why you're so down in the mouth. Nothing wrong with Clint, is there?'

'No, he's flourishing in Manchester. He's got a job and he's going to college.'

'Holy Mother of God! Has he got himself a brain transplant as well?'

For the first time since meeting Bob I felt my guard relaxing fractionally. I was still angry with him for not coming back sooner, though.

I pointed the car back towards Wilmslow. Bob hadn't asked to be taken anywhere in particular so, in the stubborn mood I was in, I intended to resume my journey back into town along the A34 instead of the more direct M56.

'When did you get Tony's message?' I asked.

'Tony who?' he snapped, clearly picking up my vibes now.

'You know, the dwarf henchman who delivered that money to me?'

'Tony? That wasn't Tony. That was No-nose Nolan. I've never called him Tony, though his mother may have. I call him No-nose if I'm feeling pally and "Thingy" most of the rest of the time. He gives our Clint a good run for his money in the No-brains Stakes. Since when have you started getting so friendly that you call him Tony?'

'Since I asked him to get in touch with you on Monday.'

'And he said he would?'

'Yes.'

'Was he stoned?'

'He had been.'

'Listen, Dave, I'm no more likely to tell No-nose where I'm going than I am to be elected the next Pope. Much less likely, to tell you the truth, considering what a good man I must be to provide strange life-forms like No-nose Nolan with the odd crust. The man is a null point, a complete cipher, and a back marker in the race of life. Get it? He's been wandering round Cheetham Hill like a stunned wombat ever since he had his accident.'

'Who did tell you to come back, then?'

'Dave, have you been on the wacky baccy with No-nose? I came back when my lawyer told me he'd cut a deal with Customs, and before you ask I haven't been

373

having a holiday while you looked after our Clint for me. I've been toiling in foreign parts trying to ensure that I had a business to come back to when I returned to Manchester.'

'Oh.'

'Yes, oh. And now I get back I find my oldest mate is talking to me as if he's just had a load of hard core shovelled down his throat by a JCB. What is up?'

I didn't say anything, not because I was choked up but because I was manoeuvring the car round a tricky roundabout.

'Pull in over there, mate,' he said, indicating the Holiday Inn. 'Something's been going on and I want it sorted.'

There were no hot meals being served when we arrived in the lounge of the Holiday Inn but there were sandwiches and soft drinks. Bob ordered a pile of sandwiches and I discovered I had an appetite. I hadn't eaten much since breakfast.

'Not to put too fine a point on it, Dave, if it's not Clint it must be your job. So who the hell is standing on your corns this time?'

I told him the whole thing from the beginning, only omitting the names of Lee Parkes and Jamie Piercy.

'Jee-sus, Dave!' he exclaimed when I'd finished. 'Have you got a death wish or something?'

'No.'

'Were you thinking of going back to sleep in your office tonight?'

'Where else?'

'Dave, I've known you a long time but I never thought you were stupid. This Thompson has been trained to kill people in dozens of different ways. If you think you can fend him off by sleeping with a gun under your pillow, you're crazy.'

I shrugged my shoulders. He was probably right but I didn't feel like admitting it.

374

'Where is this intercepted conversation with the mysterious dope dealer?'

'On the desk in my office.'

'Right, this is what we'll do. We'll book in here for the night and while you're getting settled I'll go and collect it from the office.'

'But . . .'

'If your cross-dressing friend Thompson is hanging around disguised as a lap-top dancer or whatever, he'll be looking for a six-foot-tall idiot with dark curly hair not a short-arsed carrot top like me. With any luck he'll think I'm a copper. Give me the gun.'

I passed him it under the table.

When he got back I was asleep in the room we'd booked. I woke with a start as Bob shook my shoulder.

'There was no sign of anyone but that doesn't mean he wasn't there. Did you know central Manchester's heaving with transsexuals, by the way? After what you said about this Thompson, every woman I saw looked dodgy. I made sure I wasn't followed back here.'

'Right,' I mumbled.

'Come on, Dave, snap out of it!' he ordered.

'A lot of Turkish Cypriots have moved into the drug scene in Manchester,' Bob informed me twenty minutes later. He was poring over the intercepted message. 'This could be one of them. See where he tells the guy that he's a Muslim but gets annoyed when he's called a Paki? The swear words that they can't translate could be in Turkish.'

'Or Albanian, or Arabic, or one of dozens of other languages.'

'My money's on a Turk. They have businesses on the side, like importing fruit and veg from northern Cyprus, and this guy's promising to pay off half his debt in merchandise. That could be fruit and veg. They've got one of the biggest wholesale market trading set-ups in Europe in Amsterdam. It's a perfect way to change

375

some of this unwanted sterling into nicely laundered guilders.'

'Don't you know his name?'

'What am I? A human card index? I don't know him but I know who to ask.'

'Great!'

'Hang on, Sherlock. There's a price to be paid for this information.'

'Name it!'

'Dave, get a grip, will you? It's not me you have to pay but this guy who knows where our Turk is.'

'We're saving a kid's life. Surely . . .'

'Dave, you don't know that. Look, with these drugs importers it's like being in the English Premier League . . .'

'Don't talk to me about soccer,' I moaned.

'All I mean is that everything's done to gain an advantage – slagging off a ref, winding up the opposition's manager. It's just the same in this world. They're all in competition. Hell, I should know.'

'OK, you've got to stop looking at this from the perspective of an honest man. We've got this Turkish fruit seller who's sitting on a mountain of cash and there are people who know who he is and what game he's in and we want them to tell us his name, right?'

'Right.'

'They could probably do that straight off after reading this interesting piece of paper.'

'Right.'

'And you think anyone would do that to save this kid from Mr E?'

'Right again.'

'Dead wrong! Those people may or may not be his friends. If one of them sees an advantage to himself by not telling us then he won't.'

'A kid's life's at stake!'

'We're not dealing with the NSPCC here. These are

dealers in hard drugs all trying to pile up their first few millions. Sentiment is a word they've crossed out of their dictionaries. They can and will kill any member of their own family who gets in the way, so one of them might think the fruit seller's kiddie is a reasonable price to pay to take her daddy out of the game.'

'Lovely world.'

'It is. Why do you think I got out?'

'Someone was grassing you up, according to Brendan Cullen.'

'Yeah, and it's taken me weeks to get that sorted. From now on I'm out of grass and into tobacco and who do you think benefits from that?'

'Not the Chancellor of the Exchequer!'

'Not him, true, but who does?'

'The bloke who grassed you up?'

'Precisely, but he doesn't know what's going to hit him. After what I've done to him he'll be lucky if he has a pot to piss in let alone pot to sell. I've been spending some time in various warm places making sure that certain people will be very, very unwilling to sell him even enough weed to roll himself a spliff.'

'Can't you get into some honest line of work, Bob?'

'Dave,' he said with a grin, 'you sound like my mother, God rest her soul. I need you to keep me straight.'

'But tobacco smuggling . . .'

'The Government could stop it tomorrow by lowering the duty. The fact that they don't suggests to me that they're prepared to accept a degree of smuggling. It's not as if people wouldn't get hold of cigarettes anyway. All I'm doing is making them available at a lower price.'

'Bob Lane, friend of the poor,' I joked.

'If you like. It's true enough.'

'You don't smoke yourself, though.'

'So what? Tobacco's never been banned, and if you're

377

so moral what are you doing investigating a kidnapping that led to a child's death without informing the police?'

'Well, it just sort of happened that way.'

'Precisely! You drifted into it and now you're stuck with it until you sort it. It's the same with me. You get into these things because they seem like a good idea at the time and then you can't get out so easily when things turn sour.'

'If you put it that way . . .'

'I do put it that way. The only difference between us is that you've got a nice legal business to turn to when this is over while I'm still floundering about trying to make an alternative career for myself.'

'I suppose so,' I agreed. I didn't really accept his argument. There were lots of alternative careers he could have chosen right now.

'Dave, you don't fool me. You think once a crook, always a crook, don't you?'

'I didn't say that.'

'But you thought it. I can tell.'

'No.'

'Yes. I don't mind. You don't have to be polite. It does me good to have a friend who disapproves. But let me remind you of one thing, Dave.'

'What?'

'Who was it who met me at the airport with a dirty big shooter stuck in his belt?'

'Me, I suppose.'

'Yep, that's right, partner. You were all ready for a shoot-out at the OK Corral. The difference between you and me is that I know when I'm doing wrong whereas you think whatever you do is right.'

'Thompson's got to be stopped.'

'But not by you, Dave. If you want to stay out of prison, that is. I'll do what I can tomorrow but until then let's get some shut-eye.'

27

I slept better for the remainder of that night than I'd done for weeks. We started the morning with a full English breakfast and suddenly the world seemed a warmer, cosier place than it had done at one a.m. Some of the tension seemed to have gone. Maybe I was kidding myself and it was just sleeping on a decent mattress but I did feel livelier.

Bob departed for the New Smithfield Market on Ashton Old Road and I headed for Pimpernel Investigations. It was when I'd parked the car and started walking to the office that the world began to feel a great deal less cosy than it had done in a nice warm hotel. What was to stop Thompson walking into my agency and blasting all and sundry? Nothing much that I could think of. The man's methods were draconian as his victims had already discovered. Why shouldn't he clear up a few loose ends at Pimpernel Investigations? He'd told Crockett that he was heading back to the South Seas, so why not add a few more crimes to his list before he went?

I've been in these situations before and in the end you finish up suspecting everybody and jumping at your own shadow. In the days when I was on my own I could always find somewhere to lie low, but how do you protect an organisation with twelve full-time staff and various part-timers?

'There's only one way,' I told Celeste when she arrived at eight-fifteen. 'Put a notice up in the window saying

"Office Closed for Renovation" and leave a telephone number.'

'Dave, have you any idea how many telephone enquiries we deal with in an average day? We can't leave the phones unmanned.'

'Celeste, have you heard of your namesake, the *Marie Celeste*? A sailing ship that was mysteriously found with not a soul on board yet everything in full working order? Tables laid with meals and everything?'

'Yes,' she said sulkily.

'We don't want the Mystery of Pimpernel Investigations, do we? A detective agency found with all its phones working and not a soul to answer them.'

'That's what I'm saying, we've got to be here.'

'No, we've got to be *not* here,' I said firmly. 'It's easier to recover from a few days of flat business than it is from a bullet in the head. Anyway, this has happened before. Where do you think all those businesses went when the IRA bomb went off outside Marks & Spencer's? You're the one who's always telling me that we live in an electronic age. Book a suite in the Manchester Conference Centre, take your secretaries with you and get the telephone company to transfer our calls there.'

'We're on four lines and then there are all the files,' she protested. 'The wages calculations . . .'

'Do it, Celeste!' I ordered. 'I want this place shut down by nine.' I enjoyed cracking the whip for once.

It was actually nearer ten before the last of the office staff had departed in taxis to our new improvised headquarters and I was able to lock the door. I felt as if a heavy stone had been lifted off my chest. I looked up and down the narrow street. There was no sign of the ambling islander either as his own ugly self or in any kind of fancy dress.

When I reached the room in the Manchester Conference Centre at the back of the University near Sackville Street,

Celeste was already at work informing all staff who could be reached that salary slips would be delivered by taxi and they weren't to go near the office.

'This looks bad,' she moaned. 'It looks as if we can't pay our bills.'

'Not at all,' I assured her. 'A lot of businesses change their offices frequently. It would look a lot worse if that maniac had burst in and shot somebody. Most of our staff keep in touch by mobile phone, anyway.'

Speaking of mobile phones made me start fidgeting with my own. Bob was taking his time at the New Smithfield Market.

'Michael phoned,' Celeste said, 'he's staying in London over the weekend because the record office is open on Saturday and it won't be worth his while to come up here just for the Sunday.' She looked thoroughly miserable about this.

'Fine,' I replied. I couldn't work out what the problem was with her and Michael. 'I trust him, you know. Did he say what he's working on?'

'He's investigating the family history of Mel Parkes. Apparently she came from quite a wealthy background.'

Celeste looked very unhappy and I was about to ask what the problem was when she asked me a question.

'Dave,' she said in a half whisper, 'what do you think about inter-racial marriage?'

I took a deep breath and allowed myself to wonder what was coming next.

'I only ask because when I took Clint to the flat I couldn't help seeing that your dead wife was a black woman. I'd never realised before.'

'Elenki was a medical student at the University. An African girl.'

'Yes. Do you think inter-racial marriage works, though?'

I stared at Celeste, trying to work out what was going on in her head.

'I must have done or I wouldn't have given it a try,' I admitted. 'Mine didn't last too long because she died.'

'My mother says it's an insult to the black community.'

'My mother and father were very hostile. My dad said he didn't want any coffee-coloured grandkids. As it happened he didn't get any.'

'How sad,' Celeste said so soulfully that I wondered once again if she was volunteering to supply the deficiency.

'They came round eventually but it was too late,' I added.

'Marvin "Shit For Brains" Desailles says all these adverts where you see a black man going with a white woman are just racism. They're insulting to black women – though you'd think he'd be the last one to talk about insulting women.'

Her eyes started to fill with tears.

'He has a right to a point of view,' I said diplomatically. 'In your case it would be the black men who were being insulted and as Marvin isn't interested in women anyway, I don't see what's grieving him. Some would say that it's only the business of the couple involved.'

'Do you really think that?' she asked hopefully. 'It's Michael . . . I've been seeing a lot of him, or I was until you started sending him to London the whole time. He wants me to move in with him but I've said I won't unless he marries me.'

'Oh!' I gasped, and took a deep breath, thankful that vanity hadn't compelled me to tell her I was already spoken for.

'I've seen so many of my friends move in with their boyfriends and then they move out again a few months later. My mum's all in favour of me moving in with Michael – she thinks I'll soon get sick of being with a white guy. She's a racist like Marvin really. But I won't get sick of him. I want to marry him.'

'Celeste, why don't you finish early and go down to

London and help Michael to finish up there?' I suggested. 'The firm will pay,' I added grandly.

After that the temporary office began humming, little trills of song began to emerge from Celeste's corner and the others were beavering away so hard that I soon began to feel redundant.

My mobile chirruped and I eagerly keyed the menu button and clamped it to my ear.

It wasn't Bob.

'DCI Cullen here, Mr Cunane, calling from Bootle Street Police Station,' Brendan Cullen said formally. 'We were wondering if you'd care to step round to Bootle Street to help us regarding an incident? We've been to your office but you appear to have shut up shop.'

The stilted way he was speaking sounded as if he was reading the words off a prompt sheet.

The first thing that went through my mind was that Brendan was pulling some kind of practical joke. Did he think I'd forgotten where he worked? Then I realised that he must be speaking in the presence of another senior officer. His words were intended to tip me off to keep my distance. If there's one thing the senior ranks of the GMP enjoy more than massaging the crime statistics it's playing internal politics. I wondered if it was me that was in trouble, or Brendan for slipping me the McAteer file.

'Do I need to bring my solicitor with me?' I asked. For once in my life I'd nothing in particular to reproach myself with, though that's never stopped the police from finding something which they can reproach me with. I could only think that my visits to Mollingtree hadn't gone unnoticed.

The line went dead for a minute while Bren conferred. There was nothing joky in his tone when he replied: 'That's entirely up to you, Mr Cunane. There are no charges currently pending against you but you may face charges as a result of our inquiries and so you are fully entitled to exercise all your legal rights. At the moment we're simply asking you to step round here to clarify certain matters.'

There was something in his tone. It was almost as if he was willing me to bring a solicitor with me. One thing was certain: I wouldn't have an inkling about what was going on unless I did as he was asking.

'Very well, DCI Cullen. I'll be round to see you as soon as my solicitor can be contacted.'

'Make that twelve o'clock sharp, would you, Mr Cunane?' Brendan said with a touch of the iron hand in the velvet glove. 'With or without your legal representative.'

I agreed.

'Those stupid pigs!' Celeste cried. 'As if we haven't enough trouble because they let the riff-raff of the world walk round our streets killing people, they have to get on your back.'

'Get Marvin to meet me at Bootle Street before twelve,' I said mildly.

'Will I be able to go to London now?'

'Peter can come in and see that everything's finished up here,' I told her. 'Anyway, I'm not expecting to end up locked in the cells.'

'You never know with that lot,' she said comfortingly.

Half an hour later I stood alongside the white limestone façade of Bootle Street Police Station examining the ashlar masonry for fossils of extinct forms of life. There were plenty embedded in the stone and plenty behind it too, especially in the offices of the senior ranks.

Marvin arrived by taxi on the dot of twelve and we went in together. He and I hadn't exactly been what you might call 'best buddies' recently but as we walked up to the desk he insisted on going through the full handshaking, hand-patting, and finger-counting routine as if we were long-lost brothers. He only does it to annoy the police. He was looking a lot more like a solicitor today. He still had locks but he'd shortened them and they were tucked under a small leather pill box hat. He was wearing a well-cut dark blue suit, a white shirt with button-down collar and silk tie, and gleaming black leather shoes. The image he projected now was of an aide to the Secretary General of the United Nations, or of a rising black politician.

'You look as if you mean business,' I said out of the corner of my mouth as we were led upstairs to be interviewed.

'Hey! They think I'm the bee's knees down at the old Black and Blue. I've done so much networking there that my phone's not stopped buzzing with offers of work. Ethnic's flavour of the month with some of these big firms. They'd pay me fifty grand a year just to sit in an office so everyone can see how multiracial they are.'

'I appreciate the privilege of your representing me.'

'I'm not joking you! These dudes are on the lookout for a tame black guy but I don't think I'm tame enough for them yet.'

'I'll just have to put up with your little ways for a while longer then.'

'Sorry about that, Dave,' he said with a Cheshire Cat smile.

We were ushered into an interview room where we met Cullen and Detective Sergeant Munro. Munro is a hopelessly trendy young man. The last time I'd seen him he'd been sporting a four-button brown suit and dyed yellow hair. This time the hair had reverted to what I took to be its natural mousy brown shade and he was wearing a blue V-neck sweater and cargo pants, without shirt or tie. If I didn't know better I could have thought he'd just dropped by to deliver a pizza. He thought he was very cool.

Brendan was in a navy blue suit and looked just a trifle sweaty.

'This is an informal interview, Mr Cunane,' he said. He rolled his eyes heavenwards as he spoke.

385

'Yeah, we can see that,' Marvin replied, examining Munro with a nasty expression on his face.

'We won't be recording anything,' Brendan stressed. He seemed nervous and I understood what he was telling me. There would be other unseen listeners.

'We appreciate that,' Marvin said, 'but I will be advising my client not to say anything that you might put a wrong construction on.'

'It's all right, Marvin, let's hear what they've got to say.'

Munro led.

'Do you know a Mr George Andrew St Joseph Crockett of the Phoebus Health Club?'

I considered this question for a long time. Crockett. Not the Smathers, not McAteer, and not Charlie Costello. Neither Brendan nor Munro gave the slightest sign of impatience. Marvin nudged me. 'Do want to confer in another room?' he asked.

I shook my head.

Finally I said 'Yes, I know him.'

'Do you know Mr Crockett's current whereabouts?'

'Just a moment,' Marvin intervened. 'Mr Cunane has admitted that he knows this Mr Crockett but why should he know the man's whereabouts? Are you imputing something to my client? If you are, I shall advise him not to answer until formal charges are laid.'

'No one's charging your client,' Munro replied icily. 'We are simply seeking his assistance in locating Mr Crockett.'

Marvin drew me back for a whispered consultation: 'I don't like this. I think they suspect something heavy's happened to Crockett and they're trying to pin it on to you. Say nothing.'

I was burning up with eagerness to know what had happened to Judder but you don't arrive at the nick with a legal adviser in tow who can talk the hind-leg

386

off a Philadelphia lawyer and then start shouting the odds yourself.

I nodded.

'My client declines to respond,' Marvin said.

I looked at Brendan. He seemed pleased with this reply in so far as I could assess the Sphinx-like smile that hovered on his lips.

'When did you last see Mr Crockett?' Munro asked.

'Mr Cunane . . .' Marvin started.

'No, it's all right. I met Mr Crockett at his club some time ago and then last weekend I attended a party there on Friday then met Mr Crockett at a pub on the Saturday and again at his club on Sunday.'

'So you were well acquainted with him?'

'No, I merely met him several times to discuss some private business.'

'Was this private business concerned with the extortion of money by menaces?'

Marvin started to get out of his chair and to pull me along behind him but Brendan Cullen intervened for the first time: 'Detective Sergeant, perhaps you'd like to rephrase that question?' he suggested urbanely.

Munro didn't look in the least upset by his superior's request and I realised that the police knew nothing about what was going on.

'Did Mr Crockett express concern to you that someone was trying to extort money from him with menaces?' Munro asked.

'No,' I replied.

My words produced a cool little smile from Munro.

Marvin sat down again.

'Did Mr Crockett in fact try to seek your services to protect him from such threats?'

'No.'

Munro indicated disbelief by the merest inclination of his head.

'Were you and an associate present when Mr Crockett had security equipment installed at his club?'

'Yes.'

'Did he explain to you why he required such elaborate precautions?'

'He said there'd been a lot of break-ins and that he was going to have the same level of security as that enjoyed by Sylvester Stallone although he was not able to resort to firearms in defence of his property or person. I advised him to spare himself the expense and to phone me if he felt threatened but he declined and I then left.'

'Did Mr Crockett give you some written material contained in an A4 envelope?'

'He did,' I agreed cautiously. There was no point in denying it as they'd obviously been briefed by Crockett's celebrity protection team.

'At last,' said Munro with a sigh of relief. 'We believe that paper contains instructions on how to enter Mr Crockett's premises and we wish to do so now. There's no suggestion of foul play but we have reason to believe that Mr Crockett may have met with an accident in his private quarters and we'd be obliged if you would release the information.'

I was fairly stunned by this information. I made no reply. Kimball Smathers, Keeley Smathers and now Judder Crockett? Spring-cleaning on a grand scale.

'Say nothing,' Marvin whispered. 'Something's happened to this geezer and they're on a fishing trip to tie you into it.' The interval this consultation provided gave me the opportunity to come up with a story that Brendan might believe.

'Mr Crockett has been attempting to raise funds for expansion of his club. The paper he gave me was simply some financial material. If I knew my way into the penthouse I'd be happy to help you, but I don't.'

This time it was Munro and Brendan who held a whispered conversation.

'Mr Cunane,' Brendan said, 'it would be disingenuous of me to conceal that Mr Crockett hasn't been seen for the last two days and that there are concerns in some quarters that you know something about this.'

'Outrageous!' said Marvin.

'If you'd let me finish, Mr Desailles,' Brendan retorted calmly. 'I'm satisfied that Mr Cunane's connection with Mr Crockett is wholly innocent. However, he was present when this mysterious sealed chamber was constructed in Mr Crockett's quarters and we would be highly gratified if he could assist us in gaining access.'

I looked at Brendan as the strained smile slowly faded from his face. Whatever he knew or suspected he wasn't trying to fit me up. It was almost as if he was throwing the ball my way and waiting to see how far I'd run with it. In the midst of all my dealings with Crockett at the weekend I'd found time to drop a hint to Brendan about extortion cases and he'd sent me those notes about McAteer. Could it be that he thought Crockett was the extortionist? Did he know something about links between Charlie Costello and Crockett that I wasn't aware of?

I held a whispered conference with Marvin.

'If this is a fishing expedition I want to try catching something too. I need to know what's happened to Crockett.'

'As long as I come with you,' he agreed.

'Mr Cunane will be happy to cooperate,' Marvin announced, 'as long as I'm allowed to accompany him to make sure that the rash young man here makes no further attempts to incriminate Mr Cunane.'

'What are we waiting for?' asked Brendan. The rash young man, Munro, looked slightly annoyed at Marvin's description of him.

We could have made the short journey to the Phoebus Health Club on foot but that would have been undignified for the police so we went by car with sirens sounding.

At the club there were officers on the pavement but the place was functioning normally.

There was such a long wait for the lifts that we walked through the building and up the internal stairs. This time I had more opportunity to inspect the various activities than when Anna Pietrangeli had whisked me straight up to the restaurant floor. On a Friday afternoon the club was particularly busy as people of all ages toned up their muscles for the weekend. There was weightlifting on the ground floor, step aerobics on the first floor, every kind of mechanical muscle bender on the second floor, and massage and skin toning on the third floor. The place was heaving with people. At just under a thousand pounds for a year's membership for a couple the place must have been raking in the cash. No wonder Judder wanted to expand. The religion of the body beautiful looked set to go on indefinitely.

We arrived at the fourth floor where several uniformed officers were waiting accompanied by a number of workmen. Heavy drills and mechanical chisels lay about on the carpeted floor. The door had been forced open.

'Lead on, MacDuff,' Brendan invited with a hint of his old geniality. 'You know your way round here. I don't.'

I went up the stairs very cautiously behind a uniformed officer. There was no saying what booby traps might have been rigged. Thompson had trained with Special Forces even if he did prefer his ancestral weapon on occasion. When we reached the roof level the scene was tranquil. The koi carp still swam beneath their net as placidly as ever. All the gravel had been raked back into place with no sign of the previous disturbance. The only incongruous note was the concertina wire festooned all along the edge of the roof.

'Expecting visitors, was he?' Brendan asked with a nod at the wire. 'Did he think they were going to climb up the outside walls?'

'It was possible,' I said, 'so he took precautions.'

'Not enough, by the look of it.' The door of the penthouse was slightly open. 'Anybody been in here?' he asked his officers and the workers.

'No, we forced the door below and then we waited for you.'

Brendan, Munro, Marvin and myself entered.

The place had been trashed again, only this time it wasn't just a matter of tipping things out on to the floor. Furniture was smashed and splintered. There was every evidence of a thorough search having been made. The bronze statue had been broken off its plinth. Everything that might have concealed an object was broken.

'I wonder what someone was looking for?' Brendan asked. 'I spy with my little eye something beginning with "c". Is it a chair, is it a cupboard? What do you think, Mr Cunane? Could it be a club? C for club? Oh, but then we're in the club, it's all round us, isn't it?'

I gave Brendan a startled look. Was he a mind-reader? The same thought had occurred to me. Had Thompson come back to search for his implement of execution and had Crockett tried a spot of blackmailing of his own account? As good a guess as any, I thought. Brendan had far greater resources to help him find things out about the residents of the Phoebus Club than I had and if he'd decided that Thompson had killed Charlie Costello then that was all to the good. There was no way he was going to find out about *why* Thompson and Mr E had killed Charlie unless they told him. It all figured now, the summons to Bootle Street. Brendan hoped to jog my conscience into telling him what Charlie had been up to when he was killed.

I felt cold fingers running up my spine.

I could tell him everything . . . even Bob's theory about the Turkish Cypriot drug dealer . . . and they might well catch Thompson and Mr E in the act, but on the other hand if Mr E had his sources inside the police force they might not. All I would have done would have been to warn him.

391

Brendan had tipped me the wink that he wasn't the only person listening to our conversation in Bootle Street. Was that why he'd brought me here now? Had he thought it out so many steps ahead? Did he expect some word for his ears alone in the privacy of this club?

If so, he was going to be disappointed. Having come so close to the point of discovering who Mr E was I couldn't take the risk of handing everything over to Brendan and the police. If Mr E decided to ditch the operation against the Turkish Cypriot, Thompson could be discarded at his leisure. He was my lead. He was the one I hoped to spot. If Mr E sent him back to Fiji I'd have lost my chance. All Mr E needed to do was to shake another enforcer down from the trees and he'd be back in business. I still hadn't a single decent clue as to who Mr E was. I had to go ahead on my own. It wasn't simply a matter of protecting Jamie Piercy's reputation.

I looked round the room. Apart from being smashed to pieces there was only one incongruous note. Someone had been smoking in here. I bent to look at a crushed cigarette butt.

'Leave that to the professionals, *Mr* Cunane,' Munro snapped. He plucked the butt up with a pair of tweezers and put it into a plastic bag.

'Don't they have any security videos of who came up here?' I asked Brendan.

'Unfortunately not. The relevant tapes for yesterday are missing. Let's do what we came here for. Do you know how to get into Crockett's security room?'

'It's supposed to be resistant to all efforts at forced entry and to be able to survive an earthquake,' I said.

We walked up to the balcony. The gaping hole in the wall had been repaired and plastered over. Access to the secure room was through a door that had been cut into the side wall of Crockett's bedroom. The door was locked. 'You're going to need explosives to get in there,' one of the locksmiths explained. 'It's like a bank vault.' He indicated the reinforced hinges which had covers over them to prevent anyone chiselling them off.

'It doesn't look all that strong,' Brendan sniffed. He's never been a great admirer of things transatlantic.

'The idea is that you shut yourself in there and then you radio for the LAPD to come and rescue you. It's not built to withstand a siege.'

'That lot! They didn't exactly cover themselves with glory in the O.J. Simpson case. That poor woman could have used a secure room.'

'They cost tens of thousands of dollars. State-of-the-art.'

'You'd better get on with it then,' he said to the waiting workers. 'Mr Crockett has angina. He might be lying on the floor inside there in need of attention.'

We withdrew to a corner of the roof while the technicians blew the hinges. It was a surprisingly small explosion, more like a crack than a decent bang. The carp didn't even stir.

When we got into the room it was pristine. There was no sign that Crockett had ever been in it.

'Looks like this did him a fat lot of good, doesn't it?' Brendan commented. He was on the point of dismissing us when a policewoman came running up.

'They've found something at the back, sir,' she said breathlessly. 'A body.'

Munro glared at her for announcing this in my presence.

'Wait on the street,' Brendan said to me.

Access to the rear of the Phoebus Club was via a very narrow alley two doors down from the actual club. It was just wide enough to allow a car through. We waited at the street end inside the police cordon.

After a few minutes Munro came trotting up to us.

'Can you identify the body?' he asked.

I followed him down the mephitic little lane. It's interesting how these city centre buildings only have one decent face which they present to the world. Steel girders were visible in the wall like bare ribs. Ghosts of older buildings had left their outlines in the rough brickwork of the former insurance office. There were piles of rubbish, vents emitting steam and large refuse containers everywhere. It seemed that the workers in the nearby buildings weren't very good at aiming their rubbish at the bins. There was as much piled up on the ground as in the bins.

It was behind one of these that the grisly remains of Judder Crockett lay in a messy pile.

'That Crockett?' Brendan asked laconically.

I nodded. The thick brushed-back hair was unmistakable.

'The rats have been at him by the look of it,' Brendan said.

Munro did take a look and then recoiled. He clamped a handkerchief to his mouth and tried to hide his revulsion behind the previous cool expression. He couldn't hide it. He turned green, ran to a corner and puked.

'Sorry, sir,' he muttered shamefacedly when he came back.

'Don't apologise for being human, Munro,' Brendan said. 'It's when the sight of what human beings can do to each other doesn't affect you that you need to apologise.'

I agreed but kept my mouth clamped shut. I was wondering if this was why we'd been brought here. Brendan must have suspected something. It doesn't usually require a Detective Chief Inspector to come out and look if some citizen's failed to show up for work. He'd been expecting to find Crockett's body, only the location came as a surprise to him. That meant he must have his own sources of information, probably staff at the club. Maybe Eos the Dawn had shed a little light. I couldn't help but look at Crockett's sad remains again. Only one side of his body showed visible injuries apart from where the rats had been at him.

The four of us stood contemplating the grim evidence of mortality. It could just as well have been me lying there. Music from an aerobics class drifted down to us. Traffic noises filtered along the narrow alley from the street. There was a clatter of cutlery being loaded into a dishwasher high above. Life went on but not for George Andrew St Joseph Crockett. The wind blew a crisp packet across his face.

I'd never wished the man ill, I told myself. Certainly not anything like this. Didn't I warn him the last time I spoke to him?

'It looks as if he's come off there,' Brendan said, pointing to the roof of the Phoebus Club, 'and then hit this wall and gone down behind the bins. It's no wonder the body wasn't spotted sooner. We'll have to check when these bins are emptied.' We peered at the blank back wall of the building which backed on to the Phoebus Club. Sure enough, high up, there were signs that something had disturbed the fine coating of dirt and dust on the bricks.

'Do you think he jumped?' Munro asked.

'You've seen it,' Brendan replied. 'There's a six-foot-high fence of concertina wire round the inner edge of that roof. Does he look as if he climbed over that?'

Munro shook his head.

'Pace out the width of this alley,' Brendan ordered.

It was at least twelve feet.

'No one could have jumped off that roof and then hit this wall unless he had wings. Some bastard picked Crockett up and slung him over the fence. Some very strong bastard, eh, Dave?'

I didn't speak. I knew this was the moment that Brendan must be expecting a revelation from me but he wasn't going to get it. It was better to say nothing than to lie to an old friend.

I shrugged.

He looked at me searchingly. There was just the faintest trace of a grin on his face.

'OK, Mr Cunane, thank you very much for all your help. You've been most enlightening,' he said. 'Don't leave town without letting us know, will you?'

'Why not?' Marvin demanded fiercely.

'You never know, we might have some more questions for Mr Cunane and we don't want to have to go looking for him, do we?' Brendan said with a cheeky grin.

Marvin and I walked back up the slight incline from the club towards Deansgate. The streets were filled with people anticipating the weekend by heading into the innumerable bars and restaurants. The Black and Blue Club was just round the corner.

'Fancy a drink?' Marvin suggested.

'Yeah,' I murmured. A brandy would go down very well.

We crossed Deansgate and turned the corner into Peter Street. I was just about to tell Marvin that I was not going into Loony Leary's Liquor Store under any circumstances when my mobile rang.

It was Bob.

'I've got a name,' he said. 'Mehmet Celal, and he lives in Wilmslow with his wife and teenage daughter.'

28

I phoned Peter and told him to meet me at the leisure centre car park in Wilmslow. Bob was already on his way there.

'What about me?' Marvin asked. 'Shall I come?'

'Thanks for what you've done today but I need you to keep plugging away at the legal profession.'

'You don't think I look the part for Wilmslow, is that it? Too black for the white hinterlands?'

'To be honest, Marvin, yes. Your appearance is too distinctive for undercover work. It's not that you're black but if Mr E was at the Black and Blue Club or one of the other places where you've been looking for disgruntled lawyers or coppers, and then he spotted you trudging round Wilmslow, he'd be warned wouldn't he?'

'You just shoved me into that club to stop me getting under your feet, didn't you? Not that I'm complaining, joining that place is going to be the making of me, but you did, didn't you?'

'Marvin, I sent you there because that's where Charlie Costello spent his days and nights. The fact that Charlie almost certainly knew him is the only lead I have to Mr E's identity. OK, Charlie knew most of the criminals in Manchester but I had to start somewhere. You're one of my top men.'

'OK, I'll believe you, thousands wouldn't,' he said. I could tell he was pleased with my answer though he didn't care to show it.

He promised to keep in touch via the mobile. We parted. He headed back towards the club and I went to where I'd left the car. On the way I phoned Janine to let her know that things were bubbling.

'The very man!' she said when I contacted her.

'What?'

'I've just received a summons for doing over ninety on the A34 last Saturday at four in the morning. How do you explain that?'

'Well, obviously it was me,' I said defensively.

'You were going to see that Italian piece out in Heald Green, weren't you?'

'I was but . . .'

'But nothing, Dave Cunane, you just can't keep your trousers zipped, can you? You let me start feeling all lovey and tender towards you and then you go off after other women. You're diseased!'

She disconnected before I could reply.

I redialled but there was no reply.

I phoned her mobile number, again no reply.

I stopped and keyed in a text message to her. She'd have to turn her mobile back on sometime. The message read: ZIPPER WAS ZIPPED SATURDAY LOVE DAVE.

Once in the car I debated stopping off in Chorlton to straighten things out but the call from Bob was too urgent. I joined the rush-hour traffic queuing up along the Princess Parkway to flow into the commuter arteries. It was queues all the way. A queue to get on to the M60, then another queue to get off that on to Kingsway and a slow crawl through Cheadle towards Wilmslow.

Peter and Bob were in the car park at Wilmslow in their separate cars looking at their watches anxiously when I arrived. They'd never met. I pulled up next to Bob's hire car and Peter came over to us.

Introductions didn't take long.

'So what's the plan?' Bob asked. 'He lives on the other

side of Wilmslow out near Lindow Moss. I've already driven past and I didn't see any white vans.'

'What about at the house?'

'There were two cars there. A Mercedes and a Toyota Land Cruiser.'

'We've got to go there right away,' Peter said.

'Hang on. If they are under observation we don't want to tip Mr E off by arriving as a delegation,' I argued. 'It's better if I go on my own. What's the SP on this Celal?'

'Mehmet Celal isn't your average humble fruit and veg merchant,' Bob explained. 'He describes himself as a food broker and has an office near Victoria Station in Shudehill. He has good contacts with the citrus industry in northern Cyprus. You remember they had a civil war there?'

'I know all about the Cyprus Troubles. My dear papa was in the military police there during the EOKA campaign.'

'Yeah, well, this is the follow-on from that. The Greeks wanted *enosis* or union with Greece which would have meant the Turkish minority being kicked right off the island. The Turks were about eighteen per cent of the population. When we pulled out, the Brits that is, Greece and Turkey nearly had a war over it. In the end the Yanks stopped it but the Turkish Army invaded and grabbed thirty-eight per cent of the island.'

'Nice deal!'

'Be careful what you say about that. Apparently they're very touchy. The Turkish bit is now separated from the rest by the Green Line but the relevant part for Mr Celal is that the Turks grabbed the section that has the citrus-growing industry and although no other country has recognised what they call the Turkish Republic of Northern Cyprus, they've been doing very well with fruit exports. Mehmet Celal is closely connected to the growers. If you want a few truck loads of oranges for juice or marmalade or whatever all he has to do is pick up the phone and the growers will load a refrigerated lorry on to the Gazimagusa to Mersin ferry.'

'Gazimagusa?' I asked.

'That's what they call Famagusta now. Mersin's in Turkey and they send them on from there across the Bosphorus Bridge to Europe and into New Smithfield Market in a few days.'

'Or to Amsterdam,' I said.

'That's right. Oh, and guess what? Mr Celal does quite a bit of trans-shipping. He's just as happy to deliver you a cargo of tulips from Amsterdam in one of his nice refrigerated lorries.'

'There must be a good profit in that, especially if there's something else besides flowers in the load. So what are you saying? Is he shipping heroin into Amsterdam from Turkey, or is he picking it up in Amsterdam, or what?'

'You'd have to have the whole of the intercepted conversation to know that. Cocaine is flowing into Amsterdam from South America. The place is the drug crossroads of the world, especially since the Schengen Agreement abolished the internal frontiers within the European Union. The bit of the transcript we have doesn't say exactly what they're dealing in, heroin, cocaine, amphetamines, Ecstasy or what. But it's obvious that Mr Celal is in an excellent position for smuggling with contacts in Turkey, still a prime heroin producer, Europe and the UK, and a legitimate business as cover. The opium base from Turkey is processed in another country, Bulgaria or somewhere else in the Balkans, not in Holland.'

Peter had been listening to all this quietly. Now he piped up: 'This is all very interesting, but while we're chewing the fat here Celal's kid could be being grabbed.'

'True enough, but we don't want Dave walking in there completely clueless,' Bob argued.

'Thanks!' I said.

'No, listen, it's all very well getting sentimental about Celal's daughter but this guy is making a vast profit on drugs. Hard drugs, real killers. How many kids die every

400

time this bloke moves a lorry loaded with drugs into the country?'

'Do you know anything about the daughter?' I asked.

'Nothing, except that her name's Yasmin, she's fifteen, and she goes to a private convent school for girls at Bowdon called Loreto. I don't know anything about the wife.'

'I'm going to see him,' I announced. 'You two drop me off and come in after me if I don't phone in ten minutes.'

Celal lived in a detached house on Pear Tree Lane which itself backed on to Lindow Moss. It was all nice expensive property round there if you didn't mind being directly under the flight path for Manchester Airport. Celal hadn't been exaggerating when he told his Dutch business colleague that he lives 'just around the corner from the airport'. It must have been handy for his business.

It was a big house with a double gateway from the road and two large new vehicles parked on the gravel drive to show just how well Mr Celal was doing in the fruit broking trade. Although the nights were getting lighter it was gloomy and lonely when my friends dropped me on Pear Tree Lane. I looked up and down the street. There was no sign of anyone watching but then with Mr E there wouldn't be. I stood in the shadows for a moment. Delise Delaney, my archaeologically inclined former girlfriend, had been mad with enthusiasm when the body of Lindow Man, a two-thousand-year-old Druid sacrifice, had been recovered from the peat bog just a couple of hundred yards away from where I was now standing.

The sheer incongruity of it all struck me. Two thousand years ago an excited bunch of tribesmen had sacrificed one of their leaders to ensure good harvests or some such. He must have felt much as I did now before the dagger struck, only certain that he was going to be reborn among the gods of the Celtic Otherworld. Here I was, two thousand years later, going to try and save the life of an unknown girl and to catch the killer who'd been giving me sleepless nights for weeks. I just hoped that he hadn't got a dagger waiting for me.

My feet seemed to make a dreadfully loud crunching noise as I walked towards the house. All the lights were on. As I walked up to the door a man stepped out from behind the Toyota Land Cruiser and came up behind me. He pushed something hard and metallic into the small of my back. I almost jumped out of my shoes. He patted my arms and jacket but missed the pistol I was carrying in my trouser pocket and then pushed me forward.

The door to the house opened just as I was about to collide with it and I tumbled inside. Another shove sent me down on to the carpet. I looked up and two extremely angry Turks glared down at me. The older man who I took to be Celal was squat in build and broad-shouldered. His face was unusual. Olive-complexioned, it was shaped like a beer mug, narrower at the bottom than at the top. The crown of his head was flat and he had greased black wavy hair. His eyes were dark and well spaced, like little black buttons, nose small and flat, perched above a massive handlebar moustache and a squared-off chin. He had a thick roll of flesh where most people keep their neck.

The foreign appearance was lessened by the expensive grey check suit he was wearing which looked as if it had been cut by a Savile Row tailor. He was about fifty years of age and looked as tough as one of those iron bollards they tie aircraft carriers up to.

The other man, also olive-complexioned and dark-haired, was much younger and, if anything, looked even tougher and nastier. When he opened his mouth I saw that he had an extra tooth between the two upper front incisors. It gave his rugged face an extra degree of ugliness.

'You've come about Yasmin, you scum!' Celal said, and launched a kick at me.

I rolled out of the way and pulled out the 9mm pistol.

402

'Calm down,' I barked as I struggled to my feet. 'I know nothing about Yasmin.'

Both men backed away but in different directions to present less of a target. This was not going the way I'd intended. I held the gun between two fingers and put it down on a table beside me.

'I'm a private detective,' I shouted, throwing my ID towards Celal.

He picked it up, examined it and then threw it on the floor.

'Bastard! You've come to spy on me.'

'Read the ID. I'm a *private* detective.'

'Not police?'

'No, private.'

'I don't trust you. You're a spy.'

'Would I walk up to your door if I was? But I do have some idea about what's happening. Yasmin's your daughter, isn't she?'

'How do you know?'

'What's happened to her?' I asked desperately. His disbelief was like a granite wall.

'You know because you've got her.'

'No, I'm a detective trying to track down a gang of kidnappers. They've got your daughter, haven't they?'

Every word I said seemed to make things worse. They say you should stop digging if you're in a hole but I couldn't. I needed him on my side.

'No! Get out of my house. You're a spy.'

Just at that moment an inner door opened and a tall, youngish man appeared. This one had a round face and curly blond hair and there was something Irish-looking about him. He was carrying a shotgun and it looked as if he knew how to use it.

'Shoot him, Darko!' Celal ordered. 'He's not from the police.'

Darko hesitated to obey, not from unwillingness, but

because Celal was in his line of fire. In those few seconds the front door was kicked open and Bob Lane appeared framed against the evening gloom. He made an interesting picture because he was clutching an Uzi sub-machine gun in his pudgy fingers. He was also wearing a bullet-proof jacket.

If he'd touched the trigger there'd have been general mayhem which might have been unfortunate for me as I was in the middle of the room. Instead he suggested, 'Why don't we all sit down and have a nice chat?'

There was a lengthy wait before Mehmet Celal's intelligence kicked in.

He looked at me, he looked at Darko and he looked at Bob. A word or a movement from him and I would be lying dead on the floor. From upstairs in the house there came the sound of deep-throated wailing. It was one of those surreal little moments that stay etched in the memory. My eyes focused on a large brass plate on the wall. It had some Arabic lettering inscribed in blue enamel. For some reason the colours and shapes were extraordinarily vivid. I think I could draw a reasonable copy of it even now.

Finally Celal spoke.

'You are not from the kidnappers?'

'No fear, mate,' I said. 'I'm being paid by the family of one of their victims to track them down.'

'You work against them?'

'That's right.'

'I need proof. Anyone could have this,' he said, disdainfully kicking my ID towards me. 'I'm not afraid of your friend's gun. The only reason I didn't order Darko to shoot is because you looked at that,' he pointed to the brass plate with the Arabic letters, 'but I still need proof. Are you a Muslim, brother?'

'No,' I said. 'I was raised as a Catholic.'

'No matter. If you had been a man of ill will your eyes would not have rested on those words when you were in danger of sudden death.'

'Why not?'

'It is our Muslim profession of faith. "*There is only one God, Allah, and Muhammad is his prophet*." A truly evil man could not have looked at that without flinching. As for your associate, him,' he said, indicating Bob who was still fingering his Uzi, 'I know him. He is a dealer like me.'

'And I know you, cocker,' Bob returned cheerfully.

I tried to think of some way to win Celal's confidence. The man probably had more reason than most to be nervous if, as the transcript had stated, he was sitting on a mountain of cash.

I very slowly drew my mobile phone out of my pocket. Celal watched closely while I phoned Jamie Piercy. As I keyed in the number I was hoping against hope that he would answer. The Reds were at the Theatre of Dreams tomorrow so he ought to be relaxing at home in Alderley.

He was.

It took me a few minutes to persuade him to come round to Pear Tree Lane and establish our bona fides.

Meanwhile Celal lit a disgusting cheroot and blew smoke in our faces.

While we waited I acquainted myself with my surroundings. The stand-off was taking place in a very large lounge which was furnished with heavy reproduction Jacobean furniture. Celal's own origins were indicated by a few concessions to the Orient. There were carpets hanging on the walls, expensive-looking ones though I'm no judge, and one corner of the room was taken up with large cushions for reclining. A hubble-bubble in elaborately tooled and inlaid brass was ready for use among the cushions. Apart from photographs of heavy-set Turks on the massive sideboard there were no pictures in the room. Some brilliantly coloured Eastern ceramics, blue and yellow predominating, and brass work inscribed with Arabic writing completed the décor, clashing with the Olde Englishe furniture.

East was meeting West, and it was the East that had the upper hand. Even if Bob fired there was no way he could kill the man with the shotgun and also deal with Celal and the other man before they got me.

Twenty minutes is a long time. We'd all relaxed to a certain extent when Jamie arrived. We heard the car turn into the drive with an impressive spray of gravel from its massive wheels. Still Celal maintained his disbelieving frown. He exchanged a glance with the gunman whose finger tightened on the trigger of the shotgun pointing at my head.

Luckily for me when the soccer star stepped into the room his charisma was firmly fixed in place. That is, his identity was blindingly obvious even to the impervious Turk.

Jamie was wearing an open-sleeved army-style vest, designer jeans and Reebok trainers without socks. He had a gold chain round his neck. Celal, Darko and the other man, who I learned shortly after was called Kemal, immediately recognised him. Jamie gave them the shy little smile which has made him the nation's darling.

I think if it had been almost anyone else – a uniformed copper, a priest, even the Prime Minister – Celal would have maintained his suspicious attitude. But for Jamie, the dark looks melted like snow in summer. Such is celebrity, I realised with a shock, as the firearms disappeared and Celal received him with open arms.

'I came just as I was,' Jamie said apologetically. Celal reverently ushered him to a massive sofa and we all sat down. The Turk lit another of his cheroots but Jamie immediately showed signs of discomfort and Celal deferentially put it out.

I passed on an edited version of the kidnapping and subsequent death of Jamie's niece and the sad fate of Eric McAteer to the Turkish drug smuggler.

'This baby dies, and they killed this boy,' Celal lamented.

'What hope is there for my Yasmin? She is all I have since her mother died.'

'I thought that was her mother upstairs.' I said, nodding towards the stairwell from which the sound of crying hadn't ceased to echo since my arrival.

'That one is not Yasmin's mother,' Celal informed me gravely. 'Yasmin's mother died four years ago and I remarried. That may have been a mistake. That one is not much older than Yasmin. I hoped for children from her but she seems to be barren. She should have picked Yasmin up from the school but instead she stayed in her bed as she often does. Those scoundrels met my daughter in a taxi. That one will send a taxi for Yasmin if she remembers. Sometimes Yasmin has to ring me.

'My poor child, she must have got into that taxi with complete trust and now this . . . Darko! Bring the box.'

Darko, a Serb, not a Turk or an Irishman, I found out later, brought a box from the kitchen. It was cold to the touch. I opened it. It contained a little finger neatly severed almost at the knuckle. I looked at Celal. His face was set like stone.

'You're sure that's Yasmin's?' I asked.

'It is hers. There is a scar on the tip where she cut herself when she was ten. I myself applied the dressing to it.'

I suppressed a shudder. This was a new wrinkle from Mr E but he seemed to be on a learning curve. Perhaps he thought the Turk was too tough to surrender without some tangible evidence of the fate in store for his only child.

'Put it back in the freezer,' Celal ordered.

There was a moment of silence broken only by the sound of sobbing from above.

'Your wife seems very upset,' I commented more for something to say than any concern.

'I have had to whip that one for her negligence and she cries now from the pain in her back and because she seeks to please me, but if my beloved Yasmin does not return

407

to me she will learn the meaning of true repentance,' he said in a matter-of-fact voice. He lit another cheroot. Jamie went and stood by the window.

It seemed that the second Mrs Celal was in serious danger of a fatal mishap if Yasmin didn't return.

We sat round a low table drinking Turkish coffee supplied by Kemal while we learned the details of this latest kidnapping.

Yasmin finished school over in Bowdon at three forty-five. At four Celal received calls in his office at Shudehill, central Manchester. The usual routine was followed, coarse threats from one and smoother promises from the other. He immediately dispatched Darko to the school from where the Serb informed him that other girls had seen Yasmin getting in a taxi. They didn't remember the company but the driver wore a peaked cap and was bearded. The headteacher was all for phoning the police until Celal himself spoke to her on the phone and informed her it was a mix-up.

As Mr E had calculated, Mehmet Celal didn't require help from the fuzz any more than Lee Parkes, or Howard McAteer, or others whose names I didn't know, had.

Another call demanded one and a half million pounds for the return of Yasmin, and as a warning that the kidnappers were serious informed Celal that he would find his daughter's little finger in a box on the gatepost of his home.

Celal then returned home with Kemal, retrieved the box and put it in the freezer. Presumably he'd then relieved his feelings by chastising the unfortunate Mrs Celal with a handy whip. He'd been waiting for the kidnapper's next call when I turned up. In the circumstances his response to my ill-timed visit was quite mild.

'What are we going to do?' Bob asked.

'Do?' Celal responded bitterly. 'We can do nothing. I don't have one and a half million in cash to give them. The girl must die.'

His eyes flickered towards the stairs. Mrs Celal might very soon be lying in the peat bog where Lindow Man had been found.

I looked at Celal. He wasn't the sort of punter you'd go out of your way to pick a quarrel with, or even engage in a conversation about the merits of Turkish football teams.

Choosing my words carefully, I asked him how much money he did have.

'One million and fifty thousand,' he said, 'in used notes; fives, tens and twenties.'

'Are you prepared to leave things in my hands if I can raise the rest of the ransom and get your daughter back?' I asked.

His eyes were completely expressionless. I understood that I was asking him to give up his ill-gotten gains but if he truly loved his daughter . . .

'Yes,' he answered without hesitation. There are plenty of men who'd have hung on to their million in cash and said goodbye to their daughter.

'Good,' I said. 'Go and shut your wife up . . . sorry, I mean, tell her to stop that wailing. It's not conducive. Bob, go and bring Peter in from where you left him.'

'He's waiting to call the police as soon as he hears the sound of gunfire,' Bob retorted with a chuckle as he went to the door.

'And, Bob,' I added, 'lose the Uzi somewhere, will you? That's making me nervous too.'

'Bloody lucky for you I had it, though, in't it?' he said over his shoulder.

'Jamie, can you help with the money?' I asked the soccer star.

'I've got money in the bank but I don't use cash much.'

'When's the deadline?' I asked Celal.

'I must have the money by four a.m. Saturday.'

'Jamie, can you phone your bank and see if they can make

409

some arrangement? This may be the only chance we'll ever get to catch these people.'

'There's money there but I don't have five hundred thousand in the bank,' he said.

'How much?' I asked bluntly.

'I'm worth plenty, my agent and accountant could tell you, but it's all invested.'

'How much can you prise out of the bank tonight? No questions asked?'

'About one hundred and twenty grand.'

'Do it then,' I invited, 'and, Jamie, when you've done that, get on to Lee and tell him we need whatever he's got. It's the only way he'll ever see what he lost. Tell him he's got to take a gamble.'

Jamie raised his eyebrows and retreated to the Turkish corner of the room. To my surprise he lounged easily on one of the big cushions, phone in hand.

Bob came back in at that point, Peter right behind him.

'The road's clear,' he said. 'Do you want me to check the Evergreens to make sure they haven't got the girl there?'

'Yes, we'd better make sure, but how are you going to get in without climbing over the fence? We don't want you ripping your suit.'

'Thompson isn't the only one who can make copies of keys,' he said with a smile.

I sent him off knowing that Mr E would never return to the same base he'd used before, but it gave Peter something to do.

'Bob, can you raise some cash?' I asked. 'It's this girl's only hope.'

'I don't know, Dave. What with all this travel and what not, I'm a bit depleted.'

'I heard about what happened to you,' Celal said. 'I can do much to help you.'

Bob looked at him thoughtfully but made no reply.

'I can probably scrape up seventy,' he said to me, turning his back on Celal. Then he went out.

'What's the matter with him?' the Turk asked.

'You tell me,' I said.

Celal made a gesture with his hands which I took to mean that he didn't know.

Jamie came over.

'I'm getting the hundred and twenty grand. The bank in Alderley Edge is going to open specially for me. Lee's said he'll find another hundred and twenty but he wants to come round. I'll be back soon.'

'Wait,' I said. I was scribbling numbers on a pad but Celal beat me to it.

'That's one million three hundred and sixty thousand we got,' he said. 'Still not enough.'

Jamie scratched his head and then flapped his hands.

'Yeah, I know,' he said brightly. 'I can ask my dad.'

He went back to the recliner cushions and settled down with the phone again. Celal paced nervously round the room.

'Why don't you go and rub some oil on your wife's back?' I suggested.

'You are a funny man, I think, Mr Cunane,' he replied.

'No, I'm dead serious. These people would probably have arranged for her to have an accident en route if she *had* gone to pick up Yasmin. They leave nothing to chance. Anyway, in England we'd regard a fifteen-year-old as being well able to come home by herself. Isn't there a school bus?'

'I did not think it was fitting for my daughter to come on the bus. There are no teachers, no holy sisters, there. The other girls might do bad things: swear, smoke, look at boys,' the drug dealer explained.

'OK,' I agreed, 'but I still don't think it was your wife's fault. These people were targeting you. They knew you had money.'

'Yes,' he said thoughtfully, 'and you did too. I wonder how that was?'

'I might tell you when this is over.'

He walked towards the stairs, then turned back. 'I'm not a Christian, Mr Cunane,' he said deliberately. 'I've no intention of forgiving and forgetting if these men who have maimed my beautiful child should come into my power.'

Looking at his expression I remembered history lessons about the nineteenth-century Ottoman sultan who liked to while away a boring afternoon by shooting his subjects from the windows of the Topkapi Palace with a high-powered rifle.

The phone rang before Celal could make any further theological points. It was the moment I'd been dreading, the moment when I would either save this girl's life or end up with very serious egg on my face.

I picked the phone up and spoke.

'Who is this?' the cultured or at least educated-sounding man on the other end asked. That voice was achingly familiar.

'I'm acting on behalf of Mr Celal,' I said. 'We have the money.'

'I hope for the girl's sake you're not the police. Because if you are you've caused her death and this is the last time you will hear from me. Who are you? You've two seconds to tell me.'

'My name's David Cunane . . .'

'The bungling detective! Hah! Perhaps not so bungling after all if you've found your way to Mr Celal's house. Or did he find you?'

'You could say that,' I confirmed. Anything that increased Mr E's confidence in his own infallibility could only be for the good. 'The word's gone round among certain people.'

'And you are the detective to the criminal community? There's a certain rightness in that, I feel. A bungling amateur to help the wrongdoers in our midst who think they can make an easy living from crime. You have the full amount?'

'We're assembling it, no problem. It'll take time. Some of the money's coming from other parts of the country.'

'Excellent, but it must be ready by four a.m. or the girl dies. It will take some time for us to count it and then she will be returned to you unharmed in daylight hours.'

'No,' I said.

'What do you mean, no?'

'It can't work like that. First, I need to talk to the girl now. Second, for one and a half million we swap the cash for her direct. No waiting until tomorrow morning.'

Click! He broke the connection.

My whole body was tingling as if I'd received an electric shock. This was the dangerous moment I'd been fumbling my way towards since I took the job on. Celal stared at me and then turned away to hide his anger.

'You bargain with my daughter's life?' he growled.

'The only way of keeping Yasmin alive is to swap her directly for the money. Any other way and he'll kill her. I told you what happened to the little boy. We'd better hope that he's confident of his disguise. If he is, he may risk it. It's Yasmin's only hope.'

I must have been convincing because Celal made a fatalistic gesture with his hands and went upstairs. There were no sounds of beating so maybe he was applying a little oil to his wife's back. I felt far less certain than I'd sounded.

Brendan Cullen had suggested that extortionists are resistant to the slightest deviation from their set pattern. My hope was that with Thompson keen to leave the country maybe they'd take the risk for the money and let the girl live. Her chances were no better than fifty-fifty, less probably. It depended on Thompson really, how eager he was to have his travelling money.

Jamie came over.

I'd forgotten about him.

'You're a cool character, Mr Cunane,' he said. 'This is like a penalty shoot-out.'

'God, no!' I exclaimed. 'Not against Germany!'

'Funny! We've improved, honestly. They make us practise it a lot now.'

'That's all right then.'

'I wish you'd been with me and Lee that night they took Cheyenne. I loved that child. I don't think I could take it if this one dies too.' He showed me a framed photo of a young girl. 'That's her. Beautiful, isn't she? Got everything to live for,' he said sadly. 'I'm going now. My dad's going to raise a hundred and forty grand as a loan to me. He's bringing it up from Essex but it'll be in gold bullion – bars and Krugerrands. Do you think they'll accept that?'

'I think so,' I assured him. I remembered several bullion robberies from which the full amount had never been recovered, but maybe Jack Piercy had come by his money honestly. I was in no position to quibble.

Jamie moved with that unexpected turn of speed that is his hallmark. Seconds later I heard the Ferrari's roar. I looked at the photo he'd handed me. I could appreciate why her father guarded her. She had delicate features and a beautiful smile. Her hair was jet black and her eyes dark and luminous in a flawless olive skin. There was something fragile about her that was very appealing. The thought that Thompson might be killing her at this precise moment was not something I wanted to dwell on.

The phone rang again. I let it ring for a moment. I didn't want them to feel I was hanging on their every word even though I was. From above I heard the sound of footsteps as Celal came downstairs. I let the phone ring, ring, and ring again. Then I picked it up.

'Are you asleep, you bastard?'

It was the rough-voiced male I'd guessed was Thompson.

Lee had described this caller as having a local accent, and so he did, but the exaggerated twang was just how someone might imitate a nasal Manchester voice. I detected a faint trace of New Zealand or Australia – the South Seas anyway. It was Thompson all right.

'Are you there, Cunane?'

'Yes,' I answered in as relaxed a voice as I could muster.

'When this is sorted I'm going to find you and rip your fucking head off and shit down your neck, you bastard!'

'Nice!' I said with a laugh. 'Very descriptive! You'll have to catch me first, though, won't you? Remember, I'm not a baby or a little boy or an old man or even one of your friends, am I? I'll be waiting for you.'

'You shit! You'll hand that money over like we say or the kid's dead now.'

'Temper, temper! First I need to know she's alive. Second I only hand the cash over for the girl direct. Get it, thicko?'

He hung up.

'You were goading him,' Celal accused.

'Yes. He may be tempted to agree to hand Yasmin over if he thinks he can get a crack at me. It's worth a try.'

Celal shook his head and went back upstairs. A few minutes later he returned with a parcel. He set it down on the low table and then left the room. I wandered round. Darko and Kemal took up station near the parcel. I hoped to find a drinks cabinet but there wasn't one, this being a Muslim house. There were some fine vases that looked very old. Celal came back with more parcels and then more. Eventually he said, 'It's all there. That's a million in cash on the table, and fifty thousand on the floor there.'

It made a fair-sized pile, all right, but not a mountain.

He looked at me expectantly.

I had nothing to say. I could have asked him why a man who dealt in drugs drew the line at Scotch whisky. But that wouldn't have been polite. I tried to smile respectfully but he must have detected some unspoken reproach in my eyes.

'Why are you doing this? Risking yourself for a stranger?'

'It's a job. I'm getting paid by Mr Piercy's brother.'

'But this man will kill you if he can lay hands on you.'

'You can get killed crossing the road.'

'Crazy man!' he said, and turned to checking his bags of cash. Each bag had a figure written on it.

'You think I'm trash, don't you? A drug dealer? Worse, a foreign drug dealer.'

I didn't say a word.

'Your friend Lane is a drug dealer.'

I didn't answer that. I strode over to the window and watched the last of the sun disappearing behind Lindow Common. He followed me. It was a beautiful sight.

'You don't know what it's like to be completely at someone's mercy. The Greeks had us by the throat. Our brothers from Turkey saved us but they'll leech us dry. I'm building up a fortune to help my own people in Cyprus. With this money I can start industries in the TRNC, build hotels, give people jobs.'

'But why drugs?' I murmured. 'Aren't the oranges enough?'

'They will get their drugs from someone else if not from me – from the Sicilians or the Colombians. The West is rotten. People have no spiritual values. They just live for the day.'

This seemed to require a response. If arguing kept both our minds off our troubles so much the better.

'I don't think people are any different from what they were a hundred, maybe even two thousand, years ago,' I said thinking of that mob of Celts howling for their chief's blood at Lindow. 'I think you drug dealers have created a market for your product just like the sellers of baked beans or any other consumer item. You prey on the vulnerable.'

His face darkened at this. His hands shook, whether from nervous reaction or suppressed rage at being challenged in his own home I wouldn't have cared to judge. Eventually he calmed down.

'I keep some alcohol for medicinal reasons,' he said. 'Do you want a glass?'

I nodded and he trotted off. I wondered if he was going to come back with some rubbing lotion in a green bottle but he returned a moment later with a bottle of Glenfiddich and two glasses. We drank whisky together and waited in silence. He smoked one of the inevitable cheroots.

'If Allah sees fit to give me the life of Yasmin, I will get out of this business,' he said after a long while. 'I never meant to become so involved. It started with a few small deliveries then it snowballed. I have the distribution network, you see, and whatever you say, I don't think your government wants to stop the trade. If they did they could easily cut off all contact with the countries where drugs are produced.'

I nodded my head wisely and that seemed to pacify him.

Peter came back with the news I'd expected about the Evergreens.

Eventually the phone rang. It was eight o'clock.

'Cunane,' Mr E said. 'We might be willing to trade provided one condition is met.'

'What condition?'

'You deliver the money in person and wait while we check it on the spot.'

'You'll hand Yasmin over to me alive and well?'

'As well as can be expected. Our little surgical intervention was regrettable but necessary . . .'

'Is she alive? Let me speak to her.'

417

'That's a problem, Cunane. She is alive but she may not be able to speak.'

'What have you done to her besides cutting her finger off?'

'Just say she's in shock. Distressed.'

'I speak to her now or you don't get a penny,' I insisted. My heart was in my mouth. I was trying to visualise what state the poor girl was in. It didn't take much imagination.

'She only speaks to you and only in English, I'm not having her babbling to her father in Turkish. I'll phone again.'

Celal's face was ashen. He was trembling.

'Has he killed her?' he demanded. Kemal and Darko were alert. Maybe like faithful hounds they could detect their master's distress. I don't know what they'd have done to me if I'd said yes.

'I'll need to identify her. Tell me some bit of information only you and she know,' I said urgently.

'When she was little she had a teddy bear with one eye. She used to call it Momo.'

Moments later the phone rang again. This time a girl spoke.

'Where's Daddy?' she wailed. 'I want to talk to my daddy.' There was no trace of a Turkish accent. She sounded like any other local teenager.

'Are you Yasmin?'

'Yes.'

'I've got to ask you a question.'

'Is Daddy coming for me?'

'Soon. Hang on, you'll be home soon. Did you have a toy with only one eye?'

'My teddy.'

'What was your pet name for it?'

'Momo,' she said, and then gave a shriek and went off the line.

418

'Very clever, Cunane,' Mr E cut in. 'Now to business. You will put the money in four of the largest size light-coloured Samsonite suitcases you can buy. They must be suitcases with wheels and pulling handles. Clear?'

'Yes, but one hundred and forty thousand is going to be in gold bullion.'

'You'd better not be trying to rig up any kind of transmitter. I'll have detection equipment with me.'

'No. We could only get gold to make up the full amount.'

'Very well. There must be approximately equal amounts of cash and gold in each case. You will place the suitcases on an airport-type luggage trolley and strap them on. You will fix the brake of the trolley by wedging it with a stick so that it freewheels on its own. Do you understand?'

'What if the money doesn't all fit in four cases?' I asked. Celal's pile looked pretty big.

'We're not amateurs, Cunane. This has been tested. If the bullion takes more space you will carry the excess by hand in an extra case but the bulk of the money must be on the trolley.'

'Right.'

He cut the connection.

I phoned Bob and told him to buy four Samsonite cases on his way back. Celal sent Darko and Kemal round to the airport in the Land Cruiser to pick up a trolley.

Lee Parkes arrived with his money and Jamie's.

'You'd better be right about this Cunane,' he said. 'Or you're dead. I'll be back after four.'

He didn't say a word to Celal.

'He is the man who pays you?' the Turk asked when Lee had gone.

I nodded and he muttered something in Turkish. It didn't sound complimentary. He went back to fumbling with his worry beads.

Bob arrived and we began counting the money and

packing it into four equal piles. It was two a.m. before Jamie arrived.

'You didn't go to Essex for that?' I asked as he lugged in a heavy case.

'No, we met halfway. It's no problem with the Ferrari.'

We packed everything up. It fitted into four suitcases.

The next call came at three-thirty a.m. I was to take the money and the trolley in the Land Cruiser, drive slowly along the A34 in the Manchester direction and wait on the hard shoulder before reaching the interchange with the airport link road. I was to go alone.

'Let us come with you,' Bob argued, indicating himself and Peter. 'We can hide.'

'No, I daren't risk it. He'll be expecting a trick.'

'At least take the Uzi.'

'Apart from the fact that I've never fired one in my life, Mr E wouldn't come within a mile of me if he saw that.'

'This could just be a set-up while they kill you,' Peter said. 'After all, they've got rid of everyone else who might lead the police to them.'

As a compromise I agreed to take the Heckler & Koch. I tucked it into the back of my belt where it wasn't too visible and set off. Jamie was the only one who wished me good luck.

The wait on the A34 seemed to stretch on for ever. The road wasn't deserted but what traffic there was didn't seem related to Mr E — a couple of milk lorries, and bread vans making early deliveries. The extortionist could have been observing me from the car park of a DIY store at the side of the road. My mobile rang at three fifty-five precisely.

'Drive towards Manchester through the next three roundabouts and stop just past the third,' Mr E ordered.

I cruised forward. The third roundabout wasn't a road junction. It only led to a small building development away on my right but there was a white van parked on the hard shoulder in the Wilmslow direction. It was dark but the air was clear and dawn was on the way in the eastern sky. There were no markings on the side of the van this time. I wondered what might be appropriate – 'Extortco'?

I stopped. The phone rang immediately.

'Unload the money on to the trolley, fasten it securely and then push it round the roundabout until you're facing in the Wilmslow direction behind our van. Any sign of company and the girl's dead.'

My heart was beating like a metronome gone wrong but I did as I was told.

I pushed the trolley across the roundabout where only a few hours before I'd queued with hundreds of other commuters. It was deserted now. I found myself facing the rear of the white van.

The back door opened. A large figure got out. It was Thompson, bald head on display with no attempt at disguise. My fingers strayed towards my gun. Thompson helped another figure out. In the grey pre-dawn light I made out that it was a slightly built female. She was wearing school uniform, a blazer and skirt. There was a grotesque mask over her face, fastened on with heavy silver tape wrapped round her head many times. She staggered until Thompson caught her by the arm.

Another person got out of the side of the van. He was wearing a Margaret Thatcher mask that completely covered his head. I realised that the thing taped to the girl's head was another of the same masks.

'Push the trolley forward,' he shouted.

'No, bring the girl,' I yelled back.

In the open air there was something familiar about the man's voice. He was someone I'd met and not all that long ago.

'The trolley, Cunane,' he shouted angrily.

'The girl first, then the money,' I shouted back.

'I'll break her fucking neck if you don't shift,' Thompson screamed. He bent over the girl.

421

'No,' I yelled defiantly.

Then Mr E came forward and the pair held a whispered conference. They made the girl sit down. Next Thompson got in the van and drove it fifty yards down the road.

'How's that, Cunane?' Mr E shouted. 'Were you frightened of my large friend?'

'You're weird,' I said. 'Just let her go and you can have the money.'

'This isn't Weirdsville, Oklahoma, Cunane. Everything's severely practical. Shove the trolley so it freewheels towards me and I'll start her on her way.'

His words staggered me. I felt my knees go weak but I couldn't give any sign of recognition. I waited until the girl was moving. She was completely blind and wandered into the middle of the carriageway. I gave the trolley a mighty shove and it freewheeled towards Mr E. He grabbed it. Thompson ran forward. I had the gun in my hand now but I was occupied in rescuing Yasmin who had stumbled again.

Thompson was on his knees. He opened one case and held up a gold bar in triumph.

I half carried Yasmin down the road, my one thought being to put some distance between myself and the extortionists. She couldn't run. They'd hobbled her legs with tape. I picked her up and slung her over my shoulder. As I did that I saw Thompson slinging the suitcases into the back of the van.

Mr E gave me an ironic salute.

I had the gun at the ready waiting for Thompson to attack but he didn't. He just got in the van and they drove off. I loaded Yasmin into the Land Cruiser. She seemed to be breathing easily through the lips of the Thatcher mask and was swaddled with so much tape around her head and neck that it would have been impossible to remove it there and then without hurting her. Her clothes were not disarranged so it was possible Thompson hadn't raped her. Her hands were also bound together with tape and I couldn't see where they'd cut the finger off. There was a strong smell of brandy.

'Just a few minutes now,' I shouted.

She made some inarticulate sounds and I guessed that her mouth was taped under the mask.

I drove back to Pear Tree Lane. The way they'd positioned me meant that I had to go all the way down to the next interchange in the Manchester direction and turn back towards Wilmslow from there. When I was finally moving in the right direction past the exchange site the extortionists were long gone. Only the trolley remained at the roadside as evidence that the event had ever happened. I noted that the spot chosen was out of range of the cameras that had caught me speeding on this same road. Whatever you thought about Mr E, you had to admire his cunning.

Back at Pear Tree Lane there was a large reception committee waiting. Jamie passed me a glass of whisky on the doorstep while Celal helped the girl inside.

A moment later he came screaming out of the house.

'She isn't Yasmin!' he howled, dancing with rage. I pushed past him into the living room. They'd cut the Thatcher mask off to reveal the bruised and battered face of a middle-aged woman.

29

Kemal and Darko both had guns in their hands, but it was Lee Parkes who took command of the situation.

'You bloody fool, Cunane. You've let them get clean away with all our money and you haven't even got the girl. Face it, that man's a lot smarter than you are.'

'He may be but I think I know who he is . . .'

'You're all talk! You said you'd get him the first time I spoke to you. I should have saved my money.'

'Lee, that's not fair,' Jamie interjected.

No one took any notice of him. Lee glared at me.

'You're a con artist,' he snarled. 'I don't know which is worse: being blackmailed by the scum that killed my Cheyenne or being done over by you. I ought to smash your face in, Cunane.'

'I've a fair idea of who he is and where to find him,' I insisted.

'More of your lies,' he snorted. 'I expect the next thing you'll say is that you want another hundred grand?'

'That's what this all comes down to with you, doesn't it, Lee? That's all it's ever meant to you – money!'

'You bet your fucking life it does! In fact, it *is* your fucking life if I don't get that money back.'

'No cliché unused when it comes to making threats, eh, Lee?'

Mehmet Celal had given up trying to untie the woman when he saw that she wasn't his daughter. He turned to me now. 'You know who this man is because you're working

424

for him. You think I'm some simple peasant who you can cheat!'

'You're in exactly the same situation now as you would have been if I hadn't turned up at your door.'

This kind of logic wasn't welcome. He ground his teeth, spat on the floor in front of me and then started flexing his upper arm muscles like a wrestler and rubbing his hands together in anticipation of breaking my bones.

Peter and Bob came and stood with me while we faced down the angry Turk and his two henchmen. Bob didn't have his Uzi. The only firearm we possessed was the pistol and I'd left that in the Land Cruiser.

'Listen, you Muppet!' Bob shouted. 'They've gone off with seventy thousand of my money as well. Do you think I'd have given that to Dave if he was in with this extortionist?'

'That just shows you're expecting to get it back,' Lee said with a sneer.

'Impeccable logic,' I commented. 'Perhaps you'd like to explain why I returned here with this poor woman if all I wanted to do was bilk you?'

'Your mate double-crossed you, that's why. It's obvious to a child.'

Lee positioned himself near Celal and his men but at some distance to the rear of them. Jamie stood in the doorway flapping his hands indecisively.

Celal turned to Lee. 'He's tricked us all. This man was sent here to make sure we handed the money over.'

'You always jump to the wrong conclusions, don't you?' I asked. 'Is this how you came to beat your wife up?'

'You're working for that kidnapper. You admitted that you know him. Tell us the truth. He's not going to come and save you.'

'I'm not working for him and you'd realise that if you thought with your brain instead of your bank balance. It's

425

just that when he spoke he said something unusual and I guessed who he is.'

Lee gave a cynical laugh at this.

'Give him a chance to explain,' Jamie said. 'I believe him. Why would he come back here if he wasn't straight?'

'Forget it, Little Brother,' Lee shouted. 'You're not on a football pitch now.'

'Listen to Mr Jealous,' I said sarcastically. 'Jamie's the only one of you who's said anything sensible.'

I knew I was arguing for my life. Celal was the type who preferred to bury his mistakes and as for Lee Parkes, I was now certain that there'd always been more to this than personal revenge as far as he was concerned. He had something to hide, and guessing that I had suspicions he'd decided to shut my mouth for ever.

The thing hung by a thread. Celal looked at me. He'd only to say the word and there'd be three corpses lying on the parquet floor. Darko the Serbian hatchet-man was fingering the trigger of his shotgun lovingly.

'You sit there,' Celal said to me, pointing to one of the low chairs. 'You two,' he said to Bob and Peter, 'lie face down with your hands behind your necks. Darko, shoot the first one to make a move.'

We obeyed quickly. Lee made as if to sit on the same side of the table as Celal.

'No, you're a shit!' Celal told him. 'You stand, and if you open your mouth Kemal will give you a smack.'

'That's nice! I put up one hundred and twenty grand for your kid and this is the thanks I get,' Lee grumbled.

'A small amount. I make more than twice that in clear profit most months,' Celal replied calmly. Kemal stood over Lee and he shut up. 'You, footballer!' Celal instructed Jamie. 'You come and sit with me. You, I trust.'

He lit up a cheroot and began puffing smoke in my direction. I blew it back at him. Jamie sat down beside the Turk, facing me. He gave me a slow wink and

426

began fanning the smoke away. Celal put the cheroot out.

'Cunane, tell me where this man is with my money and my daughter,' Celal said wearily.

'It's not that simple,' I began.

Kemal worked the slide of his automatic and placed it against my temple.

'It's simple,' Celal stated. 'Simple as a bullet in the head.'

'Have it your own way, then,' I said as jauntily as I could. The gun was withdrawn.

'I told you that Lee's daughter was kidnapped and I started following up possible leads. Well, I found a couple of cigarette butts on the street where a white Vauxhall Rascal van had been parked while the gang kept Lee's house under observation. At first I thought there were three men in the gang. The cigarette smoker who'd kept the house under observation, the ambulance driver who stopped the nanny in the street, and the heavy, later identified as Thompson, who threw her in the ambulance. It is him, by the way.'

'Get on with it,' Lee growled.

'Later I found another couple of fag ends up at Alderley Edge where the money had been handed over. They were the same brand.'

'Sherlock fucking Holmes!' Lee sneered.

'Shut up,' Celal said coldly.

'Yeah, belt up, Lee,' Jamie agreed. 'Anyone would think you don't want him to tell us the story.'

'I wonder why?' I said to Jamie.

'Talk to me, not them, if you want to live,' snapped Celal.

'Right, sweetheart,' I murmured. Kemal gave me a rap with his gun but desisted when Celal signalled.

'OK,' I continued, 'while I was searching the street a young woman ran past, purely accidentally as I then

427

thought, a casual jogger. She said she'd seen the man in the Rascal van and came into my office to help an artist draw his picture. Only she didn't. She gave us a completely useless portrait that threw us off the scent. I think *she* was the person in the van and the third member of the gang.'

'And that's it?' Lee interjected. 'Shoot the bugger, Celal!'

'Kemal, shoot this man in the leg if he opens his mouth again,' Celal commented coldly. 'Give him a choice of which leg. For your sake, Cunane, I hope you have more to say.'

'Oh, plenty, Chief! I was just filling in the background for you.'

'What is the name of this woman?'

'She has an Italian name.'

'An Italian?'

'I don't think she's just off the boat from Sicily, mate, if that's what's worrying you. It's just an Italian name.'

'Even so, I meet many Italians in my work. Tell me her name.'

'No, names come later.'

'Did you say no?'

'That's correct, no. If you want to listen to this story you can shut up. If you don't want to listen, shoot me now.'

'You know, Mr Cunane, I thought you were crazy before when you said you were going up against these men just because this shit here,' he nodded at Lee, 'had paid you money. Then I thought you were a cheat, trying to make sure you got all my money. Now, I'm beginning to think you're crazy again.'

'What do you want me to do? Pull funny faces to prove it?'

'You're quite insane,' he said. 'I only need to click my fingers and you're dead.'

'We're all dead eventually. Isn't there something in that book of yours about that?'

'What book? he growled suspiciously.

'The Koran.'

'Insolence!' he bellowed. 'You ought to be shot for that but first I will hear what you have to say.'

'Right, well, I followed various leads and we came up with the name of Thompson who was then minder to a health club owner called Judder Crockett.'

'Wait, I've heard of him.'

Kemal came over and whispered something in his master's ear.

'Crockett has been killed?' Celal asked.

'Yes, by our mutual friend Thompson.'

'This Thompson is no friend of mine.'

'Figure of speech, Chief.'

'Finish the story,' he said impatiently.

'Fine. For a while I was convinced that the late Crockett was the extortionist and while I was in that deluded state the lady with the Italian name turned up and did her best to make sure I stayed that way. It was while I was with her that I used a certain individual turn of phrase which our extortionist friend just repeated to me. As soon as he said it I knew I'd met him before in the company of this woman. He's a PE teacher who works in a local school.'

I finished and folded my arms. It didn't sound much even to my ears.

'You solve your cases by guesswork then?' Celal asked. He seemed genuinely interested. 'A turn of phrase?'

'I'm not a policeman trying to gather incontrovertible evidence. I follow leads where they take me and I'm convinced that this PE teacher is our man.'

'This isn't enough.'

'You'd have to get inside my head for the rest.'

'He's lying!' Lee yelped. 'Can't you see?'

Celal nodded at Kemal who knocked Lee to the ground with an easy movement and pointed the gun at his legs.

'Left or right?' he asked in heavily accented English.

'Shoot him and I don't say another word,' I announced.

'Yeah, leave him alone,' Jamie echoed.

'Why do you want to save this piece of rubbish from harm?' Celal asked me. 'He's calling for your blood.'

'That piece of rubbish is my employer,' I said. 'He's going to get a bill for my services and I want him to be around to pay it. Lee Parkes never welches on a deal, eh Lee?'

'Kemal, teach this man a small lesson,' Celal said.

Kemal batted Lee across the face with his gun. Lee groaned and clutched his head. He stayed on the ground. Jamie didn't seem very upset by this treatment of his relative. Not as much love lost between those two as I'd once been led to believe, I thought. He remained motionless in his seat.

'Cunane, I can't believe you'd be willing to risk your life on such a small amount of proof,' Celal said in a conversational tone.

'There's more, but it's background.'

'I'm not in a hurry,' he said.

'You ought to be if you want to save your daughter.'

'First I need some answers. Tell me about this background.'

'Little things mainly but they build up a picture.'

'Tell me!'

'Yesterday I visited Crockett's place . . .'

'*You* killed him?'

'No! I was there at the invitation of the police. Crockett was killed by Thompson.'

'You say!'

'He had this morbid fear of the man who'd been blackmailing him and had fortified his home which is situated on top of a high building. He had barbed wire, an armoured door and a massive steel room where nobody could get at him before he had time to summon help.'

'So how did he die?'

430

'He trusted the woman I spoke of. I'm sure she got him to open up and then she let Thompson in. I found one of her cigarette butts in there. Thompson threw Crockett off the roof.'

'This woman is evil.'

I nodded.

'Another thing that made me think was the kidnapping of Eric McAteer. Any kid would have run screaming at the sight of Thompson and the extortionist isn't much prettier. I think it was the woman who lured that kid out of the playground while his mother was talking to someone.'

'And the phoney ambulance which they used to kidnap Cheyenne? I think this woman was driving it while the extortionist and Thompson were in the back with the nanny and the baby.'

'They let the nanny live?'

'Yes, because the extortionist wanted her to spread a false description.'

'You think Yasmin is still alive?'

'That would fit the pattern. They don't kill their victims straight away.'

Celal stared fixedly at me. His face showed signs of doubt.

'A PE teacher – what is this?'

'Physical education . . . you know, press-ups, games and sports.'

'This is not possible.'

'He doesn't need to have been a PE teacher all of his life.'

Celal held a whispered conference with Kemal. I'd had enough. I stood up. Kemal wagged the gun at me. I ignored it and continued walking towards the door. Kemal chambered a round in his automatic. He fired and a bullet thudded into the door in front of me.

I turned round. Kemal was aiming the gun at me, his boss at his side.

'Celal,' I said, 'I know where this woman lives. I'm going there now and I'm going to find out where the extortionist lives. If he hasn't already killed Yasmin she'll be there or else I'll find a clue as to where they've got her. I've had enough of playing games with you. My life won't be worth living anyway if I don't find this creep so shoot me or let me go.'

Jamie came and stood beside me.

'Yeah, I'm with Mr Cunane. You'll have to shoot me as well,' he said in that reedy London accent of his. Funnily enough it sounded a lot more robust now.

Kemal looked uncertainly at Celal who nodded affirmatively. For a heart-stopping second I thought he was ordering his man to shoot us both but Kemal put the gun away. I remembered then, Turks nod when they mean no.

'We come with you,' he said.

'No. You can come but not them.'

'We keep your friends here then.'

'No, they come with me.'

'They stay!'

There was an explosion of sound from behind him at this. Bob sat up, ignoring Darko who had the shotgun levelled against his head. He was red-faced and angrier than I'd ever seen him.

'Celal!' he yelled. 'Were you born stupid or have you been sampling too many of your own products? You're delaying Dave. Can't you see he's trying to save your daughter and seventy thousand pounds of *my* money?'

'One man stays,' Celal insisted.

In the end we left Lee with Darko and Kemal. I retrieved my pistol from Celal's Land Cruiser. Peter, Jamie, Bob and Celal all squeezed into my Mondeo but not before Bob had retrieved his Uzi.

I drove the short distance to Heald Green. The street lights were still on but full daylight was only moments away. I went up to the door of Anna's flat over the Spar shop. I used a piece of plastic card to open the door. We all pounded up the narrow stairs and burst into the living room. It was completely bare apart from the carpets. I went in the bedroom and it was the same . . . no four-poster bed. In the kitchen there was a small table with an ashtray on it. I picked up one of the butts. It was Silk Cut.

Celal examined it.

'So where is my daughter?'

I scratched my head.

'Over here, Dave,' Bob said pointing out of the back window. There in the small backyard was an old Vauxhall Rascal van.

'That shows she might be coming back,' Peter said.

'But when?' I added.

The phone was still connected.

I dialled 1471 for the last number.

'*Telephone number 0161 648 9201 called at fourteen-thirty hours . . .*'

I wrote the number down.

'You can bet that was the extortionist calling to check if she was ready to roll.'

'Are you going to call and ask him if he's this PE teacher?' Celal asked incredulously.

'No,' I said. 'We don't want to tip him off. He thinks he's free and clear. We've just got to hope they're putting off killing Yasmin.'

I looked at my watch. It was six-twenty. I felt sick to my stomach. Why had I expected there'd be some nice fat clue at Anna's home? Hadn't Mr E always been ultra-careful? I sent Peter down to check out the van. There was nothing except that she'd left the key in it. Peter waved it at me. I shouted to him to bring the van and charged down to my own car.

'Where now?' Celal asked.

'The school,' I muttered.

It took us fifteen minutes to arrive at Wilmslow Green High School. Traffic was beginning to flow along the A34 but not enough to impede our journey. There were security cameras covering the car park so I parked on the road. As we watched a downtrodden-looking middle-aged woman walked slowly across the car park, went up to the main door, rang a bell and was admitted by a man in a brown overall.

'Cleaners,' I said. 'We've got to get in there and find out the address.'

'Yeah, it would help if we knew his name,' Bob drawled.

'Geoff Smith.'

'I'll tell you one thing for free,' Bob said, 'if we all go storming in and try to get into the office they'll have the police there in five minutes.'

'What else do you suggest?' I said, wracking my brain for another way.

'I'll just go and ask,' he said.

'And they'll tell you?'

'I'll feed him a sob story. Long-lost brother. Heard he teaches here. Mother's dying. I'm telling you, we'll get a better result than by trying to force our way in there.'

'Oh, for God's sake, try it then,' I snapped, my nerves were on edge.

I watched Bob trudge his way across the car park trying to look humble and inoffensive. He rang the bell. There was a long wait and then the brown-overalled man and the downtrodden-looking woman appeared at the door. They came out and spoke to Bob at length. The man appeared to be pointing somewhere.

'We're in luck, mate,' Bob said when he came back. 'That's the caretaker and she's his wife. There are no cleaners in today as it's Saturday but they open at seven for a local gymnastics club in the sports hall. The place is in use from seven until one. They don't know where this Smith lives for certain but they think somewhere in

Cheadle. They've heard him talking. However, the best is yet to come. Mr Smith himself comes here at seven to coach for an hour.'

When Bob told me that my long-sought target was so near the hairs on the back of my neck stood up. I could feel them under my shirt collar. There was a metallic taste in my mouth. Every nerve in my body screamed to me to do something active.

I looked at my watch. It was six forty-five. Even as I looked a Volvo pulled into the school grounds and two girls in leotards got out. They went to the entrance, found it locked and returned to the car.

'The caretaker will tell him that someone's looking for him, won't he?' I asked in despair.

'Don't lose your bottle now, Dave. I specifically asked him to do that and he refused. He and the wife are off for their breakfast as soon as the first adult club member arrives.'

'Why wait?' Celal asked. 'When this Smith arrives we grab him, drag him to a quiet place, put a bullet in his leg and then tell him he gets another and another until he tells us where Yasmin is.'

'What do you think, Dave?' Bob asked. 'It might work.'

'No,' I said. 'Every time we've got close to this guy he's had a fall-back plan. I'd say he's got one now. He's like a very elusive wild animal. He never makes a move without testing the ground with all his senses first. We have to wait and follow him back to his home and take him when he's not expecting it.'

'Crazy!' Celal argued, then subsided when no one else agreed.

Peter, Celal, Jamie and I got into the Rascal van and drove to the leisure centre car park leaving Bob on surveillance duty in the Mondeo. He was the only one of us we could be sure wouldn't be recognised by Mr E. I still found it hard to think of him as Smith.

435

Jamie, our celeb, remained in the van but Peter, Celal and I got out. Celal lit up the inevitable cheroot.

At 7.05 Bob phoned on the mobile.

'You were right, Dave. He's come in a sports car, an old green MG. He cruised all round the car park before stopping in the emptiest part of it. Then he walked up to the entrance, looking over his shoulder the whole time, took out his mobile and spoke to someone. A right long-legged, windy-looking bollocks he is too. If we'd picked him up he'd have missed the call and Thompson and your Italian woman would have got away.'

'He's at the school,' I said to the others.

Gradually the car park began to fill up around us with early shoppers and workers. We attracted some stares but most of them were intent on their own business. Tension mounted by eight a.m.

'We go!' Celal said angrily.

'Bob will be following him. If we start a convoy there's no chance that Smith won't notice it,' I said, but it was hard to stand still.

The phone chirruped at 8.15.

'Its Cheadle Hulme,' Bob said. 'A road called The Loop, number twenty-one. You can't miss it, there's a great big white van backed up against the garage door.'

'The Loop,' Peter repeated in wonder when I told him. He set off. 'That's only a few hundred yards from where I live. It's this curious street that winds round in a circle from the main road. There's been a lot of trouble because some developer wanted to build houses on the inner space. It's a wildlife jungle. Big trees and kids' dens and things. The residents have stopped the developer in his tracks the last I heard.'

'Sounds like the right address for a nutter,' Jamie said.

'This is no nutter. He's extremely cunning but not mad. If he was mad he'd have been caught long before he got on your brother's case.'

436

'Yeah,' Jamie agreed. 'Not mad, just bad!'

We parked out of sight of the address. Bob was waiting for us.

'Same thing again,' he said. 'The geezer drove round this Loop twice and checked out parked vehicles. I just had time to turn off before he drove back and saw me. Talk about paranoid! Anyway, he drove the sports car round to the rear of the house and then came back, looked in at the garage through a side window, and went in the front door. The upstairs curtains are still closed.'

This time I couldn't restrain myself. There was nothing to be gained by further caution. I checked my pistol. Bob took the Uzi out of the boot and covered it with his jacket.

'These might be some use,' he said, pointing to the bolt cutters I'd been carrying round in case I met another chained gate as at the Evergreens.

Peter picked up the bolt cutters. Celal had a gun.

Although The Loop lived up to its name it wasn't continuously curved, it was more like an irregular pentagon and number twenty-one was on one of the sharper corners. I decided that it wasn't a good idea for all five of us to walk up to the house in a body. We converged from different directions.

I was the first to arrive. There was no garden gate. The house was a poorly maintained semi. There was oil-stained gravel leading to the garage doors and a separate flagged path to the house. The front was heavily screened by an overgrown privet hedge and an apple tree obscured the door. The lawn looked like a ploughed field because someone had obviously backed a heavy vehicle on to it several times.

We assembled one by one and waited against the side of the house for a minute to get our breath back. The other four were out of sight of the street but I scanned neighbouring houses for any sign of curtains twitching.

There was nothing. Our arrival hadn't been noticed. Further down the street people were getting in cars so I signalled the others to move round the back of the house where they wouldn't be seen from the road. The back garden was a suburban nightmare. The MG was parked right up against a fence and there were bits of other vehicles all around, engines, axles, and gear boxes just thrown any old how. It was an open-air car repair centre or automobile graveyard. Behind the fence sycamore trees loomed up from Peter's wilderness and screened this ugly mess from any neighbours who might object.

I peeked into the living room. It was empty.

'Check the garage,' I whispered.

This was an unusually large and long structure of ramshackle construction. Although it seemed to have been cobbled together from two or three smaller timber-framed garages an attempt had been made to make it secure. There were heavy mesh grilles over the two side windows facing us and the front double door was secured by a large chain.

Bob looked in at the window nearest the road.

'There's one of those old-fashioned Mercedes,' he whispered, 'but there's space for at least another two small cars in there.'

I heard a sound from within the house, a toilet flushing. If Aaron Thompson had come round the corner then I think I'd have shot him without blinking. Luckily he didn't. There were no more unwelcome noises, just the creaking of branches and the distant hum of traffic on the A34.

'Here,' Peter hissed. He pointed to the second garage window. Positioned on a chair in a gloomy corner I could just make out a shape. It looked like an old dressmaker's dummy draped over a chair. The posture was odd. I strained my eyes to see, cursing that I hadn't brought a torch. It was the girl, Yasmin. She was taped to the chair and the odd posture was due to the fact that she was slumped forward with her head lolling. She looked as if she was dead.

Hardly daring to breathe we went round the back of the garage. There was an ordinary small door secured by a padlock through a sturdy metal hasp.

I checked the garage door for any possible burglar alarms or booby traps but it was clear as far as I could tell.

Bob held the padlock while Peter cut it.

The door swung open and a shaft of light fell on Yasmin. She was naked except for panties and lashed to the chair with that same silvery tape that the unfortunate decoy woman had been swathed in. There was tape over her mouth and tears and mucus had dribbled over it from her eyes and nose. Celal was cursing solidly under his breath in Turkish. He seemed frightened to touch his daughter. I moved closer and felt her neck. There was a faint pulse.

'She's alive!' I whispered, and winced at the sight of her left hand, roughly bandaged with a piece of dirty rag.

All five of us moved at once. Bob had a penknife and I had the Swiss Army tool that Judder Crockett had generously given away. We cut the girl free. It seemed to take for ever. She started moaning when she was released but her eyes remained shut. Bob raised her eyelids.

'They've doped her with something. She's out of it.'

Celal took his coat off and we wrapped that round her, but when he picked her up we heard something else, a faint sound like a runner panting hoarsely or a steam train a long way away. There was a deep inspection pit in the concrete floor of the long garage with an inspection lamp handy. I switched it on and shone it into the dark void at our feet.

Aaron Thompson lay face down at the bottom of the pit. He was making the panting noise. The reason was obvious. There was a deep wound across the back of his head and the implement that had caused it lay beside him. It was the stone club I'd last seen on the wall above his bed in

439

Crockett's penthouse. Crockett must have handed it over before he died, or had Thompson found it in whatever hiding place Crockett had concealed it in? Whatever the truth, it wasn't in hiding today. It was the same size as the deep groove in Thompson's skull. Blood had pooled under his head. Whoever had struck the blow had intended to kill him but failed.

Celal had his gun out.

'Shall I kill him now? It would be a mercy.'

'Take your daughter home,' I whispered fiercely. 'We'll deal with things here.'

'This isn't finished,' he vowed.

'Jamie, go with him and bring the van as near to the house as you can without letting them see you from upstairs. You go first.'

'Yeah, right,' he replied. He turned and made one of his rapid exits. Celal followed a few minutes later. We just had to take the risk of some nosy neighbour raising the alarm if they saw him carrying the girl. We waited in silence while Celal disappeared round the hedge. We heard the van doors shutting.

'There's something creepy about that Jamie,' Bob commented. 'Here one minute, gone the next. He's like a ghost.'

'It's a handy skill for a striker,' I agreed.

'What about him?' Peter asked, pointing at Thompson. 'He needs medical attention.'

'He can wait until we get Smith and Pietrangeli sorted.'

Peter seemed inclined to argue.

'He's killed at least four people that we know about,' I said fiercely. 'He can wait his turn.'

We gave Celal and Jamie a moment to get clear with Yasmin and then left the garage. The back door of the house wasn't locked. I paused to think about that. Smith had entered via the front door. Did it mean the back door was a trap for the unwary? I decided that leaving it unlocked was just a handy means of escape or else plain carelessness. Even Mr E was human. I opened it ever so slowly on to a filthy kitchen overflowing with blackened pots and plates jammed on to a small unit. There was a large smelly bin overflowing with rubbish. Whatever else he was, Mr E wasn't fastidious about his domestic arrangements, a serious offence in my eyes.

We tiptoed out of the kitchen into the narrow hall and through into the living room. There was a faint rhythmic sound coming from above. If we hadn't already found Yasmin it would have beggared belief that major crimes had been planned from this house. A real criminal mastermind shouldn't have been living in such shabby surroundings.

But he was. It was perfect concealment.

I looked round the room. The sofa had a spring protruding. The old-fashioned floral wallpaper was yellow with age and peeling. If he was looking for camouflage he'd achieved it but I believed this room was the real Smith. This was what the man amounted to: a seedy but highly cunning criminal who was capable of killing children or anyone else who might give him away.

I remembered telling Lee Parkes that criminals gave themselves away by spending money or through their friends. Smith hadn't spent a penny of his loot and his only criminal contact appeared to be Thompson, who was now lying in what looked like a concrete grave.

Had he boasted of his departure for Fiji just once too often? Or was the attack on him just another piece of Mr E's housekeeping?

We listened to the sound vibrating from the ceiling for a moment. The rhythmic noise was joined by a creaking of bed springs.

'I know what that is,' Bob said with a smile. 'We'll never have a better chance to catch them both with their pants down.'

Smith's pants were certainly down when I put the gun

441

to his head. Anna had her arms wrapped round him and her eyes tight shut. It took Mr E a second to realise what was happening and in that second Bob yanked him off the bed by his hair and on to the floor. There was a celebratory bottle of champagne on the bedside table and beside that a packet of Silk Cut cigarettes. Anna hadn't managed to kick the habit.

She opened her eyes and her mouth formed a perfect O of surprise. She made a gurgling sound and made as if to pull the crumpled sheet back over herself.

'No,' I said, ripping it out of her hand. 'You're going to get the same amount of modesty you allowed Yasmin.'

She gave a yelp of outrage.

'Get the curtains drawn downstairs,' I ordered Peter. 'We're going to have a little chat with these two love birds.'

Bob ripped the flex off the bedside lamp and tied Smith's hands up behind his back. He jerked the bonds tight and Smith squealed in pain. I've never seen anyone look so frightened. His mouth was working and he was drooling with fear. This was the moment all his careful plans had been devised to avoid. As my attention was momentarily distracted Anna launched herself from the bed. She tried to rake me across the face with her fingernails extended but by reflex I pulled away in time. Bob grabbed her and pulled her down. She tumbled on to the floor on top of her lover. Bob put his hand on her neck and pressed her face into the linoleum-covered floor while she struggled and cursed.

'Do you want this one trussed up as well?' he asked.

'Better safe than sorry,' I muttered. I tossed him the cord out of a threadbare dressing gown and he tied Anna's hands behind her back. She started screaming but Smith spoke to her.

'Shut up, bitch,' he hissed. 'I told you we should have killed Cunane after he saw us together at the school but you had to be clever.'

Anna shut up.

'Thanks a bunch, Anna,' I said.

Bob jerked them both to their feet. They didn't make a pretty sight and by unstated agreement Bob and I searched for something to cover up their nakedness. Bob draped the dressing gown round Smith while I wrapped Anna in a dirty oil-stained old mac that had been tossed into a corner.

'Are you going to get the police?' Smith asked nervously.

Bob gave that sinister laugh at this. 'You must be joking, mate. Police, after what you've done? Mehmet Celal's on his way. He's been sharpening his carving knives. He's keen to relieve you of your marriage tackle and I think that's only the beginning. He's a brutal bugger is old Mehmet.'

Smith buckled at the knees at this but he rallied himself.

'The money's all packed up in the van,' he said desperately. 'There's more than three million pounds and it's all yours if you give us a head start on him. You can tell him we got away.'

Bob appeared to consider this offer seriously. He stroked his chin thoughtfully.

'What do you say, Dave, a three-way split with Peter?' He winked at us.

Smith's offer had certain attractions. It wasn't the money. I was dreading the moment when Celal really did torture these two to death. He'd been ready to shoot me or Lee Parkes for nothing at all. Now that the people who'd inflicted terrible harm on his daughter were available he was certain to give his sadistic instincts full play.

I've only once killed and then it was two men who were trying very hard to kill me and the woman I was protecting. It was done in self-defence and I knew that I was morally justified but there haven't been many days since I shovelled the clay into their unmarked grave that I haven't regretted the necessity. If there was any way I could avoid more killing I wanted to find it. Still, it was hard to get the image of that boot lid being slammed down on little Cheyenne out of my mind, or of Eric running screaming to his parents' home only to be deliberately run down.

'Take her downstairs for a minute, Bob, while I have a chat with the criminal genius here on his own,' I said.

It was as if I'd turned a light on. Hope flared in Smith's narrow-set eyes. Bob raised his eyebrows in surprise but he did as I asked him.

30

It was just after nine that I pushed Mr E into the living room downstairs. I'd spent half an hour in his company and felt soiled.

'Meet ex-Detective Sergeant Smith, late of the Greater Manchester Police and the National Criminal Intelligence Service,' I said when I pushed him ahead of me. I gave him another shove and he landed on the sofa alongside Anna. Three faces turned to stare at me. One of them, Anna's, with hope; the other two, Bob's and Peter's, with expressions somewhere between mystification and suspicion.

'You've not done some sort of deal with him, have you?' Peter asked.

'Such as what?'

'I don't know. Have you?'

I shook my head.

'They must be handed over to the police,' Peter said severely.

'And that would defeat everything we've been working for,' I said angrily. Peter can be just a bit too sanctimonious at times.

'I still say leave 'em for Celal,' Bob insisted. 'He'll sort the problem out.'

'Come over here, you two,' I said. The three of us gathered in the hall doorway where we could keep an eye on our captives and talk out of their earshot.

'Listen, Dave,' Bob said, 'whatever you're going to do, you'd better do it quickly. Celal will be back with his boys soon, not to mention Lee Parkes. They're going to take the problem out of your hands.'

'Call the police and get an ambulance for Thompson as well,' Peter insisted, pointing to the phone at the end of the stairs.

'If the police arrived here now who do you think they'd arrest?' I asked patiently. 'Us or the two innocent householders in there, one of them ex-job? They'd have us for assault and those two would swear blind we were the ones who brained Thompson.'

'But the girl . . .'

'Is unconscious and Celal's unlikely to welcome a visit from the police. He might even deny he knows anything about this.'

'We can't handle this on our own, Dave!'

'We may have to. Didn't you hear Smith up there? The first thing he said when we grabbed him was were we getting the police? He wants us to. He's probably got some convincing story to tell them.'

'We've done nothing illegal.'

'You've been walking round for weeks giving out Thompson's picture to all and sundry. Now someone's brained him and you turn up. It wouldn't take the brightest copper on the force to come up with the idea that you were looking to kill him.'

Peter looked horrified.

'They wouldn't do that,' he protested feebly.

'Ring them and see,' I said, gesturing to the phone.

He made no move to pick it up.

'What about Thompson though?' he said eventually 'I feel bad about letting him lie there.'

'He'll have to wait until we've sorted the other two out,' I snapped. I felt no great concern for the Fijian.

'What about these two, then?' Bob piped up. 'A bullet in the head for both of them?' He held up the Uzi.

'Do you feel like doing it?'

446

'Well, it would be kinder than what Celal will do to them,' he said defensively. He made no move towards the two captives. I knew well enough he was no more capable of shooting two captives in the head than I was.

'So what are we going to do then?' Peter asked.

'Smith suggests we give them each ten grand and they'll go to Brazil. He says we can watch them right up to the moment they get on the plane.'

'Are you mad?' Bob asked. 'They've probably got money salted away and the first thing they'll do when they're free is get themselves a hitman and rub you out, double quick. Then they'd be back in business.'

'I've thought of that but what alternative is there? I can't shoot them in cold blood.'

'You could pay someone else to do it. I know a few blokes who'd jump at the chance.'

'Talk sense,' I growled.

Bob's always had this practical side to him. He studied my expression. 'No, perhaps not,' he agreed, 'but letting them both walk out of here is a seriously bad mistake.'

'I haven't agreed to anything yet.'

I took a look at Smith and Anna. They'd both got their colour back and had recovered from the shock of being captured.

'Made your mind up yet?' Smith enquired.

'Come on, Dave,' Anna added. 'You know you're not going to kill us or leave us for that horrible Turk. Let us get dressed and we can all go to the airport together. Think of it. There's over three million pounds in untraceable used notes in that van. You could all live in luxury for the rest of your lives.'

'Yes,' Smith agreed. 'We'll promise not to come back into the UK.'

'Will that be a promise like the one you made to Howard McAteer that he could have his son back if he handed over all his money?'

447

'McAteer was a scumbag! He was living in the lap of luxury off his drug dealing. He had no right to expect that his family would be secure. I wasn't to know they'd both go to pieces. Other people have lost a kid and got over it.'

'Why did you have to run the boy down?'

'He'd seen Anna. He could have described her,' Smith said as if that explained everything.

'You bastard!' Bob snarled. 'I'm not sticking around here to listen to this piece of filth justify his dirty game.'

'You don't understand,' Smith protested. 'Apart from you lot nobody knows what I've been doing. The police don't have any of it down as crime. Nobody will ever miss the money. You can have all that money free and clear of any risk if you just let us escape to Brazil. You can tell Celal we got away. He doesn't know the money's in the van.'

'Tape their mouths up,' I said angrily.

Both our captives began shouting at once. Smith tried to struggle to his feet off the low, sunken sofa but Bob pushed him back and brutally wrapped the tape round his mouth. Anna submitted only slightly more tamely. She tried to bite Bob until he cuffed her.

'He's right about Celal,' I said when Bob had finished. 'Bob, you take the van to Chorlton and dump the money in my garage.'

'Are you going to keep it?' Peter asked, round-eyed with horror.

'Will you stop thinking the worst of your employer?' I asked, and patted him on the shoulder. 'If I have the money and I give Celal every penny back that he's lost . . .'

'And don't forget me, mate,' Bob interjected.

'I'm sure you don't intend to let me. If Celal and Lee Parkes and Jamie and hid dad get back what they've shelled out there's a chance, just a tiny chance, mind you, that they might let me sort out the problem of our two master criminals in a civilised way.'

'Such as what?'

'They want to be flown out to Brazil for a new life,' I said loudly. 'That gives me an idea. We can fly them to anywhere we like and I've heard that there are certain countries where you can have people imprisoned in exchange for a nice cash payment. Yemen, Burma, Bolivia, North Korea . . . there's quite a number of places where they like hard currency and don't ask too many questions about locking people up.'

Smith started struggling fiercely when he heard this.

He obviously found the idea credible enough though it had only just come into my head.

I went over to him. 'I only promised I wouldn't kill you or let you be killed,' I told him. 'A new life in a new country was your idea. It's just going to be in a prison somewhere unpleasant rather than in a flat at Copacabana.'

Smith struggled so hard I thought he was going to choke himself on the gag and save us all a lot of trouble. He didn't. Bob came over with the gaffer tape again and lashed his legs and arms up like an Egyptian mummy.

'Handy stuff this.'

'What about her?' I asked, nodding at Anna. She was sending me love messages with her eyes. They were lovely, those eyes. Sadly, the only thing they put me in mind of was Judder Crockett trustingly letting her into his penthouse.

'The female's often deadlier than the male,' Bob agreed, and lashed her up like her partner.

'Dave, I can't drive that van on my own,' he said in a whisper. 'I'd find the steering wheel was turning of its own accord and somehow I'd end up in Amsterdam or Rome. I wouldn't want to do it, but it would just happen. It's nice of you to trust me with your last three million quid, Dave, but . . .'

I phoned Celal's number.

Jamie Piercy answered.

'Listen, Mr Cunane, I'm sorry I won't be able to help you any more today,' he said apologetically. 'I've got to report to the club soon.'

'Will you be all right?'

'Yeah, I'll be fine. I often don't sleep the night before a game. It keeps me on a fine edge.'

'As long as you don't fall asleep on the pitch.'

'Yeah, right. Better not do that. Well, Mr Celal's taken Yasmin to a private clinic. She's in a pretty bad way. He told me to tell you he expects to have his money back as well.'

'Nice guy!'

'Yeah, but I promised I'd get me dad's money back too.'

'That's all right. I'm sorting it right now,' I assured him. 'What about Lee?'

'He was hurt pretty bad. He's gone to hospital to have his face stitched up. I feel a bit guilty about that.'

'Don't!' I said forcefully.

'Yeah, well, he is my brother. I'm the only one here now. Said I'd hang on until you called.'

'Right. What about that woman we brought in last night?'

'Oh, her. She's a prostitute they picked up last night. They got her blind drunk. She knows nothing about all this. Thinks it was a stag-night trick that went wrong. Celal gave her some money and she went off in a taxi.'

'Fine, well, we'll have your money at Lee's house by this evening. We're going to have to meet to decide what to do about you know who.'

'Christ! I'd forgotten about them,' he said, sounding frightened.

'Good luck with the game,' I said and hung up.

I turned to Peter.

'Will you be all right guarding these two on your own for about an hour?'

450

'I suppose so,' he said unhappily.

'Will you or won't you?'

We looked at Smith and Anna. They weren't going anywhere. The more they squirmed, the deeper they sank into the ruined sofa.

'Will you take the Uzi?' Bob asked him.

'No, it's no use, I wouldn't be able to shoot them anyway. If they start trying to wriggle away I suppose I could drag them back.'

'Good! We'll be back in an hour and we'll find a way to get Thompson to a hospital and some place to keep these two locked up. Don't let anybody in.'

'I'm not an idiot,' he said.

We went to the van. I took a look in the garage before we left. Aaron Thompson was still breathing in the pit. I know it was callous of me, but I hoped he'd be dead when we got back. There didn't seem to be any way he could recover from the wound which his good friend Smith had inflicted on him.

Bob was right. Driving a large van stuffed with cash was an odd sensation. I don't know how these security firms manage to get away with so few robberies by their own staff. There must be a lot more honest people about than popular opinion suggests. Anyway, temptation aside, it only took us twenty minutes to get to Chorlton.

I pulled the van up alongside my garage, got out of the cab and opened the door.

'This isn't right,' Bob said sheepishly. 'It's not respectful. You can't just stash three million pounds in an ordinary garage.'

'Why not? It's all parcelled up.'

'No, I wouldn't be able to sleep for thinking about it.'

'Do you want to drive round to the bank and make a deposit? Can you see their faces when we start heaving the dosh in by the sackful?'

'Don't be funny, Dave. You shouldn't joke about three million pounds. Think of all the things that could buy.'

'"Can't buy me lurve"!' I sang.

The truth was I felt liberated since leaving Cheadle.

'Dave, get serious! What're we going to do?'

'We'll lug it upstairs to my place. Janine can buy herself a designer dress.'

'She could buy herself a fashion house!'

In the end, he stayed on guard and I struggled upstairs with the first consignment of cash. I'd carried two suitcases up and had just taken the key to the flat out of my pocket when Janine appeared. She looked at me and then at the suitcases.

'Are you moving out?' she asked. There was something about her expression that told me she expected me to say yes.

I shook my head.

'The case is solved,' I said with a smile.

'Hardly that,' she said grimly, 'you've had a pile of faxes about your friend Parkes. It seems he's something of a criminal himself. Go in and see.'

I went into my flat. Clint was in the living room.

The faxes concerned applications made to the London District Probate Registry by a solicitor on behalf of Lee Parkes. The first application was before the death of little Cheyenne, the second after. It appeared that Mel Parkes, née Morgan, was a very wealthy woman, sole heiress of Richard Morgan who had sold his chain of record shops for five million pounds back in 1976 and then invested the money carefully. Mel was his only child. He'd died in 1994, Mel's mother in 1997. Mel married Parkes in 1998.

I read the pages with mounting surprise. Although relatively little had been said about Mel, the impression Lee had given was that she was from the same background as himself. Nothing had been said about her being independently wealthy. Come to think of it, there were precious

452

few reminders of her in the Parkes home, just the one photo and that wasn't in a prominent spot. Lee had allowed me to think that he'd paid for everything and that the money stuffed in his safe was his illegal earnings.

There was worse to come. When Mel died the fortune went to her child, not to her husband. Trustees had been appointed to administer the estate and to pay Lee a monthly sum to provide for his daughter. The amount paid was generous but it would cease when Cheyenne came of age. Then Lee would receive a much smaller sum, unless of course he could persuade his daughter to increase it. However, if Cheyenne died then Lee was the sole heir to the estate apart from a few bequests to various animal charities.

Cheyenne's death had made Lee Parkes a very rich man.

I dropped the cases in a corner and tried to work out what this meant. Lee had refused to pay five hundred thousand for the child's return and I'd always assumed that even if he had paid he'd still have found his daughter left in the boot of a stolen car, but would he? I now had the means to find out.

'So what do you think, Zipperman?' Janine asked with a smile. 'Does this complicate things too much?'

It took me a second to remember what she was referring to. It complicated things all right, particularly as I had two people trussed up like chickens waiting for Lee Parkes, among others, to come and pass judgement on them.

It crossed my mind not to tell her anything but then I found myself talking, gabbling out the whole story.

'You can't be serious about dumping them in a foreign jail?' she said when I'd finished. 'Not unless you send Lee Parkes off with them.'

'We don't know that he did anything,' I said grudgingly.

I don't exactly feel loyalty to a client so much as to the job but it was hard to admit to myself that I'd been so

453

deceived. What could I do about it? Insist that the next time I took on a personal case the customer submit himself to a lie detector first?

'Dave! Of course he did,' Janine said after studying my confused face. 'He must have arranged with Kimball Smathers for the baby to be kidnapped, knowing that the child was unlikely to survive. He's a callous brute. The only thing I'm not sure about is this – did he also arrange for Kimball and Keeley Smathers to be shot?'

'I don't know but I'm going to find out,' I said grimly.

I took Clint downstairs with me for a joyful reunion with his brother and with his help we soon shifted the pile of cash upstairs. Clint moved the furniture to make a space in my living room.

'I'm not happy about this,' Janine announced.

'I'm not going to keep it,' I said quickly.

'Damn right you're not!' Bob agreed. 'Seventy thousand of it's mine.'

'That's not what I meant,' Janine insisted. 'I'm not happy at the thought of you going back to that house in Cheadle to deal with that pair. If this wretched Turk does decide he wants vengeance then you'll be an accessory, and how are you going to cover that up?'

'I can't leave Peter on his own. I said we'd only be an hour and it's nearly that now.'

'Why don't you phone him and order him to get out? Let him tell them that they're free to go but the Turk's on their trail. They'll disappear then, won't they?'

'I've already thought of that,' I said, 'but it means that our security – you, me, the kids, everything – is dependent on whatever Celal decides to do. Of course, he said he'd pack up drug smuggling if he got his daughter back . . .'

'In a pig's ear he'll give it up,' growled Bob. 'Did you hear him bragging to Parkes about how much he makes in a month?'

'What if you tell Brendan Cullen?' Janine asked.

'What can he do?' I exploded. 'There's no evidence except for Yasmin and we don't even know where she is now. Probably having surgery to sew her finger back on.'

In the end we unpacked the suitcases and counted out Bob's money then sorted out the separate piles of cash: Jamie's, his dad's, Lee's and Celal's. Bob bunged his into the bread bin in my kitchen.

'I trust you, Dave,' he said playfully, 'but if that money goes walkabout, you're toast!'

When we went downstairs to the van, there was a problem. Clint refused to be separated from his brother again. He came along with us, sitting in the back with Celal's share of the ransom money. We called at the house on Pear Tree Lane but it was deserted. Even the unseen Mrs Celal was absent. We drove on the short distance to the house in Cheadle. The Mondeo was where I'd left it. The key was still in the ignition. We transferred Celal's cash to the boot of the Mondeo and left Clint in the car to guard it.

I crunched the van up over the gravel path and got as close to the door as I could. I expected to see Peter at the window but there was no sight of him. The curtains were still drawn.

When we reached the back door there was a trail of blood leading from the garage across the concrete path and up the step, then on through the kitchen into the living room. There we found Smith and Anna still lying on the sofa bound with the gaffer tape as we'd left them but now very much dead. Their heads had been beaten in and the perpetrator, Aaron Thompson, lay on his back on the carpet. His eyes were wide open and staring but he also appeared to be dead. There was none of that awful gasping for breath that he'd been doing before. I gaped at him for a moment. His chest was not moving. He was clutching the stone club with which he'd been struck down earlier. More blood had spilled from the awful wound at the back of his head on to the worn carpet of Smith's living room. It was obvious he'd somehow crawled out of the garage into here and dealt with his former partners as they'd tried to deal with him. He'd had a lot more success than they had.

'Oh, shit!' Bob said.

'Where's Peter?' I asked, hardly daring to move my eyes lest they come upon the corpse of my senior detective.

Bob crashed up the stairs into the bedrooms.

'He's not up here!'

I dashed out to the garage. Peter was lying at the bottom of the inspection pit, groaning and clutching his arm. With Bob's help I hauled him out.

'Where's Thompson?' he gasped. 'Has he got away?'

I didn't trust myself to speak. We helped Peter into the house and he saw the same spectacle we'd seen a moment earlier. He gave a groan. 'I went to give him some water. I couldn't bear the thought of him lying in that pit on his own. When I got there he seemed to come round. He drank the water and then I turned to see if I could get him up the ladder and he hit me with that club. He broke my arm and I passed out.'

'Lucky for you that you did,' Bob said. 'If you'd struggled with him, you'd likely have ended up like they did.

'Right, we're out of here,' I said.

'No,' Bob interjected, 'we must have left our prints all over the place. We'll have to wipe the place down. I don't know about yours, Dave, but my prints are on file.'

I nodded agreement and despite the pain that Peter was in we had to leave him sitting at the bottom of the stairs while we tried to remove any trace of our presence. It took twenty minutes. We hadn't touched much. During the brief clean-up neither of us noticed any files or materials relating to Smith's extortion racket. There were many mobile phones which Bob gathered up, at least twenty. He put them in a carrier bag.

'There must be something we've missed,' he said.

456

'He must have had a personal phone book. I know! The attic.'

There was no attic as such, only a dust-filled roof space. As I peered round among the rafters I felt my desire to get out of the house growing stronger by the second.

When we reached the back door the first thing I saw was the side of the white Transit van.

'God!' I groaned. 'What are we going to do about that? It's got our fingerprints all over it.'

'Bloody hell, Dave! I'm not going down for a murder I haven't committed,' Bob said. He sounded panicky. Peter loomed up behind him, his face grey with pain.

I had to come up with a solution, and quick, before everything unravelled.

'Bob,' I said, 'take Peter to the Casualty Department at Cheadle Royal. Use the white van and then come back here and reverse in so that the doors are up against the garage.'

'Setting fire to the bloody place is the best idea,' Bob suggested.

'Great! What happens when they find three charred bodies in the remains? That's the surest way to make certain that the police do a thorough forensic check,' I said. 'Look, we've not been thinking straight. We're bound to have left some trace of ourselves somewhere in the house. Brendan Cullen already has me linked to Thompson. It won't take them five minutes to identify his body and then they'll pull me in.'

'Get a really good fire going,' Bob argued. 'There's petrol in the garage.'

'No,' I said. 'Take Peter and then come back with Clint. I'll clean up a bit better when you've gone. We'll load the bodies in the van and then think of something else.'

'You'd better think of something good, Dave. I'm not going down for this.'

I waited until they were clear and then fetched the petrol

457

out of the garage. I didn't intend to set fire to the house but I knew that it was a very good method of removing the bloodstains from the pit, the concrete path and the kitchen floor. I set to work with a petrol-soaked rag. Twenty minutes later there was no visible trace of blood. I didn't kid myself a forensic examination wouldn't turn up some trace but I meant to ensure that no one ordered such an inspection.

Thompson's killing of Smith and Anna had taken place while they were both crouched in terror on the ruined sofa. I tried but it was hard to work up much sympathy for them. I reckoned Anna must have been in the van when they ran little Eric down. The main splash marks from their shattered skulls had gone into the sofa. Thompson's own blood had run on to the filthy rug he was now lying on. There were tiny drops on the walls but everything was already so dirty they didn't show up much. I worked out my next move.

I felt sick. I went to the filthy toilet and vomited. I told myself it was the petrol fumes.

The job I'm in has hardened me to some extent but this solution to the problem of what to do with Smith and Anna wasn't the one I'd have chosen.

It was getting on for an hour before Bob came back. Clint was still in the car down the road. He had the Gameboy with him.

'Well?' Bob said. I could see that he wasn't in the mood for pleasantries.

'We carry them through the garage and into the back of the van. The sofa and that carpet go too. Next week, I phone a house clearance firm to shift the rest of the furniture and then we put the house on the market. Smith owned it, the deeds are in the house.'

'You're crazy, Dave!'

'No, it can all be done over the phone. We can give an accommodation address.'

'That still leaves us with three bodies to dispose of, and suppose someone reports Smith missing? His school . . .'

'Listen, what Anna told me about him being head of department was all lies. Smith told me. He was on a temporary contract and she was a supply teacher. I don't think he had many friends apart from Anna. According to Brendan Cullen, the guys who do this sort of crime aren't involved in a network of criminals. There was just him, Anna and Thompson. No one's going to miss him. Even if they do, what's the problem? People leave their homes and clear off all the time. The point is, if we don't have a big fire-raising exercise no one's going to start searching here, are they?'

We got to work.

31

I drove the van into the car park of B&Q just off the A34. Bob followed me with his brother in the Mondeo. The bodies were well covered and screened by the sofa if anyone started peering through the back window. It was the best I could do for the time being. Then I got in the Mondeo and Bob drove us to the house on Pear Tree Lane.

Bob and I didn't say much to each other while we waited for Celal to return. It was Clint who did all the talking. He described the stables and the horses and his daily routine in such minute detail I formed a picture as clear and complete as a Vermeer. Every experience, no matter how commonplace, seemed so vivid and important to Clint. Bob said a little about his Caribbean journeys.

It was four o'clock before Celal rolled up. There was a young woman with him, the second Mrs Celal. She was a fleshy-looking blonde with full, almost pendulant lips. They did nothing to diminish the generally sulky aspect of her face but I suppose she had reason to be less than thrilled with life. She had no visible bruises but there was something about the stiff way she walked that suggested discomfort. The bodyguards were also there. They took up position on either side of the front door while Mrs Celal tottered inside.

Celal stood on the gravel path fingering his moustache. Eventually he lit a cheroot and came over.

I waited until he approached and rapped on my window.

'You have something for me?' he suggested. His tone was mild.

I stepped out of the car and unloaded his money from out of the boot. Bob got out of his side of the car and gently laid the Uzi on the roof. Neither of the bodyguards moved a muscle. Clint wound down his window and smiled at them. Apart from the sub-machine gun it could have been a pastoral scene. Behind us magpies and pigeons flew among the trees of Lindow Common.

I opened one of the cases to show the wads of cash.

'You'll want to count it, I suppose?'

'Meaning what?' Celal asked aggressively.

'Meaning that you'll want to check I haven't stolen some of your precious money. That's what this is all about, isn't it, money?'

Celal's face assumed the slightly worried expression of a walker with a wasp buzzing round his ears. He spat the cheroot out of his mouth and then reassembled his face into to what he must have imagined was a friendly smile.

'My daughter is all right,' he said. 'They haven't violated her but the surgeon isn't certain whether he'll be able to graft her finger back on. The wound on her hand was untreated for so long . . . his hope is that he will be able to.'

I continued to open the cases for his inspection. There were three of them.

'No,' he protested, 'this isn't necessary. You keep one of the cases. Pick whichever one you want.'

I got back in the car, leaving the three cases where they were. He came round to my window. 'OK, I was rough on you back there,' he said, nodding towards the house, 'but you must admit it was suspicious. I get a demand for ransom and then a detective turns up out of the blue and says he's tracking down the same blackmailer. It was suspicious.'

'Yes,' I agreed. 'It was.'

461

'I see,' he said. 'I've offended you honour. Now my honour demands that I find some way to repay you.'

'You know how to do that. You said it yourself last night.'

'That was a promise to Allah, not to you. It's between me and Allah,' he said defensively, then glared at me. 'You must take some gift from me or you'll be insulting me. Wait here.'

I shrugged.

He turned and ran back into the house.

'Ho hum,' said Bob, suppressing a yawn.

Celal returned with one of the beautiful multicoloured ceramic plates I'd admired earlier.

'Take this,' he said, thrusting it at me. 'It's very rare Iznik pottery.'

'Thanks,' I said, passing it back to Clint who cradled it on his knee. I started the car. Bob got in.

'Wait, Mr Cunane, there's one more thing. This Smith . . . what of him and that bitch?'

'They're taken care of,' I said casually.

'Taken care of? What do you mean?'

'They won't be troubling anyone again.'

'You make a joke? I don't believe you could have taken care of them in the way I would have taken care of them. You've let them go free?'

'No,' I said. 'Actually, Mehmet, I was hoping you could help me there. There are three bodies in that white Transit van of theirs. We left it at the B&Q car park down the road. It might be awkward for all of us if they were found.'

He gave me a quizzical glance and then nodded to Kemal. I handed him the keys of the van.

'You go now, Mr Cunane,' Celal said respectfully. 'I'll clear up for you.'

We drove off.

'You've got your nerve, haven't you?' Bob said. Then he gave a barking laugh. 'Well, the bugger was ready enough

462

to kill us all in his living room so he must have his ways of disposing of unwanted corpses.'

'That's what I thought.'

'Where to now, Chief?'

'Food, I think,' I said, 'and then the Parkes mansion.'

We called at a McDonald's in Wilmslow and watched while Clint chewed his way through a stack of Big Macs. The coffee was good. I needed it. I'd had about four hours sleep in the last forty-eight and I felt light-headed. It took us the best part of two hours to satisfy Clint's appetite. He collected several toys from Happy Meals which he said he was going to give to Lloyd but I noticed that he was pretty interested in them himself.

There were no lights on when we arrived at Lee's house and rather than park in his drive I drove back to the main road and waited in the spot that the late Anna had used when she was observing in the Rascal van. For the sake of something to do we listened to the sports reports. The Reds had only managed a draw but Jamie was responsible for the last-minute equaliser that saved them a point.

'That's nice to hear, innit?' Bob said ironically. 'They can't blame us for making them lose.'

Clint played with his McDonald's toys. Bob and I drowsed in turns.

Eventually a car passed us and the lights went on in the Parkes residence.

'Shall we go now and catch him on his own?' Bob asked.

'No, we'll wait for Jamie to show as well,' I muttered. 'Both their names are on my contract.'

Later I was jerked out of the half sleep I'd fallen into by the throb of the Ferrari 550 Maranello engine as Jamie swept majestically past us. I gave Bob a shake and he woke up.

'God!' he mumbled, stretching his arms. 'I feel more like having twelve hours' sleep than a set-to with the Brothers Grimm.'

'You're right, we'll make them wait for their money.'

I reversed the car and we went back to McDonald's for another round of coffee. I felt slightly restored, at least enough to hold my own with the brothers. Clint found space for another couple of Big Macs.

As we returned to the car a mobile phone rang.

Bob and I checked our pockets but it wasn't one of ours.

'Christ, it's one of these buggers,' Bob said, pointing to the bag of phones in the foot well on his side of the car. He started frantically sorting through them before finally clamping one to his head.

'It's Celal! He wants to speak to you.'

All sorts of thoughts had shot through my mind such as that Smith had another confederate, so it was with relief that I spoke to the Turk.

'How did you get this number?' I demanded.

'It is the number Smith used on his last call to my house. He must have got careless and forgotten to block it. You're a hard man, Cunane.'

'Whoa!' I spluttered. 'I'm not responsible for what you found.'

'As you say, my friend,' he said with a conspiratorial chuckle. 'They brought their deaths on themselves and I'm not grieving over them.'

'Wait a minute . . .' I said.

'No, they are taken care of and nothing more need be said. They will find an unmarked grave on some lonely hillside in the Balkans. You're a hard man. Mr Cunane, and a clever one too, I think,' he said courteously. 'You made no demands but I shall continue to consider an appropriate reward for you.'

Then he broke contact.

'He thinks we killed Smith and Pietrangeli,' I told Bob.

'No, Dave, he thinks *you* killed them.'

'This is the last thing I wanted.'

464

'Serves you right, Chief,' he said unsympathetically. 'You couldn't resist telling him you'd taken care of them, could you?'

'I didn't mean . . .'

'In his world what you said means only one thing. Anyway, not to worry. Respect, eh! It'll go round in the circles he moves in that Dave Cunane isn't a man to be dissed.'

'No!'

'Yeah. A whisper here, a nod and a wink there.'

I was in something of a daze when we drove to Lee Parkes's home.

'Do you want us to stay in the car, Squire?' Bob asked in a mock deferential voice. 'While you take care of business, like?'

'Like hell I do!' I snapped. 'I might need witnesses.'

'I don't want Clint seeing anything unpleasant,' Bob replied.

I looked at him.

'Just teasing, mate!' he said with a grin. 'Celal will probably never mention what happened to another living soul.'

'Probably not,' I agreed despondently.

Clint carried the remaining suitcase containing the three hundred and twenty thousand belonging to Lee. Jack Piercy's gold bullion was in a separate container and Jamie's hundred and twenty grand was in two carrier bags. I was carrying that load, Bob was holding the Uzi.

'Here, what's this?' Lee snarled when he opened his door to this spectacle. 'Them two aren't coming in for a start.' He pointed at Bob and Clint. Lee's face was heavily bandaged.

'Right, lads, back in the car,' I said happily. 'Mr Parkes can call round for his money when he's in a better mood.'

'Now just hold on, that's *my* money,' he said hastily.

465

'It's money all right, but whether it's *your* money is quite a different question.'

'What do you mean?'

'I know you gave Jamie *your* one hundred and twenty thousand last night but the money before that, the two hundred thousand . . .'

'What do you mean?'

'I've no way of knowing that you actually handed it over. They left Cheyenne to die . . .'

'She'd have died anyway. She had leukaemia, poor little mare!'

'She wouldn't have died so soon, though, would she, Lee? So maybe you didn't pay any ransom. Maybe what Jamie thought were parcels of money were just bundles of scrap paper.'

'I knew it!' he screamed. 'I knew you were bent. You're trying to cheat me out of my money.'

He ran forward shouting, 'Give me my money! Give it to me!'

Bob cocked the Uzi and Lee stopped in his tracks.

'You bastard, Cunane!' he cursed.

Jamie appeared behind him.

'It was real money,' he said, 'I helped him to count it out.'

'I don't know, Jamie, there's an awful lot of counterfeit stuff about these days. Are you sure it was the genuine article?'

'Yeah,' he muttered, flapping his hands. 'I can't believe you're doing this, Mr Cunane. You've got my money and my dad's there. My money's still in the bank wrappers and Dad's is gold bullion unless you're going to say the Krugerrands are fake?'

'Stranger things have happened.'

'Can't we talk about this?' he pleaded. 'My dad will go mad if he doesn't get his money back.'

'Yes, talk, that's a good idea,' I said. 'You two give me

some information and then you get the money. That sounds like a good idea.'

Lee had been gibbering to himself during this conversation. Now he strode up to the house and flung the front door wide open.

'Come in then, you bastards.'

'Lovely,' Bob commented. 'I don't know about you, Dave, but I've seen my mum and dad's marriage certificate. I wouldn't like to swear about these two, though, would you? The older one looks like a right wrong side of the blanket merchant to me, with his face all banged up like that. You could almost say he looks like a crook.'

Inside, we sat in the big lounge. Clint sprawled on one of the low sofas but Bob and I pulled over stools from the bar counter. It struck me that the room had no character at all. It was like an airport lounge. Lee and Jamie faced us across the expanse of fitted carpet. The money was piled up on our side of the room but neither of the brothers made any attempt to claim it. That might have had something to do with the fact that Bob had laid his Uzi on the bar counter and his hand was resting about three inches from the trigger.

'I know who you are, Lane,' Lee said to Bob, 'so don't you start handing me any of this moral shit like Cunane.'

'Nice,' Bob replied. 'I like it.' His hand moved a shade closer to the Uzi.

'OK,' I said, hauling the bullion and the carrier bags over to the football star. 'This belongs to you, Jamie.' I opened the case containing the bullion.

'Thanks,' he muttered. 'I knew you were only joking. Are you going to give Lee his?'

'Oh, no! There's still a question about who the rest of the money belongs to.'

'It's mine!' Lee shouted.

'Tell us where you got it from, Lee, and I'll think about returning it.'

'I got it off those Malaysian Chinese, I told you. Some I won on the horses.'

'Try again, Lee,' I said patiently.

'All right,' he muttered. 'Some of it was Mel's but she was my wife.'

'Some of it? Just some of it? How much would you say – a thousand?'

'Some of it was hers. Some of it was mine. We were married.'

'I know you were married but Mel went to a great deal of trouble to ensure her fortune was kept out of your sticky fingers. She set up a trust to look after her money for Cheyenne, didn't she?'

'So what?'

'So, you're asking us to believe that you were so helpful to them that these Chinese gamblers paid off all your debts and handed you at least half a million for a few tips on match results and names of some players who were hard up?'

'There's big money involved in the Far East,' he said desperately.

'And they're very generous?'

'Yes,' he muttered sullenly.

'You're lying, aren't you? I don't think there ever were any Chinese. You were screwing the money out of Mel and playing a game with Jamie. You needed to spin him that yarn about the Chinese to explain why you were suddenly so rich, didn't you? You didn't like to tell him you'd got it off your wife.'

'I knew Mel had money,' Jamie said. 'Her old man was a millionaire.'

'But you didn't know that Lee was entirely dependent on her, did you?'

He shook his head.

'Come on, Lee. Tell us, was the money from the Chinese or was it from Mel?'

'There's no law against a man taking money off his wife.'

'No, but you were greedy, weren't you? You wanted to play the successful gambler. You wanted more and more, and when she wouldn't give you more, what happened?'

'It wasn't my fault! I told her not to drive that Porsche but she insisted . . .'

'Where was she going?'

'She was going to Mollingtree.'

'Why? Did she want to ask Kimball Smathers how much of her money the pair of you'd got through that day?'

Lee hung his head.

'You know, Lee, I wouldn't be at all surprised if someone hadn't done something to that Porsche. They're like racehorses, those high-performance cars. One little alteration here or there and the thing's all over the road.'

'You'll never prove that,' he snapped. The reply came back so quickly I was certain I was right. An innocent man would have been flustered and indignant.

'Why not? Did you have the car crushed?'

'None of your damned business! The car was inspected by the police. They were happy to believe it was an accident.'

'They did say the brake linings were badly worn,' Jamie said. 'You told them you'd warned her not to use the car but she insisted.'

'I did warn her but Mel was headstrong, you know that.'

'But the Volvo was her car, why did she take the Porsche?' Jamie probed.

Lee was at a loss for an explanation, his face purple with rage.

'And you did have the car crushed,' Jamie added thoughtfully. 'It wasn't an insurance write-off.'

'So?' Lee replied defiantly. 'I'm supposed to have the car my wife died in sitting outside the house to remind me what happened to her?'

Jamie shifted away from his brother as if he had an infectious disease.

'When Mel died you thought you'd inherit all her money, didn't you?' I continued. 'But she'd changed her will, making Cheyenne the sole heir. That was done just two weeks before her unfortunate accident. I wonder why?'

'I don't know. The woman was stupid!'

'She was stupid not to tell you she'd changed her will leaving Cheyenne as the sole heir, instead of you. Maybe there would have been no point in killing her if she'd told you that. But you didn't know about the will so she had to die, didn't she? It must have been a blow when you found you were only getting enough money to look after your daughter. I bet you hit the roof.'

'You've no idea what I did.'

'Yes, I have. You discussed the situation with your old mate Kimball Smathers. He's dead now so we'll never know which one of you first came up with the idea of getting rid of Cheyenne, but it must have been him who told you that he knew a crazy Fijian who'd grab the child for a few quid and see that she died on cue.'

'Rubbish! You're just guessing. Cheyenne was very ill, she could have died at any time.'

'But not soon enough to suit you. They've made great strides in the treatment of leukaemia. Many children now make a full recovery.'

'She could have recovered,' Jamie said resentfully. 'The doctors were talking about a bone marrow transplant. I'd have been ready to give some.'

'What was it, Lee?' I asked. 'Were the bookies pressing you?'

'This is all guesswork.'

'That's right, and my guess is that the simple contract killing of your own baby went wrong. Smith and Thompson checked up on you. Found out from Kimball Smathers that you had a safe full of cash.'

Lee pulled a sour face at this suggestion.

470

'He told them, didn't he?' I pressed. 'It had to be him.'

'Kimball had a big mouth,' Lee admitted.

'So they decided to relieve you of the lot. Why shouldn't they? Who could you complain to? *Please, officer, I was paying this man twenty thousand to snuff my child's life out and he insisted on five hundred thousand.*'

'You should be writing fiction, Cunane!'

'No, that's what you're good at, Lee. Smith must have thought it was his lucky day when you fell into his lap.'

'If you're so clever, tell me why I paid two hundred grand for Cheyenne?'

'That's simple. It had to be a kidnapping, didn't it? Anything else would have involved the police immediately. Thompson could hardly have killed the baby in the street without causing a major hue and cry. If he'd broken into the house and killed her, there'd still have been a mammoth fuss and publicity was the last thing you wanted, wasn't it?'

'You're so sharp, Cunane, you'll cut yourself.'

'And there was the will. The police always check up on wills and money and things and you'd have been suspect number one as soon as they got sight of Mel's.'

'You think you're so clever but you can't get round the fact that I paid them two hundred grand to give Cheyenne back. Jamie saw all that.'

'Jamie saw what you wanted him to see. I expect your idea was that if anything went wrong, like the police getting involved, you'd have your famous brother here as a witness that you were doing everything for your child a distraught father should.'

'I did. I paid them two hundred grand.'

'Yes, to kill her! It was a lot more than you wanted to part with, wasn't it?'

'No!'

'You had to pay two hundred thousand because you were

471

afraid that otherwise they'd return Cheyenne to you, safe and well!'

'You never stop talking rubbish, do you?'

I shrugged my shoulders. Perhaps I was talking rubbish but my words were having an effect on Jamie. He was looking at his brother with a new expression on his face.

'You didn't want to pay five hundred thousand and you didn't want to pay two hundred thousand either,' Jamie said slowly. 'You didn't want to pay anything, did you? It's like he says.'

'No, it's not!' Lee pleaded. 'Honestly, I'd have done anything for that kid. You know that.'

'I know I had to snatch that money out of your hands,' Jamie said fiercely.

'It wasn't like that,' Lee beseeched his brother. 'You've got to believe me. Cunane's a liar.'

'Then there's the late Kimball Smathers,' I said. 'I paid him a visit and he thought you'd sent me to punish him and collect the extra money you'd been forced to hand over. He let you down twice, didn't he? He found you the wrong contract killer and he told him you were loaded.'

'Smathers was a greedy idiot!'

'Greedier than you? Why should you be the cat that got all the cream? I bet Kimball was biting the carpet when he found out Thompson had screwed you for two hundred grand. What did you pay Kimball? A couple of thousand?'

'Kimball was a mate. He'd never have done anything like you said.'

'He was your mate. Now he's dead mate!'

'What a funny man you are, Cunane,' Lee said self-righteously, 'but I had nothing to do with that.'

I looked at him. Apart from a clear admission by Lee I had no way of finding out whether he did or didn't have something to do with the Smathers killings. Thompson, Smith and his girlfriend were dead but Lee didn't know

472

that. I decided to plough on. If nothing else I was convincing Jamie that his brother wasn't a knight in shining armour.

'Do you know what a "cut-out" is, Lee?' I asked.

'Why should I answer your riddles?'

'Because this money walks out with me if you don't,' I reminded him.

'I don't know what a cut-out is, unless you mean some kid's game?'

'I don't think you're that naïve, but I'll tell you. A cut-out is included in a criminal plot as a safety device. Your mate Smathers was one. Only Kimball Smathers stopped being safe, didn't he?'

'I don't know what you mean.'

'He told Thompson too much about you. It's because I don't think he told you much about Thompson or Smith that I'm prepared to give you the benefit of the doubt about killing him. When I told you about Charlie Costello you were frightened enough to leave the country in case you were also on their list, and Thompson and Smith had more to gain by Kimball's death than you did.'

'So now there's someone I didn't kill?'

'Maybe there is, but Kimball's and Keeley's deaths were highly convenient for you. Charlie Costello was killed with a stone club, an affectation of Mr Thompson's. The police are already looking for a man who kills with a stone club. They know about Thompson and in the end they'll find out that Smathers was the only person Thompson knew when he came to England. If Kimball Smathers were still alive the police would have found your connection with him and somehow I don't think Kimball would have done too much lying for you.'

'Jamie,' Lee said, ignoring me, 'he's got all this worked out in his head like some kind of fucking Sherlock Holmes. It's crap. If I'd wanted Cheyenne's death covered up why did I bring Cunane into it?'

'That's a laugh!' Jamie said bitterly.

473

'Listen, bro,' Lee said desperately but Jamie wasn't listening. 'I've got to get out of here,' he whined pitifully. 'Help me, they want to kill me!'

'You're going nowhere, Lee!' Jamie shouted. 'No one's going to kill you. *You* didn't bring anyone into this case. It was me! I brought in Cunane. It was me who wanted to find out who kidnapped Cheyenne, and all along it was you!'

Jamie did another of his rapid movements but this time it was towards Lee. Before either Bob or I could move a muscle he had his hands clamped round his brother's neck.

Clint was the one who prised him free. Lee remained on the ground gulping air and Jamie flung himself on to a chair, weeping bitterly.

'What are you going to do?' he gasped eventually.

'About Lee? What can I do?'

'Not just about him, about those two you've got trussed up in Cheadle? You'll have to get the police.'

I suppose it's a tribute to what an instinctively law-abiding bunch we all are that so many of us believe calling in the police is the solution to any problem.

'It's not so simple,' I told Jamie. 'Mr Smith is himself a former policeman, and as your brother has said, I've no proof. This is all guesswork. A good brief would laugh us out of court, assuming we ever got there.'

'So Lee's free and clear?' Jamie asked indignantly.

'Looks like it,' I said. 'All he's going to get from me is an itemised bill, and he'd better pay it in full.'

'But what about the other two? They cut that girl's finger off. They killed that man in the pit, Thompson.'

'No,' I said, 'that was one of their few mistakes. He crawled out of that pit, went in the house and knocked the pair of them on the head before dropping dead himself.'

'So they're all dead? The three of them?'

I nodded.

'That's a bit hard to believe. Are you sure you didn't take money off them to let them go or something?'

I shook my head.

'Hard to believe or not, Thompson killed the pair of them.'

'God!' he muttered, looking at me with a peculiar expression.

'There's something else,' I said. 'Lee encouraged you to go along with all this Chinese bookmaking stuff by threatening to reveal the story of how you deserted your wife and child.'

'That wasn't my fault!' he blurted out. 'Me dad . . .'

'Did Lee threaten to reveal that story?'

'He dropped hints, like. Said he was the only one who knew all the facts about me. He said the *Sun* or the *Mirror* would pay him at least a hundred grand for the story.'

Jamie shook his head. We looked at Lee who was sitting up and rubbing his neck. His eyes were fixed on the suitcase full of money.

'If only you hadn't tried to make me as corrupt as you are,' Jamie said to his brother sorrowfully. 'Why did you have to make me think I was bent?'

'You've had it so easy,' Lee growled. 'You had Jack Piercy looking out for you, seeing you got all the best chances to make it in the game, and what did I get? Henry and Maureen Binns were so hard up it was a struggle for them to put food on my plate, let alone gravy.'

'That wasn't my fault,' Jamie said. 'I stuck by you through thick and thin.'

'It wasn't your fault,' Lee agreed. 'But do you know what really happened? Did you ever wonder why they favoured you and not me? The first night I was with the Piercys, my mum and dad's big friends, I wet the bed and cried. It wasn't much for a little kid who'd just lost his parents but it was enough for those stinking rich swine.

475

They sent me back to Social Services. They couldn't cope with two of us, so they picked you.'

'Yeah, well,' Jamie said miserably.

'And what have you done ever since?' Lee asked rhetorically. 'I'll tell you. You've licked their hands like a grateful little puppy. You even took their name instead of our dad's.'

'I was only a little kid. I can hardly remember our parents. I clung to you, I looked up to you . . .'

'You needed teaching a lesson.'

'Why? What harm have I ever done to you?'

'You needed teaching to stand up for yourself. Maybe I'm not so perfect but you're a walking lie . . . the big, bold football star. The only thing you ever did without asking Jack Piercy first was to get Ashleigh pregnant and marry her, but when Jack told you to ditch her you couldn't do it fast enough.'

'I was only a kid then.'

'Yes, that's you. Always a kid. I think the public ought to know more about your real character. They've built you up as this Cliff Richard of the soccer world, Saint Jamie, England's darling. I'll see that the papers find out the truth about you!'

'No, Lee,' I said. 'You won't do that because as soon as you open your mouth the media will start sniffing round you for any more dirt they can find, and you know there's plenty.'

He didn't actually gnash his teeth at this but he certainly fumed silently.

'I suppose you think you're very clever,' he said at last, his words sharp as knives. 'Are you going to turn me in to the police?'

'I've told you, all I want from you is the payment of your bill.'

Lee shook his head disbelievingly.

'The money?' he asked.

'Take it and welcome,' I said, kicking the case towards him.

Lee tried to struggle to his feet but something seemed to have snapped. He flopped back and started sobbing like a child.

The rest of us left the house together. I helped Jamie to stow his father's gold in the back of the Ferrari.

'Are you going to Essex tonight?' I asked.

Jamie looked back at the house and scratched his head.

'Lee was right about one thing. I am too tied to Jack Piercy's apron strings. The old scumbag can sweat for his money. If he hadn't made me leave Ashleigh, Lee would never have been able to put the screws on me. It was because I lost my own kid that I was so fond of Cheyenne.'

We watched Jamie drive off and then got in our own car. Bob casually tossed the Uzi down on the back seat next to Clint.

'Are you sure that's all right,' I asked nervously.

'It'll be OK,' he said dismissively. 'Are you sure you believe Lee didn't have any contact with these Chinese bookmakers. I mean, they do exist, don't they?'

'They exist,' I agreed wearily. 'My main aim was to get Jamie to see that Lee's been ripping him off all his life. Lee was probably into the Chinese for all he could get.'

'But Jamie thinks . . .'

'Jamie really does think he's the Cliff Richard of soccer. Is there any harm in that? Or would you rather leak this to the press and give them two or three days of sensational headlines? This way Jamie won't ever let Lee blackmail him again, even if he dared to try.'

Bob punched my shoulder.

We drove to Chorlton. Bob was going to book into a hotel with Clint and I was looking forward to having unimpeded access to my own bedroom. When we got out of the car I saw with horror that Clint was playing with the Uzi.

'Put that down, Clint,' I said urgently.

'He's all right,' Bob countered.

Clint pointed the gun at me, cocked it and pulled the trigger.

Nothing happened except that both brothers started laughing like drains.

'It's a replica,' Bob explained when he could finally speak.

'You went in Celal's house and held off his bodyguards with that!' I said weakly.

'Yeah, it worked perfectly, didn't it?'

I was too tired to argue but I felt as if someone had walked over my grave.

When I got upstairs I wanted to climb into bed and sleep for a week but Janine was waiting for me and she had other ideas. About sleep, that is.

Epilogue

I did sleep later for the best part of a week. Janine, the children, Naomi and myself took a break in Majorca during Whit. I needed a break because solving the case had left me with almost as many problems as I'd had before.

There was the immense pile of money remaining for one thing. The only victim whose name I knew for certain was Howard McAteer. I'd spent half an hour trying to get Smith to tell me more about what he'd done but it wasn't long enough. He was too skilled at evading questions to give me much useful information. I called round to McAteer's house in Gorton. He wasn't in.

'He's got a job shelf-stacking at Tesco,' a neighbour informed me.

I'd considered all kinds of variations with McAteer, ranging from not giving him the money to arranging some sort of pension, but this news made me happy. I left a note under his door telling him to phone. He could come and collect his money. Ill-gotten or not, it was his and I wanted out of the problem of looking after it.

Even when depleted by all the paybacks there was still well over a million pounds in cash. I kept it in my bedroom. The answer came to me one night just before I fell asleep. Cheyenne Parkes had been suffering from leukaemia. I decided to divide the money and give half to the Christie Hospital and half to the Francis House Children's Hospice in Didsbury. My mystery gifts made the national news on television and all the front pages. The money was

479

investigated but the police couldn't prove that it was the proceeds of crime and so the institutions kept it.

Clyde Harrow pestered me relentlessly about the promised TV interview with Jamie. I was half inclined to tell him to go to hell. Jamie now believed that the gambling syndicate story was just a scam by his brother and I wasn't anxious to rake up more muck, particularly since Lee had emigrated to Las Vegas, but a promise is a promise. Jamie's career had gone from strength the strength. The Reds won the League and the European Cup in which he scored twice.

I was a bit shy about approaching him but when I did, he fell on my neck.

'Mr Cunane,' he said, 'I've been thinking of something like this for a while and we both know old Clyde. He wouldn't try any snide tricks, would he?'

'Oh, no, Clyde would never do anything underhand,' I agreed, without a trace of a smile on my face.

'It'll give me the chance to put my side of what happened, you know, like with my wife. The lawyers have sorted out a divorce. They found Ashleigh after your man gave them the details. You'll never guess what happened to her.'

'No,' I said.

'She became a nun. Still is one.'

Clyde Harrow came round a few weeks later. Frustration and annoyance were written all over his chubby features.

'What's up? I asked, attempting to forestall his wrath.

'You, Cunane, "you whoreson, cullionly barbermonger".'

'Here, hold on!'

'*Lear*, Act Two, Scene Two. It's all your fault.'

'What is?'

'That I'm committed to do a programme on Master Piercy that amounts to little more than a work of hagiography. Sorry, I forget your ignorance . . . as now scripted it's the life of a saint, an hour-long commercial celebrating the virtues of Saint Jamie of Alderley Edge'

'So what's wrong with that?'

'You led me on to believe that he was up to something and now it turns out that his great "problem" was nothing more than a youthful indiscretion with a girl who subsequently become a nun. A nun, I ask you! I've had to include a saccharine-flavoured interview with her about her work in Africa and she won't say a word against Jamie either. It comes out as a sort of cross between *Match of the Day* and *The Sound of Music* . . . two young people who've dedicated their lives to the service of others.'

'You were expecting juicy revelations of scandal?'

'You led me on, you cunning reptile.'

'Don't start again! It's hardly my fault that Jamie turned out to be purer than the driven snow. You should be happy. Think of the wonderful publicity for the Beautiful Game.'

'There is that, I suppose,' he said gloomily. 'It'll certainly do nothing for my reputation as a hard-hitting documentary producer. I've already been approached by the religious channels in the USA. "A plague on both your houses!"'

'*Romeo and Juliet*,' I snapped, before he could supply the provenance.

He left without another word.

As it turned out the documentary was a great success. Jamie was invited to meet the Prime Minister soon after it was screened and sent on a tour of youth groups throughout the country, exhorting them to take up soccer and give up drugs, drink and gambling.

There was happiness all round including an outbreak of wedded bliss when Celeste married Michael. My prospects of the same remain as remote as ever. Celeste became pregnant soon after the ceremony and gave in her notice at Pimpernel. Peter became office manager and more or

481

less runs the whole show now. Levonne is very happy with his regular hours.

Almost the first thing Peter did was to part company with Marvin. He didn't mind. He got another job at a solicitor's in John Street.

There's talk of the firm 'going public' again. The insurance work is still expanding. I have my doubts. As it is now, although I get bored with office work, I still own the firm and can set my own agenda, but who knows what might happen if I have a load of shareholders shouting the odds behind my back?

Bob Lane was so happy with Clint's progress that he kept him on at the stables in Carrington. He bought a house nearby in Urmston and Naomi Carter lodges with them. She combines housekeeping for the brothers with working as a part-time nanny for Janine. Clint is attending special classes and has managed to start reading, so who knows where his progress will end?

One Saturday afternoon in July the follow-up from the police came as I'd known it would. I was alone in the flat when a familiar voice on the intercom demanded admission. It was Brendan.

'Have you got some of that Lagavulin left, Dave?' he asked when he'd settled himself on my sofa.

I primed him well with the Scots nectar.

'Shall I tell you a story?' he began.

'What if I say no?' I replied.

'I'll tell you anyway, but I think you know part of it. Once upon a time there was this policeman . . .'

'Not yourself?'

'Listen, Dave. We'll call him Smith because that's a nice anonymous name, isn't it? Hardly enough to identify a real person. He was a well-qualified man, was this Smith, much brighter and better educated than most of the plods of his era although his background was ever so humble. Smith's

482

father was a coal miner in Beswick, north Manchester, back in the days when they still had coal mines in Manchester. Hard to remember that far back, isn't it? But Smith had a good memory, he never forgot his origins.

'His memory served him well because he won a scholarship to Manchester Grammar School where he rubbed shoulders with a lot of other clever scholarship lads who went on to all sorts of posh jobs. There's a fair percentage of them from Manchester Grammar School. Head of this, head of that, you name it. Just like Eton in a way. Smith's contemporaries did well. Anyway, our man had a few knocks on the way up.

'When he was in the sixth form getting ready to go on to Oxford or Cambridge his father was killed. There are pensions and compensation and things these days, but even so his mother had a hard time. There were other children, none so bright as Smith himself, so it was decided that he should leave school and take a job to help support the family. We don't know what he thought about that but he did as he was told. He got a clerking job in a solicitor's office in town. He didn't earn all that much but at least he wasn't a drain on his widowed mother and he did make all sorts of contacts that were useful to him later.

'Now in a real fairy story this is where the Fairy Godmother comes in, waves her magic wand and sends your man off to Oxford or Cambridge, or even to both of them, and then he resumes his miraculous progress to the top. Prime Minister Smith, Managing Director Smith, Lord Smith of Beswick. Except that didn't happen for our Smith. He never found his Fairy Godmother. Instead, he went to Salford University. Nothing wrong with that, you might say, and that's true, but BA Salford doesn't have quite the ring of MA Oxon, does it? Even worse, his degree was in engineering, hardly the high road to fame and fortune in this country.'

'There was George Stephenson!' I interjected.

'Who's telling this story?' Brendan asked crossly. 'He's the exception that proves the rule. Name another famous engineer.'

'Brunel.'

'Clever sod, aren't you? Anyway, those two apart, engineering isn't a highly paid job in this country. Most people think it's got something to do with filling in holes in the road and at the start of your career as an engineer you have to accept quite low pay. This didn't suit our Smith. He had a girlfriend, she was pregnant and clamouring for him to put a roof over her head. In those days the police still got allowances for that kind of thing so he joined them. Things went quite well for him. He wasn't "fast-tracked" or anything but he quickly made it into CID and then became a sergeant. On the domestic front things weren't quite so rosy. His son was killed in a traffic accident and his wife became severely depressed and left him, taking the other kids. Still, he had his career and firmly believed he was destined to become Chief Constable. It's sad, but other people got the same impression that he was destined for the top and in the job there are ways to block someone you feel is a bit too bumptious for their own good. That's what they did to Smith. He found himself blocked not because he was stupid but because he was clever.

'He left CID and went into NCIS and found himself blocked again so he left the job.

'He started a small electronics company but that went bust. This was during the period in the early nineties when interest rates hit the roof. We can imagine how peeved Smith was at this development. He tried to become a property developer but that didn't work either. Then he went into part-time teaching. He had maths from his engineering and a PE qualification, and it was during that period of his life that he went completely out of control.'

484

'What did he do, chalk his headteacher to death?'

'I think we both know what he did, Dave.'

'What?' I asked blandly.

'I'd dearly like to ask him, but he doesn't seem to be around any more. Nor is Thompson, nor is a young woman who attached herself to Smith.'

'I don't know why you're telling me all this.'

'I'm telling you because we found a connection between Thompson and Smith.'

'Oh, yes?'

'And something very curious happened.'

'Do tell,' I said, pouring him another generous dram of Lagavulin.

'It all boils down to clubs, Dave. Smith knew Charlie Costello. He was a member of the Black and Blue Club. The chromatography finally came through with an identification of the stone particles found in poor Charlie Costello's skull. They came from New Zealand greenstone, a basaltic rock used to make a type of stone club called a *patu*. The Maoris used to have them as war clubs but they're found all over the South Seas.'

'Interesting,' I murmured.

'Now, listen to the really interesting bit,' he said. 'One of these *patus* has turned up in a local junk shop, of all places. A curator at the Manchester Museum bought it. He reported it to the police because he thought it might have come from another museum. Authentic specimens are quite rare apparently. The stone matches the particles from Charlie's skull but that doesn't prove anything because the same stone was used to make so many clubs.'

'That's a shame.'

'Isn't it? The junk shop proprietor can't remember which of several house clearances it came from but one of them was Smith's house in Cheadle Hulme.'

'Makes you think, doesn't it?' I commented.

'It does. I'd dearly like to think Thompson headed off back to his native islands and that Smith and his lady are lolling on some Pacific beach, but somehow I think someone put a spoke in their wheel.'